PENGUIN BOOKS

THE SHELBOURNE ULTIMATUM

D1396254

The Shelbourne Ultimatum

ROSS O'CARROLL-KELLY
(as told to Paul Howard)

Illustrated by
ALAN CLARKE

PENGUIN BOOKS

PENGUIN BOOKS

Published by the Penguin Group
Penguin Books Ltd, 80 Strand, London WC2R ORL, England
Penguin Group (USA) Inc., 375 Hudson Street, New York, New York 10014, USA
Penguin Group (Canada), 90 Eglinton Avenue East, Suite 700, Toronto, Ontario, Canada M4P 2Y3
(a division of Pearson Penguin Canada Inc.)
Penguin Ireland, 25 St Stephen's Green, Dublin 2, Ireland (a division of Penguin Books Ltd)
Penguin Group (Australia), 707 Collins Street, Melbourne, Victoria 3008, Australia
(a division of Pearson Australia Group Pty Ltd)
Penguin Books India Pvt Ltd, 11 Community Centre, Panchsheel Park, New Delhi – 110 017, India
Penguin Group (NZ), 67 Apollo Drive, Rosedale, Auckland 0632, New Zealand
(a division of Pearson New Zealand Ltd)
Penguin Books (South Africa) (Pty) Ltd, Block D, Rosebank Office Park,
181 Jan Smuts Avenue, Parktown North, Gauteng 2193, South Africa

Penguin Books Ltd, Registered Offices: 80 Strand, London WC2R ORL, England

www.penguin.com

First published by Penguin Ireland 2012
Published in Penguin Books 2013
002

Penguin Ireland thanks O'Brien Press for its agreement to Penguin Ireland
using the same design approach and typography, and the same artist,
as O'Brien Press used in the first four Ross O'Carroll-Kelly titles

Typeset by Jouve (UK), Milton Keynes
Printed in Great Britain by Clays Ltd, St Ives plc

ISBN: 978-0-141-04852-9

www.greenpenguin.co.uk

Contents

Prologue

Wake up!

I'm like, 'What?'

'I said wake the fook up! Where are you?'

I'm actually walking along – believe it or not – Westmoreland Street. And that's, like, Ronan in my ear.

'Hey, Ro,' I go, 'I'm only, like, five minutes away from you.'

He's not in the mood to be bullshitted, though. 'You said that to me fifteen minutes ago, Rosser.'

I'm like, 'I know. But, like, this time I *really* am?'

The line goes dead. He's not a happy rabbit. Which for some reason, I immediately know, is bad news for me.

I walk across O'Connell Bridge and onto O'Connell actual *Street*? It's been a while since I've had the pleasure. The old sign for Bailey's Irish Cream, I notice, has been replaced by one that says *Cash 4 Phones*, and that should be, like, a forewarning of how things have changed. As in, it's no longer the O'Connell Street we all know and try to avoid insofar as we can.

I walk past McDonald's. Except it's not *even* a McDonald's any more? It's, like, a cash-for-gold outlet. Which throws me for a second. Then I notice that so is the old Supermac's and suddenly I'm thinking, okay, I know we're all supposedly in the shit, but could things have really gone this far downhill in the six months since I was last here?

I cross Middle Abbey Street and have a quick look across at Clerys, which, I notice, is no longer a deportment store. It's now basically a four-storey mobile communication technology superstore where you can buy second-hand – or 'previously loved' – phones. And so is the Happy Ring House, by the way.

It's, like, what is happening to this town?

I pass a gang of four scrawny fockers in hoodies leaning in the

I

doorway of what was once Eason's and they stare at me, trying to make eye contact as, like, an excuse for kicking the basic shit out of me. It's nice to see that some of the old northside traditions have survived.

I put my head down and just keep walking.

When I pass the GPO, I stop – I know I probably shouldn't, but I can't *help* myself? – and I end up taking a look down Henry Street. And I feel my body go instantly cold. Because it suddenly hits me. The entire northside of Dublin City Centre is one giant, sprawling slum, where there *is* no law and the only businesses still operating are those dealing in smelting stolen gold and fencing stolen phones. Although Zerep *is* still Zerep, I notice.

I'm passing a shop called Ch-ching for Bling, where the Gorda Station used to be, when all of a sudden some dude comes staggering towards me with, like, a paper cup in one hand, then in the other a piece of cordboard with the words 'Haven't Eaten For Three Days' written on it in, like, black morker pen. I just happen to look at his face and I end up having to do an actual double-take.

'Christian?' I go. 'Christian!'

Except he doesn't answer. He just, like, staggers past me, like he hasn't actually heard me, and I'm about to follow him when all of a sudden I hear the sound of a horse clip-clopping its way down the other side of O'Connell Street, past what *used* to be the Gresham Hotel but is now a shop called – very clever this – Celu Phonz.

There's, like, crowds of people lining the street and they're all, like, cheering and wolf-whistling the figure sitting on the horse's back. I realize suddenly that it's Erika – as in my half-sister? – and she's, like, totally naked, with only her long hair protecting her modesty and her kaboobers. She's, like, waving to the crowd – the way you see, like, the Queen do – and then, for whatever reason, I end up looking at the horse's face. And it freaks me out because it's, like, Fionn. I shit you not. It's, like, a full-on horse, but with Fionn's actual face grafted onto it.

I feel a hand suddenly touch *my* hand, then fingers sort of, like, stroking my orm, the exact same way that . . . *she* used to.

'How are you feeling today?' I hear a voice suddenly go. It *is* her.

It's, like, Sorcha. 'Better, I hope. You definitely *look* better? They gave you a bath last night – well, a good wash . . .'

I'm thinking, okay, what the fock is going on here?

'They've *all* been in to see you, Ross. Fionn and Oisinn have been here pretty much every day. They've been, oh my God, *so* an amazing support to me as well. Oisinn's very upset. He thinks he could have maybe done something to stop it. Erika as well. She can't stop crying. Christian's never off the phone looking for updates. And JP arranged, like, a prayer meeting for you – here in the ward? I don't know if it did any good. It's just that a lot of the orticles I've been reading online say that coma victims respond well to, like, *positivity?*'

Coma victims? Is that what I am? What the fock?

'Your dad and Helen were in this morning. And Ronan. Well, Ronan's here pretty much all the time. He's broken up, Ross. He keeps shouting that he wants justice. He says if you die, there's going to be blood on the streets.'

Die?

'But we're trying not to think like that. The doctors are very hopeful. They're saying it could be, like, fifty-fifty. You lost a huge amount of blood, but there was no actual brain damage.'

There's, like, twenty seconds of silence then. I can nearly *hear* her hoping.

'I'm trying to think of other news. My friend Claire from Bray and her husband, Gareth, are thinking of setting up an organic bakery and coffee shop on the Quinsboro Road called Wheat Bray Love? They both – oh! my God! – *loved* the book. Probably because they first met each other while they were doing the whole travelling thing?'

I go to say something horrible about the two of them – focking saps or something like that – but nothing comes out.

'They're only going to be selling foods that promote, like, wellness,' Sorcha goes. 'That's provided the bank gives them the two hundred thousand euros they need to borrow . . .'

Hope it all goes tits-up on them. I want to say it, but I can't.

'Oh my God, don't even talk to me about the banks. *So* don't.

3

Do you remember whenever it was that the Government decided to, like, bail them all out? They said we were faced with the nightmare prospect of putting our cords into an ATM and being told that we'd no actual money. Two and a half years on, Ross, I've lost my shop in the Powerscourt Townhouse Centre, the bank is still threatening to repossess the house and I put my cord into an ATM this morning to be told, guess what? I've no actual money!'

She laughs, except not in a good way.

'I'm sorry I haven't brought Honor in. I just figured, you know, it's no way for her to see you. Best to wait until you're well again. It's been hard enough trying to explain to her that her daddy was . . .'

I hear her voice falter.

'. . . her daddy was shot.'

Shot! I was shot! Yes, there's a familiar ring to that alright.

I hear her sobbing. Jesus. The shit I put this girl through and look at her. Still here. Still hanging her stupid hopes on me.

She puts something into my ears. Feels like it might be earphones. Then I hear the clickwheel of her iPod turning and she goes, 'I made, like, a playlist of songs that are, like, *our* songs?'

Then suddenly I'm listening to *Secret Gorden*. We're talking Bruce Springsteen here. What even movie was that from? *Jerry Maguire*. That was it. Might have been the first flick we ever went to see together. It *was* the first flick we ever went to see together. That little cinema in Glasthule that's now gone. Was it called, like, the Forum?

Always loved that line. *You've gone a million miles – how far'd you get?*

I lose myself in the song and then I suddenly find myself back on O'Connell Street, waiting to cross the road over to what used to be the Ambassador. Buckets of Blood and Nudger are standing outside, both in monkey suits. They haven't aged well. Buckets goes, 'Name?'

I'm like, 'Fock's sake, Buckets. I'm Ro's old man. You've known me for *how* long?'

Nudger touches his earpiece. Someone's obviously talking to him

4

through it. He looks at me like it's taking every bit of strength he has to stop himself from just punching my jaw loose.

'Folly me,' he goes.

He leads me through an expensively corpeted hallway to a lift that's made out of, like, *gold*? He presses the button. He says nothing during the ride to the third floor. That'd be his trademork, of course.

The doors ping open and I'm in this humungous office. And I'm suddenly staring across the biggest desk I've ever seen at my son at twenty-four years of age. And I instantly get it. This entire city is under his control.

'Hey,' I go, 'how the hell are you?'

He looks the same, except he's got a little bus driver moustache, which comes as no real surprise to me – he's been threatening to grow one since he was eight. I notice he also has this, like, *Samurai* sword in his hand? I get the impression that he's pretty handy with it, if and when the need arises.

He points the thing *at* me. Then, with one eye closed, he stares at me along the length of its blade. He goes, 'No fooken smalltalk. What did you get?'

And I'm like, 'That's the funny thing, Ro – bit of a slow morning actually.'

'Empty out yisser fooken pockets!'

Which I do, as quickly as my shaking hands will let me. Three iPhone 12s and a Motorola Bravo. I drop them in a pile on the table. Ronan stares at them, his eyes wide.

'That it?'

I go, 'Dude, I've been out since, like, eight o'clock this morning . . .'

'And this is what you fooken bring me?'

'It's all these warnings in the papers and on the radio. People are being more – I don't know if it's a word – but *vigilant*?'

'I give you the best patch in this city . . .'

'I know.'

'Foxrock Choorch to Donnybruke viddage . . .'

'Ro . . .'

'The fooken Balsamic Vinegar Belt.'

'And I'm grateful.'

'And this is alls you bring me?'

'Ro, please . . . I *need* this job?'

'You're no good to me, Rosser.'

'Ro, please. Me and Sorcha, we've got debts. Honor's going to be going to college soon. There's fees and blah, blah, blah.'

'Ine soddy, Rosser.'

'Ro, I'm your actual father.'

He looks at Nudger. No words pass between them. But somehow he manages to, like, convey the order to fock me headfirst out onto the street. I end up putting up a serious fight. Well, I actually lie on the floor, while Nudger grabs me by the legs and storts dragging me along the corpet towards the lift. I stort, like, wriggling, then holding on to random pieces of furniture to make it horder for him. But then he thinks of a solution to that problem. He's suddenly standing over me, one hand gripping the front of my shirt, the other formed into a fist, which is, like, cocked and ready to launch.

I close my eyes and then I hear it. Another familiar voice. It goes, 'Well, this is a fine how-do-you-do, isn't it, Kicker?'

And I think, what the fock? It *sounds* like he's in the room. Except, like Sorcha, I can't actually see him and I can't actually talk to him.

'A year ago, it was *you* at *my* hospital bedside,' he goes. 'Now it appears the roles have been reversed. Well, I'm here for you, old chap – that's what I wanted to say. And obviously worried. I mean, *everyone* is. Including your godfather. Old Hennessy. Asking for you, naturally – you probably don't need me to add that detail.

'They do say this helps, you know. With people in, well, *your* situation. I said it to the doctor – she's one of these lady doctors, Ross – I said, "Would it help his condition any if his Old Dad – as he likes to call me – sat by his bedside and chatted away to him?"

'She said it couldn't hurt to keep him in the loop re what's been happening – events and so forth. Well, the big news, I suppose, is that which concerns your mother. She is, as I speak, Ross, sitting on a long-haul flight bound for the city of Los Angeles – Tinseltown, don't you know! It seems someone or other is interested in making a movie based on this latest book of hers. *Mom, They Said They'd Never Heard of Sundried Tomatoes*. And they want *her* to write the blooming well script! Yes, she rang me from Heathrow. All terribly exciting, don't you think?'

Jesus. Please. Someone put a focking pillow over my face.

'In other news, poor old Jim Mansfield's in trouble. The current economic what's it. Poor Jim, eh? Still, it's an ill wind and so forth. I've made – let's just say – subtle inquiries to the receiver as to the likely fate of certain *effects* of his? He has a Ming vase, you know, as well as a set of duelling pistols that are supposed to have belonged to, I don't know, George Washington or one of those chaps . . .'

He suddenly stops talking. There's, like, five seconds of silence at first, then he storts literally screaming the walls down. 'Doctor! Doctor! Quickly! Doctor!'

I hear, like, a rush of feet and the room is suddenly full of voices.

'He spoke,' I hear the old man go. 'He bloody well spoke.'

I can all of a sudden hear this, like, beeping sound that I wasn't *aware* of before? It's obviously some kind of machine, monitoring my something or other. Someone's pressing buttons.

'It was clear as a bell,' the old man goes. 'He said, "Fucking vulture." Although I can't think what he meant. I expect it's the effect of the drugs . . .'

'Get him out of here,' a woman's voice shouts.

'Will he not want to see a familiar face,' the old man goes, 'when he wakes up?'

'Out!'

I hear him being bundled out of the room. He says this is a fine old carry-on, then mentions how much money he spent in health insurance contributions last year – why, I have no focking idea.

Then a door slams behind him.

A woman – I'm presuming this doctor he was banging on about – puts her lips next to my ear and goes, 'Ross! Ross! Ross!' in, like, a really *urgent* way?

I open my eyes and I end up being nearly blinded by the light. I end up having to keep blinking until I can eventually bear to keep them open.

The first thing I notice, typically, is that the doctor is an absolute cracker. If I had to say she looked like anyone, it'd be Minka Kelly. I've never been so happy to see a pretty face. She smiles at me and goes, 'Welcome back.'

I look around me. I'm in, like, a hospital room. Vincent's Private would be my guess.

I'm there, 'I can't tell what's a dream or what's real any more.'

She smiles. 'You've just woken from a coma,' she goes.

'How long was I out for?'

'Ten days.'

'Someone . . . someone shot me.'

'Yes, we know. Do you have any pain, Ross?'

'I don't know . . . oh my God, yeah.'

'Okay.'

'Jesus Christ. My stomach. Fock.'

'It's okay, Ross.'

'And my legs.'

'I'm going to increase your morphine dose.'

'Jesus focking . . .'

'It'll take a moment to kick in.'

'Oh, fock . . . am I bad?'

'What?'

'As in badly hurt?'

She's like, 'Just rest, Ross. You're lucky to be alive.'

Who shot Ross O'Carroll-Kelly?

The dude is built like a focking petrol pump. I'd say when he crosses the road, it's the traffic that looks both ways. He's, like, sitting on a chair at the bottom of my bed, staring at my medical chort, even though it's pretty obvious from his expression that he hasn't a clue what it all means. 'How are you feeling?' he goes in this, like, really *friendly* voice?

I'm like, 'Er, I don't know,' because I'm still a bit actually groggy.

'You were having a nightmare.'

'Was I?'

'You were moaning in your sleep anyway. Unless it's pain. Are you in pain at all?'

He's a Gord. That'd be my guess. They all talk the same way, don't they?

'Might be a combination of the two,' I go.

My eyes drift to the window, which looks out onto the golf course. The snow is really coming down out there. I can just about make out a tiny piece of red cloth on this, like, undisturbed blanket of basically white and I realize that it's the top of the flag on the third green. Which means there must be, like, four feet of snow out there.

'Detective Sergeant Shane Harron,' he goes.

Told you.

'Yeah, no,' I go, 'the doctor said you'd been in once or twice alright. I can't . . . I can't remember anything.'

He's like, 'You have amnesia.'

'I don't even know if it's, like, *proper* amnesia? It's just those ten or fifteen minutes in Regina's kitchen . . .'

'They're missing.'

'It's actually freaking me out.'

He nods, then sort of, like, smiles patiently at me. 'Look,' he goes, 'I've had some experience of trauma-related memory loss. What the mind can't process, it chooses to bury. I expect that's what the nightmares are about.'

'What do you mean?'

'Your mind is conflicted. It wants to remember, but at the same time it doesn't.'

'Oh.'

'I've had one or two cases like this before.'

He seems actually alright.

'Look,' he goes, 'I'm not going to put pressure on you. I know it could take weeks for you to retrieve that vital clue. But this is an attempted murder investigation, Ross.'

'I know.'

'We walked into that kitchen to find you on the floor, bleeding out like a piece of – what's the word I'm looking for? It's the way the Jews like their beef . . .'

'I don't know – is it, like, a kebab thing?'

'Halal. That's the word I'm looking for. You were bleeding out like a lump of halal beef. You lost nearly five pints of blood. Do you know how many pints of blood are in a human body?'

'How many?'

'Eight.'

'Doesn't sound like a lot.'

'Huh?'

I hate the way Gords and teachers say that even when they've heard you.

'I'm just saying, it doesn't sound like a lot.'

'Well, that's all there is. Eight pints. Do you remember the snow that day?'

'It's one of the last things I *do* remember?'

'It was the first day it fell. The ambulance had a hell of a job getting up the Malahide Road. People saw the bit of snow falling and they panicked. Decided to get out of town. There was mayhem.

The ambulance very nearly didn't get to you in time. It's only by the grace of a few minutes that this isn't a murder investigation.'

I'm there, 'I want whoever did this to be caught.'

'I'm glad to hear you say that. Do you think if we talked that it might, you know, jog something?'

'We could certainly give it a go.'

He stands up, checks the corridor outside, then closes the door. He walks over to me and sits down on the side of the bed. I hear the thing creak under his weight.

'We have a chief suspect,' he goes.

I'm like, 'Who?'

'The individual who phoned the emergency services from the house. A nineteen-year-old girl.'

I automatically say her name. 'Hedda Rathfriland.'

'So you remember some things.'

'I remember her.'

'Well, it's a start. Is there any particular reason why she'd want you dead? And bad enough that she'd pull the trigger herself?'

'No. I mean, we had a bit of a thing. Sex and blahdy blah. I'd imagine you've already found that out.'

'She told us you were, eh, intimate.'

'Well, I red-corded her. And she was obviously upset. But I wouldn't have thought enough to want to kill me.'

He smiles and at the same time shakes his head. 'The female of the species . . .'

I laugh, even though it hurts to. I'm like, 'You're preaching to the choir.'

'*She's* saying that's how she found you. I'm telling you this informally, of course. She's saying she walked into the kitchen and found you lying on the floor, shot in the stomach. Her father's gun was on the table – wiped clean, by the way. There was no one else in the house but her.'

I nod. I'm there, 'The last thing I remember is walking into the kitchen . . . I'm not sure if you've found this out yet but I was also – whatever you want to call it – *sleeping* with her mother as well.'

'We're aware of that, yes.'

'Well, we actually broke up. It was really the whole age thing. And obviously the fact that I rode her daughter, which didn't go down well. I actually went back to the gaff that night to clear out my stuff.'

'So you were in the kitchen . . .'

'Yeah, no, Regina bought me a cor. It was, like, an Audi A8. Anyway, I decided I should possibly give it back. So I went into the kitchen to leave the keys on the island.'

'Go on.'

'I remember *being* in the kitchen. And the next thing . . . the next thing I remember . . . is waking up in this bed . . . Why can't I *focking* remember?'

'Don't get frustrated, Ross.'

'Why can't I remember?'

'You're doing great. *Really* great. Let's go back. Earlier. What else do you remember about that day?'

'Yeah, no, it was snowing, like you said. I was in Blackrock.'

'What were you doing in Blackrock?'

'I was supposed to meet Terry and Larry – as in, Terry and Larry Tuhill?'

He's like, 'What?'

'Terry and Larry Tuhill. They were these, like, *neighbours* of mine?'

'The gangland fellas?'

'Yeah, no, they actually lived next door to me. In, like, Ticknock.'

'Sure that was the same day the two of them were murdered in their car.'

'I know. That's why they didn't show up to our meeting.'

'Go back, go back – why were you meeting them fellas?'

'Like I said, we were neighbours. And there'd been – to be honest – a bit of a misunderstanding between us. So it was supposed to be, like, a clear-the-air thing?'

I watch his eyes suddenly narrow. 'What kind of a misunderstanding?'

'Okay, I'm going to say it. For some reason, Larry was under the impression that I, again, *slept with* his girlfriend. And cords on the table here, I actually *did*? In the focking stairwell one afternoon.'

The dude's jaw just drops. He whips his mobile from the inside pocket of his – let's call a spade a spade here – sports coat. He dials a number, then holds the phone to his ear. While he's waiting for a response, he goes, 'Had they threatened you at all?'

I'm like, 'They'd more than threatened me. They trashed my focking gaff.'

'You're saying *they* did that?'

'Yeah. They also totalled my old cor. *And* they burned out my van. I *was* in the old document-shredding game.'

Someone obviously answers, roysh, because he suddenly goes, 'Bart. New line of inquiry . . . yeah, I'll see you back in the station in an hour.'

A spasm of pain suddenly rips through my, I suppose, abdomen. He reaches for the call bell. He's like, 'Let's get you something for that pain.'

I'm like, 'Thanks.'

He goes, 'You've done great, Ross. Really great. If anything else should occur to you, I'm leaving my card here on your bedside locker. No matter how insignificant you think it might be – do you get me?'

I'm there, 'I do, yeah.'

She hasn't cried. Not once that I've seen. Even though she's been coming here three times a day since it happened. What she does instead is she keeps the conversation moving swiftly along to avoid ever having to *go* there? She storts looking through my Get Well Soon cords, stacked high on my bedside locker, going, 'Oh! *My* God! *Mister* Popularity? Ross, I haven't heard of half of these people.'

'Sorcha,' I go, 'come and sit down.'

She's like, 'Louisa de Groot? Why is that name familiar?'

She still gets jealous, even though the divorce was *her* actual idea?

'Sorcha, come on, sit down,' I go. 'Talk to me.'

She sits on the side of the bed.

'Ross,' she goes, 'you look like shit.'

I just smile. I'm like, 'So would you if you'd been fed through a drip for nearly three weeks.'

She looks well, it has to be said. She's had her roots done and she's wearing her good Isabel Marant jacket with jeans, a white tee and a hefty whack of *Prada Infusion d'Iris*, which has always done it for me.

I'm there, 'So how's Honor?'

She just smiles – sort of, like, *sadly*? – and goes, 'Honor is Honor,' and I know straight away what she means. She *can* be a bit of a bitch and I'm saying that as her father.

She goes, 'I'm sorry I haven't brought her in, Ross. I mean, I *agonized* over it? It was actually my dad who didn't think it was a good idea for her to see you . . . Well, you know . . .'

Her old man hates my actual guts.

I'm there, 'Hey, it's fine. And *I'm* fine as well, by the way.'

Which *is* true. I took the full brunt of the blast in the stomach. Like the dude said, I had, like, massive internal haemorrhaging and they had to, like, transfuse me at the scene. It took a team of, like, seven surgeons to basically save my life. I've lost nearly half of my stomach and nearly a metre of my lorge intestine. On the upside, the shot managed to miss all of my vital organs, including – dare I say it? – the most vital one of all. According to the doctor, it was a case of, like, *millimetres*? But I did also take a fair bit of shrapnel in the tops of my legs.

I'm a real mess under all this bandaging. I had a look while one of the nurses was bathing me. My beloved six-pack, which once stood out from my middle like the ridges of a kitchen draining board, is a mass of stitches and scabs and staples and collapsed muscles. You could read my stomach like a focking Google map. But, given the fact that someone shot me from less than ten feet away, you'd have to say that I got off lightly.

I'm like, 'What did you tell Honor? About what happened?'

She goes, 'I just said you'd been in an accident.'

'Probably all over Mount Anville by now, though, is it?'

'No – all the schools are closed because of the snow. Which is, like, a blessing, I suppose.'

I'm there, 'Oisinn and JP called in this morning. Fionn was in last night. They're all worried about me. Christian's rung me from the States practically every second or third day since I woke up.'

'You have amazing friends,' she goes.

There's, like, a moment of silence, then she goes, 'Have you remembered anything yet – as in, who did it?'

I just shake my head. 'They're saying I probably will eventually.'

Sorcha looks away. 'Because do you know what the papers are saying?'

'Papers?'

'Ross, it's been all *over* the papers? "Former Schools Rugby Star Shot!"'

'Did it actually *say* stor?'

'What?'

'It definitely *said* stor, did it?'

'It said *former* stor.'

'Hey, that's still stor. I'll take it.'

I'm putting, like, a brave face on shit and she knows it.

She's like, 'Are you interested in what it *also* said?'

I'm there, 'Okay, what?'

'It said you were part of a mother-and-daughter love triangle.'

I laugh. Again, torture.

'What paper did it say that in? I bet it was that focking rag that Foley writes for. I'm going to say it to him the next time I see him.'

'It said you were having ... *relations*, simultaneously, with a sixty-year-old woman – who I'm presuming is Regina Rathfriland, since it was her kitchen floor you were found bleeding to death on – and her teenage daughter, who was the one who called the ambulance ...'

'Definitely sounds like One F's crowd alright. Oh, he'll have filled them in on some of my previous, of course.'

'And one of the theories they're working on is that the daughter shot you with her father's shotgun in a fit of, like, *jealousy*?'

'Well, the Feds think there's a possibility it could also be gang-related.'

She nods. 'I read that somewhere else. Because those two gangsters who lived next door to you were shot on the exact same day. Ronan's theory is that you were all, like, *witnesses* to something?

And that one of these – I don't know – *hoods* had to, like, pop a cap in the three of you – to guarantee your basic silence.'

I can't tell you how funny it is listening to a girl from the Vico Road talk street.

That's when I reach for her hand. 'Sorcha,' I go, 'you're unbelievable – do you know that?'

She rolls her eyes. She thinks I'm spinning her a line here.

I'm there, 'I'm serious. You're in this hospital morning, noon and night. My old dear hasn't come to see me once, by the way. Wouldn't bother her hole coming back from LA to see her son who's on his, like, deathbed.'

'In her defence, Ross, there's – oh my God – chaos at the airports at the moment.'

'But *you're* here, Sorcha – despite everything.'

'Well, the Rock Road wasn't actually bad. It's, like, the salt air. I remember that from geography.'

'I'm not talking about the snow, Sorcha. When I say everything, I mean everything I put you through. Cheating and blah, blah, blah. Focking up our marriage. And yet I wake up after, like, ten days in a coma and the doctor tells me that the first person to arrive at the hospital after the ambulance brought me in was my still technically wife. Talk about amazing friends.'

She shrugs – just one shoulder. 'We said we'd stay on good terms, didn't we? We're co-parenting our daughter . . .'

'Sorcha,' I go, giving her hand a light squeeze, 'you don't need to come up with excuses for giving a shit about me. I'm just saying it's nice, that's all. No one's ever cared about me the way you do.'

She tries to make a joke about it. She nods at all my cords. 'I find that very hord to believe. You seem to have a lot of fans.'

She hasn't even seen the ones in the drawer, by the way.

'That's just sex, Sorcha. Birds I've been with. Birds I nearly ended up being with. What *we* have is different.'

I notice, like, a tear glisten in her eye, then I realize that she's actually welling up.

'Hey,' I go, 'it's okay, Sorcha. It's okay to cry,' and that's when the floodgates come crashing open.

'I thought you were going to die,' she goes. 'They wouldn't tell me anything, Ross. The Gords. When they rang. All they said was that you'd been shot and that you were in a critical condition. And that you had massive trauma and that they were going to have to perform . . . emergency surgery. And all I could think about was that last time I saw you. That afternoon, when you called to the house. You seemed so . . . so scared, Ross. Like someone was chasing you or something. And all I could think about was all the things that I should have said to you and now . . . and now I'd never get the chance.'

'Hey, it's okay.'

'Then I ended up having – oh my God – *such* a row with my dad.'

'A row?'

'I rang him and told him you'd been shot. And do you know what he said, Ross? He said it was only a matter of time.'

'Hey, he's never been a supporter of mine, Sorcha – we *knew* that.'

'Then I asked him to drive me to the hospital and he just said no. He's never said no to me in my entire life, Ross. He said if someone shot you, he was going to be a suspect and he'd have to get his alibi straight. He said hundreds of people all over Dublin would be on the phone doing the exact same thing. I was like, "*Oh* my God! How can you joke about a thing like this? He's Honor's father and he might actually die!"'

'Hey,' I go, pulling her close to me, 'I didn't die. That's one thing you need to maybe realize.'

She ends up seriously losing it then. The whole grief thing. She throws herself on top of me on the bed – Jesus Christ! – forgetting, of course, that it's only some pretty slick needlework holding me together. Her head is buried in my shoulder and she's trying to say something, but she's crying so hord that I can't understand a single word coming from her mouth. I want to tell her to get up for a minute, or at least move, because I'm literally in agony here. Except I don't. I just grit my teeth and let her lie there on top of me, with my stitches at practically bursting point, until she's cried her eyes dry.

*

The doctor who's a ringer for Minka Kelly lays her cold hand on my forehead. 'You're hot,' she goes.

I give her the full eye contact. I'm like, 'You're not so bad yourself.'

She smiles. I honestly think she's a bit smitten. I reach for her fingers.

She goes, 'What are you doing?'

I'm there, 'I'm not a fool, you know. I've seen the way you look at me.'

She looks away. But she doesn't deny it. And that's always the giveaway. She takes a breath, then she looks at me and goes, 'Just give me a second, okay?'

I let go of her hand and she turns away. I'm like, 'Where are you going?'

'To get some protection,' she goes.

She walks over to this, like, long cabinet on the other side of the room.

I'm like, 'Protection?'

I've never been able to say the word without laughing the two final syllables. But then all of a sudden I'm *not* laughing? Because she's standing at the foot of the bed pointing a sawn-off shotgun at me.

I go, 'Please! No!' except I don't get to even finish my sentence, because she laughs, then pulls the actual trigger. There's, like, a loud bang, followed by a scream, which comes from me. And then I'm suddenly awake again, staring at the ceiling, trying to remind myself where I am.

'Thee'll be got,' I hear a little voice go. It's Ronan. 'That's alls Ine saying, Rosser. Thee'll be got.'

I look up. He's sitting on a chair beside my bed with his little hord-man face on him. I can't help but smile. It's so good to see him.

I'm like, 'It was just another bad dream, Ro. Might be this morphine they have me on.'

'Ine just saying,' he goes, 'whoever shot you, Rosser, thee'll be hunted down and dealt with.'

'I'd prefer if you just concentrated on your school work,' I go, 'and forgot about avenging my near-death.'

Talk about lines you never thought you'd say to your son.

I'm like, 'But hey, the good news is that I could be out of here for Christmas.'

'Seerdious?'

He's delighted. He can't hide the fact. But I still feel unbelievable guilt about what I put the kid through.

'Out by Christmas,' I go. 'Obviously, there'll be physio and blah, blah, blah. But mork my words, I'll be doing sit-ups by the time the Six Nations storts. Getting the six back!'

'You look shit, but.'

'Thanks, Ro.

'Ine just saying, Rosser.'

It's only then that I notice that his voice has broken. When did that happen? I didn't cop it the last time he was in. He's huge now as well – almost as tall as me, if I was up and out of this bed. He's nearly fourteen, of course. Not a little kid any more, which I have to admit makes me sad.

'So how's your old dear?' I go. Tina's back *dating* Tom McGahy, the principal of Ronan's school. It's a pretty sensitive subject. 'Is she still going out with that prick with ears?'

He actually surprises me by going, 'Ah, Tom's alreet, Rosser.'

I'm there, 'Er, *you* seem to have changed your tune.'

'He's good to me ma. And, well, he's arthur getting me into that course – the one thee do for kids with exceptionoddle abidities.'

'The weekend one in DCU?'

'Yeah.'

'Fionn did that same course. So you're *actually* gifted now? The last I remember, you were, like, one or two IQ points off.'

'Thee tested me again.'

'And you were over the limit? Well, fair focks – I have to say it. Who'd have thought an idiot like me would sire an actual brainiac? I'd say that one must bend McGahy's head.'

He helps himself to my Lucozade. I'm not a fan of the stuff anyway. 'Here,' he goes, 'do you know who else is on me course?'

'Go on, who?'

'Do you member Shadden Tuite? She's a boord off me road.'

I remember hearing about Shadden alright. He rebounded into her orms after he finished it with Blathin. 'So she's another smortie, is she? You'd have to ask yourself is there something in the water on that side of the city. Aport from obviously lead.'

He suddenly goes, 'I'd luven you to meet her, Rosser.'

And I'm like, 'Yeah, big-time – let's arrange it.'

'She's outside, so she is. In the coddidor.'

'What's she doing out there?'

'Ah, she dudn't want to interrude. I'll go and get her, will I?'

'Go and get her big-time. Jesus.'

Off he toddles. I end up having a little chuckle to myself. He's an exceptional kid alright. I don't need any test results to tell me that.

'Er, Rosser,' I suddenly hear him go, from the door of the room, 'this is Shadden.'

I look up expecting her to be – and this is my own prejudices coming through – just another piece of northside batter, one of those girls who even says 'Hello' like she's being accused of something. But I couldn't be more wrong. She's actually a pretty little thing. Small and blonde with glasses – except trendy glasses, not the focking Rovers Return beer-mug kind that Fionn wears. She's possibly a year or two older than him as well. And manners? You've never heard anything like it.

'Hello, Mr O'Carroll-Kelly,' she goes – get this – shaking my hand. 'It's *so* nice to finally meet you. Ronan talks about you *all* the time.'

She talks – I'm not shitting you here – like a kid from a focking *Nornia* movie. She's good stock, in other words. I didn't even know there *were* private houses on Ronan's road.

I laugh. I'm there, 'I hope it's all good shit he says about me, is it?'

'Oh, yes,' she goes. 'Oh my God, he showed me the video of that rugby match you played.'

It's obvious which match she's talking about as well. I look at Ro. 'Did you?'

He gets embarrassed, of course. He hates anything that punctures his whole hord-man image. He's like, 'Leave it, Rosser.'

She goes, 'You were obviously an amazing rugby player, Mr O'Carroll-Kelly.'

I like this girl. You know the way sometimes you just get a vibe?

'Well,' I go, 'that medal was actually taken off me on a technicality. The whole methamphetamine business. And blah, blah, blah.'

She's like, 'That doesn't matter. No one can ever take away from you what you did on the day.'

Okay, I'm going to have to wipe this stupid look off my face – I'm grinning at her here like she's a focking monkey on a tricycle. I'm like, 'Thanks very much, Shadden. That's an amazing boost for me to get.'

'How are you feeling?' she goes. 'Ronan was – oh my God – *so* worried about you.'

I'm like, 'Hey, I'm well on the mend, don't you worry about that. I might be back on solids in a week or two. Did he tell you I've been out of the bed two or three times walking? *With* crutches, of course.'

She smiles at me. 'Well, thank God you're alive. Anyway, it was lovely to meet you, Mr O'Carroll-Kelly. I better go. I've got a lot of studying to do. You do, too, Ronan. We've both missed a lot of school with the snow.'

As they're leaving the ward, I catch Ronan's eye and I mouth, like, four words to him: 'You have struck gold.'

The nurse is no scene-stealer. Being brutally honest, she actually looks like Boris Johnson with tits. But when she tells me that I'm being dischorged – a full week before Christmas – I feel like nearly *kissing* her?

'Well, why not?' she goes. 'The doctor's very happy with you. And you'll be able to get around with the crutches.'

She has a face like a Solero left out in a hundred focking thunder storms.

I'm there, 'The doctor also said there might still be bits of, like, *bullet* still inside me? I think the phrase she might have used was *fragments*?'

She smiles. It's pretty obvious she fancies me, the poor girl. 'One or two pieces,' she goes, 'that you'd nearly struggle to see with a microscope. They're not a danger to you.'

'Well, thanks,' I go, 'for looking after me.'

She's actually a ringer for a Munster fan I hatefocked the night they won their first Heineken Cup and I'm wondering is she possibly a cousin?

She's there, 'Do you have somewhere to go?' her eyes – I'm not imagining this – tracing figure eights on my chest. I'm thinking, okay, eyes up here, lady! 'Do you have someone to care for you?'

'Yes,' this voice suddenly goes. 'He does.'

It's honestly like something from a romcom – one with Ginnifer Goodwin and possibly Gerard Butler in it. Sorcha is suddenly standing at the foot of the bed, with her head cocked to one side and a look of the old Sacred Hort of Jesus about her face.

She goes, 'Me.'

She looks incredible, I'm going to have to say it, in just her Louise Kennedy bodycon black dress, her Claudia Schiffer soft grey cordigan and the Carvela ankle boots that I let her stick on my credit cord last Valentine's Day but which she never paid me back for. And, I notice, she finally has the statement fringe she was always threatening to get whenever she got all silly and self-conscious about her forehead.

It's obvious she heard they were letting me out before *I* even did?

I'm there, 'Sorcha, it's cool. I can go back to Rosa Porks.'

'Er, I don't *think* so?' she goes, then storts picking up and folding various items of my clothing that are scattered about the place. The nurse takes this as her cue to fock off – accepts there's nothing here for her. 'What, back to that apartment of yours? It was destroyed, Ross.'

'Yeah, no,' I go, 'but the old man fixed it up. Or paid someone else to. He was in here this morning. The point is it doesn't look like a bomb hit it any more.'

'That may or may not be true,' she goes, stuffing my clothes into her Louis Vuitton Monogram Canvas Pegase, 'but there's no way you're going back there to spend Christmas on your own. And the fact remains, Ross, that you're going to need – oh my God – round-the-clock care.'

Sorcha, of course, would try to get the last word over an echo. Arguing with her is as pointless as a pulled pube. So I end up just swinging my legs out of the bed and grabbing my crutches. I manage to work myself into an upright position. But then I feel this sudden pain in my guts, like I've been stabbed, and I end up just roaring, then my crutches go crashing to the floor and I fall back onto the bed.

Sorcha has a practical shit-fit.

'Ross,' she goes, 'will you stop being so – oh my God – proud! You're going to have to accept, like, *help* from people?'

She bends down to pick up my supports, as they're known in here. I put my orm around her shoulder and she helps me to slowly stand, then five minutes later I'm picking my way across the cor-pork of Vincent's Private, towards Sorcha's Hyundai Santa Fe, with a giddiness about me that I soon realize is excitement at the prospect of seeing my daughter again.

It's been, like, a month.

'I told Honor you were coming home,' Sorcha goes, as if reading my mind. We're stopped at a red light outside Bianconi's. 'I told her you were going to be possibly staying for a few weeks – just until you're well enough to look after yourself.'

I'm there, 'How is she? Is she okay?'

Sorcha looks away sadly and tells me she's getting worse. 'She's so cheeky, Ross.'

I'm always the first to defend her, of course. Fathers and daughters. 'I still think it might be just a phase,' I go. 'Something she'll possibly grow *out* of?'

She's there, 'I hope so.'

I'm like, 'I do sometimes wonder was it something *we* did, though. Did we possibly spoil her? Or was it even us breaking up?'

'You had sex with our daughter's nanny in *our* actual bed,' she goes. The light turns green and she leans on the accelerator. 'It would have been far more damaging to her growing up in a home full of lies and deceit, Ross.'

I'm there, 'I'm not saying you were wrong to fock me out, Sorcha. But it's still going to affect her, isn't it? Having no strong male role model around, twenty-four-seven.'

I stare out of the passenger window. Booterstown bird morsh zips by.

Sorcha goes, 'Sometimes, the way she speaks to me . . .'

I'm like, 'I'm wondering is that maybe the way all kids speak to their olds these days?'

She shakes her head. 'It's not, Ross. I look at other mothers with *their* little girls . . .'

'Okay, what mothers are we talking about?'

'Well, Katie Holmes – just as an example. There's a photograph of her in one of my magazines – I think it's on the back seat there. Her and Suri are in the Häagen-Dazs Café in Miami. The two of them just, I don't know, hanging out, like actual best friends. The way *I* always was with *my* mum?'

I'm there, 'Come on, Sorcha. It's a photograph in a magazine. Suri Cruise could be a little focking wanker for all we know.'

She doesn't want to hear that, of course. Neither of us says another word until we reach the right turn at the bottom of Newtownpork Avenue.

Then I go, 'By the way, I met Ronan's new girlfriend.'

She's like, 'Oh my God, he told me he was seeing someone. What's her name again?'

'Shadden Tuite. And before you leap to the same conclusion I did, I've got to tell you, Sorcha, she's a great kid. I'm already a huge defender of hers.'

'Apparently she's, like, sixteen.'

I laugh. 'He obviously has a thing for older women as well!'

It ends up being a tumbleweed moment. It'll be a while, I suppose, before the whole Regina Rathfriland thing becomes a laughing matter.

She goes, 'So what's she like?'

The filter light turns green but she doesn't notice. Someone behind us in a blue Nissan something-or-other gives us a beep. Sorcha makes the turn, then says sorry in the rear-view – even puts her hazards on to apologize. And that's when I cop it, the reason I like Shadden so much – she's exactly like Sorcha was at that age.

'She's just one of life's good souls,' I go. 'That's the definite vibe I got.'

She pulls up outside the gaff and I give her a smile that says – basically – home, sweet home. She gets instantly defensive then. She goes, 'Remember, Ross, this is only for a few weeks – until you're back on your feet.'

I go to open the cor door, except she jumps out, rushes around to the passenger side and helps me get myself vertical again.

'I have to say,' I go, 'that I've been looking forward to this moment more than anything.'

I pick my way up the gorden path. Sorcha puts the key in the door and in we go. The hall is empty except for Linh, the Vietnamese nanny, who, by the way, is so focking ugly it'd make you want to weep. She was Sorcha's choice. No one can say the girl didn't learn from experience.

Linh goes, 'Wewcome hom.'

I'm like, 'Thanks, Linh. It's good to be back. Now, where's that beautiful daughter of mine?'

All of a sudden, Honor comes pegging it out of the living room, going, 'Daddy! Daddy! Daddy!'

She throws her orms around my legs – like her mother, forgetting how badly injured I actually am. Sorcha cops my reaction and goes, 'Honor, be careful!'

But I'm like, 'It's fine, Sorcha. It's really fine,' and I end up just stroking her hair and holding the kid close. Yes, it's agony. But it's nothing compared to the agony of nearly never seeing her again.

'*Sur-prise!*' they all shout.

And it genuinely is. I was wondering why Sorcha was so keen for me to go out and meet JP for a pint, rather than spend Christmas Eve at home with her and Honor. They've arranged, like, a surprise porty for me in Kielys. And they're all there. We're talking Oisinn, JP and Fionn. We're talking Ryle Nugent. We're talking One F obviously. We're talking Erika, Chloe, Sophie, Amie with an ie. All the old crew.

Gordon D'Arcy and Shane Horgan have even shown their faces and you'd have to say fair focks.

There's, like, a banner hung above the bor that just says 'Welcome Home, Ross O'Carroll-Kelly!' and there's, like, a round of applause when I walk through the door, which then turns into a chorus of 'Legend! Legend! Legend!'

The vibe is very much one of, like, hero worship?

I end up just standing there, on my crutches, lost for basic words. Oisinn storts *actually* crying. He's like, 'Dude, I didn't think I'd ever see you walk through those doors again.' He's always had a soft side, though you'd never have known it watching him play rugby. I think he might also be shit-faced.

I put my orm around his waist and I laugh. I'm like, 'It's okay, Big O. Come on, I'm still here. Let's just celebrate that basic fact.'

JP tells me I look like something out a focking horror movie and I tell him he should see me stripped to the waist! We high-five – apologies to no one – and I tell him thanks for the prayers, they were much appreciated and obviously worked.

Then, a lovely moment, Fionn gives me a hug and tells me it's great to see me out of that bed at last. Then he goes, 'I'm hoping you'll still be my best man.'

He's still supposedly marrying my sister.

I'm like, 'Dude, I was the one who kicked off the riot at that battle re-enactment of yours. You said it yourself, I was the reason you lost your job in the Institute.'

He just shrugs, like it's not a major deal any more. 'Look, I know what I said at the time. But what happened to you . . . I mean, what *nearly* happened. It just puts everything in perspective.'

I'm pretty sure the word is *prospective*, but I let it go. I'm just like, 'Of course I'll still be your best man. Provided it goes ahead, of course.'

I just think it's necessary to add that in.

Fionn just rolls his eyes, then Erika arrives over, looking tremendous, it has to be said, in a tight-clinging red dress that really shows off her Cha-Chas and I'm saying that as her brother. She leans in, gives me an unbelievable hug and tells me it's lovely to see me and she seems to genuinely mean it.

She's like, 'I was so worried about you.'

It's only then that she even *acknowledges* Fionn's presence? He wishes her a Merry Christmas, then goes to kiss her, except she turns her face and presents her cheek to him. Then she cops his disappointed reaction and tells him she's just put on lippy.

He nods like he understands. The poor focker's in for a serious land, take it from someone who can read the signs.

JP sticks a pint in my hand, which I'm not allowed to drink, of course. I've been living on, like, probiotic yoghurt and energy drinks. But even just the feeling of holding it is nice.

Various people – Kielys regulars a lot of them – stop by to, like, pat me on the back and tell me they're delighted I pulled through and they hope the Gordaí catch the bastards who did it.

'Are you having any counselling?' Erika goes.

I laugh. I'm there, 'Counselling?' basically playing the tough goy.

'Ross, someone shot you. You nearly bled to death on that stupid bitch's floor.'

'But I don't *remember* any of that?'

'Maybe that's why you need counselling.'

JP throws his thoughts into the mix then. 'She's right, Ross. You might think you're fine. But shock is a funny thing. It can just all of a sudden rear up and bite you on the ass.'

Oisinn just goes, 'Everyone's saying that it was that girl who shot you.' Like I said, he's mullered. 'Is it true you were doing her *and* her old dear?'

I laugh. Jack the Lad. 'Yeah. But they still don't know if that's why I was shot.'

'I think it was the Westies,' Oisinn goes. 'They burned your van out. I saw that myself.'

Fionn's there, 'But they were already dead by the time Ross was shot.'

'But they might have hired someone to do it, Dude – as in, like, a contract killer.'

'I don't think a contract killer would have hit him in the stomach from ten feet away.'

I end up just shrugging. 'Look, until I remember something, it's all just speculation.' Then I raise my glass. 'But in the meantime, here's to just being alive.'

They all raise their glasses, then someone – probably One F – shouts, 'Speech!' and there ends up being, like, a chant of it from everyone in the bor.

It's like, 'Speech! Speech! Speech! Speech!'

And of course I've never been one to disappoint a crowd. So I end up just putting the pint down on the bor, clearing my throat, then going, 'Okay, first of all I want to say thank you to everyone for coming out tonight. I know it's Christmas Eve and most of you would probably be here anyway. But the reception I got when I walked through that door earlier, it was real hero-worship stuff and I just want to let you know that it was genuinely appreciated.

'They say that people who go through what I went through – as in, like, a near-death experience? – are never the same again. It changes you. Makes you want to live for the moment. And as soon as I'm well again, that's what I fully intend to do. *Carte D'Or*. Seize the day.'

That gets a massive cheer and a round of applause. Then I move on to my thank yous. There's, like, a real Oscars vibe to it.

I'm there, 'I know a lot of you were worried about me. My friends here. Oisinn. JP. Fionn. My sister, Erika. My amazing soon-to-be-ex-wife, Sorcha, who's at home tonight with our beautiful, beautiful daughter, Honor . . .'

I hear my voice wobble a bit.

'. . . my son, Ronan. Even my old man. They were in and out of the hospital like I don't know what. Talking to me while I was out of it. Praying for me when it was looking like it was maybe touch and go . . .'

I look at JP. He's telling Fionn that I'm storting to lose it. He's possibly right.

'. . . It probably hasn't even hit me yet. As in, how close I actually came to dying. How close I came to, like, never seeing this place again. To never seeing my friends again. My family . . .'

Shit. I'm crying.

'How close my kids came to growing up without a father . . .'

Suddenly, roysh, I can't even speak. My chest feels heavy, like something is pressing down on it, and I can't form words.

I hear someone go, 'He's having a panic attack or something.'

JP storts a round of applause – fair focks – just to get me out of there. Oisinn drags over a low stool and tells me to sit on it. Fionn orders a packet of Hunky Dorys, then tips the crisps all over the floor and tells me to breathe into the bag. And all the time I'm just, like, bawling my eyes out and I don't even *know* why?

Erika crouches down beside me and wipes away my tears with her hand. Then she turns to Fionn and goes, 'Go outside and see can you get him a taxi.'

'Oh! My God!' Honor goes. We're watching *PS I Love You* on DVD, by the way – one of her, like, Santa presents? 'Hilary Swank has teeth like a rocking horse!'

I laugh so hord, I end up nearly choking on a mouthful of scrambled egg – my Christmas dinner, by the way, and the first actual food I've had since the shooting. Where does she even *get* these lines?

'You, er, possibly shouldn't talk about people like that,' I go. 'Even though it's a cracking quote, in fairness to you.'

She's like, 'But look at her mouth, Dad! Hashtag – does your dentist *hate* you?'

The doorbell rings. I'm thinking, who the fock is that at, like, ten to twelve on Christmas morning?

'Honor,' I go, 'there's someone at the door,' meaning, of course, get up off your orse and answer it because I'm still recovering from being shot in the focking stomach here. She looks at me like I've served her stew and told her it's cassoulet.

'Er,' she goes, 'DILLIGAC?'

I'm like, 'DILLIGAC? What does that mean?'

'Er, do I look like I *give* a crap?'

'Oh,' I go. 'Fair enough,' and I end up having to grab my crutches, struggle to my feet, then hobble out to the door. I can see through the glass that it's my old man and Erika.

'Here he comes!' the old man roars, loud enough for half the focking neighbourhood to hear. 'Ross O'Carroll-Kelly! As I live and breathe!'

I open the door. 'Fock's sake,' I go. 'Take it down a decibel or five hundred, would you?'

He doesn't even bat an eyelid, just throws his orms around me and goes, 'Merry Christmas! Still the same old Ross, eh? With your banter and your what-have-you! Oh, it's good to see you home!'

Erika gives me a hug then. She looks *and* smells amazing – again, if that doesn't sound too weird. 'Are you okay?' she goes.

I'm like, 'Why wouldn't I be okay?'

'You got a bit . . . emotional in the pub last night.'

She says it with a smirk on her face. Is she being a bitch? It's always hord to know with Erika, although experience would suggest yes.

Honor comes running out into the hall and goes, 'Merry Christmas, Granddad!'

Honestly, it's like someone performed a focking personality transplant on her sometime in the last ten seconds.

The old man picks her up and goes, 'Merry Christmas, little one. Come here and give your granddad a GBH!'

Honor laughs. 'Oh my God, that is so lollers. Big Hs and Ks, Granddad.'

'Big Hs and Ks indeed. IWALU.'

'IWALU, too.'

I end up just going, 'Sorry, am I having a focking stroke here? What the fock is everyone talking about?'

The old man cracks his hole laughing. 'Sorry, Kicker. Helen bought me one of these – quote-unquote – texting dictionaries. In order to better understand my beautiful little granddaughter here. Well, it's all the rage, you see, what with all this Twitter and what-have-you-got. I could easily tell you to GWI, of course. In other words, get with it!'

Honor laughs again. 'Oh my God, LMFAO, Granddad!'

'LMFAO indeed, little one. Even ROFL. With a generous helping of CSL.'

'Oh my God! YASF, Granddad. YASF!'

I turn around to Erika. I'm like, 'Jesus focking Christ . . .'

'Where's Sorcha?' she goes.

I'm like, 'Mass, if you can believe that. Foxrock Church. With her old dear and her granny.'

That'd be a Lalor family tradition. She actually tried to persuade Honor to go – 'Four generations, Dorling!' – but Honor ended up having a total shit-fit and telling her she didn't believe in God.

She's not even six years old yet.

'By the way,' the old man goes, 'what are you doing for St Stephen's Day, Ross?'

'I don't know. There's bound to be an Indiana Jones or a Bond on. Are you going to Leopardstown?'

'I doubt it'll be on, with the snow and everything. I wondered if you didn't fancy taking a drive with us – Erika, Helen and I. We're going to Powerscourt, don't you know!'

'Why are you going to Powerscourt?'

'Because the famous Ritz-Carlton has emerged as a possible venue for your sister's nuptials!'

I look at Erika and just laugh. I possibly shouldn't. But then *she* was a bitch to *me*. 'You're still keeping that up, are you?'

She just stares at me, roysh, coldly.

She's like, 'What?'

'I'm just making the observation,' I go, 'that you're leaving it pretty late in the day to pull the corpet out from under the poor focker.'

The old man genuinely hasn't a clue, by the way. 'Pull the carpet?' he goes. 'What are you talking about, Ross?'

Sometimes I think I'm the only one who actually knows the real Erika.

'Ignore him,' she goes. 'He's being nasty.'

I'm there, 'Hey, Fionn's one of my best friends. I'm only saying it as the man who's going to end up picking up the focking pieces.'

She's not a happy bunny. 'And to think,' she goes, 'I actually felt sorry for you in that intensive care unit.'

The old man puts Honor down and storts playing this game with her where she has to guess which hand the fifty yoyo note is in. She guesses right at the second go, then takes the money and sticks it in the pocket of her bubblegum-pink Lucky Brand jeans. Her old dear will shit fifty focking colours if she finds out.

Then *he* suddenly goes, 'Step outside, Ross? I have a little surprise for you.'

I'm there, 'A surprise? What are you shitting on about now?' deciding to just hear him out.

He goes, 'It's your Christmas present, of course – come on, it's parked outside on the road.'

Porked outside? It's obviously a new cor. I keep forgetting that I don't have wheels any more. Erika brings Honor into the living room to watch the rest of *PS* and I make my way out into the gorden on my crutches. It's pretty slippery underfoot, it has to be said – there's, like, black ice on the path.

The old man follows me out onto the road. The only thing porked outside, though, aport from his Kompressor, is a flame-red Lamborghini. I turn around and look at him and he's grinning at me – honestly – like a man being electrocuted.

I'm like, 'You're ripping the piss.'

He's there, 'Merry Christmas, Ross! Do you like it?'

'Like it? It's a focking Lambo!'

I open the driver's door, hand him my crutches, then manage to swing myself painfully into the thing. It's got that brand-new cor smell. Fock knows what it must have set him back. I run my hand along the polished leather interior and the walnut detailing.

I'm too in shock to even say thank you. But then I don't get a chance to anyway because he suddenly brings up something else.

'I said some things, Ross . . .'

He's standing next to the driver's door.

I'm there, 'Forget about it,' because I've a good idea what's coming and I know I'm going to die of focking embarrassment here.

'No, no,' he goes, 'it has to be said. That day at the Aviva, Ross, when I discovered you'd been . . . Well, when I discovered that you'd been taken advantage of by that wretched Rathfriland woman . . .'

'Can we not just leave it?'

'I wish I could. But I said some things. Said you were no son of mine. Said I never wanted to set eyes on you again – well, I'm sorry, Ross.'

Jesus. He has me actually feeling sorry for him here.

'Look,' I go, 'you were upset. I know she pretty much extorted one point seven mills from you to keep Erika's name out of her divorce proceedings. And then you found out that I was . . . well, you know. Blah, blah, blah.'

'But I should have known, from my own dealings with her, how bloody manipulative the woman could be. And how innocent *you* can be. Not to mention trusting of people.'

I wonder does he actually believe that shit.

'I did realize it later,' he goes. 'Mature reflection and so forth. I thought, Of course! *She'll* have taken advantage of him! I thought, Yes, I think I rather owe the chap an apology. But then I heard that you'd been shot. I mean, shot! Oh, I still can't get my head around it. And then you were in a coma. And I thought, what if I never get the chance to tell him how sorry I am?'

I end up having to comfort *him*. 'It's fine,' I go. 'It's in the past,' and then I'm like, 'Come on, sit in here beside me,' which is what he actually ends up doing.

It's some focking cor – there's no doubt about that.

He sort of, like, flops into the front passenger seat. It's very low to the ground. I turn the key in the engine and give it a few revs. It's got the power of a focking Boeing 747.

'So,' he suddenly goes, 'anything shifted yet?'

I'm like, 'Sorry?'

'Upstairs. You know, the old memory? Or are you still struggling to recall events?'

I'm like, 'I wish people would stop asking me that. It's all pressure, you know?'

'Sorry, old chap. It's just, well, whoever it was who pulled that trigger, they belong in a bloody well prison cell. I expect you've heard one or two of the stories doing the rounds.'

'Of course I have.'

'Paper never refused ink and what-not. Do you want my theory, Ross? Do you want to know what *I* think happened?'

'Go on?'

'Well, nothing half as salacious as our friends in the media are suggesting. No, I think you walked into that house and interrupted a robbery.'

'A robbery?'

'Yes, sir! Stumbled in while it was in progress – quote-unquote – then acted the hero, no doubt.'

'It's possible, I suppose.'

'Well, I'm sure the Gords will crack the case eventually. Oh, by the way, Hennessy said don't let them interview you without him being present. Isn't it lovely to know, Kicker, that you've got your godfather looking out for you?'

I'm like, 'Er, I suppose.'

'Well,' he goes, 'what do you think of the car? Don't keep me in suspense.'

It's at that exact moment, bang on cue, that a Coca-Cola can – full, by the way – comes flying through the air and smacks off the front windscreen. It bursts as well, sending a spray of Coke all over the front bonnet. I don't even see who did it. But I can totally understand, at a time like this, with the country in a serious jocker and a thousand people emigrating every week, according to Sorcha, how seeing someone sitting in a bright red Lambo is going to piss people off.

So what can I do except turn around to the old man and go, 'I focking love it.'

I'm like, 'Merry Christmas, Dude. Hey, we missed you in Kielys last night.'

Except Christian answers in, like, a low voice that makes me think that I've maybe got the time difference wrong. Maths was never my thing.

I'm there, 'Whoa, is it the middle of the night over there?'

'No,' he goes, 'it's eleven o'clock in the morning.'

'And you're still in bed?'

'I'm not in bed. I'm in work.'

He's still managing the *Star Wars*-themed casino in Vegas.

I'm like, 'You're *working*? On Christmas Day?'

He goes, 'It's the holidays, Ross. One of our busiest times of the year. Anyway, how are you doing? You're out of hospital, I gather.'

'I certainly am. Back eating little bits. Pegging it around on these crutches as well. Going to be storting physio in two weeks.'

He goes, 'God, I was worried, Ross,' in, like, a really *serious* voice?

I'm there, 'I was worried myself.'

'I thought you were going to . . .'

'Hey, I didn't. So don't go all morbid on my ass, okay? Come on, let's talk about something else.'

Christian's like the brother I never had. I know he feels the exact same way about me.

He goes, 'Lauren says you're back living with Sorcha. Is there any possibility of you two . . .'

I actually laugh. 'Nah. Although don't get me wrong, if I thought there was a focking sniff of it, it'd be *on* like Donkey Kong. But yeah, no, this is just Sorcha being Sorcha – basically the most caring person I've ever known. What about your life? How's Lauren? How's little Ross?'

'Ah, we're same-old, same-old. Ross is great. He's a little chatter-box.'

'Well, he was bound to have the gift of the gab being named after me, wasn't he? What about work? How are things there?'

'Obviously not great at the moment. The recession is really biting the tourist trade hard here. Numbers are way down on what we projected.'

'Dude,' I go, 'if anyone can turn it around, you can. We're all proud of you over this side of things. Me and the goys were actually saying it when I was in the hospital. Out of all of us, you're the only one who's still doing well for himself.'

There's, like, a five-second gap, roysh, before he goes, 'I, er, better get back to it, Ross. I've got meetings all day.'

Meetings? On Christmas focking Day? That's what it's like to be a high-flyer, see.

I'm there, 'I'll talk to you soon. And, hey – may the Force be with you.'

But he doesn't say it back to me – possibly for the first time ever. The line just clicks and he's suddenly gone.

I don't have time to think about it, roysh, because it's at that exact moment that I hear the front door slam. And the next thing I know, Ronan's stuck his head around the kitchen door. He's there, 'Alreet, Rosser?'

I laugh. He'd put you in immediately good form – he's just that kind of kid.

I'm like, 'Hey, Ro. Merry Christmas.'

He's there, 'Merry Christmas yourself. Whose car is that peerked outside?'

'Which one?'

'The Lambo.'

'It's mine. Christmas present from the old man.'

'Why is someone arthur writing "Wanker" on the side of it?'

I'm like, 'What?'

I hobble on my crutches over to the window. He's right. It's written in, like, white paint – huge capital letters as well – on the driver's side.

It's just like, 'WANKER'.

He goes, 'Do you think it was the same feddas what shot you?'

I'm there, 'I don't think so. It's just there's a lot of people going through a lot of shit out there and they hate seeing anyone still doing well.'

'You're going to need a spray job, Rosser. Do you want me to have a woord wit Nudger?'

'Nudger? I thought he burned things and made it look like an accident.'

'He's a conflagration consultant, yeah.'

I laugh. 'That was the phrase. I still have his business cord somewhere.'

'He also paints cars, but. It's a side-loyen of his.'

'Good to have something to fall back on, I suppose. Yeah, no, ask him to look after it, will you?'

'I will so. Be me Christmas present to you. Haven't got athin else for you.'

'Hey, it's cool. That'll do nicely. Although make sure to specify that it's a paint job I'm looking for, not the other thing.'

'Feer denuff.'

He looks around him and goes, 'Sorcha and Honor home?'

I'm like, 'No, they went to Sorcha's old pair's gaff for, like, tea and they're still not back.'

He's all disappointed. He loves his sister.

'They'll be back any minute,' I go. 'Then we can do presents.'

I bought Ro and Honor a laptop each, so they can, like Skype each other.

I hop over to the fridge. I'm like, 'Do you want, like, a Coke or something?'

He goes, 'Er, I'll have a beer, if you've got one.'

He's only chancing his orm, of course. But then I think, fock it. It's Christmas. And they say that about the French, don't they? They give their kids wine with their dinner from the time they're, like, three years old or something ridiculous – which is why they grow up to, like, *appreciate* alcohol? So I throw him a can of the old Dutch master.

'Have you athin udder than this piss?' he goes and, of course, I end up just cracking up laughing, even though it still hurts, by the way.

I'm there, 'Hey, if it was good enough for me at your age, it should be good enough for you. And if Sorcha walks in, you better focking hide it. She wouldn't be a big fan of kids drinking. This is the girl who used to go to Wez sober, remember.'

I grab one myself, at the same time thinking, these are the precious moments of being a father. First tooth. First steps. First words. First can.

He throws back the first mouthful like a seasoned drinker – which I suspected he was anyway.

I'm there, 'I didn't get a chance to say it to you, by the way. Shadden. Fair focks. It has to be said.'

He goes, 'Do you like her?'

'Like her? She's perfect. She's obviously a major fan of mine as well. Yeah, no, she actually reminds me of Sorcha when *she* was a teenager?'

'Me ma dudn't approve, but.'

Of course, I can hordly believe my ears. 'What do you mean, your ma dudn't approve? What, is it the age thing?'

'No, she just dudn't like her family.'

'Oh, yeah,' I go, 'that'd be typical focking Finglas, of course. If you're not claiming the dole under three different aliases and toilet-training your kids at gunpoint, you're considered a snob.'

I knock back a mouthful. I can't believe Ro's nearly three-quarters of a can ahead of me.

He's there, 'She wants me to finish it wit her.'

'Well, I hope you told her to fock off,' I go. 'Yeah, this coming from the woman who's having sex with your headmaster.'

'She said she'd prefer if I just concentrated on me studies.'

'Studies? You're only thirteen.'

'Thee think I should sit me Judinior Ceert. a year early, but.'

'Whoa, whoa, whoa! *They* think?'

'Yeah.'

'And by *they*, I'm presuming you mean *him*?'

'Yeah. See, Ine so far ahead of the udders in me class. Tom says Ine arthur reaching Judinior Ceert. stantort already.'

'Sorry, I'm just wondering how *he* suddenly gets a say in how my son is raised.'

'Ine well able for it, Rosser.'

'That may or may not be true. I still think it's time that me and your so-called mother had words.'

There's, like, silence for about a minute. Then, suddenly, out of nowhere, he goes, 'Ine glad you're home, Rosser.'

I smile at him and I go, 'I am too.'

You look at Ronan's friends – Nudger and Git Burden, Buckets of Blood and Gull. You listen to his hord-man spiel. And now with the deep voice and the extra inches he's suddenly sprouted. And you forget sometimes – as Tina clearly has – that he's still basically a child.

I suddenly hear Sorcha's key in the door.

'Okay, hide the beer,' I go.

I hear Sorcha ask Honor who she's texting and Honor goes, 'Are you deaf or are you just having, like, a senior moment?'

I go, 'Come on, Ro. Come and see what I've got for you under the tree.'

Detective Sergeant Harron rings. Wants to know did I have a nice Christmas. I'm actually still having it. It's only, like, the day after Stephen's Day. That's the thing about cops. They never switch off.

He's there, 'You're still very sore, I'd imagine.'

'It's unbelievable,' I go. 'It's like there's a knife stuck permanently in my stomach. Then anytime I move . . .'

'Here, will I tell you something? There's two fellas here in Malahide remembers you playing rugby?'

'Really?'

'There's a fella, Neil O'Gorman, he went to St Munchin's. He played against you in a friendly. Then David O'Mahony – he retires this year – he remembers you playing against his son, although I don't know what school he went to.'

'It's nice that people still remember all the amazing things I did on the field.'

'Oh, Neil says he can't understand how you didn't make it in the game. It's a pure mystery to him.'

'That's a lovely thing to hear.'

'Anyway, I thought I'd just give you a ring. See had anything occurred to you.'

'Nothing. It's, like, the more I *try* to remember, the more . . .'

'That's okay, Ross. You can't force yourself to remember. It'll only come back to you when your mind is good and ready to let it.'

'Do you think?'

'Like I said, I've some experience in this area. Anyway, let's hope 2011 is a better year for you. Happy New Year.'

'Yeah, no, Happy New Year.'

Sorcha tells me not to move because it'll only end up hurting. And there I am, roysh, lying on the sofa pretty much naked, while *she's* kneeling on the floor beside me, running her tongue over her top lip like she does when she's concentrating on something really hord. She throws her hair behind her shoulder and goes, 'It's a long time since I've done this.'

'Hey,' I go, 'I could probably do it myself.'

'Ross, there's no *way* you could do it yourself.'

'Or that nurse in the hospital could do it. The big, ugly one.'

'*Excuse* me?'

'Sorcha, she did offer.'

She gets suddenly protective when she hears that. She definitely picked up on the vibe in the ward that day. 'Look, I *said* I'd do it and I'm *going* to do it?'

She's talking about changing the dressing on my stomach wound, I probably should point out.

'I still can't believe you're being so secretive about what you're doing tonight,' she goes.

I'm there, 'I'm going to this porty in my old man's gaff. Same as you and everyone else.'

This is, like, New Year's Eve, by the way.

She goes, 'No, but, like, *beforehand*?'

She heard me on the phone an hour ago ringing for a taxi.

I'm there, 'I'm just, er, going to see a friend of mine.'

She's there, 'A female friend?'

'Yes,' I go, 'you *could* say she's a female friend.'

She storts pulling at the plaster slowly and I can feel the hairs on my stomach and chest being ripped from their actual sockets. Is she doing it on purpose?

I'm like, 'Jesus focking Christ!'

'Sorry,' she goes. 'Actually, the best way to do this might be to just . . .' and then, without any warning at all, she suddenly rips the thing off in, like, one sudden pull.

I let a major focking roar out of me. Although Sorcha's reaction is even worse. She suddenly sees the mess that the gunshot made of my once stunning ab region and jumps back after literally screaming.

I don't know what she was expecting to see. But it's like it's only just occurred to her what actually *happened* to me?

'Oh my God!' she's going, with her hands over her mouth, like she thinks she might spew. 'Oh my God! Oh my God!'

It honestly looks like someone just dropped a sixteen-inch Domino's Wisconsin Six Cheese pizza on my belly.

She goes, 'How could . . . how could somebody do something like this to you?' and she's suddenly, like, filling up again.

I'm there, 'That's why I said – do you remember? – we should have just gone back to the hospital? That's why I'm *on* Plan B plus options, Babes.'

But she shakes her head. And then she's suddenly got, like, her *determined* face on? 'No,' she goes, 'I can do this.'

I'm there, 'Are you sure you're okay with it?'

She goes, 'Er, I was in the Order of Malta for two years, Ross.'

I tell her I remember. I was there when she barely missed out on a Meritorious Service Medal, that time in Leopardstown, when a horse got out of its paddock and ran amok in the crowd. She did unbelievable work that day helping the injured and definitely deserved it. In fact, I was the one who suggested she tell them to shove it up their focking holes when she didn't get it. Which is exactly what she did – except in obviously a nicer way.

She storts picking the little bits of fluff out of my wound. I can tell she wants to gag. I'm like, 'Try not to think about what you're doing.'

She suddenly goes, 'You're still having nightmares, aren't you?'

'Who told you I've been having nightmares?'

'I can hear you through the wall, Ross. *And* I heard you had, like, a meltdown on Christmas Eve.'

'Focking Erika and her big mouth,' I go. 'Let's talk about something else, can we? Thinking about it makes me depressed. I haven't really asked you how *you* are – as in, *actually*?'

'I'm fine. I've been listening to a lot of Noah and the Whale and really, like, *enjoying* life? Taking it as it comes.'

'Well, that all sounds good.'

'Plus, you know Erika has asked me to be her bridesmaid? And I've got an – oh my God – amazing dress for the big day, which I'm, like, determined to fit into, even if it kills me.'

I laugh. I'm like, 'Yeah, I wouldn't go swearing off the focking snack boxes just yet, Babes. There's not a chance in the world of that wedding ever happening.'

'Why do you keep saying that, Ross?'

'Because I know my sister. She's punching well below her weight and deep down she knows it.'

'Well,' she goes, 'I wonder do you really know Erika like you think you do. Oh my God, Ross, the *actual* change that's come over her since she got together with Fionn. She used to be, like, *so* materialistic. *And* a bitch.'

'Like I said, I remain to be convinced.'

She grabs this bottle of, like, disinfectant solution that they gave us at the hospital and tips some of it onto this bit of, I don't know, cloth.

'What about work-wise?' I go. 'Anything stirring?'

I'm not being a wanker here, but it might be a while before I'm back earning again and I'm not sure how long I can keep making the old vagimony payments.

'I'm actually happy,' she goes, 'just to wait until the right thing comes along.'

'Would you not just, I don't know, take any old job in the meantime?'

Aaarrrggghhh!

She puts the disinfectant on my open wound without even a word of warning.

I'm like, 'Fock's sake! Go easy with that shit, will you?'

She's like, 'I'm sorry!'

Then she goes back to dabbing at it, except lightly this time. 'Hey,' she suddenly goes, 'did I tell you about my shop?'

She means, presumably, her old unit in the Powerscourt Townhouse Centre.

I'm like, 'No.'

'They're turning it into of one those, like, *discount* stores that are becoming suddenly popular?'

'You've got to be shitting me. Please tell me you're shitting me.'

'I'm not. I saw them putting the sign up over the door yesterday. Euro Hero.'

'Jesus Christ. What are the other traders doing about it? I'm presuming they're up in orms.'

'They're not doing anything as far as I know.'

'What the fock is happening out there? Has everyone just, like, given in?'

'Ross, I'm fine with it.'

'I don't know how you *can* be.'

'Well, I really am. My shop was one of Ireland's most amazing, amazing boutiques. But it's a part of my life that's in the past now and it's time I possibly moved on.'

She finishes disinfecting my wound, then she reaches for the new dressing, with a happy little smile playing on her lips.

'Here, I'll give you a laugh,' I go. 'Tina doesn't approve of Ronan's new girlfriend.'

She's there, 'Oh my God, why not?'

'Probably because she speaks well. She says please and thank you and it's an honour to you meet you, Mr O'Carroll-Kelly, you were definitely an amazing rugby player back in the day.'

'Tina must have her reasons, Ross.'

'You know what they're like in that estate of Ronan's. You teethe your kids on a Glock and you can't fart without every focker in the room wanting to stand up for the national anthem. They hate anyone who tries to rise above it.'

'That's, like, oh my God!'

'That's exactly what it is. And I'll tell you another thing that's pissing me off. McGahy's pushing Ronan to sit his Junior Cert. in June.'

'Oh my God, he's only in, like, second year.'

'Yeah, that'd be *my* basic point?'

'He'd probably be well able for it, Ross. He was telling me himself that he's *actually* gifted now?'

'I just don't agree with the idea of them, I don't know, fast-tracking him through school. He's still a kid, Sorcha. Just because McGahy had no focking childhood.'

She strips the new plaster out of its wrapping. Something suddenly occurs to me. 'Hey, by the way, what do your old pair think of me being back living here?'

She gets suddenly sheepish. 'I haven't told them yet. I didn't want to spoil my dad's Christmas.'

You have no idea how deep his hatred for me runs. I'm there, 'He'll shit focking giblets when he finds out.'

'Well, I was thinking of telling them both tomorrow – in the restaurant . . .'

The Lalors always have dinner in Roly's on New Year's Day. Another family tradition.

After a long pause, she goes, 'Will you come with me?'

I'm there, 'Er, is it not, like, a family thing?'

'You're Honor's father, Ross. You'll always be family.'

I think – as you always have to do with birds – okay, what's *actually* going on here? At a guess, I'd say she's still pissed at her old man for refusing to drive her to the hospital. And unveiling me as her new lodger in the middle of a crowded restaurant is her way of getting him back. So she's basically using me. But I end up agreeing, mainly because I can't wait to see the focker's face when she breaks the news.

Sorcha's mouth suddenly drops, then she – I *think* it's a word – *recoils* in pretty much horror? 'Oh my God,' she goes, 'you're getting turned on. You're *actually* aroused.'

I stort laughing. It turns out she's right. I'm like, 'I'm sorry, Babes.'

'Make it go down. I mean it.'

'Yeah, no, it doesn't *exactly* work like that, Sorcha? It's not like your leg or your orm.'

'Oh my God, Ross, I told you – nothing is going to happen between us.'

'I never said it was. But you're fiddling around down there. And this thing wouldn't know the difference between Mila Kunis and a focking ice-cream van.'

She gets up and literally runs out of the room, going, 'You're disgusting, Ross. Oh my God – you are *so* disgusting.'

But in her voice, I can hear, like, a hint of laugher and I know that deep down she's actually flattered. As for me, I'm just pleasantly surprised to discover that, despite everything, the thing still works.

I stare at her through the window of the restaurant, shovelling chunks of minted monkfish escabeche into her mouth and I think, so this is life under NAMA, is it?

She actually looks well for a woman of sixty-whatever-the-fock-she-is-now – although I do still wonder how I ever went there.

Hedda is sitting opposite her, turning her porcini and spinach risotto over with her fork, without actually eating it – but all the time *scowling*? Hedda hates her old dear. But then I suspect Regina is none too fond of Hedda at the moment either. She obviously doesn't want to see her go to jail, though – that's why she's keeping her close, I imagine.

I knew they'd be here. It's the opening night of *Le Petit Bedon*, the new restaurant in Sandycove that Arnaud, one of Regina's old chefs, has just storted up. They've been friends since forever and I knew she'd be there to support him.

There's, like, accordion music coming from the restaurant. That and laughter. I stand outside in the shadows and continue just watching the free-and-easy way that Regina exchanges banter with the couple at the next table. Not a care in the basic world. From the papers and probably the Gords, she'll know that I can't remember what actually happened. Which puts them in the clear.

My phone suddenly rings and I answer it. It's the old man. His opening line is, 'Powerscourt it is, Ross!'

I'm like, 'What?'

'The venue for your sister's nuptials. The Ritz-Carlton. It's settled. Oh, I know it has its critics. A blot on the landscape and a permanent monument to a nation's folly, etcetera, etcetera. But who cares if you can see it on a weather map. The ballroom has to be seen to be believed. And you can tell your pals not to be fretting about the expense. Helen and I will be paying for everything. Rooms. The lot.'

'Somehow, I still think you're money's safe.'

'Where are you, by the way? The party's in full swing, Ross. Your good lady wife is here. All your pals.'

I just go, 'Yeah, I'm on my way. I'll see you in a bit,' and then I hang up.

I *could* pick my way into the restaurant and make a scene. But I think, no, just leave them to enjoy their New Year's. I'm playing the long game here. You see, I've been lying to the Feds. I've been lying to Sorcha. My old man. My friends. Everyone. Because I remember what happened. I remember everything so focking clearly that the memory of it still sends me cold. These two will be hearing from me soon enough. Regina Rathfriland and her batshit crazy daughter. The girl who pulled the trigger. The girl who tried to kill me.

Totes Recall

You can probably picture Sorcha's old man's face when he sees *me* hopscotching my way across the floor of Roly's to the quiet corner table where he's already sitting with Sorcha's old dear and her sister – Hafnium or Arnica or whatever the fock she goes by.

He goes, 'What the hell is *he* doing here?' loud enough for the entire restaurant to hear.

Sorcha's old dear, who's always tried to give me the benefit of the doubt, touches his shoulder and goes, 'Come on, Edmund – let's hear what Sorcha has to say.'

And he looks at his eldest daughter – the apple, literally, of his eye – waiting for an explanation. Sorcha takes a breath – she did that presentation skills course with Terry Prone, so this'd be very much her area – and goes, 'Ross has moved back in. It's just for a few weeks – until he gets back on his feet again.'

His face turns instantly red – it looks like his whole head is about to explode. I'm not helping matters, of course. I can't wipe the focking smirk off my face.

'Getting *him* out of the house,' he goes, with a real viciousness in his voice, 'was the best day's work you ever did. And now you're going to undo all of that by letting him . . . *insinuate* his way back into your life like the bloody . . . *disease* that he is.'

'Dad!' Sorcha goes, then nods at Honor, who's standing between us – the message being, hey, not in front of the kid.

He's still steaming, though. Prick.

'Hello, Darling,' Sorcha's old dear gives it.

And Honor goes, 'Hi, Grandma,' in her little butter-wouldn't-melt voice, then runs around the table to her and gives her a hug. She puts on a good performance – there's no doubt about that.

Sorcha asks a passing waiter if we can squeeze in another chair and the dude says no problem at all. And all the time, Sorcha's old man keeps just staring at me. Needless to say, he's very much in *favour* of the whole divorce thing? But, equally, he knows the power I have over his daughter. Over both of his daughters, to be fair to me.

The sister shoves up her chair and makes room for me beside her.

'I was, like, *so* worried about you,' she goes, as I put my crutches down and manage to manoeuvre myself into a sitting position. 'When I heard you got shot, I was just like, *"Oh! My God!"* Wasn't I, Sorcha?'

Jesus Christ. She's had a focking breast job. Although that's possibly the understatement of the century. I heard a rumour she went travelling around Australia for a year and came back with a new rack. But you've honestly *never* seen heffers like these. She reaches across me for the wine menu, making sure to give me a good eyeful. It doesn't escape her old pair's attention either.

'Honor,' Sorcha goes, 'what are you going to have to eat?' and, at pretty much the same time, she turns to the waiter and goes, 'You *have* a children's option, don't you?'

Honor, without even missing a beat, looks up from her menu and goes, 'How is the halibut done?'

The waiter's obviously a bit thrown – not even six years old, remember.

'It's, em, stir fried,' he goes. 'With baby bak choi, shitake mushrooms, soya and ginger. Oh, and a sesame seed dressing.'

Honor's there, 'I'll have that, thank you,' at the same time closing her menu, 'with the sesame seed dressing on the side . . . and some iced water, please.'

Sorcha's old man just keeps staring at me.

The rest of us give our orders then. I ask for just the veggie soup, because I've no real appetite at the moment, what with only having half a stomach and everything. Might end up having some ice cream afterwards. Who knows?

'So,' the sister, totally out of the blue, goes, 'have you found a job yet, Sorcha?' and she's being a definite bitch from the way she says it. 'Or are you still on the dole?'

They're some crack, the Lalors.

Sorcha obviously decides to just take the high road. 'Yes, I'm still waiting for the right thing to come along, thank you.'

Her old man – you can see how proud of her he is – goes, 'Don't you worry, Sorcha. You won't be out of work for long. What, with *your* qualifications?'

I just go, 'An Orts degree,' without even thinking. And of course it's pretty much impossible to say those words without sounding like you're ripping the piss.

He just glowers at me. At least I *think* it's glowers? 'And what have you got?' he goes.

Sorcha's like, 'Dad!'

'You didn't even get your Leaving Certificate, did you?'

I'm about to tell him that it's never actually held me back, but I decide to take a leaf out of Sorcha's book and be the better man. 'Whatever,' I just go.

Sorcha's sister leans across me again, this time for the walnut bread. Her chitties are taking up half the table – there's literally nowhere for the waiter to put our drinks. I catch her old dear trying to – I don't know – *communicate* something to her with a frown.

'She's telling you to button up that shirt,' her old man goes, big serious voice on him. '*Two* buttons – at the very *least*.'

Sorcha looks at her, narrows her eyes and goes, 'Yeah, it's a *family* restaurant?' finally getting her dig in.

He tries to make conversation then.

'I'm telling you,' he goes, 'the next General Election can't come soon enough. There's a genuine sense of revolution in the air. They're saying that Fine Gael could win as many as eighty seats. What are your own feelings, Sorcha?'

She shrugs her shoulder. 'I just think that change is – oh my God – *so* needed,' she goes, except she doesn't make eye contact with him. Then she turns to her old dear. 'It's just such a pity that no one here has been able to re-create the whole atmosphere that surrounded Barack Obama. I'm talking about the whole *Hope* thing?'

She's definitely still pissed at him. It's genuinely the first time I've ever seen it.

'Well,' he goes, 'Fianna Fáil can take what's coming to them. And I'm saying that as someone who's voted for them all his life. Your mother and I feel very let down by them. Very let down.'

I clear my throat and every head at the table turns to me. They're all waiting for me to say something, I don't know, *significant*?

'I'm actually going to go for a hit and miss,' is what I *do* say. I catch *him* just shaking his head. The day I married his daughter must still rank as the worst day of his life. I reach down for my crutches and I manage to, like, lever myself upright.

The sister, of course, is up on her feet straight away – obviously sees an opp. 'I'll help you,' she goes.

Sorcha's there, 'He doesn't *need* help.'

'Sorcha,' the sister goes, 'there's, like, *stairs*?'

Hilarious. This dude thinks his precious daughter married *beneath* herself? There I am – picture the scene – making my way downstairs, as fast as my crutches can carry me, to the jacks, with the sister – I think it's a word – *tottering* behind me on her four-inch Loubs and her focking moo moos hanging out of her shirt, and my soon-to-be-ex-wife, of course, roaring, 'He can go to the toilet by himself!' for everyone to hear.

The sister then follows me *into* the actual gents. Some family, huh?

I go into Trap One and I quickly slam the door. I whip open the old chinos and I sit down. That's when she storts banging on the door, going, 'Are you okay in there? Ross, let me in!'

I'm like, 'Er, I'm having a hit and miss in here?'

'Let me help you.'

'Yeah, no, I'm *pretty* sure I can manage by myself.'

The next thing, roysh, I see the lock turning. Jesus focking Christ. The mad bitch has stuck, like, a fifty cent piece or something in the focking screw head and is opening the actual door from the outside. I go to stick my foot out and, of course, that sends, like, a rip of pain across the tops of my legs, which causes me to pretty much *howl*?

She bundles the door open and she's suddenly on top of me. She's there, 'Oh my God, I *knew* you needed help?'

I manage to struggle to my feet and pull up my chinos. But she locks the door and then stands in front of it, blocking my way. 'Hey, slow down,' she goes. 'What's the rush?'

She's wearing *212 VIP* by Carolina Herrera – it's impossible to miss that detail in the close confines of a toilet cubicle.

'Look,' I go, 'in about ten seconds' time they're going to be wondering is something going on. And your old man hates me enough as it is, remember.'

She basically ignores this. 'I saw you looking at me,' she goes. 'Looking at my breasts.'

'Yeah, they're, er, pretty difficult to miss,' I go. 'You're focking bouncing them around the table like Shaquille O'Neal.'

She laughs – *and* in a really flirty way. She's a serious honey. I've always said that about her. 'Do you want to do it?' she goes.

I'm like, '*Excuse* me?'

'As in, *it*. You can be as quick as you like. You don't even need to worry about me.'

Now, I've been around a few corners in my time, as you're no doubt aware. But even *I'm* shocked at that. 'Are you talking about . . .'

She laughs again – except it's actually more of a *giggle*? She makes a grab for the goods, but I pull away, deciding to be basically strong. 'Look, I'm not having sex with you in a restaurant toilet while my wife and daughter are sitting upstairs. I don't know what kind of a focking sleazebag you think I am.'

I end up just getting off with her instead and having a bit of a go of her honkers. I feel terrible for doing it, especially after everything Sorcha's done for me. But then I'm a dirtbag. Love me or hate me, you'd have to say that about me.

Five minutes later, we're on our way back to the table and I can straight away see – even from the other side of the restaurant – that Sorcha is in tears. And naturally my first instinct is that she somehow knows what just happened.

I end up going into, like, *über*-defensive mode. I'm there, 'Babes, nothing happened between us,' at the same time wiping my mouth for possible lipstick traces.

'What do you mean nothing happened between you?' her old

man practically roars at me. 'Of course nothing happened between you! What the hell do you take my daughter for?'

There's things I *could* say, but I don't.

Sorcha looks at the sister – I couldn't be a hundred percent sure she's not called Ophelia or something like that – and, literally bawling, goes, 'Did *you* know about this?' her make-up all over her face, like she slapped it on pissed.

The sister's like, 'Know about what?'

'About them selling the house.'

I presume she's talking about the family gaff in Killiney. The sister obviously hasn't a breeze. She's like, 'Our house?'

Sorcha's there, 'Yes. Honalee.'

The old man goes, 'I'd prefer not to talk about this in front of outside parties,' meaning me – possibly also explains why he waited until I went to the shitter to break the news to Sorcha. 'We'll discuss it further when we get home.'

Sorcha goes, 'Well, it's not going to *be* home for much longer, is it?'

The sister goes, 'Oh my God, why are you selling the house?'

'I told you,' he goes, 'I will not discuss it in front of *him*.'

But the old dear ends up saying it anyway. 'We have some financial problems,' she goes, 'like a lot of people out there.'

Of course I end up saying completely the wrong thing as per usual. 'I honestly don't mind you discussing this in front of me. As in, there's no shame in it.'

'Shame?' he goes. 'How fucking dare you!'

This dude's, like, a family law barrister, bear in mind. He'd obviously have to keep his cool on a day-to-day basis – yet every time I open my trap, he looks like he wants to crush my focking head under his John Lobbs. 'I'm not ashamed of a damn thing. Especially where *you're* concerned.'

Sorcha turns to the sister then and goes, 'They borrowed money to buy bank shares.'

The sister wouldn't be the brightest crayon in the box, yet she knows exactly what that means. Her jaw just drops.

'They *borrowed* money,' Sorcha goes, like she's still trying to ger her own head around it herself. 'Basically remortgaged the house.

To buy bank shares. And guess *which* bank they bought the shares in, everyone?'

It doesn't focking matter, of course. They're all focked.

He goes to put his orm around Sorcha's shoulder. He's a lot focking braver than I am. She just pulls away. 'Don't touch me!' she just goes. She loved that gaff, you see. 'How could you have been so stupid?'

'We were naive,' the mother tries to go.

Sorcha ends up just roaring at her. And I've never heard her raise her voice to her old pair before. 'You were greedy.'

The old man, I notice, has barely even touched his traditional Kerry lamb pie. 'Maybe we were,' he goes. 'Look, I was planning to retire early. Wanted to make it as comfortable as I could for your mother and myself. Those shares went through the roof, you know.'

'I can't believe you've known about this – how long, two and a half years? And you've kept it to yourselves. That's the house I grew up in!'

I'm still standing up, by the way – as is the sister.

'We thought we could trade our way out of it,' *he* tries to go. He's digging a serious hole for himself here – that'd be my analysis. 'We were sure the villa in Quinta do Lago would hold its value.'

'And you were wrong.'

'Yes, we were wrong. If you want to hear me say it, Sorcha, I'll say it. But we can't just bury our heads in the sand either. We have to deal with it and that's what we're attempting to do.'

Sorcha just shakes her head. 'All of my childhood memories,' she goes, 'the happiest moments of my actual life, are wrapped up in that house . . .'

'But you'll always *have* those memories.'

'You told me I'd always have the house! You said it'd always be a refuge for me. On the morning of my wedding day – do you remember that? – you said that when things inevitably went wrong with Ross, my old bedroom would always be there for me.'

Like I said, the worst day of his life.

He just goes, 'We are where we are, Sorcha,' which is what every focker seems to be saying these days when they're giving you bad news.

It's only at that point that I remember Honor and I'm suddenly worried about how she might be taking it – all these adults shouting the odds in front of her. But she's sitting there, quietly texting away on her little phone with a look of, honestly, complete and utter boredom on her face.

I go, 'Don't worry, Honor. It's just the grown-ups talking about the whole current economic thing. Blah, blah . . . Blah, blah, blah.'

She doesn't even look up, just goes, 'Whatevs.'

The sister's only storting to get her head around what the whole thing is going to mean for her. 'Oh my God,' she goes, 'that's also, like, our *inheritance*?'

'And we're very sorry about that,' it's the mother who goes. 'But whatever the rights and wrongs of it, your father and I have got ourselves into a situation where we owe more money than we're ever going to earn. We can either *choose* to sell the house or the banks are going to force us to sell it.'

'Have you even thought about where I'm going to live?'

This is the sister, again.

'We're looking at apartments,' the old dear goes. 'Another few years and that garden was going to be too much work for us any- way. A lot of people out there are downsizing.'

'So, what, I'm going to be living in, like, an apartment with you?'

The old man ends up going suddenly ape-shit with her. 'You're twenty-six years of age! Do you not think it's time you stood on your own two feet?'

She's like, '*Excuse* me?' the same way Sorcha does when she's riled.

He goes, 'How many courses have we paid for you to do?'

'Edmund,' the old dear goes, trying to calm him down.

'And you haven't worked a bloody day since you left school.'

'Er, I've done *Smirnoff* promotions?'

He obviously doesn't consider that work, roysh, because he goes, 'And meanwhile, it was your mother and I who paid for you to go gallivanting around Australia,' and – hilarious – he nods at her top tens. He *actually* nods at her top-ten hits. I notice that.

He turns on Sorcha then. This is a father and daughter, bear in mind, who've never exchanged so much as an angry word in their lives. But, like I told you, this row was brewing. 'And how much money did I put into that blasted shop of yours?' he goes.

Sorcha's there, 'It was actually a *boutique*?' feeling the sudden need to defend herself.

'How many years was I writing cheques to cover your losses? I must have given you half a million euros to keep that . . . silly place open.'

She's like, 'Silly?'

This is one place you do *not* go with Sorcha.

He's there, 'Yes. Because it never turned a five-cent profit, even during the best economic years this country has ever enjoyed.'

'Oh! My God!'

'And you two *dare* to ask about your inheritance? You've already had it!'

The next thing I hear is the sound of, like, chair legs scraping off the floor. Sorcha stands up. 'Ross, Honor – we're going.'

Honor looks up from her iPhone and goes, 'Er, our *mains* haven't even arrived yet?'

And for once Sorcha actually loses it with her. 'I said we're going!'

She turns to me and goes, 'You bring her. I'll be waiting in the car,' and off she storms.

This is a definite first. I always end up being the villain at Lalor family dinners. I've just snogged my wife's sister in the jacks and had my hands all over her wobblesteaks. Yet for once I'm somehow *not* the most unpopular man at the table.

'Hey, don't worry about it,' I tell her old man. 'I'll talk to her for you.'

He just goes – this is in front of Honor, by the way – 'I don't want anything from you, except for you to disappear from our lives forever.'

The old man's on the phone, banging away in my ear, going, 'So it looks like the Government is poised to fall, eh?'

I go, 'Hmmm,' but only because it's quicker than going, 'And this affects me *how* exactly?'

He's there, 'Yes, it turns out that poor old Brian Cowen played a round of golf with your friend and mine a few weeks before the big Anglo meltdown. Now the opposition are demanding to know what they talked about. Well, if I know Seanie like I think I do, he'll have been ribbing the chap about his golf game. Oh, gamesmanship isn't the word, Ross. He used to say to me, "Charles, if you grew tomatoes, they'd come out sliced!" This was *as* I was about to tee off! I mean, have you ever heard the like of it?'

'Hmmm.'

'How's the car running, by the way?'

'Well, obviously I haven't driven it yet. Still too sore. Hurts to press on the pedals.'

'Your legs?'

'And my stomach.'

'Oh, dear. Plenty of time, though, eh?'

'Someone painted the word "Wanker" on the side, by the way.'

'Good Lord,' he goes, then he sort of, like, tuts to himself. 'Still a lot of misdirected anger out there.'

'Mate of Ronan's is coming out today. He's going to do a job on it.'

There's a beep on the line.

I'm there, 'I've got to go. I've another call coming through.'

It ends up being Tina. She must have got my message from earlier. Her opening line is, 'What do you want, Ross?'

There's no Happy New Year, how are your injuries, or I'm really glad you didn't die.

So I just go, 'I want to know what the deal is with Ronan being made to sit his Junior Cert. a year early.'

She's like, 'No one's *making* him do athin. It's just that he's so feer ahead of the rest of he's class, it dudn't make sense for him to wait anudder year to sirrit.'

'Okay and what about his childhood?'

'What?'

'I'm just saying, Tina – he's sitting his Junior Cert. at fourteen. Probably do his Leaving at fifteen. He'll have a focking degree by the time he's properly shaving. Pordon me but I'm just worried he's going to look back at the childhood that he never got to enjoy and go, "Okay, what was the focking rush?" '

'Tom thinks he'll get bored if he waits anudder year . . .'

'Oh, Tom! Of course. Because he's his dad now, isn't he?'

'Ross, Ine just arthur coming off a sixteen-hour shift at the hospiddle.'

'And let me guess – is it Tom who wants Ronan to break it off with Shadden Tuite?'

'No, *Ine* the one who wants him to break it off wirrer.'

'Why?'

'Because I doatunt like the family.'

'What, because you think they're snobs?'

'What?'

'Just because they don't shop in Aldi and ride around on ponies, you think they're looking down on you.'

'I doatunt think they're looking down me.'

'So what is it, then? I think, as his father, I'm entitled to ask.'

That's when she suddenly loses it with me. 'His *fadder*? Yeah, and a fine example you're settin um.'

'Sorry?'

'Ine the one who had to look arrum, Ross, crying heself to sleep at night, thinking he's daddy was going to die . . .'

'Hey, it wasn't my fault I ended up getting shot. Don't try to turn that one around.'

'I *read* the papers . . .'

She does. Tina's priorities when she's doing the weekly shop are tabloids, then cigarettes, then food.

'The fooken caddy-on of you. That auld one. Her thaughter. Laddy Tuhill's fiancée . . .'

'They weren't actually engaged.'

'Caddying on like a doorty animal. What kind of an example is that to set your son? You're *no* kind of fadder.'

And before I get a chance to say a word in my own defence, she just hangs up.

I must be mad. Must be. I'm up at, like, eleven o'clock on a Saturday morning to get fitted for a suit for a wedding that's never going to focking happen.

I mean, when's she planning to dump his orse? Is she going to let this thing go all the way to the altar?

I say this to JP as we're standing outside the suit hire place, waiting for the others to arrive. He just shakes his head and tells me to let it go. He's like, 'They're in love, Ross. Everyone's saying it – they've never seen her this happy before.'

I laugh. Can't help myself.

'Dude,' I go, 'I know the girl. She's never cared about men. All she's ever cared about is herself. And her lifestyle. Expensive holidays. The best of restaurants. Good clobber. What was it they used to call her, back in the day?'

'Shop and awe.'

'Shop and awe. That was it. And what kind of lifestyle is *he* going to provide for her – er, an unemployed teacher?'

'That's horsh, Ross.'

'Well, you know me, J-Town – I've never been afraid to call it. Look, I love them both. But they're just not suited. *She* likes the good life. *He* has socks with the days of the week on them. His idea of excitement is wearing Thursday's ones on a focking Wednesday.'

He has no actual comeback to that. In fact, he doesn't get a chance to say anything, because all of a sudden Fionn is walking up the Main Street – we're in, like, Blackrock, by the way – accompanied, I can't help but notice, by his very, very tremendous sister, Eleanor.

She's obviously come along to give us, like, a *woman's* take on shit?

I've always had a serious thing for Eleanor. That goes way back to when people used to think she looked like Carolyn Lilipaly. And the word on the grapevine is that she's back single again, having just broken up with her long-term boyfriend. He apparently took her to Paris for their five-year anniversary and produced a hunk of ice. She supposedly said yes – it was in, like, a restaurant – but then burst into tears when they got back to the hotel and told him she didn't think that he was the one.

I give her a big smooch on either cheek and a long, lingering hug – just to let her know that I'm there for her. If anything she's *better* looking than she was the last time I saw her? I don't know if you can say the same for Carolyn Lilipaly – you never really hear of her any more, do you?

'So,' I go, smooth as a focking Ken doll, 'are you still doing that thing you were doing, as in work-wise?'

She gives me a huge smile and goes, 'Immunology – yes.'

I pull a face like I'm seriously impressed. Which I probably would be if I knew what the fock it was.

'By the way,' I go, 'thanks for the Get Well Soon cord. It actually meant a lot to me.'

'Well,' she goes, 'when Fionn told me his friend had been shot, I was like, Oh my God!'

'A lot of people were, Eleanor. A lot of people were.'

'And how are you now?'

'Hey, I'm on the big-time mend. The stomach's healing. They say it's possibly the most painful part of the body to get actually shot in.'

She looks down at it. She's like, 'Oh my God, poor you!'

'That's not my belly sticking out, by the way. It's all, like, bandages and shit. Just to, like, protect the area.'

'And you're on crutches.'

'Yeah, no, I took a bit of buckshot in my thighs, especially the right one. They had to go in there and dig it out.'

'And Fionn was saying they still don't know who did it.'

'No, unfortunately. But, er, again, thanks for the cord. Knowing that the likes of you were thinking about me was one of the main reasons I pulled through.'

I've still got it. There's no doubt about that.

A definite look crosses her face then. See, she's always thought of me as just a friend of her little brother's. Now, I can almost hear her thinking, hey, I'm a single girl – why *not* have a slice of that?

Fionn has to immediately break it up. It'd kill him, of course, the idea of me bulling her.

'Oisinn's running a bit late,' he goes, all businesslike.

He's having, like, four groomsmen, by the way. Christian's going to e-mail his measurements from the States when we pick out what we want.

'I said we'd go on ahead and get ourselves sorted,' he goes.

So in we go.

It's me who ends up getting measured first. The owner of the shop gives me just a standard monkey and I hop my way into the little fitting room and throw it on. Then I lever myself back out into the shop. Eleanor's eyes, I can't help but notice, are out on literally stalks. A tux has always suited me. Every girl says it.

JP gets measured next, while Fionn storts going through the racks and I stand there, James Bond-stylee, offering Eleanor the benefit of my relationship experience while at the same time giving her full eye contact – a trick of the trade.

'Possibly the best advice I can give you is to get back in the game,' I go. 'And I'm saying that, Eleanor, as someone whose marriage is over and is currently unattached himself. You need to have some fun – preferably with someone who's in the same situation as yourself, showing you the ropes.'

'I've been out on one or two dates,' she goes. Then she laughs – you'd have to say *bitterly*? – to herself. 'Let's just say there are a lot of assholes out there.'

I just shake my head, with my big sincere face on me, and go, '*Why* do men hurt?' which would be a line of mine, then I punch the door of the fitting room – I don't even *know* why? It just seems like the right thing to do at that particular moment. She *seems* pretty impressed, though. The dude who owns the shop isn't. 'Yes, can you *not* do that,' he goes. 'And by the way I still have to measure your neck.'

'It'll be XXXL,' Fionn goes, all pissy with me. See, it's okay for *him* to be with *my* sister, but not the other way around.

'It will,' I go, giving Eleanor the raised eyebrow. 'And let me tell you, the rest of me is in proportion!'

Fionn goes, 'Ross, will you come over here and please help me?' determined to, like, separate us. I go over to him, while JP wanders over to her and soon the two of them are locked in one of those pointless conversations you hear where they're just basically asking each other, do you know this person, and do you know that person, and then, when they hit on someone they both know, going, 'Oh my God, small world! Talk about three degrees of separation!'

Fionn ends up being seriously focked off with me. He saw the way his sister was looking at me – and still is, across the floor of the shop – and he knows I'm going to nail her the second I'm physically up to the job.

'Look,' he goes, his voice dropping a note or two, 'she's not in a good place at the moment. I'm talking about emotionally, mentally.'

I'm there, 'Hey, I'm just trying to be a friend to the girl. I'm a people-pleaser. It's one of my major weaknesses.'

'She's very confused is what I mean. I don't think she's even sure she did the right thing finishing it with David.'

'She will be, Fionn. She will be.'

I've always found low self-esteem in women a major turn-on.

'Ross,' he goes, suddenly turning on me, 'are you ever going to start acting like a responsible human being? I mean, have you learned nothing?'

I'm like, 'From what?'

'From being shot.'

'I'm not following you.'

He's like, 'Just . . . forget it.'

It's at that point that Oisinn suddenly arrives into the shop. He's hanging from last night. The last time I saw him, he was getting into a taxi on Leeson Street with a woman who had a face like Mary Byrne's knee.

'How'd you get on?' I go, still laughing at the memory of her.

One of the amazing things about Oisinn is that he never tries to talk *up* his conquests? Like any good golfer, he declares his fouls. You've got to respect that.

'That's the last time I go home with a Disco Divorcée,' he goes. 'Woke up with a five-year-old kid at the foot of the bed saying he wanted his cereal. Suddenly felt very old. Thought, is this the future for us?'

Fionn says is there any chance we could maybe concentrate for, like, ten seconds so he can pick out something to wear for his wedding day. The shop dude asks if he's decided whether it's going to be tails or not.

And I end up having – I'm going to be honest here – a bit of a moment. I'm looking at us. The four of us. Me, Fionn, JP and Oisinn. And I'm thinking, look at us. Still together. Our lives have changed a fair bit in the last few years. They're certainly a lot shitter. Between us, you'd have to say, we've seen it all. Unemployment. Divorce. Bankruptcy. Near-death.

Oisinn was once Ireland's one-hundred-and-seventy-third richest man – now he's not even allowed to own a bank account. Last Resort Asset Reclaim, the repossessions business that JP ran with his old man, is about to go into voluntary liquidation – they're being sued by a fifty-five-year-old Blackrock housewife, who claims that JP drove her repo'ed Lincoln Navigator back to a motor dealership with her still sprawled across the bonnet. There's talk of, like, six figures. And as for Fionn, he's out of work and – like I said – in for the land of a lifetime.

But we're still all friends. I end up getting a bit emotional, I'm going to be honest, thinking about how close I came to never actually seeing them again. Fionn says that Erika's decided against tails because they cut off your legs and I get this sudden flash of, like, memory. Father Fehily is standing on the sideline in Castlerock – I think it was Terenure, putting us under serious pressure – and he's just going, 'Endure! Endure! Endure!'

And that's what we do. And we do it together. And none of these so-called rating agencies that you sometimes hear about can put a value on that.

I'm, like, picking my way through the waiting area of St Vincent's Private when I hear my name suddenly called. That's when I see him. What was his name again? Something Harron. Detective Sergeant. He's leaning against a pillar next to the elevator bank, with a coffee in one hand and a doughnut in the other. Actually, there might not have been a doughnut – that might be just my prejudice.

He's like, 'How are you doing?' because I think I mentioned that he's actually pretty sound.

I'm there, 'I'm good, er . . .'

'Shane.'

'Shane, yeah. I was just in for a check-up.'

'And how's she healing? The body.'

'They seem pretty pleased with me. Still one or two pieces of shrapnel in my legs that they couldn't get at, but it's supposedly not a problem.'

'Jesus, it's a miracle your liver and kidneys didn't get it.'

'Yeah.'

'Huh?'

'I'm agreeing with you.'

'Are you wanting a lift somewhere?'

'Er, no, it's cool, my wife's actually here. She's just bringing the cor around.'

I go to move away, roysh, except he follows me. 'Well, I just wanted to touch base with you anyway. See has anything occurred to you.'

I'm like, 'Nothing at all. It's still, like, *fock!*'

'Well, we've ruled out Terry and Larry Tuhill as suspects. I thought you should know that.'

I end up just stopping in my tracks. I'm like, 'Why?'

'Well, they'd been dead about four hours when you were shot.'

'But could they not have, like, ordered it?'

'But why would they have used a gun that was in the house? Professional hitmen tend to carry their own. And, to be brutally honest about it, if it was one of them fellas, you wouldn't be alive today.'

I'm there, 'Unless the dude was about to kill me, but I, like, pushed the gun downwards before it went off.'

'Are you saying that's what happened?'

Jesus, he's like Columbo, getting me to suggest, like, scenarios and eventually reveal my own guilt.

I'm there, 'No. Like I said, it's still an actual blank.'

I stort moving towards the electric doors. He follows me.

'No, this has all the hallmarks of a crime of passion.'

'I better go. I think Sorcha's porked in the drop-off zone.'

Out of the blue, he goes, 'Isn't it a fine life they have?'

I'm there, 'Who?'

'Regina Rathfriland and that daughter of hers. Living it up in the Shelbourne.'

'The Shelbourne?'

'That's where they're living these days. I expect they don't want to go back to that house. Too painful maybe.'

'The Shelbourne, though. I thought Regina was, like, hundreds of millions in debt.'

'That's life under NAMA for you. Taxpayers paying the bill and that crowd still living it up like nothing ever happened. Make you angry, wouldn't it?'

'Yeah.'

'Huh?'

'I'm *saying* yeah?'

'It's like you nearly in the mortuary and the person who pulled the trigger walking around, free . . .'

He knows. And he probably knows *I* know. The doors port in front of us. He's like, 'Remember, Ross, if you think of anything . . .'

The bank told Claire from Bray and that tosspot she married what they could do with their Wheat Bray Love idea. Proper focking order as well. An organic bakery and coffee shop in Bray, selling foods that promote wellness? That's the kind of madness that *has* the country in the shit it's in.

Sorcha thinks it's – oh my God – *so* unfair. 'Er, sorry, *remind* me who it was again who bailed the banks out?' she goes. '*And* we recapitalized them. That's, like, *our* money. And they're refusing to lend it to small and medium business people, Ross, who could provide actual employment.'

I say nothing. I just ask her if she wants the last spring roll.

'No, you have it,' she goes.

She leans forward and grabs it for me. It's still too sore to stretch.

It's, like, a Saturday night and we're sitting in watching celebrities skating. Kerry Katona. That bird off *Loose Women*. Then Richard and Judy's daughter. And one or two others who used to be in stuff. I suppose this is, like, a snapshot of what it would have been like had we stayed married.

'By the way,' she goes. 'What's going on between you and Eleanor de Barra?'

I'm like, 'Who?

'Er, Fionn's sister?'

'Oh. Nothing. Why?'

'She obviously has a thing for you?'

'Why do you say that?'

'Are you friends with her on Facebook?'

'Er, no.'

'Well, I am. Even though I probably wouldn't know what to say to her if I ever bumped into her in the street. Anyway, she must have been doing a search for you this afternoon – except she accidentally typed your name into the line where it says, "What's on your mind?" So Ross O'Carroll-Kelly came up as her actual *status*?'

I laugh. The girl clearly has it bad for me.

Sorcha's there, 'It's the new social faux pas apparently. There was a whole thing about it in *The Dubliner* only, like, two weeks ago.'

'Yeah, no, I met her last weekend when we were getting fitted for our suits. I thought I picked up a vibe alright. Jesus.'

I'm trying to make out is she jealous. I think she *definitely* is?

'What I *would* say,' she goes, 'is be careful.'

I'm there, 'It's nice to know you still take an interest in who I end up *being* with.'

'Don't flatter yourself, Ross. I'm just saying she's just broken up with her boyfriend of, like, five years.'

'That's because she didn't love him any more.'

'Well, what I heard was that she did love him, but she wasn't *in* love with him?'

I often think it must be exhausting being a girl.

I tell her I'll be careful, then. She asks me if she can lie length-ways on the sofa and put her feet on my lap. It's a thing we used to do. She's always loved having her feet massaged. I take off her slip-pers and do my duty.

She seems sad. I pick up on it. She *has* been, I realize, since the huge borney with her old man that day in Roly's.

'Have you spoken to your dad,' I go, 'you know, since?'

She's like, 'No,' and she says it in, like, a super-defensive way.

I hate seeing the girl down, which is why I say what I say next. 'Do you think you should maybe give him a call?'

She goes, 'Oh my God, you think I'm being hord on him.'

I'm there, 'No. I just think, you know, it's two weeks later and you're obviously miserable.'

'Ross, you heard the way he spoke to me in that restaurant. He's never raised his voice to me in my actual life.'

'Which shows you how much pressure he must be under. Look, I know he's never been my number-one fan. He blames me for ruining your life, which is fair enough – but he also chooses to ignore some of my amazing, amazing qualities. I mean, I'm the last one who should be defending him . . .'

'And yet you are?'

'All I'm saying is you're the apple of his actual eye, Sorcha. And you love him as much as he loves you. I mean, all the shit he's already going through – him *and* your old dear. Losing their life savings. Having to sell their gaff. And now it's the middle of January and you're still not talking to them.'

'He described Sorcha & Circa as silly. Ross, you heard him use that word.'

'Be honest, what are you most upset with him about – that or the fact that he's having to sell the home you grew up in?'

She stares into the distance for a good sixty seconds. In fact, I wonder is she going to even answer. Then she goes, 'I guess I'm just coming to the realization later than a lot of girls that my dad isn't Superman.'

I laugh. 'Hey, Superman had his enemies. But he didn't have every focker in the street telling him to stick his money in bank shares. Or telling him to buy investment properties in – where was it again?'

'Quinta do Lago.'

'Quinta do Lago. Jesus. It's hord to even say the name now without smiling. Anyway, the point I'm trying to make is that, yeah, your old pair focked up. They focked up in a major way. A lot of people did . . .'

She reacts to that like she's been stung. 'Oh, no you don't, Ross. Don't you dare give me that "We all portied" line. Some of us actually *didn't* lose the run of ourselves?'

I'm just remembering the time she paid some Chinese dude in Crumlin nine hundred snots to have her Tao recentred while his wife burned eucalyptus candles and played *Bridge Over Troubled Water* on the Tibetan bells in the kitchen.

I decide not to mention it, though.

'Look, Sorcha,' I go, 'you know as well as anyone that there's very little going on between my ears. My head is like a focking snow globe. I mean, Tina's right in a way. Who am I to be dishing out advice to anyone? But Father Fehily used to say this thing – perfection is something we seek in everyone else but never in ourselves.'

She looks away. 'That *is* an amazing quote.'

'See, I wrote a lot of them down. The only writing I ever did do in school. Can I tell you something else, Sorcha?'

'What?'

'I was always jealous of your relationship with your old pair. I mean, I honestly would have liked a bit of what you always had. And I'm telling you this for nothing – you do not want to end up the way I am with mine.'

'You're getting on better with Charles these days.'

'It's better – there's no denying that. But *she* didn't even come home to see me in the hospital, remember.'

'Fionnuala loves you, Ross.'

'That woman's not capable of love. All she's interested in is collagen, Bombay gin and doing evil. Seriously, Sorcha – you should possibly think about giving your old man a break.'

I obviously manage to get through to her, roysh, because she suddenly stands up and says she probably owes it to him to give him the chance to apologize.

She goes out to the kitchen to use the house phone. I continue watching the skating. Hilarious. When I saw the headline in the paper, 'Kerry Katona on Ice', I did wonder was she back on the drugs.

Sorcha comes back and says he's coming over. She's actually like a different girl – giddy as a kitten, all of a sudden. 'I'm going to have a shower,' she goes. 'I look a total mess. Oh my God, Ross, where are *you* going to go when he comes?'

She knows he won't want to be even in the same room as me.

I'm like, 'Sorcha, calm down. I'll go upstairs and watch TV with Honor and Ro.'

She throws her orms around me and tells me I am *the* most incredible person she's ever met in her life and that it – oh my God – *hurts* her that some people can't see that there is actual good in me.

Half an hour later, there's, like, a ring on the doorbell. I manage to get myself upright and make my way out to the door on my crutches.

Sorcha's old man looks at me like I'm a used tampon in a hot tub.

'Come in,' is all *I* go.

He's there, 'I don't *need* an invitation from you to enter my daughter's home. Let me tell you something, I rue the day she let you back in here just as much as I rue the day she ever met you.'

There's a great smell coming from the kitchen. Sorcha's obviously baking.

'She's in there,' I go.

He looks me up and down and goes, 'Huh!' like I'm rubbish.

I manage to, like, lever my way up the stairs, then I stand on the landing and watch Honor and Ronan through a crack in the door. They're watching *Keeping Up with the Kardashians*.

'Which one's that?' Ronan's going.

Honor's like, 'That's Kourtney. Oh my God, she's *such* a skank.'

'She's nice, but.'

'She's still a skank, Ro. That much is obv. Oh my God, you *have* to watch *Kourtney and Khloé Take Miami* with me. I've got them all, like, Sky Plussed.'

'Bang one on so.'

And standing there on the landing, listening to my son and daughter hitting it off like I don't know what, I know that it doesn't actually matter what Sorcha's old man thinks of me. I actually haven't done a bad job after all.

★

70

Focking hilarious. The old dear thinks that lol means lots of love.

She just texted me from LA, going: 'Poor Delma's husband. His lung has collapsed. Lol.'

I'm cracking my hole laughing at this, thinking I hope nobody ever focking tells her.

'Who's that?' the old man goes.

I'm there, 'That pickled trout you used to be married to.'

'Oh, she's coming home, Ross. FYI, as my lovely granddaughter would have it. Some time in February. Did I tell you?'

I just shrug – let him know that I don't *give* a fock either way.

'Anyway,' he goes, sort of, like, ushering me into his study, 'come in, come in – your godfather's here, don't you know! We're listening to the election results.'

Hennessy's sitting in the corner. He acknowledges me with just a dead stare. The old man hands me a glass of XO big enough to disinfect a hospital.

I'm there, 'What election?'

The old man laughs – totally over the top, by the way. 'What election? Did you hear that, Hennessy? An acerbic commentary on the futility of a political establishment beaten down by their European technocrat betters! Well, our old friends have been decimated, Kicker. Only one bloody seat in Dublin. Soldiers of Destiny, how are you! Well, let's see if Enda fares any better running the country . . .'

Hennessy takes occasional swigs from his brandy and keeps staring at me. It actually storts to freak me *out* a bit?

'I mean, Fine Gael!' the old man's still going. 'They were nearly bloody wiped out in 2002. Electorate didn't want them. Of course, the way people talk now, you'd think poor old Bertie seized power in a *coup d'état*. Oh, well – to happier things! The day grows ever nearer, Ross!'

'What are you talking about?'

'Your sister's wedding, of course.'

I just shake my head. 'I just can't believe we're all still pretending.'

'Let me tell you, Kicker, it's going to be the day to rival the nuptials of a certain royal couple who are soon to be conjoined in – quote-unquote – holy matrimony. No expense spared and what-not.

I've said it to Erika. The best of flowers. The best of wine. The best of food. Don't even tell me the price. All this talk of austerity – go hang! This is going to be the happiest day of my life – along with the day, of course, when the person, or persons, who shot my son are hunted down like the dogs they are. On which subject . . .'

I sense Hennessy taking a sudden interest. He, like, pauses mid-sip and looks at me over the top of his glass.

The old man goes, 'Still nothing?'

I end up having a bit of a freak attack with him. 'You ask me that every time I focking see you.'

'Well, we're all just anxious, I expect, to see the perpetrators put behind bars where they belong. And no one more so than your godfather here.'

Hennessy finally focking speaks. 'That's right,' he goes. 'I've got to tell you, I'm more intrigued by this case than anyone. And that *includes* the cops.'

'Well, hopefully something will occur to me,' I go. 'Although, then again, it might *never*?'

Hennessy goes, 'I just find it extraordinary, Charlie. Someone shoots the boy. But there's no head trauma. I mean, all he's really lost is a lot of blood, half his stomach and ten days out of his life. Yet he wakes up with no memory of what happened whatsoever . . .'

'Well, you know what the mind is like, Old Scout. A fragile piece of apparatus.'

'I'm just saying it's odd. Like something from a movie.'

'Oh,' the old man goes, 'there's no doubt about that.'

And Hennessy – still staring me out of it – goes, 'Not even a good movie.'

Someone's had another go at the Lambo. This time they've daubed the words 'ANGLO – YOU PLAYED, WE PAID!' in white paint across the front bonnet.

Which means another focking spray job. This is before I've even driven it once, remember.

They've also cracked open the sunroof and filled the cor with bags of, like, rubbish – we're talking to actual *bursting* point here?

I pick my way into the house and I end up hearing one of *the* weirdest conversations I've possibly *ever* heard? Ronan is in the kitchen, interviewing Sorcha for a job. At least that's what it sounds like.

'Can you think of perroblem,' he goes, 'that you've encounthered in the past at woork and tell me perhaps how you dealth with that perroblem?'

I'm still trying to get used to that deep voice of his.

'Well, firstly,' she goes, 'I'm really glad you asked me that. My previous job, as I told you, was as the owner, manager and chief buyer for Sorcha & Circa, a boutique specializing in both contemporary and vintage lines. I've always believed that the best way of dealing with any challenge is to, like, meet it head-on? So, just as an example, a couple of years ago, I was supposed to be the first shop in Ireland to stock this – oh my God – amazing, sassy, red lace skater frock that went really well even with just gold *gladiators*?

'Anyway, I'd told everyone – including *Image* magazine? – that no one else in Ireland was going to be, like, stocking it. The next thing I heard, there was a shop in, like, Ashford that was supposedly going to have them as well. I thought, Oh! My God! They're going to make, like, a total *liar* out of me? So I rang up the supplier and I said, "Okay, I'll double the size of my initial order if you promise not to give them to that other shop." And that's exactly what ended up happening – I got them exclusively!'

I push the kitchen door. They're both sitting at the table, one opposite the other. *She's* wearing her good Alexander McQueen trouser suit. And *he's* just having a flick through her CV, nodding – you'd have to say, thoughtfully.

I'm just like, 'What the fock?'

Sorcha just flicks her hand at me, as if to say, not now, Ross!

'Very good,' *he* just goes. 'One mower question. Do you have any weaknesses, do you think?'

She smiles at him. 'That's a very good question and thank you for asking it. I *can* be a bit of a perfectionist? If I do something – oh my God – it *has* to be done right. And I tend to expect the same standard of care and attention to detail from *everyone* I work with? Also, sometimes I can be a bit impatient. If I'm given a deadline by which to have a task or project completed, I tend to work flat-out to try to get it finished *ahead* of time?'

'Okay,' I go, 'I'll refer you to my earlier question, which still stands. What the fock?'

'I have a job interview,' Sorcha goes. 'Ronan is just helping me to prepare.'

'Hey, that's great,' I go. Then I turn to Ronan. 'Hang on – it's not with Nudger, is it?'

He rolls his eyes. 'No, it's not with Nudger.'

'I'm not saying *who* it's with,' Sorcha goes, 'because I don't want to, like, *jinx* it? But I'm actually very excited.'

I'm there, 'I can hear that in your voice.'

She wanders over to the fireplace and checks her lippy in the mirror. She looks well, it has to be said.

'I had an – oh my God – *amazing* chat with my dad last Saturday night, Ross. Okay, I'm still upset about them selling the house. Of course I am. I mean, there's, like, a tyre swing in the gorden that's been there since I was, like, a little girl? I mean, I can't even bear the thought of someone else's daddy pushing them on it. But my dad *is* right when he says we can't just bury our heads in the sand and pretend it's still 2004.'

I'm there, 'You're possibly right.'

'Okay,' she goes. 'Wish me luck.'

Me and Ro, at the exact same time, go, 'Good luck.'

I follow her out to the front door. 'By the way,' I go, then I drop my voice to practically a whisper, 'what's *he* doing here? Not that I don't want him here. I'm just saying he's here a lot lately, isn't he?'

She smiles. 'Isn't it *so* cute?'

'What?'

'He just wants to be around you.'

'Do you think?'

'Oh my God, Ross, you got shot. You could have been killed.'

'I suppose.'

'Plus, he has something he wants to ask you.'

'What?'

'I suppose I *should* give you a heads-up. Tina rang.'

'Tina? What the fock did *she* want?'

'She says Ronan's worn out, Ross, travelling back and forth across the city to go to school every day.'

'That's because they're pushing him too hord – her *and* McGahy.'

'She says she thinks it'd make things a bit easier for him if he lived a bit nearer to his school.'

I end up totally flipping.

I'm like, 'She's not moving him to Belvo, Sorcha. I'd rather see him put in care.'

'She doesn't want him to move to Belvo. She wondered – well, Ronan wondered as well – if he could possibly stay here a couple of nights a week.'

'Here? In your gaff?'

'Just on the nights when he has a lot of studying to do. He's wearing himself out, Ross.'

'I suppose he's only, like, ten minutes away from the school here. Well, how do *you* feel about it?'

'Oh my God, Ross, I love Ronan. So does Honor. And we've plenty of room.'

I'm there, 'Okay, that's that settled, then.'

I wish her luck again and off she trots. Then I head back inside.

Ro's sat at the kitchen table, already hord at his homework, I notice. He has, like, his books spread out and he's, like, scribbling away furiously. 'What's that?' I just happen to go – again, just showing an interest, like any father would.

He's like, 'Maths. Ine trying to woork out the coordinate geometry formula for this triangle here . . .'

I just nod and pull a face as if to say, hey, we've all *been* there – which *I* focking haven't, of course.

'Then I've to prove anutter theorem using congruent triangles . . .'

'Er . . .'

'Don't woody, Rosser, Ine not gonna ast you to help me.'

I have to admit it – I *do* suddenly breathe easier.

'Here,' he suddenly goes, 'I've something to ast you?'

'What is it?'

'Would you moyunt if I sted over the odd night, Rosser – durding the week. I do be bollixed going over and back to Finglas every day.'

'If Sorcha's cool with it, then so am I.'

'She said you'd probably luven to have me here.'

I just smile. She wasn't wrong. She wasn't wrong at all.

Eleanor's pretty surprised to see me at her door. She just stares at me, her mouth slung open like an elephant looking for buns.

'Ross,' she goes.

I'm like, 'Hey, Eleanor,' playing it cool *as*.

She doesn't know where to look or what even to say. Eventually, she just blurts it out. 'Look, I'm sorry about the whole Facebook mix-up. I am actually *so* embarrassed about it. What happened was that I was searching for . . .'

I'm just there, 'I *know* what happened, Eleanor. You were curious.'

She just sighs. She knows there's no point in even denying it. 'Yes,' she goes, 'I *was* curious.'

I'm there, 'Hey, no crime has been committed.'

She's like, 'I mean, some of the stories that Fionn told me about you over the years . . .'

That specky fock. See, he was *always* terrified of what's about to happen.

'And then that day when I met you in the suit shop, you just seemed so . . . so different. I mean, even to the way *I* remembered you.'

'I won't deny it, Eleanor. I've done a lot of growing up.'

You get days like that – don't you? – where you're just on fire.

'You just seemed so genuine,' she goes. 'I mean, listening to me going on and on about David can't be anyone's idea of fun . . .' I didn't even tell you the half of it, by the way. 'But for the first time in a long time, I felt like someone was actually *listening* to me.'

I nod and try to look all – I don't know – *meaningful*?

'And some of the things you said, Ross, about how not all men are assholes and I just need to become better at spotting the good ones . . .'

'That's a genuine belief of mine.'

'Well, it was also just what I needed to hear.'

I give her a smile – a real Ross special. 'What I'm taking from all of this,' I go, 'is that you're interested.'

My dick might have gotten me nearly killed, but I think the lesson from this is that I'm probably never going to change.

She laughs. 'Er, I think curious was the word I agreed to.'

'Hey, you say, "Tomato", I say, "Are you going to ask me in for a coffee?"'

She just shakes her head – this guy! – then opens the door wide enough for me to get in on the crutches. I let her lead the way to the kitchen.

Being an immunologist obviously keeps her in shape because those Hudsons fit her so well I want to give her a round of applause.

And that orse is God's work.

The complete and utter wanker that I am, of course, I couldn't resist the temptation to ring Fionn about five minutes ago and let him know exactly what I was about to do.

I was like, 'Here, Fionn, what number is your sister's gaff again?'

She lives in Morningside, by the way, this little estate of mock-Tudor houses off Carysfort Avenue, which they built after demolishing an estate of real Tudor houses. Blackrock would be very much like that.

He went, 'Why do you want to know that?'

And I was like, 'Well, it turns out I made a bit of an impression on her a couple of weeks back in the suit hire place.'

The volume of his voice suddenly dropped.

'Ross,' he went, 'Erika and I are just meeting with the priest at the moment. Can this wait?'

I was like, 'The question is can she? She's seriously gumming for me, Fionn – you should have told me. I presume you heard about the whole Facebook thing?'

He ended up totally losing it with me. He was like, 'Ross, do not have sex with my sister.' Hilarious. This was in front of the man who's supposedly going to marry him and *my* sister, remember. 'Ross, she's a real mess at the moment, mentally. I'm asking you as a friend. Please. Do *not* have sex with my sister!'

I was like, '*Carte D'Or*, Fionn! *Carte D'Or!*'

Then I hung up. He didn't even need to tell me the door number, by the way. There's only, like, twelve houses in the estate and I spotted her little red Honda Fit in the driveway pretty much straight away.

'You're still on the crutches, then?' she goes, probably wondering, deep down, whether I'm up to the task. I've got to be honest, I'm pretty curious myself.

I'm like, 'Yeah, no, I'm storting the physio next week, though. Nice gaff, by the way.'

'Well, one of the few positives to come out of my break-up with David was that we actually *underborrowed* during the whole boom? I mean, we're *in* negative equity obviously – isn't everyone? – but we're not as bad as other friends of ours who've split up.'

I've a focking horn on me like the UCD water tower.

'So you're actually *selling* the gaff?' I go, keeping the conversation ticking along.

It's all port of the act.

She's like, 'Well, obviously, if we're not together any more . . .'

I'm there, 'Interesting. *Interesting . . .*'

She switches the Nespresso on – it's the exact same one that Sorcha got as a present from Claudia Carroll for, like, kitting her out for an Ireland AM interview a couple of years ago.

Her mobile suddenly storts ringing. She checks out the screen and goes, 'Oh my God, it's Fionn!'

The sneaky focker.

I suddenly realize I'm going to have to skip a step or two in the old seduction routine here. I make my move before she gets the chance to even answer it. I make a sudden lunge for her, dropping my crutches, shoving her up against the Ariston double-door fridge freezer and throwing the lips on her in a big-time way.

She *pretends* to be shocked at first?

Then she obviously just thinks, hey, I'm actually loving this, because I hear her drop her phone – it actually shatters on the floor – then she's suddenly running her hands through my hair and going at me like *she's* the focking Cookie Monster and my lips are Chips Ahoy!

I unbutton my shirt – forgetting, of course. She sort of, like, moves back a bit when she sees all the padding. Doesn't dampen down her passion, though.

She's like, 'Would it not hurt – you know – if we did it?'

And I go, 'Eleanor, it would hurt if we didn't.'

Cheesarama, I know. But it does the job. Because sixty seconds later she's kicking off her kitten heels upstairs and I'm going about the job of putting the bright back in her eyes.

Off come the chinos and, again, she basically pauses when she sees the tops of my legs, especially my right one, which is still heavily bandaged. I think she's scoobious as to whether I'm going to be able to perform here. As am I. But then I find a position that's comfortable for me and we get down to business.

No problems achieving and sustaining, I'm happy to report.

She ends up being pretty good. Birds who've just come out of something long term usually are – especially when they're, as Fionn says, emotionally damaged. As it happens, I don't hear any complaints from her either. She digs her nails into my orse for the entire episode and pulls funny faces like the bird who signs the Sunday morning repeat of *Hollyoaks*. Whilst screaming as well, loud enough to melt the wax in my ears, giving it, 'That's it, Ross! That's it! Oh my God! Oh my God! Ohmygodohmygodohmygod . . .' all the way to the finish line.

Then we collapse in a sweaty heap and, to cut a long story short, we both end up drifting off to sleep.

I wake up to the sound of a key in the door downstairs. And of course my initial reaction is that it's obviously *him*, arriving at the scene of the crime an hour too late. I even laugh to myself. And Eleanor – who *was* snoozing soundly with a big focking contented smile on her face – suddenly opens her eyes and asks me what's so funny.

'Your brother's downstairs,' I go.

She's like, 'What?'

'Oh, yeah. See it's okay for him to ride my sister but not okay for me to ride his. Would have been even funnier had he walked in half an hour ago when you were swearing like a docker.'

She's like, 'What are you talking about?'

That's when I hear a voice that definitely *isn't* Fionn's call up the stairs. It's like, 'Are you home or not?'

I sense what's coming as surely as one of those cats you hear about who fock off out of it when there's, like, an earthquake in the post. In fact, I'm already pulling back the sheets when she goes, 'Shit! It's David!'

On go the shirt and chinos. Ask your questions *while* you're getting dressed – that's one of the most valuable lessons I've learned in my life. I'm going, 'I thought you two had broken up,' as my feet find my Dubes like they're guided by satnav.

I'm suddenly feeling no pain.

She's there, 'We *have* broken up.'

'Well, what the fock is he doing here? What the fock generally in fact?'

'We still *live* together, Ross.'

'You've *got* to be shitting me.'

'I told you, we're in the process of selling the house.'

'But you didn't tell me you were still both living in it. Jesus focking Christ.'

'You didn't give me a chance. You weren't in the door five minutes and you had your tongue in my mouth.'

'You were the one who suggested we take it upstairs.'

'I didn't expect him home until half-five.'

'It *is* half-five.'

'Oh my God, I must have fallen asleep. Ross, you're going to have to find a way out of here without him seeing you.'

'Yeah, that *had* crossed my mind as well. What the fock did you think I was going to do, Eleanor – pop down and ask him if he had any johnnies for round two?'

'I mean, he's already been hurt enough . . .'

She's still lying in the scratcher, by the way.

'He's not the only one,' I go, holding up my crutches. 'I've just come *out* of focking hospital, can I just remind you?'

'Oh my God, if he found out that I brought a stranger into our old bed . . .'

I can't stand around listening to her focking idiot blathering any longer. I decide it's time to exit this seriously focked-up scene.

Now, in all my years as – I'd *like* to think – Ireland's leading philanderer, I've climbed through more windows than all the career burglars in Mountjoy's D Wing. Yet there's still nothing quite like the shock of discovering – as in this case – a focking locked one. I feel along the windowsill for a key, except there isn't one there.

And all the time, roysh, Eleanor's still going, 'I mean, I know we said we were going to lead separate lives until the house was sold . . .'

I fock my crutches away and I actually run for the bed, already in a half-crouch, getting ready to throw myself under it. Except when I whip back the valance, it turns out to be one of those ones with, like, *drawers* built into the base?

I'm thinking, thank you, Jim Langan – this is the focking legacy you've left us.

The wardrobe is my next thought, obviously being an old hand at this. Oh, yes – many are the mornings I've spent stuck behind a sliding door, farting myself two jean sizes thinner, while trying not to breathe in case it sets the hangers tingling. Except this time when I open the wardrobe doors, they turn out to be all, like, *shelves*? There's no actual standing room in there.

And now I'm really storting to panic. But that's when Eleanor suddenly comes up with an idea – one that even I'd be proud to call my own. 'Say you're here to fix the heating,' she goes.

I'm like, 'What?'

She jumps out of the bed and storts throwing her clothes back on.

'It's broken,' she goes, stepping into her shoes. 'The radiators won't heat. I was supposed to call a plumber.'

Before I can say another word, she grabs me, puts my crutches back in my hands, drags me out onto the landing, throws open the door of the hot press and tells me to just *try* to look like I know what I'm doing.

Then she tips down the stairs and I'm suddenly listening to them talking in the kitchen – bickering actually.

'There was no milk,' *he* goes, 'for my breakfast this morning.'

She's there, 'If you wanted milk, David, maybe you should have *bought* milk.'

'I did. Except *someone* decided to have a hot chocolate before they went to bed.'

'Oh, that's a good idea. Why don't we start putting our names on the various items in the fridge now? That'd be so amazing, wouldn't it?'

I'll tell you something – she's certainly gotten over the guilt she was feeling, like, two minutes ago. She's busting the poor focker's balls in a major way. I think I read somewhere once – or maybe I saw it on TV – that birds are good at turning self-loathing outwards.

'Eleanor, I don't want another row.'

'Oh – and you're saying I do?'

'I'm saying you're being passive-aggressive again – like your counsellor said you could be.'

'Oh, you're using what my counsellor says against me now, are you?'

'I can't listen to this.'

'Well, I can't listen to it either. You know what? The day this house is sold is the day I'm going to celebrate.'

Shit. The next thing I hear is the sound of him coming up the stairs. My hort is suddenly going like a focking drumroll. I'm pretty sure I've never met the dude, but I'm wondering does he possibly know me to see around.

I'm still staring into the hot press and I might as well be looking at a road sign in Irish for all I understand of it. I decide to kneel down. That way he'll see even less of me. There's, like, a boiler in front of me, so I put my hand on that, then I tut a few times, like I can't actually believe what I'm seeing.

He's standing behind me, all of a sudden. He goes, 'She finally called you, then, did she?'

I'm there, 'She did, yeah – just this arthur noon, Bud.'

I'm putting on an inner-city Dublin accent, by the way. I have no idea why I assume a plumber would talk like that. Again, probably prejudice.

'Two weeks she's been promising. But then her promises aren't worth much – I know that now. What do you think the problem is, by the way?'

'You've mebbe been togedder too long,' I go. Because most tradesmen I've met fancy themselves as comedians. 'My advice would be to get out now, Friend.'

He laughs. He actually seems alright. 'And what about the heating? It's a fault in the motorized zone valve, isn't it?'

I pull a face – the exact same one I used to pull at school whenever a teacher asked me about the theme of a particular poem or the periodic symbol for water. I don't even *know* why – because all he's staring at is the back of my head.

'It coulth be a number of diffordent tings,' I go. I'm pretty good at the accent, it has to be said.

'Well,' he goes, 'just don't tell me I need a new cylinder. I don't know if I could take any more bad news.'

Then he says he'll leave me to it and he focks off back downstairs.

I'm still kneeling there, staring into the hot press, thinking, okay, Maestro, how are you going to get out of this one? What's the playbook here?

Then I think, well, I've got to at least *sound* like I'm working. So what I do is I take off one of my Dubes and I stort literally belting the shit out of just some random pipe with it – the plan being to do that for, like, sixty seconds, then tip downstairs and tell him I need to go back to my – I don't know – workshop to get a particular tool that I need. Then I'll be out the door and gone.

I'm actually in the process of putting my shoe back on when all of a sudden I hear *him* calling up the stairs. 'It's back working! You're a genius!'

Now, I have literally no idea what I did. Freed something would be my guess – a *bubble* maybe? Or maybe I did nothing. You know the way some things stop working, then for no reason *stort* working again?

Either way, David is definitely impressed. He's waiting for me at the bottom of the stairs. 'What was it?' he goes.

He's seeing my face for the first time, but he has genuinely no idea who I am. He mustn't be a rugby fan.

I'm there, 'It was, er, what you were already arthur saying, Friend.'

'Motorized zone valve? I knew it. I had a feeling that's what it was last time, when she got some bloody cowboy to look at it . . .'

'A bleeden joker, wha'?'

'Wasn't even a proper plumber.'

'The doort boord. Ah, well. It's sorted now, so it is . . .'

He notices me limping, then cops the crutches in my hand. 'Here, what happened to you?'

'Did it playing ball,' I go.

He nods, apparently satisfied with this. Then he puts his hand in his sky rocket. 'So what's the damage?'

I'm just standing there, thinking, I've just slept with this poor focker's ex-girlfriend in *his* actual bed – now he wants to give me money.

'Er, tree hundrit euros should just about cover it,' I go.

I'm going to hell and everyone knows it.

He's like, 'Okay. And what for cash?'

'Soddy?'

'Come on! It's the way the world's going. How much to keep it off the books?'

'Er, I don't know – *two* hundred?'

He laughs. Presumably at what a shit businessman I am. He's like, 'I'll give you two-fifty.'

He whips out a wad, counts off five fifty-yoyo notes and hands them to me. Then he thanks me – he *actually* thanks me.

Five minutes later, I'm on the crutches again and I'm heading back towards Blackrock village, having – honestly – a good old chuckle to myself. There's literally no one in the world like me.

That's when my phone suddenly rings. I check the screen and it ends up being Sorcha. 'Ross,' she goes, 'where are you?'

I'm like, 'I'm, er, out and about, Babes.'

'Swing into O'Briens and pick up a bottle of champagne, will you? Tonight, we're celebrating.'

I'm like, 'Okay. If I can manage to carry it. What are we supposedly celebrating, by the way? I'm just wondering would Prosecco do the same job?'

'I just had a phone call,' she goes. 'I got it, Ross!'

'Okay, what are you talking about?'

'I got it. The job I went for.'

'That's great,' I go. I'm actually *genuinely* happy for her? 'Although you still haven't told me what the actual job is.'

'Ross,' she goes – and this without any hint of laughter at all – 'you are now talking to the manager of the new Euro Hero store in the Powerscourt Townhouse Centre.'

'Room service,' I go, after giving three shorp taps on the door. It's a trick I picked up watching one of the Jason Bourne movies – either the second or the third.

'Room service?' comes the reply. 'We didn't order any room . . .'

The door is suddenly whipped open. Weirdly, I end up being just as shocked to see her as she is to see me, even though I *knew* I was coming here?

She's obviously just out of the Jack Bauer. She pulls her bathrobe tighter around her.

Neither of us says anything for about ten seconds. Then *I'm* just there, 'Hello, Regina.'

And she goes, 'What abycha, Ross?' because she's from, like, Belfast.

I cop her staring at the crutches as I brush past her into the room. I don't even wait to be invited.

They're in, like, a suite as well. You wouldn't focking blame them, would you?

She's like, 'Hov *yee* lost wheet?'

I laugh at the actual gall of it. 'Yeah,' I go, 'that tends to happen when half your focking stomach gets blown away. You can go off your food a bit.'

All of a sudden I hear a voice coming from the next room. It's like, 'Who is it?'

Then Regina practically freaks. She goes, 'Doant come in horr. Stee where yorr.'

Except Hedda doesn't listen to her. She walks in anyway. And when she sees me standing there, it's like she's looking at an, honestly, ghost.

She's like, 'What . . . what's *he* doing here?'

She's obviously still into the whole emo scene, just from the way she's dressed.

Regina goes, 'Ay was abite tee ask hom the seem quastion. Althoy – at a gass – ay'd see his mammary has soddenlay come back tee hum.'

I end up just, like, staring at Hedda. I can't even begin to tell you how much hatred I feel for the girl at that precise moment.

'Actually, there was fock-all wrong with my memory,' I go. 'I remember exactly what happened.'

I watch Hedda's bottom lip – with its six or seven rings stuck through it – just tremble. She's obviously shitting it. Must have thought she was in the basic clear. She turns her big, red, panda eyes to her old dear.

'There's no point in looking at her,' I go. '*She's* not going to be able to help you – especially where you're going.'

Regina ends up losing the actual plot with me then. 'Doant yee thratten may daughter. Doant yee even talk tee horr. If *yee've* onythang tee see, you see ut tee me.'

I look at Regina. I have to admit, I'm loving the sudden power. 'Believe me,' I go, 'you're in no position to go issuing orders. Like I said, I remember it all.'

I turn to Hedda then, who's bawling her eyes out at this stage.

I'm like, 'I remember you walking into the kitchen pointing your old man's sawn-off at me. I remember asking you to put it down – begging you, in fact. And I remember you pulling the actual trigger.'

Again, Regina leaps to her defence.

'She phoned yee an awmbulance,' she goes.

I end up just laughing. 'Oh, I'm supposed to be grateful, am I? My kids nearly grew up without a father. My old man without a son. My wife without an ex-husband . . .'

Regina goes, 'Just tell us what yee want and get ite.'

'Excuse me?'

'Well, ay presume you're horr tee meek demawnds of some kaind.'

'Actually, as it happens, there are one or . . . one point seven million things I'm interested in.'

'What?'

'You heard. The one point seven million yoyos you took from my old man for keeping Erika's name out of the divorce.'

'What abite ut?'

I actually laugh. 'And I thought *I* was the slow one. I want it.'

'Ay don't hov ut.'

'Horse shit.'

'*Ay* told yee, ay'm fanished. *Ay* owe hondreds e mallions. All may loans are going tee NAWMA. They're abite tee teek the hyse.'

I reach out and I grab the lapel of her bathrobe between my thumb and forefinger. It's a good weave – you have to say that for the Shelly. 'Come on, Regina, people like us are never *really* skint. Not the way ordinary people are. I mean, you're not exactly staying in the Iveagh Hostel here.'

Hedda suddenly finds her tongue. 'Bastard!' she actually roars at me. 'You focking bastard!'

The girl is three nuts over fruitcake maximum. And that's even *without* the threat of twenty years in prison hanging over her? I see her eyes move to the bottle sticking out of the champagne bucket and I can tell she's wondering what kind of weapon it'd make.

Her old dear *also* reads her mind. 'Doant,' she goes. 'He's nat worth ut.'

I look at Hedda. 'Violence?' I go. '*Really*, Hedda?' and then I shake my head, cracking on to be disappointed. 'Some emo you turned out to be.'

Then I stort making my way to the door. When I reach it, I turn around and go, 'I'm giving you a week.'

Regina's like, 'Ay'm naver going tee reez thot kaind of mornay in thot taim.'

'A week,' I go again. 'Or I tell the Feds everything.'

I go out the door and down the corridor, feeling pretty focking amazing about myself, it has to be said. I'm standing waiting for the elevator, actually congratulating myself on how well that just went, when I suddenly feel someone – or some *thing* – kick one of my crutches from under me. I fall forward, the side of my face hitting the steel door of the elevator. I feel like my stomach is about to burst open again.

'You stupid fuck,' a voice above me goes.

And of course I recognize the voice even before I manage to turn onto my back to see him. It's Hennessy.

'I knew it,' he goes. 'I fucking knew it.'

I'm like, 'Hey, I was the one ended up nearly dead. I'm entitled to compensation.'

He grabs me by the Henri Lloyd and literally drags me into the stairwell. I end up having to grit my teeth against the pain.

He goes, 'Okay, you've got some fucking explaining to do – talk fast and talk clearly.'

'I want the one point seven million yoyos that she took from my old man,' I go.

He shakes his head. 'You think Charlie would approve of you doing this, just to get him his money back?'

I'm there, 'I never said the money was for him.'

He laughs like it's the funniest thing he's ever heard.

'Hey,' I go, 'I'm going to be, like, scorred for life, you know?'

'So you want to extort the mother of the girl who tried to kill you? Take one point seven million big faces from her as the price of keeping her kid out of jail?'

'Yeah. Pretty much.'

He stares down at me, then smiles. 'So why didn't you come to me?'

I'm a bit in shock. 'What?'

'This is my fucking business. Why didn't you come to me?'

'I don't know.'

'Because you got shit for brains. Don't you know the police are going to be watching your every fucking move?'

'Do you think?'

'They know a bullshit story when they hear one! Just like *I* fucking knew! You know what will happen if they find out what you're doing here?'

'No.'

'You'll do five years. Minimum! Are you *that* fucking dumb?'

'Er, maybe.'

'So what did she say?'

'Who?'

'The fucking Widow Rathfriland. When you told her what you wanted. Said she didn't have a bean, am I right?'

'Yeah.'

'Expect that's what she's telling all her creditors. But I know where she's got that one point seven million hidden.'

'How?'

'Because I fucking paid the money over, remember.'

He smiles. Hennessy is bad to the focking bone. I don't know why I *didn't* think to ask for his help?

He holds out his hand to me. I grab it and he pulls me to my feet. I groan with the pain of it. He picks up my crutches, then hands them to me.

'I'll get you your one point seven million,' he goes. 'Leave the negotiations to me. But I want twenty-five percent.'

I straight away agree, even though I haven't a focking clue how much twenty-five percent actually is.

Of course he cops this immediately.

'It's four hundred and twenty-five big ones,' he goes. 'And you stay the fuck away from that woman in the meantime.'

3.

Meet the fockers

I've walked, like, two hundred metres on the treadmill and – honestly? The way I feel? – I could actually walk another hundred.

That's how well my recovery is going.

Even Grzegorz, the dude who's handling my physio, ends up having to say it to me. He's like, 'This may be enough for thooday.' He's from, like, Lithuania – that's why I'm doing the accent. 'You thon't want thoo ask *thoo* much of your body.'

Of course, you can imagine how a line like that goes down with me. I'm just like, 'Dude, you obviously don't know how I roll.'

He laughs. He's possibly never seen a competitor like me before. He's like, 'Eet ees important, of course, that you rebuild your muscle strength. But eet ees also important that you rest.'

'Fifty metres more,' I go, sweating like a northsider outside a shut pub.

This is in, like, the Blackrock Clinic, by the way.

He shakes his head, smiling. '*Feefty* more – then that ees eet.'

So, on I go. The work I've been doing here for the last week or so is the first actual training I've done in a long time and it's got me thinking all sorts of crazy shit. Ireland were beaten by France in the Six Nations yesterday and I'm actually storting to believe I could still do a job. Not for Ireland, obviously – that dream is possibly gone now – but for someone in the AIL, if it's even still going.

I put Jay-Z back on the old iPod and I stort imagining myself – I'm going to admit it – selling Yannick Jauzion *the* most unbelievable dummy, then shrugging off Dimitri Yachvili to put the ball under the posts and make the conversion a little easier on myself. My little daydream ends up being interrupted by a horrible screechy voice that I manage to hear even over the sound of my man belting out *Dead Presidents*.

'Jet lag is the bane – the bane! – of my life!'

I pull the earphones out of my ears. 'Crow's feet and halitosis must also be pretty high on your list,' I automatically go.

There's something about my old dear that brings out the best in me.

She's like, 'I've been awake since five o'clock, you know.'

I'm there, 'Morgan Freeman could narrate the story of your life and I still wouldn't give a fock about it. What are you even doing here?'

She lets it just wash over her, though. 'Sorcha told me where you were. I thought I might treat you to some lunch.'

I laugh. I don't even know *what* to say to that? So I just go, 'Have you let someone else have a crack at your face again?'

She smiles at me – I swear, those teeth could chew a focking cantaloupe through a set of prison bors – even though I know what she really wants to do is burst into tears.

'Yes, Ross, I had a little work done while I was away.'

'Jesus Christ, that face of yours is like the Rock Road out there – they're forever digging the focking thing up and yet it never seems to improve it.'

'I don't think there's any cause for that kind of unpleasantness.'

I don't even look at her. 'So why didn't you come home when you heard I'd been shot?'

She's not ready for the question. She sort of, like, mutters and stutters for a bit, then at the end of it, the best she can do is, 'I was finishing my screenplay.'

'Oh, and that was more important than seeing your son . . .'

'I had certain contractual obligations that I had to . . .'

'Your son who might have actually died.'

I end up practically roaring that last line at her. Grzegorz comes over and basically says, come on, we agreed fifty metres, you've ended up doing another seventy – fair focks, though – then he presses the emergency stop button and the machine slows to an actual halt.

'Hello,' *she* has the focking cheek to go, 'I'm Ross's mum.'

He's like, 'Oh, halo,' and he reaches across me and shakes her hand. 'I am Grzegorz. Pleased to meet.'

'So,' she goes, 'how's his rehabilitation coming along?' like she actually *gives* a shit?

He's like, 'Ferry gute. A lot quicker than expected, yes? Eet helps, of course, when you have a good baseline of strength to begeen weeth.'

It's an amazing thing to hear – I'm going to try to remember that exact quote.

'Anyway,' he goes to me, 'I see you again on Wednesday, yes?'

I'm just there, 'Yeah, coola boola, Grzegorz. Coola focking boola.'

He smiles. He knows I'm an animal and it's nice to get that recognition. As he turns to leave, I catch the old dear – I swear, I'm going to focking vomit here – checking out the dude's bod in a serious way.

'You're a focking disgrace,' I tell her.

She acts the innocent, of course, cracks on that we're still talking about her not bothering her hole coming to see me on my – for all anyone knew – *death*bed?

'I rang the hospital every day,' she tries to go. 'Your father promised to ring me immediately if your condition worsened. And the studio told me they would fly me home by private jet in that eventuality. I have to say, they were very good to me throughout the whole ordeal.'

'You didn't go through an ordeal. All you went through, judging from the focking size of you, was a lot of five-course dinners in The Ivy and the Polo Lounge.'

'Are we just going to continue like this, Ross? Or are we going to make an effort to be friends?'

I'm, like, towelling off my face when she says this. I'm just there, 'Friends?'

She goes, 'I've had to let a lot of things go myself, Ross.'

'As in?'

'As in, the last time I saw you, you were . . . doing whatever it was you were doing with that awful Rathfriland woman in the toilets of the O2. Jesus, it was Bublé, Ross!'

'So why are you being so suddenly nice to me?'

'Because I'm your mother and you're my son.'

I turn my back on her. 'I'm going to go and get changed.'

'Well,' she goes, sounding really desperate now, 'what are you doing for lunch?'

'Fock all. I'm going home.'

She actually *follows* me – all the way to the gents?

'Let me drive you.'

'Don't bother. I'll walk.'

'On crutches?'

'I don't need crutches. You've just seen me on the treadmill, haven't you?'

'Grzegorz said you've to continue using the crutches until you've had another two weeks of physio. I heard him.'

'Whatever.'

'So I'll wait for you.'

'Do what you want.'

I end up grabbing a quick Jack Bauer, then throwing my clothes back on. When I go back outside – I swear to fock – she's standing at reception, trying to persuade Grzegorz to touch various parts of her body and give her his expert medical opinion. You can tell from his face that he'd sooner handle nuclear waste.

'I tend to tense up,' she goes, 'when I'm at my desk. I'm a writer, as you probably know.'

'Well,' he goes, 'eet might be problem of suppleness.'

I just shake my head. I'm like, 'She's mostly made of silicon and rubber. Sit her in front of a radiator for an hour and that'll sort her out.'

Then I hobble outside. Five seconds later, I can hear *her* clip-clopping behind me, gaining ground. I decide I might as well take the focking lift from her.

'My pecs are, like, twice the size of his,' I go.

She releases the central locking on the cor. She's like, 'What an unusual thing to say!'

'Hey, I'm just pointing it out as a statement of fact.'

I pull the door open and I go to sit in. Except there's something on the front passenger seat. Of course there focking is! A big whack of A4 paper. It's, like, three or four hundred pages, tied together with, like, green string.

On the first page it says, *Mom, They Said They'd Never Heard of Sundried Tomatoes.*

'Oh,' she goes, 'was that in the car?' cracking on that she *didn't* leave it there for me to just find? 'The studio would be so mad at me if it fell into the wrong hands.'

'If someone's going to actually make this thing, I'd say it's already fallen into the wrong hands.'

I turn the page to the introduction, which I end up reading in one of those voices you always hear on, like, *movie* trailers?

It's like, '*Imagine you woke up one morning and the world as you knew it had come to an end. Zara Mesbur was a young girl enjoying a normal, happy childhood in Dublin, playing the bassoon in her school's junior orchestra and enjoying playdates with her friends, Louisa and Eily, in Dundrum Town Centre. Then came the terrible events of September 28, 2008 – and life for her would never be the same again . . .*'

'For fock's sake!' I make sure to go.

She takes, like, a *left* at the cor pork exit, which means we're going for lunch, whether I like it or not. I *am* a bit hungry, as it happens – maybe my appetite is finally coming back – so she's actually lucky.

I flick forward a few pages:

ZARA, *a five-year-old girl, enters a shop. There are a lot of sleazy-looking men standing about – clearly working class, generally idle. The atmosphere is like that of a saloon bar in the old American West. They are all unshaven and they laugh in a way that many would consider uncouth. Perhaps someone is playing ragtime piano in the background. There is a man behind a counter wearing a string vest. He has many, many tattoos. Silence suddenly descends on the shop when she walks through the door.* ZARA *approaches the man. The score should add to the tension of the moment. Everyone is waiting to hear what she has to say. Finally she speaks . . .*

ZARA: I'd like a pound of organic truffle butter, please.

The men in the shop laugh cruelly at her. They repeat the words she has spoken but in common Dublin accents. ZARA*'s eyes fill with tears. She can't understand their reaction. She speaks to them indignantly.*

ZARA: It's for my mom. We're having spicy salmon kedgeree with sweet potato latkes for brunch.

The men laugh again, uproariously, like it's the funniest thing they've ever heard. Now, it's the turn of the SHOP OWNER *to speak. He removes the toothpick from his teeth.*

SHOP OWNER: Sorry, young one – this isn't a gourmet food shop any more. It's a bleeding Subway sandwich bar, so it is.

One or two of the other men are heard to mutter, 'Sweet potato latkes!' while shaking their heads and laughing. ZARA *looks around her, taking in her surroundings for the first time. She suddenly realizes that this is no longer Pious and Greene, purveyors of fine foods. It is, like the man intimated, an American restaurant franchise specializing in reasonably priced 'submarine' sandwiches, many containing 'rolled' meats. Zara stutters . . .*

ZARA: But . . . but I must have organic truffle butter. Please. Please tell me, where can I go to get organic truffle butter?

The SHOP OWNER *shoots her a callous, stiletto-shaped smile.*

SHOP OWNER: Try 2005!

ZARA *bursts into tears and runs from the shop.*

I end up just closing it. I'm like, 'I wouldn't go keeping Oscars night free if I were you. It's shit.'

'Well,' *she* goes, 'the studio have huge hopes for it. They're calling it a post-millennial *Angela's Ashes*.'

I'm thinking how seriously difficult it is to hurt this woman, no matter how many times I go through the phases.

As we're passing the Punchbowl in Booterstown, she asks me to pass her phone to her. It's on the actual dashboard. It's a slick piece, by the way – we're talking at least a grand's worth. She goes, 'Excuse me a moment, Ross, I have an important call to make.'

She dials the number – *while* driving, by the way – spending a good five seconds looking down at her phone and not *even* at the road?

She's like, 'I shouldn't do this, of course. I'm only two penalty points away from losing my licence.'

I'm like, 'Yeah, whatever. Where are we eating, by the way? I'm focking storving, just to let you know.'

'Thought we might try out the new Bentley's. What's this they're calling it now? *Oh, hello* . . .'

Someone's obviously answered the phone because her voice is suddenly posher.

'Is that the Stephen's Green Shopping Centre? Yes, it's about this – Ross, hand me that little piece of paper there. I wrote the name down – this *Phil Lynott* exhibition that you have running . . . Well, my problem is that it's drawing a lot of people from the – let's just say – wage-bearing classes to this side of the city . . . Yes, *do* put me through to someone – that's why I'm phoning.'

I end up just shaking my head. She's only back from America, what, two focking days? She ends up getting put on hold, which is something she hates. '*Give me a home, where the buffalo roam,*' she goes. 'That'll be in my head all day now . . . Oh, the Cliff Town House – that's the name of the restaurant . . .'

She eventually gets put through to someone. I end up just staring out the window and trying to blank her voice out. We pass the Merrion Shopping Centre and St Michael's College – a banner on the wall outside says 'The Flaming Sword' – and she's still banging away in some poor focker's ear as we pull up at a red light at the RDS.

'I don't care if he *was* an icon of Irishness,' she's going. 'I'm saying that the Ilac Centre is a far more appropriate location for something like that. That's why they built it where they did . . .'

It's at that exact moment that I cop the Gord standing outside the British Embassy. One of the things that made me the rugby player I could so nearly have been was my ability to spot opportunities and to, like, *act* on them? I'd love to see some stats on it, but Tony Ward, Gerry Thornley, Derek Foley – any of the goys who saw me when

I was good – will tell you that I never, ever let a good scoring chance go to waste.

So I stort staring hord at the Gord – basically trying to get his attention. Except he's looking up and down the road. Doesn't cop me. So I just keep staring.

'I don't wish to be unkind,' *she's* still going, 'but this Phil Lynott character – whoever he is or was – seems to have a lot of followers among what I call the dispossessed. And Grafton Street is already one step away from bloody offal queues as it is . . .'

Finally, the focker looks at me. So I stort rolling my eyes and flicking my head in the old dear's direction, trying to draw his attention to her, sitting there, gabbing away with her phone clamped to the side of her big, botox-stuffed head. He screws up his face, not a clue what I'm trying to tell him.

You'd have to ask what the fock they're teaching them down in Templemore?

'Who am *I*? Well, for your information, I'm one of this country's most influential writers and opinion-formers. That's what *Who's Who in Ireland* said about me. Look it up . . .'

Shit. Up ahead, the lights turn green. The cors in front of us stort to move. I make a last-ditch attempt to tell the Gord about the crime being committed right under his nose. I make the shape of a phone with my left hand and hold it up to my ear, then I flick my head in her direction again.

This time, he finally cops it. *She* doesn't, by the way? She's just about to press on the accelerator when there's all of a sudden a tap on the front passenger window.

I, very helpfully, roll it down.

She knows she's in serious shit as well. 'I'm sorry, Garda,' she tries to go, 'it was a humanitarian call.'

This is with the phone still stuck to her ear, by the way.

'Hang up that phone,' he goes, reaching inside his jacket for his all-important notebook. 'Then pull in up ahead there.'

I turn to her and go, 'Looks like you've hit the old penalty point jackpot.'

She's suddenly grinning at him like the focking meercat off the

TV ad. 'Just to tell you,' she goes, 'I can't afford to lose my licence. Too many people rely on me.'

I'm struggling to keep a straight face throughout all of this, of course.

He's obviously not the type to take shit from anyone. He goes, 'I said hang up that phone and pull in up ahead there.'

It's turning out to be a pretty good day, I have to say.

Lindsay Lohan is going back to jail, even if she accepts a plea deal. That's according to Judge Keith Shwartz of the Los Angeles Superior Court. Honor turns up the volume. The girl is supposed to have robbed a necklace worth two and a half Ks from a jewellery store in California – this is *while* she was on probation for her two DUIs.

'And that means jail-time,' the dude on *E!* goes, 'for the star of such movies as *The Parent Trap* and *Herbie: Fully Loaded.*'

'I wonder what happened to poor Lindsay,' I go.

Honor just goes, 'Er, she's *trash?*'

I'm like, 'Do you think so? I liked her in *Freaky Friday*, I have to say.'

'She's still white trash. Oh my God, that's obv.'

I nod like she's just made a very good point. Positive reinforcement is a huge thing for kids and I'm saying that as someone who never actually got any.

Sorcha's out at a Euro Hero staff-training day, although Honor doesn't know that. Sorcha wants to break the news of her new job to her gently.

Jesus, if she thinks Lindsay Lohan is trashy . . .

It's a nice way to pass a Saturday afternoon, though, just sitting here in front of the TV with my daughter. Spending literally quality time together.

I notice that my phone, switched to silent, is ringing away on the coffee table. I pick it up and notice it's, like, Eleanor, as in Fionn's sister. That's, like, seven missed calls from her in three days. I might have known she'd be a desperate bitch.

'Jesus,' I suddenly go, 'is that Katie Price on the TV?'

Honor's there, 'Oh my God, yeah! Okay, FYI, Katie – leather trousers are *not* your friend?'

I laugh. 'Yeah, there's camel toe – and then there's the whole hoof, leg and hind quarters.'

This she finds absolutely hilarious. She even says it to me. She goes, 'Oh my God – *ROFL*?' and then follows that up my telling me that I'm lollers – and it's not often I hear that.

I'm there, 'Do you really think so? Because I can do loads more of that kind of shit, Honor.'

We go back to watching the TV. Charlie Sheen has announced that he's a warlock with tiger blood and Adonis DNA after CBS cancelled the remainder of the new season of *Two and a Half Men*.

Suddenly, out of nowhere, Honor goes, 'I like that you're living here, Daddy.'

It literally floors me. I'm like, 'Really?'

She nods.

I'm there, 'That's an amazing boost for my confidence, Honor, as well as a lovely thing to hear.'

She shrugs her little shoulders. 'It's true.'

Ronan pops his head around the living-room door. 'What are yiz watching?'

'*E! News*,' Honor goes. 'Do you want to watch it with us?' and she storts moving up the sofa to make room for him on the other side of her.

He's like, 'Er, Ine apposed to be doing an essay on the changes involved in Irish agriculturiddle life since the nineteen-thoorties.'

I actually snort. What a focking waste of a life. Honor looks at him all disappointed. That's when he suddenly sees sense.

'Ah, sure what's an hour?' he goes, then he comes and joins us. 'Moy Jaysus, is that Christina Hendricks? She looks like two bowling balls sewn into a sleeping bag.'

Me and Honor both crack our holes laughing. Honor goes, 'Oh my God, Ro, you are *so* lollers.'

It's nice. I'm just saying.

He blows cigor smoke into my face and tells me I look like shit, which is a standard conversational opener for him.

Then he goes, 'Sorcha home?'

I'm like, 'She's at work?'

'What about that smart-mouthed daughter of yours?'

'School.'

He nods, then pushes past me into the hallway – doesn't even wait to be *invited* in? I close the front door and follow him into the living room.

'Hennessy,' I go, 'can you actually *not* smoke that thing in here? Sorcha wouldn't be a major fan of the smell.'

That's actually true. I remember me and the goys had a poker night once and Sorcha moved back in with her old pair for a week until the whiff had cleared.

Except Hennessy just goes on puffing away on the thing – it's like I haven't even spoken.

'So I talked to your girlfriend,' he goes.

I'm like, 'Girlfriend?'

'That old lady you were dicking.'

'You mean Regina?'

'You been dicking *more* than one old lady?'

'No, just one. And anyway, sixty's not that old . . .'

He points the lit end of his Cohiba at me. 'Hey, I don't want to hear about your fucking perversions. I just came here to tell you, I talked to her. I told her I was going to be handling things on your behalf.'

'Oh . . . and?'

'I laid it out for her. "My client only has to tell the police that he's had a sudden flash of memory and your daughter will do ten years. Minimum." '

'And what was her basic reaction?'

'Let's just say we opened negotiations.'

'Negotiations? Well, what's she offering?'

'Fifty Ks.'

I end up totally flipping. 'Fifty Ks? For nearly focking killing me?'

'Negotiations are ongoing.'

I decide to take, like, a tough line. 'Fock that,' I automatically go. 'There's no negotiating to be done here, Hennessy. I want one point seven mills and that's the end of it.'

'Do you know the first thing she said to me when I told her we wouldn't hesitate to turn the kid in? She said, "Do it. I don't care." '

'She's bluffing. Because she practically begged *me* not to do it.'

'Maybe she had a change of heart after you left. They're not exactly friends, in case you never noticed. The girl hates her mother – still blames her for her father's suicide – and from my conversation with her, the mother feels the same way about her. One point seven million is a lot of loot.'

'So she thinks her daughter's freedom is worth, what, fifty Ks?'

'That was till I filled her in on what prison would be like for a nineteen-year-old girl. Coloured it in for her a bit. Appealed to her maternal instincts.'

'So how did the conversation end?'

'With me turning down the fifty K flat. Said we were looking for one point seven million. No fucking wiggle room. Told her to take two weeks to think about it.'

I take a moment to think about it myself. Two weeks. I suppose it *was* always going to take time. In the end, I just nod and go, 'Well, done, Hennessy – you did good.'

He brushes past me, then out through the front door, going, 'Do you think I give a flying fuck how well you think I did?'

'Here's a joke for you, Kicker,' the old man goes. This is in the kitchen of his gaff, by the way. 'I was PMPL when I heard it – that's Peeing My Pants Laughing, to the uninitiated. Heard in Mr John M Shanahan Esquire's wonderful establishment . . .'

He's wearing that focking hat – the one he picked up years ago at the Irish Open when the whole Greg Norman thing was huge. But I don't tell him what a complete and utter tit he looks in it because we're actually getting on pretty well these days.

He's like, 'Yes, I'm trying to remember the *dramatis personae* involved in the thing. There was certainly Sean Quinn – no question of that. And Seanie Fitz, obviously. Oh – and Sean Dunne. That was it. The three Seans . . .'

Helen hands me a mug of coffee and just smiles at me. Then she sort of, like, touches the old man's shoulder – letting him know that he's doing okay.

I'm actually glad he ended up with someone like her. She's a really cool person.

'So the three chaps are in a boat, Ross. And would you believe it, the bloody thing ends up sinking! I mean, have you ever heard the like of it?! So there's our friends – and I hope they won't mind me telling this joke, because they *are* all friends of mine – and they're in the sea and that's when they suddenly realize that there's only one bloody well lifejacket! So Seanie Fitz – wouldn't you know it! – he turns around to his two near-namesakes – both bloody good golfers, by the way – and he says, "Do you think you two could float?" And Sean Quinn says, "The shit *we're* all in – and you *still* want to talk about business!" '

I laugh – obviously just to be polite.

Helen picks up her cor keys and tells him she's just popping down to Terroirs for a couple of bottles. When she's gone – and not necessarily *because* she's gone – the old man turns around to me and goes, 'Oh, I gather you saw your mother.'

I automatically laugh, remembering her text from this morning. 'Huge earthquake and tsunami in Japan. Looks like a nuclear disaster could follow. Lol.'

I'm there, 'Yeah, I saw her. The state of her face, by the way.'

He sort of, like, smiles to himself. 'Oh,' he goes, 'it's wonderful to see you two getting along so well. Of course, she's going to need all of our support now. You know she's lost her driving licence.'

Again, I laugh – can't be helped.

'I know, it's shit for her. I was in the cor when it happened. I was the one telling her she possibly shouldn't be talking on her phone and driving at the same time.'

He nods sadly.

'You obviously did your best, Ross. No, I've been telling her for a long time that she needed to get herself a driver. A woman with your mother's busy lifestyle can't be expected to drive a motor car *and* keep up with all she has going on in her life.'

That's when Erika suddenly arrives in the door. And of course the old man is suddenly all about her. He storts giving it, 'Here she comes! The blushing bride!'

She smiles at him. She's wearing the same cobalt-blue Lela Rose dress that I know Sorcha wanted. Erika definitely has the body for it and I hope that doesn't sound weird coming from me.

'Ross,' she goes, her top lip curled and her teeth exposed, 'why are you looking at me like that?'

I'm there, 'No reason. I'm just thinking you look very, I don't know, Sofia Vergara in that dress. Slash, Vida Guerra . . .'

I'm babbling, I realize. I tend to do that around her.

'And Kelly-green shoes actually suit it,' I go. 'You're certainly ticking off the colour-blocking trend with the whole look.'

She looks at me like she's just caught me, I don't know, anally pleasuring myself with her toothbrush. 'You are *so* weird,' she goes.

She's obviously decided to be a total wagon to me, so I hit straight back. 'Well, speaking of weird,' I go, 'you can tell your supposed fiancé that I want a word.'

'What are you talking about?'

'I'm talking about Fionn. He never told me his sister was still *living* with that dude?'

'Ross, he told you she wasn't in a good place emotionally . . .'

'But he didn't tell me that her ex could potentially walk in while I was skronking the girl bug-eyed.'

It's hilarious the way the old man just nods his head, like I've made some really clever observation about, I don't know, the state of the economy.

Erika's face lights up. See, there's still a cruel streak in her that others crack on not to see. 'Are you saying he caught you in the act?'

'Very focking nearly. I had to pretend I was there to fix the plumbing.'

This, she *seems* to find hilarious, for some reason.

I'm like, 'Yeah, you can laugh. Now I've got her ringing me, by the way. She's left one or two messages – maybe we can go for a drink, blah, blah, blah. Doesn't understand the expression, One Night Only.'

The old man claps his hands together then. It's an obvious attempt to, like, change the subject. 'So,' he goes to her, 'do you have your felt-tip pens and your little pieces of card ready?'

I'm obviously there, 'What the fock is this?'

He goes, 'Erika's come over for an evening in with her mum and dad. We're going to attempt to do the table plan for the wedding. All terribly good fun. What's this Helen called it? Human sudoku!'

I look at Erika and I straight away suspect that *she* has other plans. She's certainly not dressed for a night at the kitchen table, trying to decide can she put Uncle Blahdy Blah next to Auntie Something Or Other.

'Can we do it tomorrow?' she suddenly goes.

The old man, of course, tries to, like, *hide* his disappointment? 'Oh, yes!' he goes. 'Yes, of course! Case of EGO, is it?'

'What?'

'Eyes Glaze Over? Well, Sunday is as good a day for something like this, isn't it?'

She's very – I don't know – *sheepish* all of a sudden? She's there, 'It's just, well, I've made plans.'

'Oh, hence the dress – of course! Young Fionn taking you somewhere nice, is he?'

'I'm not meeting Fionn.'

'Then it must be this old pal you've – inverted commas – reconnected with through this famous Twitter that's suddenly all the rage.'

I'm straight in there. I'm like, 'Whoa, whoa, whoa – what old friend is this?'

She's like, 'It's none of your focking business, Ross,' very touchy all of a sudden.

'Fabrizio,' the old man goes. 'Fabrizio Something-something.'

I'm like, 'Fabrizio Bettega?'

'That's the chap – a blast from the past, eh, Erika?'

I check out her face. From that very moment I know – as sure as I know my own name – that that table plan is going to end up being the biggest waste of paper since I sat the focking Leaving Cert.

Vodka chocolates (€2). Silly string (50c). Some movie that Angelina Jolie did when she was, like, twenty (€1) and has probably never bothered her hole even watching herself. Forty copies of it. On

VHS. Grease remover tablets (50c). Packs of sixty-four clothes pegs (€1) in the colours of the Ireland flag. Twenty-metre scart to 2 RCA phono leads (€2). Fingerless gloves, 95% acrylic, one size fits all (€1). Bottles of bath and shower gel (€1) with characters on them that *look* like *Star Wars* characters but *aren't*? Fruit jellies (€1) that taste of literally nothing. Bottles of hand sanitizer (€1) in wild berry. A movie about snooker (50c) with a young Bob Geldof in it.

I try not to let Sorcha see what I'm thinking. Except she does, of course. She can read me like *The John Deere Coffee Table Book of Big Tractors* (50c) – eighty copies of which are piled up on a table, waiting to be shifted.

'You can take that look off your face,' she goes.

I'm like, 'What look?'

'Er, the one of, like, *disgust*?'

'I wouldn't describe it as disgust. It'd be more deep shock. I just had no idea that people lived like this.'

'Well, they do. An increasing number of people are turning to discount stores, Ross, as the recession continues to bite.'

'Doesn't make it right, though.'

'Well, right or not, they're a pretty much fact of *life* now? My boss – as in, like, Mr Whittle? – he says we're providing an actual social service . . .'

We? Her first full day in the place and she's already a company woman.

She's there, 'My gran, just as an example – Oh! My God! – *loves* these shops? They're the only place she'll buy her handcream. She said in her day they used to call them huckster shops and you could buy literally anything in them, from a needle to an anchor.'

I'm like, 'What about a framed photograph of a waterfall with moving lights inside it (€5) that makes tropical bird noises when you walk past it?'

She snatches it out of my hands. 'If you've only come in to mock me, Ross . . .'

I end up feeling instantly bad then, so I go, 'Hey, I want to take that.'

'What?'

'I want to buy it.'

'Ross, I've had a long day . . .'

'I'm serious, Babes. I've decided to support you. So I'm going to take it.'

In a weird way, I actually respect what she's doing, even though – at the same time – it kind of disgusts me.

'Do you have cash?' she goes.

I'm like, 'No, I'll stick it on the old Visa. Kick it down the road.'

'I'm afraid we can't process credit card transactions for purchases of less than ten euros.'

'What?'

'It's only a fiver, Ross. Mr Whittle said it wouldn't be worth the cost of, like, *processing* it?'

'Okay, I'll take this, er, bicycle puncture repair kit (€3) as well.'

'Okay, that brings it up to eight.'

'And what about this set of six plastic coat hangers (€1)?'

'Still only nine.'

'And the pet lint roller (€1)? I'll take the pet lint roller.'

She takes all of the shit from me, rings it through the till and sticks it into a bag. She looks well, by the way. That grey Euro Hero fitted polo shirt does her a lot of favours, it has to be said. Really shows off her norks.

As she's handing me my receipt and purchases, I end up asking the question that's possibly on *both* of our minds. 'What do you think Honor's going to say?'

I look at her little face, trying to be brave. 'Well,' she goes, 'we'll know soon enough. Linh is bringing her in straight from school.'

'And she doesn't know what your new job even *is* yet?'

'Don't make such a big deal of it, Ross. It's like my dad was saying – Honor is going to have to adjust to the new economic paradigm, just like I've had to and millions of others like me.'

She's going to shit an organ. I know it and Sorcha knows it.

'Anyway,' she goes, 'I'm going to try to sugar it for her with some better news. Erika has asked her to be a flower girl for the wedding.'

I actually laugh. I can't help it. I'm like, 'Well, it's definitely not going to happen now, is it?'

Then I stort taking a sudden interest in the birthday cords (50c). I stort turning the rack, staring at them. They all say 'Happy Birthday' on the front, then they've all got, like, a specific name underneath. Except they're not normal names like John or Mary or Lucie with an ie. They're, like, Katya, Moag, Luna, Dagmar, Phibbs and Bree. Focking Del Boy and Rodney Trotter must do the buying for this place.

She goes, 'What do you mean by that, Ross?'

I shrug. 'I'm just making the point,' I go, 'that I wouldn't stort sweating it about fitting into your bridesmaid's dress. Especially now that she's got Fabrizio back in her life.'

She acts all shocked, even though it's what everyone is secretly thinking. I'm not afraid to call it. Never have been.

'Ross,' she goes, 'you're actually *wrong*? They're just old friends.'

They're more than old friends. She knows it as well as I do. Fabrizio Bettega was an old flame of Erika's from, like, back in her equestrian days. He was from, like, Orgentina? Won an Olympic gold medal for them in, like, showjumping and might have played polo for the country as well. Erika was supposedly in love with him back in the day and he was supposedly in love with her. His old man was, like, an industrialist – whatever it is *they* do – and he's supposed to have run for, like, the *presidency* of the country or some shit?

Anyway, all you really need to know about Fabrizio is that he's a definite looker, he's seriously loaded and has a way with the deadlier of the species.

Possibly a good way to describe him would be Orgentina's answer to me.

'So, what, we're all supposed to believe it's suddenly plutonic?' I go.

'She's in love with Fionn, Ross. Er, that's why she's *marrying* him?'

'Like I said, I'll believe it when I see it. And maybe not even then.'

'Oh my God, you are *so* cynical.'

'I'm just saying, does no one else think it's a bit suspicious that this dude suddenly breezes back into her life just as she's about to walk up the aisle?'

'They met again through Twitter.'

'So I'm hearing. Where he, presumably, found out that she was engaged and thought, I'd better get my orse over to Ireland – could be my last chance to get back in there.'

'Yeah,' she goes, 'now you're judging people by your own standards,' and then she storts taking baby stroller raincovers (€1) out of a box and putting them on a shelf. That's when my phone suddenly rings.

It's, like, a withheld number – definitely not Eleanor, whose calls I've been avoiding – so I take a chance and answer it.

It turns out to be just some random dude.

He's like, 'Is that Ross?'

I'm there, 'The one and only – accept no substitutes,' which is a thing I sometimes say.

Another one I do is, when I'm in the pub and I'm about to go for a hit and miss, I go, 'Beer in, beer out.'

It's then that *he* says the weirdest thing. 'I have a problem with my long element.'

I decide to go outside with it. I'm back walking without the aid of crutches now – mostly short distances, though. That's how well the physio's been going.

I'm just there, 'Sorry, say that again?'

'At least I *think* it's the long element. Every time I flick the immersion switch from sink to bath, the trip switch in the fuse box goes. Does that sound like the long element to you?'

'What the fock are you even talking about?'

'Oh, sorry, I got your number from David Bindle. He recommended you.'

'Who the fock is David Bindle?'

'He said you fixed their heating.'

Jesus focking Christ.

I end up having to think on my feet. 'I'm, er, actually pretty busy at the moment,' I go.

He's like, 'Oh,' obviously disappointed.

'It's literally non-stop for me right now.'

'You couldn't just squeeze me in? Like I said, you come highly recommended.'

It's only then that I remember the accent. 'Soddy, Bud. Like I said to ye – Ine rushed off me feet, so I am. Know whorr I mean?'

He actually gets a bit thick with me then.

'I would have thought, with the end of the whole construction boom, people in your line would have been happy to get any work they could.'

It's amazing the number of people who really want to believe that, isn't it?

'Not me,' I just go. 'In anyhow, I'd bethor get back to it, so I'd bethor. Gameball . . .'

I end up just losing it and ringing Eleanor. I'm like, 'What the fock?'

She goes, 'Hi, Ross,' all delighted to hear from me – like this is a *social* call?

I go, 'I've got randomers ringing me about their focking plumbing. What's the deal?'

'Sorry, Ross. Look, David asked me for your number. I had to give it to him. Otherwise, he would have suspected something. That's why I was ringing you – to warn you. Anyway, how are you? I haven't heard from you since that day.'

'So?'

'Well, I thought you might have at least phoned me afterwards.'

It's straight away obvious that this one is going to be trouble.

She's there, 'Are you embarrassed or something?'

I'm like, 'Embarrassed?'

'About what you said to me – while we were, you know . . .'

'Okay, what did I say exactly?'

'You told me you loved me.'

Oh, for fock's sake. Do I really need to explain that that's just one of those little white lies that men tell, like, 'Of course you're not fat,' and, 'It actually tastes like tartare sauce.'

'I have to admit,' she goes, 'I'm not where you are yet. I'm not anywhere near it. To be honest, I'm still not over the whole you-being-my-little-brother's-friend thing? But I do like you. Actually, I *more* than like you? I mean, I never thought I'd be the kind of girl who quotes Paulo Coelho books to describe my feelings . . .'

Jesus focking Christ.

'. . . but there's an amazing line in – I can't remember which of his books – but it says that if you know about love, then you must also know about the soul of the world, because it's actually *made* of love? It definitely wasn't *The Alchemist*. It might have been *By the River Piedra, I Sat Down and Wept* . . .'

Fionn has stitched me up in a major way here. This kind of crazy doesn't find love outside of *Hollyoaks*.

'Eleanor, you're breaking up,' I suddenly go.

'That's weird because I can still hear you fine.'

'No, it's no good. I'm definitely losing you . . .'

I hang up, then switch off my phone.

I wander back into the shop. Sorcha has finished putting up the stroller covers and now she's standing there with a picture of the Virgin Mary (€5) whose, like, halo lights up by sensor activation. She looks worried. I'm talking about Sorcha, rather than the Virgin Mary.

'They're on their way,' she goes. 'Linh just rang to say they've just porked in BTs.'

'Calm down,' I go.

'I *am* calm.'

'Okay, well just go on doing what you're doing, then, as if it's the most normal thing in the world.'

'There's, like, seventy-five boxes of diabetic chocolate gingers for Mother's Day (€2 each) in the storeroom,' she goes. 'Is it, like, too early in the year to put them out?'

I'm like, 'Sorcha, come on – chillax,' and I throw my orms around her shoulders and tell her that everything's going to be fine. Totally fine, in fact.

It's Linh's voice that I hear first. She goes, 'This is the place, Honor,' and I turn around to see my daughter walking into the shop with her nose, as usual, stuck in her mobile phone.

She's sort of, like, chuckling to herself. 'Oh my God,' she's going, '*LMFAO*? Deena Cortesse looks like a basketball in Uggs,' no idea at all that she's walking into a discount store. There's an argument to say that that's why they shouldn't even *be* on this side of the city. 'Er, hashtag – *who* is your stylist?'

'Hi, Honor,' Sorcha goes. 'Welcome to Mommy's new place of work.'

Honor's head goes up. She doesn't say anything for literally twenty seconds. She just looks around, taking it all in. The 2011 calendars (€1) with a picture of an Airedale terrier for every month of the year. The mechanical pencil set (€2) with the rip-off *Littlest Mermaid* pictures on the packaging. The soap (50c) that doesn't even have a name – just says 'SOAP' on the outside – and smells of Loughlinstown Hospital. The faux-bronze ashtrays (€1) with the little man standing on the side having a focking slash into it.

She takes it all in with her mouth open, then she looks at Sorcha, closes her eyes and let's *the* loudest horror movie scream out of her that I've possibly ever heard.

It's like, 'Aaarrrggghhh!!!'

'Well, you're just going to have to accept it!' Sorcha's going.

'Aaarrrggghhh!!!'

'You can scream all you like, Honor. It's like you always hear them say – we are where we are. And, like it or not, this is where we are.'

'Aaarrrggghhh!!!'

'We're all doing what we have to do to get by.'

I get suddenly worried about her, though. She's exactly like I was in Kielys on Christmas Eve. I'm like, 'Sorcha, I think she's hyperventilating.'

Sorcha's there, 'She's not hyperventilating. She's being a spoiled little . . . *madam.*'

She *is* hyperventilating, though. For once, she's not play-acting. She has genuinely lost it.

'Breathe!' I'm telling Honor. 'Breathe!'

She can't actually catch her breath, though. She's turning literally white. 'Sorcha,' I go, 'quick – get me a bag.'

But she still doesn't believe it's for real. 'They're twenty-two cents each, Ross.'

'Sorcha,' I end up having to shout at her, 'just get me a bag!'

The old dear is wearing gladiator sandals. Probably because

someone told her that they're hot right now. Well, they're not. Not on a woman of her age. *Or* with *her* legs. The last time I saw a set of pins like that, Cian Healy was hauling them down five yords from the line at the Aviva.

Oh, I make sure to draw her attention to that fact as well. I go, 'Does Russell Crowe know you've been raiding his wardrobe?'

Except she doesn't give me the pleasure, just shakes her head and smiles and reminds me that this is supposed to be a happy occasion.

It's actually the pre-wedding meet-and-greet for Fionn's and Erika's two families. Although I still fail to see why the old man included *her* on the invite list. Erika is the lovechild that her ex-husband fathered with another woman while he was still married to her. And here we all are, standing around, playing happy families in Patrick Guilbaud's.

'You're not *even* family,' I go.

She smiles without even looking at me. She has enough foundation on her face to paint the *Stena Nordica*. 'Your father and I have managed to remain dear, dear friends,' she tries to go, 'in spite of the divorce. Why that should upset you, Ross, I don't know. We were part of each other's lives for many, many years. It's only natural that he'd want me to be part of his daughter's big day.'

I watch her fake-smile Fionn's old dear across the room. We're having, like, pre-dinner cocktails before we're seated.

'At the same time,' I go, 'gladiator sandals! Are you on medication or something?'

Her face all of a sudden lights up, as Sorcha arrives over. 'Sorcha,' she goes, 'you look fabulous!' and she does the whole air-kissing thing – pure fake, of course.

Sorcha says it's just a silver beaded Belmain midi, but the old dear tells her she owns the look – from head to toe, she *owns* it – which seems to make Sorcha happy.

'And tell me about your new job,' the old dear goes. 'It sounds so exciting.'

That's a definite lie, by the way. I heard her once – on TV3's *Midday*, in fact – describe euro discount stores as the potato blight of the modern age.

'I'm just delighted to be back in retail,' Sorcha goes, putting a positive spin on it, like she does with everything. 'Okay, it's not, like, high end like I'm *used* to? But it's competitive and it's a definite challenge. *And* it's allowing me to add to my skill set.'

The old dear smiles at her, like a rat eating shit out of a tyre groove. 'And Honor,' she goes, 'how *is* she?'

Sorcha looks at me then, as if she's seeking *permission* to speak? 'She has her moments, doesn't she, Ross?'

I'm like, 'You could say that, yeah.'

She goes, 'She didn't take the news of my new job particularly well. She's worried that someone in her class is going to see me.'

'Well, children can be very cruel,' the old dear goes. She looks at *me* when she says it as well. I don't think I'm imagining it either. 'She'll see in time that you're doing your best – both of you – to put food on the table for her and to give her a good education. And outside of that, nothing really matters, does it?'

She's being weirdly nice. I take a sip of my whiskey sour and try to come up with something really horrible to say to her, when all of a sudden I feel a hand touch my elbow. I turn around and it ends up being Eleanor. The first word that goes through my head is fock – as in, I totally forgot that she was going to *be* here?

Her opening line is, 'Oh my God, no crutches!'

I'm like, 'Yeah, no, this is actually my first time even leaving the gaff without them,' but at the same time, roysh, I'm *wary*?

That's when her expression suddenly changes. She goes, 'Ross, what's going on?'

Sorcha is cracking on not to be interested, but I can tell she's got one ear on the old dear – banging on about this so-called screenplay of hers – and the other on me trying to let Eleanor down gently. So I end up having to just pull the girl off to one side.

I'm like, 'What's with all the questions?'

The best *and* worst time to get a girl is when she's just come out of something serious. I'm just remembering that.

She's there, 'You're just being so . . . so slippery.'

I decide to just level with her – easier all round. 'Look,' I go, 'I'm always a wanker to women I've just slept with. You must have heard that from Fionn over the years.'

A line like that would usually earn me either a slap in the face or a drink down my shirt. Not this time, though. I watch Eleanor's eyes just fill up with tears and I think, oh, no, please – not a crier. I'd honestly prefer a knee in the old two dots and a dash.

'Come on,' I go, 'don't do this to yourself.'

I notice Sorcha taking a *very* keen interest now. She's been in her position, of course, many focking times.

Eleanor's there, 'I can't believe I let you sleep with me.'

'Whoa, don't try to pull that one on me,' I go, trying to reason with her. 'We both got what we wanted that day. We both enjoyed ourselves. No one got shortchanged. No one got cheated. But, hey, I'm not the pot of gold at the end of your rainbow, Baby.'

That's when the tears really stort to flow. Suddenly, every set of eyes in the place is fixed on the two of us, standing aport from everyone else next to the cheese cort.

Eventually, it's her youngest brother – Lorcan's his name; he played for me when I coached the S at Castlerock – who comes to my rescue. He puts his orm around her and tells her that she's making a scene – which she focking is, by the way – and then he brings her presumably out onto Merrion Street to try to get her calm again and mop up her face.

If I had a thousand mickeys, I wouldn't give her one now.

I catch Fionn giving me a serious filthy from a good twenty yords away – he has a focking cheek, I can tell you that. The next thing I feel is a big bear hand on my shoulder and a voice in my ear go, 'I think young Eleanor might have had too much to drink, eh, Kicker?'

I laugh, letting the old man think it *is* that. 'Yeah,' I go, 'some people just can't handle it.'

'Shall we get ourselves seated?' he goes and we all end up following him over to this long table that's been set for, like, twenty-four people.

'Where the fock is Erika?' I just happen to go.

The old man's there, 'She's just pulled up outside. She was collecting this chap of hers, Fabrizio.'

At first I wonder did I, like, *mishear* him? I'm like, 'Say that again.'

'Yes,' he goes, 'this famous friend of hers – from Argentina!'

'He's actually coming to the dinner?'

'Yes, I must admit, I'm rather looking forward to meeting the chap. See what he knows about Argentina's own sovereign debt crisis of '99 to '02 and the steps the country took to remedy it.'

He sits at the head of the table and he sort of, like, gestures for me to sit to his right. I pull out the chair and pork myself next to him. I'm there, 'He's coming here tonight – even though it's, like, a meet-and-greet dinner for supposedly family?'

'Well,' he goes, 'it seems the poor chap was at a loose end. Doesn't know too many people in Dublin, you see.'

'He always has the option of focking off home to Orgentina, of course.'

'Well, as it happens, he's thinking of making Ireland his new European base of operations. He's a showjumper, of all things – did you know that, Ross?'

'Unfortunately, yeah.'

'Well, you two will obviously get on like the proverbial what's-it. Two great sportsmen – etcetera, etcetera.'

Then he's suddenly on his feet, going, 'Here they come, everyone!'

Erika is making her way across the floor of the restaurant in what Sorcha later describes to me as a green Roland Mouret dress with just red Loubs. Yeah, no, she looks well. And then walking beside her, in just beige corgo pants and a white cricket jumper – a look that, even *I* have to admit, he manages to pull off – is the man who, I'm becoming convinced, is here to steal my sister from Fionn.

He's better looking than I remember. All the birds used to say he looked like Jonathan Rhys Meyers and he possibly does, except obviously with dorker skin. He's, like, stick-thin as well, with cheekbones you could hang your focking duffle coat on and – I have to admit – a bit of a hush, I don't know, *descends* on the table when everyone sees him.

I hear the old dear, at the other end, go, 'Oh, he's so handsome, isn't he?' a disgrace and a focking traitor at the same time.

Erika brings him around the table, introducing him to everyone, and you'd nearly forget who in this restaurant she's supposedly *marrying*?

When he shakes my hand, he goes, 'Halo, Russ – a long time,' and I make sure to squeeze his hand extra tight and go, 'Would have been even longer if it had been my choice,' just to let him know that *I'm* not taken in by him.

Everyone else seems to be, though. Even Fionn, the poor focker. He even gives the dude a hug and tells him it's great to see him again, too innocent to realize that another bull seal has designs on his stretch of beach.

Sorcha also ends up getting sucked in. I hear him go, 'Sureeka,' because she would have known him back in the day, 'you are heefen more beautiful than I remember,' which is such a bullshit line.

She blushes and I suddenly remember how it was I managed to get her to take me back so often.

The table plan ends up being Sorcha, Fionn, my old dear, Fionn's old man and Helen down one end of the table; Eleanor and the brother, who are both still missing, and loads of random rellies – including one or two nice cousins – in the middle; then my old man, Fionn's old dear, Erika, Fabrizio and me at the other end. And I'm sure you can imagine the tension where *we're* sitting. Two predatory alpha males and blahdy, blahdy, blah?

I can't actually help myself. I'm on the focker's case from the second he sits down. 'I hear you're still into the ponies,' I go. I used to always hammer him on that one when he was over for the Dublin Horse Show. I used to call it Pony Club and tell him it was for girls.

Erika just shakes her head. She *knows* my form, see.

'Yes,' the dude tries to go, 'I steel ham competing for Hargentina. Also, now, I ham setting up training camp for elite showjumpers – to become trainer, yes?'

I'm like, 'Fair focks,' except obviously not meaning it.

The old man blunders into the conversation then. 'How do you think your chaps will fare in the World Cup this year, Fabrizio? I, for one, think they're capable of giving England a shock.'

He hasn't a focking clue, of course. 'You harr talking about rogbee?'

'Rugby – yes, of course.'

'I ham surry. I know nussing about thees game.'

'Oh, he knows nothing about rugby,' I go, at the same time studying Erika's face for a reaction. 'That's interesting, isn't it?'

The waiter has storted taking orders at the far end of the table. I hear Sorcha ask if the chicken is farm-assured.

Fionn's old dear gets in on the act then. She's actually sound – always was – but she's wetter than a split welly and she really lets me down when she turns around to Fabrizio and goes, 'Fionn tells me you won an Olympic gold medal.'

I'm thinking, whose focking side is she supposedly on?

He smiles. Delighted with himself. Why wouldn't he be? 'Yes,' he goes. 'I wheen een Athens – een 2004.'

She's like, 'How wonderful!' and then she turns around to my old man. 'Isn't that wonderful? We're having dinner with an Olympic champion!'

And the old man then *agrees* with her – without a focking thought for *my* feelings, by the way.

I order the West Cork king scallops with pine kernels and light garlic emulsion, followed by the Wicklow lamb with apple polenta and balsamic and cacao grue reduction – the appetite's back with a vengeance now – then I hand the menu back to the waiter and pull a face like I'm not impressed with the whole Olympic thing.

'Do you ever wonder,' I turn around to Fabrizio and go, 'how much of it was down to you and how much of it was down to the horse?'

Erika rushes straight away to his defence. 'What are you talking about, Ross?'

'Hey,' I go, 'I'm just saying that it must cross the dude's mind from time to time. If the horse had jumped like a focking donkey, Fabrizio would have won squat. But it didn't. It actually jumped well. And fair focks to it. But there must also be a part of him that thinks, "This medal really belongs to the horse – and I've possibly stolen his limelight. And I hate myself for that."'

Erika calls me an idiot, a real sign that I've touched a nerve.

He's well able to fight his own battles, though, because he turns around and goes, 'Hand what habout you, Russ?'

That's another thing I remember about him – he always refused to pronounce my name properly.

I'm like, 'What about me?'

'The last time I see you, you say to me, "I wheel play rogbee for Hyland one day." I see on TV that Hyland is playing against Hengland tomorrow. I look at team, Russ, and I ham surprised to see that you harr not playing.'

It's a low blow and he knows it. I suddenly realize that every conversation at the table has stopped and they're all, like, waiting to hear my comeback. I hope they're also getting a flavour of what this focker is really like.

'I had a lot of bad luck with injuries,' I go. 'Yeah, no – plus you had the likes of Ronan O'Gara and Jonny Sexton breaking through just at the wrong time for me.'

He smiles – except it's more like a *sneer*? He's loving my sudden discomfort. He's like, 'What a peety for you.'

The old man – the focking shame of it – comes riding to my rescue then. 'The big problem with Ross, of course, was that every coach that Ireland ever had – from Warren Gatland to Declan Kidney, by way of Eddie O'Sullivan – didn't know how to harness his talent.'

Fabrizio just smiles at me. 'Steel,' he goes, 'eet ees nice to see, Russ, that you haff never let failure go to your head.'

Erika laughs. Which means it must be, like, a dig at me. A definite dig at me. I just stare at the focker and think, Okay, you have just declared war.

'Ronan,' I go, 'I'm not going to Croke Pork.'

He looks at me with his little face all hurt. 'Why not?'

'Because those focking two or three years that the Irish rugby team spent playing there were *my* Vietnam. I'm scorred – as in, like, mentally? Yeah, no, I said when the Aviva opened that you'd never catch me anywhere near that place again.'

'But Ta Tubs are doing well in the league, Rosser.'

'Fair focks to them.'

'I've a feeding this might be their year – for the Sam and that.'

'Hey, I'm *saying* fair focks. I just don't want to go back to that place.'

I'm only busting his balls, of course. I'd walk through a focking minefield to spend two hours in this kid's company. *Or* along Dorset Street, which amounts to pretty much the same thing.

I'm there, 'I thought you went to all the Dublin games with Nudger.'

'He's woorking.'

'An orson job, is it?'

'Think so, yeah.'

'Would Shadden not go with you?'

'She dudn't like football, so she dudn't . . . Mon, Rosser, I've two tickets and no one to go wit.'

I laugh. 'I'm only pulling your chain, Ro. Course I'll focking go. Who are they even playing?'

'Dowin.'

'Never heard of them. But I'll *still* go. Even though I wish it was still rugby you were this much into. I blame McGahy for that, of course.'

This is us in the kitchen in Newtownpork Avenue, by the way.

He's in the middle of doing his homework. I'm still worried about him overworking.

I'm like, 'How long have you been at it now?'

He goes, 'Two hours.'

'Two hours? Jesus Chirst. I don't think I've ever done anything that's taken me two hours.'

'We're arthur been told that James Leerkin and the Lockout is coming up in the mocks. Ine just reading everything abourit I can get me hands on.'

There's fock-all I can say to that, except, 'Do you fancy a coffee?'

'A cappercheeno?'

'You better believe a cappuccino.'

'Yeah, I'll have one so.'

It's as I'm tipping the milk into the old Aeroccino Plus that the house phone suddenly rings. I let Ro answer it. After a little bit of blahdy-blah, he tells me it's Sorcha – and that she sounds upset.

She's upset alright. The boy knows women. She's actually in tears by the time *I* get on the phone. I'm like, 'Calm down, Sorcha. What's wrong?'

She goes, 'I'm in Debenhams . . .'

I'm like, 'Jesus Christ! I'm on my way!'

She roars at me then. 'I'm not upset *because* I'm in Debenhams, Ross!'

Three or four years ago, she would have been. It shows you how much the world has changed.

I'm like, 'What's the deal, then, Babes?'

'Honor had an – oh my God – freak attack in the middle of the Frascati Centre . . .'

Poor Sorcha's really getting a hord time from her. It sounds like a really selfish thing to say, but I'm just glad it's not me.

'You should have *heard* the name she called me, Ross. I can hordly bring myself to even say it.'

'Go on, what was it?'

'The Euro Whore-o.'

That's actually pretty clever, although it'd take a very brave man to point that out to Sorcha at this moment in time.

'Ross, you need to get down here – as in, now!'

So I end up telling Ro that he'll have to get his own coffee, then I wander outside to the Lambo. Only storted driving it last week. Nudger did a pretty amazing spray job on it the second time around, although the thing still stinks of rubbish and I end up having to keep the sunroof and all the windows open all the way to Blackrock village.

I have a pretty good idea what Honor's meltdown was about, by the way. Her mother took her out to get her flower-girl outfit and I knew there was going to be trouble from the minute Sorcha mentioned that the dress was going to be high street.

I swing into the Frascati cor pork and I spot Sorcha straight away, standing outside the main entrance, dabbing her eyes with a bit of tissue. She throws her orms around me like she's just been pulled from a burning building and I'm about to ask where Honor is when I suddenly spot her over Sorcha's shoulder. She's inside, roysh, sitting on that little bench outside the book shop, talking to someone on her phone, not a care in the world.

Sorcha pulls away from me and goes, 'There's nothing wrong with high street, Ross. Kate Middleton has been – oh my God – *championing* it? And there's a picture in *Look* this month of Sienna Miller wearing a pair of acid skinnies from just Topshop – and, like, totally rocking them.'

You can picture me, I'm sure, pulling all the right faces. It's easier all round. 'Well, you've won *me* over,' I go. 'I take it Honor is unconvinced.'

'Oh, she *stormed* out of the shop.'

'I don't know how you managed to get her into Debenhams in the first place – and I'm saying that as a compliment to you.'

'She said it's going to be designer or she's not going to do it. Ross, what am I going to do? Erika is her actual godmother.'

I'm there, 'Okay, can I suggest something?' ever the tactical master.

She goes, 'What?'

I'm like, 'There's a possibility I'm going to be coming into a few squids soon.'

'What? How?'

'Never mind that. What if I . . .'

'No.'

'If you just let me finish, I was going to say that *I'd* buy the dress for her?'

'I know what you were going to say, Ross. And the answer is still no.'

'Okay, do you mind me asking why?'

'Because I don't *want* her growing up thinking that her daddy is always going to be there to bail her out.'

It's straight away obvious what this is about. I'm like, 'Ah, you're obviously still upset about your old pair's gaff.'

She's like, 'Meaning?'

'I'm just making the point, Sorcha. Is this not more about you having your own – I don't know – illusions about your old man shattered?'

It's all very *One Tree Hill*, it has to be said.

'No, this is about the world in which our daughter is going to grow up,' she goes. 'Do you even *watch* the news, Ross?'

No, is the obvious answer. Unless it's the one that Glenda Gilson and Lisa Cannon read.

I'm there, 'Of course I watch the news.'

'We're living in a country where the Government has squandered the National Reserve Pension Fund bailing out the banks. She needs to learn that she can't go through life expecting just handouts – from the Government, from her parents, from anyone. All the old certainties are gone. Anything she gets in life, she's going to have to earn.'

'I wouldn't go that far, Babes. There'll be another Celtic Tiger by then.'

'Not in her lifetime, there won't. Now, I want you to go in there and explain that to her.'

Jesus Christ. Sometimes I wonder was I just born under a bad sign.

I push the door and wander into the shopping centre. Honor – still on the phone, by the way, presumably to one of her little friends from school – sees me coming. She's already rolling her eyes. I end up just standing around like a fool waiting for her to finish her call.

She's going, 'OMG, that is, like, *so* cool sweet awesome . . . I would *so* heart that. Hashtag – do not go without telling me first . . . Totes. Anyway, got to go. AITR . . . Yeah, awks! *Ciao* for now,' and then she finally hangs up.

'Your old dear's upset,' is my opening line.

She shakes her head. 'Is life just one big period for that woman?'

I end up laughing. I can't help it. It's just the idea of a kid coming out with a line like that.

I'm like, 'You, er, possibly shouldn't say shit like that about your mother.'

She goes, 'Why not? I've heard you say it.'

'Oh, it's one of mine, is it? Well, I'm not denying it's a cracking line, Honor. I'm just saying – you should maybe show her some *respect* and blah, blah, blah?'

'Yeah, whatevs. Tell her when she's finished her potty break, I'm ready to go into BTs and get, like, a *real* dress.'

I end up laughing again, even though I know I possibly *shouldn't*?

'Look,' I go, trying to reason with her, 'your mother's worried about the economy and the banks and the National Reserve Something Something . . .'

'SEP!'

'Which one's that again?'

'Somebody! Else's! Problem!'

I nod. 'Okay. Well, her other point is that high street is actually *in* at the moment?'

'But seriously, folks!'

'Hey. Kate Middleton. Someone else. They're all wearing it. And the other thing to bear in mind – not that I'm a great watcher of the news – is that Ireland is supposedly focked.'

'Insert sad emoticon here.'

She's a total last-word freak – definitely her mother's daughter.

I decide to change the angle of the attack then. Rugby has taught me about ninety-five percent of what I know about life.

'Okay,' I suddenly go, 'you've made some very valid points here today, Honor. So what I'm going to suggest is, like, a *compromise*?'

'A what?'

I sit down beside her. I can see Sorcha staring in. I give her a little wink. 'Look, between you, me and the glass frontage out there, Honor, there's not even going to *be* a wedding.'

'What?'

'Hey, *I've* said that from day one. There's an ex of your auntie Erika's who's suddenly back sniffing around her. He's from a place called Orgentina. The dude is a player. A serious player. He heard she's getting married and now he's come back for her. Except no one else can see it. Anyway, my basic point is that it's a waste of energy falling out with your old dear over a dress that you're never going to end up wearing either way.'

'I'm not giving in to her. She's being – oh my God – *so* lame right now. Can I just say – P and C? – I think she's actually *losing* it again?'

'Look, I know you're upset about the whole Euro Hero thing. But she's doing her best, in fairness to her.'

'Oh my God, do you *know* what would happen to my life if some-one from school saw her working in that place? Hashtag – er, social *outcast*?'

'But how honestly likely is that to happen, Honor? You're in Mount Anville, can I just remind you? The kids you know aren't going to be going into places like that. Jesus.'

'But what if they pass by the door and look in?'

'Now you're just letting your imagination run away with you. Look, I'm going to cut a deal with you here. Now hear me out. Let your mother buy you whatever focking bargain bin monstrosity she wants to buy you – bearing in mind, of course, that you're never going to end up wearing it. I'm guaranteeing you that. Then, when all this dies down, I'll bring you into BTs and buy you – let's just say – two Ks worth of clobber.'

Now, in normal circs, with an offer like that, I'd expect Honor to have my focking hand off. I know her mother would. Except Honor doesn't even respond. She just looks suddenly sad.

I go, '*Proper* clobber, Honor.'

Out of the blue, she goes, 'When are you leaving?' and I all of a sudden cop that this has got nothing to do with some, I don't know, two-hundred-yoyo dress that Sorcha wants her to wear to some wedding that's never going to happen.

I'm like, 'What do you mean, Honor?'

I don't know *why* I make her say it?

She goes, 'You don't have your crutches any more.'

I'm there, 'I know – that's because Daddy's nearly all better.'

'And then she's going to make you go again . . .'

The way Honor looks at me – well, you wouldn't understand it unless you're a separated parent yourself.

She goes, '. . . like she did before.'

See, there's a tendency to forget – because she's such a little wagon most of the time – that she's basically still just a child who can't understand why her mummy and daddy aren't together any more.

'Look,' I go, 'I'd love to get back in there, Honor. But in your old dear's defence, she felt she had a very good reason for kicking me out the last time . . .'

'It was because you slept with Eskaterina.'

'Well, your old dear's obviously decided to keep you informed about everything. Look, I could sit here and slag her off. But I'm not going to. The point is, she was a better wife to me than I was a husband to her. And she's a better mother to you than I am a father and I'm stating that as a fact.'

'No, she's not. Er, hashtag – in her dreams!'

'Honor, do you have any idea the amount of pride that she must have to swallow every morning to go and work in that focking shop? This is a girl who used to have the likes of Nadine Wai O'Flynn ringing her up looking for fashion advice. *You don't need a long frame to rock an assymetrical skirt.* Blah, blah, blah.'

'Er, yeah,' she goes, 'and now she's selling mousetraps (€2 for a pack of three) and moisturizer that smells like wet tarmac (€1 for a 500ml bottle). LMFAO.'

I'm there, 'But that's why you should maybe cut her some slack, Honor. Would you not just let her buy you the dress? Even as a favour to me. Bearing in mind that you're never going to have to wear the focking thing.'

She shrugs her little shoulders and goes, 'I'll do it, but only for you.'

It's a real cut-out-and-keep moment. She's her daddy's girl – there's no doubt about that. Then – this is, like, totally out of the blue – she throws her orms around my neck and goes, 'I don't want you to go.'

I look up and spot Sorcha coming through the main doors, with a humungous smile on her face. I manage to pull myself away from Honor, then I stand up and I stort walking towards her. I meet her right in front of Morks and Spencer.

'She's, er, going to let you get her that dress,' I go.

She hugs me then. They're definitely getting their money's worth in the Frascati Centre today.

'You're amazing,' Sorcha goes. Then she sort of, like, studies my face at, like, orm's length, and goes, 'Ross, are you crying?'

The old dear sends out a text that literally cracks me up. It's like, 'Delma's husband's lung all fixed, but now he's been made redundant. Lol.'

So I'm swinging the Lambo into a little side street in Ballybough and I'm already remembering all the reasons I focking hate Croke Pork. There's some random dude standing there with a woman, who I'm presuming is his wife. They're both wearing yellow bibs, and they're – get this – *directing* me into a porking space that I was perfectly capable of finding myself.

Dublin must be the only city in the world where the robbers dress in fluorescent colours and pick your pocket right in front of the focking cops.

By the time I get the door open, they're immediately on top of me. 'Be a tough ould game today,' *he* goes – just says it, like he's hurting no one. 'D . . . D . . . D . . . Down are n . . . n . . . n . . . nobody's pushover.'

He's got a pretty fierce MC Hammer on him.

I'm there, 'Nor am I, as it happens.'

He goes, 'B . . . B . . . B . . . Begga peerden?' the way skobies do when they're still pretending to be polite.

'Look,' I go, 'let's get one thing straight here. I've no even interest in this match. I'm only here because my son – despite my best efforts – is for some reason into Gaelic football. And I'm not giving you a focking cent, by the way.'

He's like, 'Soddy?'

He's a scrawny little focker, I possibly should mention. That's the reason I'm being so lippy with him.

I'm there, '*Soddy* nothing. This is a public street. I don't have to pay you or anyone else protection money for the privilege of porking the jammer here. End of message.'

She gets in on the act then – as in, the *wife*?

'Your keer might be wrecked when you come back,' she goes.

I'm there, 'Do you think I *give* a fock? I'm insured up the orse!'

He goes, 'You've an awful smeert m . . . mouth on you – do you know that?'

'Look,' I go, reaching into the old sky rocket for my iPhone, 'I don't have time to stand around shooting the shit with the lowest of the focking low. Like I said, I'm taking my son to this so-called match . . .'

I call up the camera app and then – this is genius, even *I* have to admit? – I take a photograph of the two of them, stood there with their mouths thrown open, like they've just seen the focking TV licence inspector coming up the path.

'There ends up being a mork on that cor,' I go, 'and I'm giving this to the Feds. I'm sure they already have your mugs on file.'

Then off I basically strut.

Ronan's waiting for me outside the Clonliffe House. 'People demanding money with menaces,' I go, 'just to let you pork. Doesn't happen at the Aviva, by the way. Dublin focking Four? Wouldn't be allowed.'

He hands me a can of Hefeweizen, which I've obviously no intention of drinking, and he tells me – his father, remember – not to be a fooken oul' one. 'Stick that in yisser jacket, be the way. And don't let the stewarts see you drinking it – udderwise thee'll take it off you.'

He's obviously got a fair few stashed about his person, judging from the focking clinking of metal on metal as he walks. It's like going to a match with C-3PO.

'Come on,' I go, 'let's just get to our seats.'

That's when he says it. 'Seats?'

This sudden feeling of dread comes over me. 'Ro, please don't tell me the tickets are for Hill . . . sixteen, seventeen, whatever the focking number is.'

'Rosser,' he goes, 'are *you* toorty-one or ninety-one? Would you not just open yisser self up to a new expeerdience?'

And that's the only reason I end up going along with it. Because he focking guilts me into it.

The Hill – as they call it – turns out to be every bit the horror show that I expected it to be. A simple question that I'm sure I've asked before – why does everyone from that side of the city fancy himself as a funnyman? It's as if life is just one big audition to these fockers until the day when someone turns around and finally goes, 'You're some fooken cadickter, you are!' and that's their life made for them.

They end up having great fun with me, of course. 'Look at dis fedda,' I hear one goy go. 'He's arthur taking a wrong turden on he's way up to the corpordit boxes!'

That'd be a flavour of the kind of humour we're talking about.

Another goy cops my Henri Lloyd, and possibly my Dubes, then goes, 'Hee-er – where'd ye peerk the yacht?' except obviously the T is silent in this port of the world.

'Just take your fooken medicine,' Ro tells me out of the corner of his mouth. 'Steer straight ahead, Rosser, and don't make eye contact with addyone, reet?'

I'm there, 'I've no focking intention of it, Ro.'

The game storts. I have to admit, roysh, I only end up, like, *half* watching it? Mostly, I'm watching Ro. The confident way he holds himself – even the way he holds his beer – reminds me so much of myself at his age.

And all I can think about is how it seems like only yesterday that we were going to see my old man in Mountjoy together and how his tiny little voice would echo around the visiting room as he shouted, 'Doorty screw bastards,' at the staff.

Now look at him. Like I said, he's like *I* was at fourteen. Loves his sports. Loves his beer – although I think I'll tell him that the next one is going to be his last. Loves the ladies. And *they* love *him*. Well, this Shadden one does anyway – certainly if the hickeys on his neck are anything to go by. He looks like he's been shot with rubber bullets.

The point I'm trying to make is that I'm really, really proud of myself. As a father, I've had my definite critics, but I don't think I've done too badly at all.

'That's Addan Brogan is arthur scoring that point,' he goes to me, filling me in on what's going on, because obviously I haven't a focking clue what I'm watching here. 'He's Burden It Brogan's brutter.'

I'm like, 'Is he really?'

Again – *showing* an interest.

The crowd goes, 'We are ta T.U. – ta T.U.B.S . . .' and Ronan's giving it as much as anyone.

I see him exchanging analysis then with the man beside him – various positional changes that some dude called Gilroy should make in the second half – then offering him a whack of his Hefeweizen.

Obviously, there'll always be a port of me that wishes it was Drico and Jonny Sexton and – yeah, I'm going to say his name – Rob Kearney that he idolized. And of course, halfway through the second half, I can't resist the urge to point out the corner where Shaggy scored his famous try against England many moons ago.

'Father Fehily used to say that Gaelic football would eventually *become* rugby – it just happened to be going through a particularly ugly stage in its evolution.'

'Will you shut the fook up about the rubby?' a voice behind me goes. 'He's talking about the rubby, lads.'

'*Who's* talken about rubby?'

'The fedda in the sailing gear.'

Sailing gear. I end up suddenly losing it and turning around to them. I just go, 'Yeah, where I come from this is actually considered *fashion*?'

'Well, wherever it is you come from,' this really hord-looking goy points out, 'you're not there now. We got rid of your bleaten crowd a couple of year ago. So shut the fook up abourrit.'

Ro just shoots me a seriously disappointed look.

'Okay,' I go, holding my two hands up. 'I've made my basic point and now I'm going to keep my mouth shut.'

The match ends. Dublin win by something-something to something-something-else. We stort making our way back to the cor.

Maybe I know what's coming and that's why I end up being *angry* more than shocked? Even from, like, fifty yords away, I can see the wheels are gone and the Lambo is up on literally blocks.

'Ah, for fook's sake,' Ronan goes.

It's nice to see that he's as upset as I am.

I'm there, 'That's the last time I'm ever crossing the river, Ro. I know I've said it before, but this time I mean it.'

He just shakes his head. 'They're apposed to look *arthur* it. Are you shewer you paid them, Rosser?'

'What are you talking about? No, I *didn't* focking pay them.'

'Why not?'

'Ro, I'm not paying protection money to some focking inner-city Phil Mitchell.'

'What, you're gonna pay for four new wheedles instead?'

I smile at him and whip out my phone. I'm like, 'Oh, I'll get those wheels back, don't you worry about that.'

'How?'

'By using a little thing called my brain. I took a focking photograph of the two of them.'

'Two of them?'

'The two skanks who tried to basically extort me.'

I call up the photograph, then I hand him my phone. At the exact same time, I see a Gord in the distance and I call him. I'm like, 'Gord! Gord!'

And of course you could knock me down with an actual feather when Ronan turns around to me and goes, 'Keep your fooken mouth shut, Rosser. That's Shadden's ma and da.'

4.

Caught us, interrupt us

They're not happy with me – the blonde more so than the brunette. Didn't help, of course, that it took them a good five minutes to persuade me that they were who they said they were. There's something about lady Gordaí that I just can't take seriously. I automatically presume they're about to do a strip. That's possibly *me* watching too much porn.

At the same time, I'm not exactly a contented temporary tent dweller myself. An hour, I've been sitting here. I only popped out for a quiet coffee in the Blackrock Buckys and I've ended up in Malahide Gorda Station, sitting behind a table in an interview room, with these two staring hord at me, but, at the same time, refusing to tell me why I'm even *here*?

'We *have* told you,' the dork-haired one goes. She's a big strapping Mayo woman, with hips so far aport they have different focking postcodes. 'Sergeant Harron has some questions for you.'

'Well, could he not have just hopped in his cor and driven out to my side of the city?'

They don't answer. I'm sensing a definite shift in the 'tude towards me.

I'm like, 'Where's my solicitor, by the way?'

'We've been told he's on the golf course,' it's the blonde one who goes. She's actually the better looking of the two, even though there's not a lot in it.

'Did you definitely ring him?' I go. 'Hennessy Coghlan-O'Hara – he's the only one in the phonebook.'

'We rang him. His secretary said he's on the golf course.'

The door to the interview room suddenly opens and in walks

Shane Harron. The two lady Gardaí leave the room without him even needing to say a word. He obviously *seriously* outranks them.

'You've been lying to us,' he goes. He's turned nasty. Obviously knows I'm ripping the pistachio. He's staring at me like a man who was promised a night with SJP but got a night with SVP instead. 'And the lies are going to stop – today!'

'I already told you . . .'

'What you told me up until now has been a pack of lies.'

'My memory . . .'

'There's nothing wrong with your fucking memory. Why are you protecting her?'

'Who?'

'Hedda Rathfriland.'

'Because I still don't know that it *was* her?'

He suddenly loses it with me. He kicks the chair opposite me, sending it flying across the room. Then he puts his knuckles on the table and leans across it, so our two noses are no more than six inches aport.

He goes, 'It was her. And you know it was her. And I'm going to get a statement out of you this afternoon.'

He stands up to his full height again, then he goes and picks his chair up from where it landed, carries it back over to the table and sits down opposite me. He doesn't say anything for a good twenty seconds. He just stares at me, breathing like Tony Soprano.

'What did you say to Aideen?' he goes.

I'm like, 'Aideen?'

'One of my colleagues who picked you up in Blackrock.'

'Oh . . .'

'Did you ask to see her tits?'

'I thought she was a stripper. I thought they both were. Look, I already apologized to them in the cor.'

'Why did you think they were strippers?'

'I thought it was a stitch-up. Look, you don't *know* my friends.'

'You know I could charge you with public indecency for that?'

'It's hordly public indecency.'

'Huh?'

134

'I'm saying it's hordly public indecency.'

All the compliments about my rugby-playing career have totally dried up, by the way.

'Fancy yourself as a bit of a ladies' man, do you?'

I just shrug. I decide not to play his game. I'm there, 'I do okay.'

He fake-smiles me. Then he goes, 'I know it was Hedda Rathfriland who shot you.'

I'm there, 'So what about the whole, I don't know, *gangland* angle to it? You're saying you've just dropped that?'

'Larry wanted you dead,' he goes, 'but he wouldn't have given the job to anyone else. Oh, I've asked around. He wanted that particular pleasure for himself. It was personal, see.'

'Whatever.'

'There was only you and Hedda in the house. There were no witness sightings of anyone leaving in the time between the shots being heard and us arriving. It was snowing. There were no footprints. So whoever pulled the trigger was in the house when we got there. Given that it would have been impossible for you to shoot yourself from that distance, that only leaves her.'

'Just because the neighbours didn't see anyone leave . . .'

'You know she took a shower between the time she rang 999 and the time we arrived? Does that not strike you as odd?'

'Not if she was checking if I was still alive, then ended up covered in blood and felt a bit, I don't know, *icky*?'

'Or covered in evidence she knew would incriminate her. No, I think we've a good enough case to put in front of a jury. All I need is a motive.'

'Like I said, if anything comes back to me . . .'

'You were giving her mother the length.'

'*I* told *you* that.'

'So Hedda thought you were one of these gold-diggers, did she? After her mother's money?'

'There wasn't any money.'

'Huh?'

'I said there *wasn't* any money? Regina's one of the people who's having to be bailed out.'

'Then you started giving Hedda the length as well.'

'Okay, do you need to keep using that focking phrase?'

'A mother and her daughter. Sure, isn't it well for you?'

Then he suddenly smiles at me, roysh, like a man about to lay down a winning poker hand.

He goes, 'We've a statement from Hedda's boyfriend.'

I'm like, 'Saying?'

'He said you rang his number *whilst* you were giving Hedda the length – just so he could hear everything.'

'There's no law against that, is there?'

'Not as far as I know. But they had a terrible row. Hedda and her little boyfriend. She told him she only did it to try to break up you and the mother. But he finished it with the girl anyway. He told us that. I don't think she's the full shilling anyway. So *she* goes back to the house and she sees your car outside. The fella who broke up her relationship. That's a good motive, I would think. I'm sure the DPP would agree with me. So she goes and gets her daddy's gun. Puts two cartridges in it. Like she saw *him* do a thousand times before. He used to take her on pheasant shoots, did you know that?'

'No, I didn't.'

'Have you heard of Cleggan?'

'No.'

'It's in the county of Antrim . . . No, this wasn't a hit. This was a crime of passion. She aimed for your balls – did you know *that*?'

'I know you're trying to trick me into saying it *was* her?'

'She only missed by about ten centimetres.'

'Well, I was told it was more like a hundred millimetres.'

'Ten centimetres lower and you wouldn't be giving anyone the length.'

He laughs – obviously delighted with himself. And that's when the door suddenly bursts open. It ends up being nearly detached from its hinges. And all of a sudden, Hennessy's big booming voice fills the room.

'Say nothing!' he roars. 'Say fucking nothing!'

I'm there, 'I *haven't* said anything. I can't remember anything,' really laying it on thick. 'Why doesn't anyone believe me?'

'Get the fuck outside to my car,' he goes, and then he turns to the Gord. 'You want to speak to my client again, you come through me.'

And the dude goes, 'Oh, I'll want to speak to him again alright. I'll see you soon, Ross.'

The phone rings about twenty times before she eventually answers it. She's supposed to live in basically a castle, somewhere down in dorkest Wicklow.

'Hellay,' she goes.

That's how posh she is – it was always hellay with her instead of hello.

'Louisa,' I go, 'it's Ross O'Carroll-Kelly.'

You possibly remember me mentioning Louisa de Groot earlier. She sent me, like, a Get Well Soon cord while I was in the hospital and Sorcha recognized her name but couldn't, like, place her? Well, Louisa was another old friend of Erika's from back in her horsey days until they fell out in a major way – over what, I've no idea. I remember she went to Alexandra College, which is probably why Sorcha – a Mountie, remember – has managed to block her out of her mind.

I haven't seen the girl for literally ten years. But she seemed pretty concerned about my welfare – enough to send a cord – and I haven't had any action since the Eleanor debacle, what, five or six weeks ago?

She seems pleased to hear from me.

She's like, 'Good God, Ross, are you alright?'

Rightly or wrongly, I'm remembering her as a sort of Alyssa Campanella lookalike.

I'm there, 'I'm great, Louisa. Well on the mend.'

'I read about it in the newspaper. How utterly ghastly.'

She talks like a character out of a period costume drama, by the way.

'Yeah, no, I got your cord. That's the main reason I'm ringing, in fact – just to say basically thanks for it.'

'Oh, don't be ridiculous – it was only a card. You're alright, though, are you?'

'Big time. I was shot in the stomach. But yeah, no, I'm actually back doing sit-ups again.'

'Well, good for you.'

'Did a hundred of them this morning.'

I'm already remembering how badly I wanted to have sex with Louisa. I don't know why it never happened before.

'Anyway,' I go, 'I just wanted to say that your message meant a lot to me. In fact, I think it was one of the main reasons I pulled through.'

She's like, 'How funny! What did I write?'

I can't even focking remember. I open her cord. It just says, 'Get well soon. Louisa de Groot.'

She didn't even sign it with a kiss.

I'm there, 'It wasn't so much what you said. It was more that you were thinking about me.'

'Like I said, I saw it in the paper and I thought, poor Ross. I always thought you were rather nice. A bit silly at times. Did you marry that girl in the end?'

'Which one?'

'Was her name Sorcha?'

'Er, I think so . . . yeah, no, actually, we did get married, being honest. Unfortunately, it didn't last, though.'

'I remember her being fabulously pretty. Is she still fabulously pretty?'

'When she makes the effort, I'd have to say definitely. Still – onwards and upwards . . .'

'She was *so* pretty . . .'

'Okay, just getting back to the reason I'm ringing. I did a lot of thinking in the hospital. Something like that – staring death in the face and blah, blah, blah – it makes you, I don't know, *re-evaluate* your life? *If* that makes any sense. I think I realized, as I was lying there, not knowing whether I was going to live or die, that I possibly always had feelings for you.'

'Good God!' she goes. 'Are you looking for sympathy sex?'

See, she was always a straight shooter like that.

I'm there, 'No, I'm actually talking about genuine feelings here, Louisa.'

'How funny! I'm not one of your silly little girls, Ross.'

'Yeah, I know that.'

'You really haven't changed, have you? *I possibly always had feelings for you.* How funny! But you must come and visit me.'

'Really?'

'Yes, no one ever visits. It gets awfully lonely down here. Mummy and Daddy are in Scotland.'

I'm there, 'I can come now if you want,' possibly a bit *too* eager.

'No, don't come now,' she goes. 'It's half-eleven at night. Come tomorrow.'

'Okay.'

'Come for supper.'

Supper? I swear to fock, it's like something you'd see on BBC2.

'Supper – not a problem.'

'You really are funny, Ross!'

Funny or not, six o'clock the following night, I'm ready to roll. I've stuck her address into the old satnav and I've pointed the Lambo in the direction of Wicklow, with a bottle of *Neuf du Plonk* from the petrol station in Loughlinstown on board and a three-pack of ponchos, ribbed – because I'm nothing if not an optimist. It turns out that Louisa lives on this humungous estate in Avoca. And when I say humungous estate, I'm not talking about the kind of humungous estate that Ronan grew up on – where kids ride shotgun on Aldi shopping trolleys and a dog with a focking tail is classed as a rare breed. I'm talking about an *actual* estate here, with, like, *deer* and shit? And smack bang in the middle of it is this, like, castle – we're talking Gothic as well.

Louisa is even better looking than I remembered her, which I didn't think even possible. She greets me at the door with a *mwoi, mwoi* and a 'How absolutely wonderful to see you.'

I give her the wine and she stares at it like I've just handed her my testicles wrapped up in a piece of tissue. See, she'd know good shit from bad.

'I'm going to have to apologize,' she goes. 'I'm hopelessly behind. I was mucking out the stables. Totally lost track of time. The supper's on, but I haven't had a chance to change.'

She's wearing jodhpurs and riding boots. There'll be no complaints from me.

It turns out we have the entire castle to ourselves. It's just me, Louisa and Sash, her little handbag dog, who clearly doesn't share Louisa's enthusiasm about me being here, given the amount of yapping she's doing in my general postcode.

This is going to sound weird, but I've always suspected that dogs – especially those little ones – can spot a player a mile off.

Louisa gives me the grand tour of the castle. It's focking enormous – and a little bit spooky actually, especially all the rooms with literally no TVs in them. It's honestly like being a character in that *Downton Abbey* that Sorcha sometimes makes me sit through.

Louisa even links my orm – actually *links* it – as she walks me around the grounds. And as the sun goes down, she explains to me the difference between hares and rabbits and points out, overhead, a red kite, this basically bird of prey that she says has recently been reintroduced to Ireland.

We end up having supper – jugged hare, if you can believe that – sitting at either end of this, like, twenty-foot-long table. Everything to her is either 'super', 'frightful', 'wonderful' or 'ghastly', although after two or three glasses of wine, she storts to loosen up a bit – certainly judging from the way she's suddenly leaning forward and giving me a flash of her baby-feeders.

She storts telling me all about her break-up with Lars, some South African dude she was engaged to, but who *I've* never even heard of, although I sit there pulling all the right faces.

'It was a ghastly time,' she goes, 'Oh, I went completely off the rails!'

'Time is a great healer,' I go. 'That'd be my favourite of all the proverbs.'

Sash storts borking, as if to say, 'It's a line, Louisa! He's spinning you a line!'

'How's Erika?' she suddenly goes. 'Shush, Sash! Is it true you two turned out to be brother and sister?'

'Half-brother and sister. Yeah, no, it's true. She's fine. She's getting married, believe it or not – supposedly.'

'Oh, really? To whom?'

'Do you remember a goy called Fionn de Barra?'

She sort of, like, narrows her eyes, then shakes her head, like she can't place him. She's like, 'No.'

I actually laugh. I can't wait to tell him that. 'Which is amazing,' I go, 'because he *did* actually play rugby. But he also hung around with the focking brainiacs. He was a Mathlete, for God's sake! I can imagine he'd be pretty forgettable – and I'm saying that as his best man and one of his best friends in the world.'

She looks genuinely incredible in the candlelight.

'I sometimes think I might phone her,' she goes.

I'm like, 'Who?'

She goes, 'Erika, of course. Silly the way we fell out.'

I'm there, 'What actually happened?'

She sort of, like, laughs to herself. 'Do you remember a boy called Fabrizio Bettega?'

I end up laughing then. It's an automatic reaction. 'I do, yeah.'

She goes, 'He was from Argentina.'

I'm seriously tanning the wine, by the way. *Her* stuff – not the piss *I* brought. I'm like, 'Just to tell you, Louisa, he's actually back on the scene at the moment.'

She perks up when she hears that. 'What, here? In Ireland?'

'Exactly. Just as Erika's about to walk up the aisle.'

'Gosh! He was terribly pretty, as I remember. I mean, I was totally besotted with him, of course. Unfortunately, Erika was in love with him as well.'

I give her my Scooby Dubious face. 'Erika's been supposedly in love with a lot of people. It was my friend Christian once. Then it was some, I don't know, chinless toff who was supposed to be related to the Royal family – no offence to you, of course. I always suspected she was in love with me as well, before she found out we were brother and sister.'

'Good Lord!'

'I think what she's really in love with, though, is money. And this Fabrizio Bettega has plenty of that, of course.'

'Is he still terribly pretty?'

'He's a good-looking goy – I won't deny it.'

'Of course, we both lost out in the end because he married Lorena Beauclerc.'

I'm like, 'What?'

'Oh, yes. French. Stunning. Like him. She was a jumper as well.'

I end up just shaking my head. 'He never mentioned a wife,' I go. 'Funny that,' delighted to suddenly have something on him.

She smiles and goes, 'Let's stop talking about sad things,' and I suddenly realize that she's actually very, *very* pissed now? And that's when she hits me with it – straight out of nowhere. 'Are we going to have sex, then?'

Talk about a fast turn of events. I mean, I've hordly used any of my lines on her and it's still only half-nine. But what else am I going to say?

I'm like, 'Er, yeah, coola boola.'

'Okay, I'm going to go upstairs, get these frightful boots off me and take a shower. Follow me up in five. It's the room at the top of the stairs.'

Of course, the only one who's *not* a happy camper with the twist the evening has taken is Sash. She storts borking at me in a seriously pissed-off way. She knows what's about to go down and she's determined to spoil the atmos.

Can I just say, at this point, that I actually quite like animals, even though some of you may be aware of my less-than-proud record when it comes to the domestic pets of one or two – or maybe three or four – previous conquests of mine. But Sash actually growls at me once or twice, so I end up doing what every red-blooded male would do if put in the exact same position.

I open the back door and I throw her outside.

Then I just stand there, looking at her through the window, while listening to the shower running upstairs, actually laughing at her, going, 'Don't mess with the best, cos the best don't mess!'

That's when it happens. I'll never forget it for as long as I live.

The first thing I hear sounds like the crack of a whip. Then, right in front of my eyes, one of the red kites that Louisa was banging on about earlier swoops down, grabs the dog in its beak and takes off with her in its mouth.

I end up standing there for, like, five minutes, totally motionless. Possibly in actual *shock* at what just happened?

And that's when I hear Louisa calling me. 'Ross, are you coming to bed or not?'

You can instantly see my dilemma, of course. Do I tell her that a bird of prey took her dog *before* or *after* we do the deed? Because *before* could put a definite dampener on proceedings.

Who'd be a man, huh?

'Do hurry up,' she goes, in that posh voice of hers. 'I'm bloody well dying for it up here!'

And my mind is suddenly made up for me.

Louisa sort of, like, baulks a bit when she sees the scors on my stomach. There's, like, one big horizontal one that goes the whole way across, then there's, like, seven or eight vertical lines that go through it. It's kind of like a Frankenstein scor, except on my belly rather than my forehead.

'How ghastly,' she goes. 'I mean, are you okay to – you know . . .'

I'm like, 'Totally. In fact, I'm going to prove it to you.'

I end up putting in one hell of a shift, especially when you consider how much my – I'm going to use the word – *conscience* is, like, *troubling* me? I keep having visions of that poor little dog in a nest somewhere being picked clean like a focking snack box and once or twice I even think I'm going to lose my – let's just say – *edge*?

But then Louisa's voice in my ear – 'Oh, this is wonderful! This really is first rate!' – gets me going again and I finish the job with her effing and blinding and yelling generally complimentary comments about my performance at the antique cornice above our heads.

And yet even that isn't half as sweet as the sound that I hear next. I'm lying there, still on top of her, trying to get my breath back, when all of a sudden I hear borking – *actual* borking – coming from outside.

I suddenly roll off Louisa. It's Sash. It's definitely Sash. I've no idea what happened. Maybe she ended up somehow killing the bird. Or maybe the bird dropped her. Or maybe the bird took her back to the nest and the other birds went, 'You're never going to focking eat all that.'

But, one way or the other, Sash is suddenly alive and my hort honestly leaps.

'He must have let her go,' I suddenly hear myself go. I just blurt it out. It's possibly relief.

Louisa sits up in the bed. She goes, 'What's she doing outside? And *who* let her go? What are you talking about?'

There's no point in even *trying* to bullshit her? She's not thick. This is a girl who did International Commerce with French in Trinity. And I can tell from her face that she's already joining the dots herself.

'Oh,' I go, trying to pass it off in a real easy breezy kind of way, 'did I not mention that a bird of prey took Sash off in its beak?'

She doesn't say anything. That's the worst thing. There's, like, a million names she could call me and I'd have heard them all before. But the silence. The, like, emptiness in her eyes. That's worse than anything.

'I'll, er, go and let her in,' I go. 'And then I'll let myself out. Unless you *want* me to stay?'

She doesn't answer. She just keeps staring right through me, not even blinking, like one of those poor fockers you sometimes see on the news, who've witnessed something seriously focking shitty.

Which, I suppose, Louisa just has.

'Is that Rossa Cadda Keddy?'

Have you ever *really* regretted answering the phone?

I'm like, 'Er . . .' actually considering *denying* it?

'K . . . K . . . K . . . Kennet Tuite,' he goes. 'Ine j . . . just ringing to apodogize.'

I'm there, 'Apologize?'

'For the m . . . m . . . m . . . miswontherstanding last weekend.'

'There was no *m . . . m . . . m . . . miswontherstanding*. You took the wheels off my focking cor because I wouldn't pay you basically protection money.'

'You got them b . . . b . . . back, but, didn't you?'

'Three of them. I don't know where you got that fourth one – it's certainly not from *my* focking cor.'

'Is it not?'

'Er, it's *smaller* than the others? It doesn't even touch the ground. Jesus Christ, I'm driving around on three focking wheels.'

'I m . . . m . . . m . . . must check the yeerd for it so. See, we took a feer few wheels that day. The p . . . p . . . p . . . peerking arowunt there does be teddible, so it does.'

I end up just freaking out. 'You don't even live around there. You live in focking Finglas.'

'I'm B . . . B . . . Ballybough b . . . born and b . . . b . . . bred, but. Anyhow, meself and Dordeen, we don't want there being addy bad feelings between us – know what I mean?'

'Not really, no.'

'For the sake of the kids and that. We're veddy fond of Ronan.'

'He's a good kid.'

'He's a f . . . f . . . fooken great kid, so he is. As I says to Dordeen tus morning – not telling you a woord of a lie – I'd b . . . b . . . b . . . bethor patch things up with that fedda – sure we mire end up being relared, wha'?'

You can probably imagine how this goes down with me. I feel like a focking lobster in Caviston's who's just caught Derek Davis pointing at him.

I'm there, 'I focking hope not. Anyway, they're way too young to be even thinking that way.'

'Veddy in love, but.'

'Love? They're only, like, fourteen and sixteen.'

'He bought her a ch . . . ch . . . chayen.'

'A chain's just a chain.'

'Has her nayum on it and everyting. Shadden.'

'Like I said, they're still just kids – still finding out what it's all about.'

'Do you know what D . . . D . . . Dordeen says to me when she sees the ch . . . chayen. Says she, "I think I'm going to be buying a hat before long." '

A hat? Jesus focking Christ.

I'd say the only hat that anyone in Shadden's family has ever worn is a focking balaclava. Because Ro gave me the full MO on the Tuites while we were waiting for them to put the wheels back on the cor. There's, like, nine of them – we're talking Kennet and Dordeen, we're talking Shadden and then we're talking six older brothers, none of whom, like their mother and father, has ever done an honest day's work in their lives.

And I know that's a bit rich coming from me.

No, the entire family income is based on things like the porking scam, not to mention the all-impotant personal injury claims. Between them, they've got something like thirty working their way through the system at the moment.

In fact, Shadden's earliest memory of her father – again, this is according to Ro – is of him drinking an entire bottle of Jameson before sawing off his index finger with a bread knife. Then he claimed he caught it in the doors of a lift and got ninety focking Ks out of some hotel or other. I'm not making that up. He's actually down to seven fingers now. The insurance companies have nick-named him Edward Scissorhands.

It pains me to say it, but Tina was right. Much as I like Shadden, I cannot end up related to these people.

I'm there, 'I still think they're very young to be getting serious. I mean, they're still in school.'

'He's v . . . v . . . veddy owult for he's age as well, but . . . Idn't he doing he's Judinior Ceert. years ahead of when he's apposed to?'

'One year, yeah.'

'*She's* the same, of course. B . . . B . . . B . . . Brains to burden. She must have gorrit from Dordeen, but. She ceertainly didn't gerrit from me. What about Ro?'

'Excuse me?'

'Does he get he's brains from you or he's m . . . m . . . mudder?'

'Probably a combination of the two. Look, no offence to you *or* your wife, Kennet, but I honestly don't think we should be talking about them being in love and, I don't know, let's all get a focking hat.'

'It'll be a anutter two or tree year – I know.'

'Two or three years? Ronan will be seventeen. Jesus Christ. They're still both kids. They've got, like, years of ahead of them. They've got school, then college, then – and this isn't a dig at you or your family – but work. They're both going to meet a lot more people.'

'D . . . D . . . Don't say that to Dordeen. She wants Shadden to be a teen berride.'

'A what?'

'She was a t . . . t . . . teen berride herself.'

No shit, I think.

'Has all sorts of fancy ideas,' he goes. 'She says we mire even end up having the engagement peerty on the boat.'

I'm like, 'What boat?'

'*Your* boat.'

'I don't *have* a focking boat. Jesus Christ, it's just a jacket and a pair of shoes I sometimes wear. What the fock is it with you people?'

'We just p . . . p . . . presumed you had a boat.'

'Well, I don't. It'd be like me going to Finglas and presuming that every focker in a cowboy hat had a horse tied up in the back gorden.'

'A lot do, but.'

'I'm sure they focking do.'

He says *the* most unbelievable thing then. This is without even a hint of embarrassment. 'S . . . S . . . S . . . So when are we going for a thrink?'

The man who took the wheels off my focking cor.

'A drink? Er, we're *not*?'

'Ah, would you go on ourra that. Do you ever thrink in Finglas?'

'Er, that would be a no.'

'Fear denuff. I'll head out your d . . . d . . . direction so.'

'What?'

He's there, 'What's the nayum of your local?'

And I'm like, 'Dude, I've got to go.'

*

Fabrizio is telling Fionn that he has the muscle definition of a man who rides a lot of horses and at the same time he's, like, squeezing the dude's upper orm – patronizing him, basically. Except Fionn can't see what the focker's doing. He's all, 'Believe it or not, I've only been up on a horse – what, twice?'

'Zees,' Fabrizio goes, 'I find ferry hart to believe. You heff gute, gute build.'

Fabrizio's other orm, I can't help but notice, is wrapped around Erika's waist. And no one seems to find this unusual – or if they do, they're certainly not saying.

What's he even doing here? That's what I have to wonder. It's supposed to be, like, Helen's birthday? Family and close friends was what my old man said. Yet when I rocked up, *he* was already here, drinking from one of the John Rocha champagne flutes that *I* bought her and telling his horseshit stories to anyone who's pre-pared to listen.

Which seems to be everyone.

They're all whispering about how handsome and how chorming he is. 'It's effortless,' I heard one of Helen's friends go. 'That's the Latino way, of course.'

He even told Helen that she didn't look anything near sixty-five, which was the exact same line that I was planning to hit her with if he hadn't got in there first.

But the orm around Erika's waist is the biggest liberty of all. And the worst thing is that *she* doesn't seem to mind. She's smiling at him, at his every, I don't know, utterance – not just with her mouth, but with her *eyes*?

I honestly feel like decking him.

Decking him and shaking Fionn and just going, 'Can you not see what's *actually* happening here?'

'So,' the old man goes, his hand on Fionn's shoulder, 'do you think Fine Gael and Labour are faring any better than the other crowd? Will they negotiate a cut in the interest rate with our friends in the IMF? Will they burn the senior bondholders? Would they dare, I wonder?'

Fionn just shakes his head. He's never been a ladies' man – I've known nymphomaniacs who only wanted to be his friend – but one thing you'd have to say about him is that he knows his shit when it comes to politics and blah, blah, blah. Whatever focking use that is to anyone.

He goes, 'You know how *I* feel, Charles. I have very little belief in the ability or even willingness of our politicians to change what's happening. I think whoever's in power, they'll do whatever the IMF, EU and the ECB tell them to do.'

'Hear, hear,' I go, trying to sound like I know what the fock everyone's talking about. Usually, I'd get away with it. Except Fabrizio recognizes it as a bluff and – this will tell you what a prick he is – he decides to call me out on it.

He's like, 'What do you mean, Russ?'

I'm there, 'Sorry?'

'What harr you agreeing weeth?'

It's basically open warfare between us at this stage.

I'm there, 'Er, basically everything Fionn just said.'

'You do not theenk that politicians can effect chenge? What about Roosevelt and the New Deal?'

Fionn tries to save me, in fairness to the focker. 'Different set of circumstances,' he goes.

Fabrizio's there, 'No, no, Fionn – I would like to hear what Russ has to say about thees.'

Jesus Christ, the all-of-a-sudden pressure. He's just, like, staring at me as well.

I'm there, 'I just think, you know, the recession and blah, blah, blah.'

He laughs. *'The recession and blah, blah, blah.* Ferry gute, Russ – I never seenk about it thees way!'

'Well,' the old man goes, 'you'll have to get used to that, Fabrizio, where this chap is concerned. Ross is what's known as a lateral thinker. Famous for it.'

'Ferry lateral,' Fabrizio goes, thinking he's focking hilarious. 'Yes. Ferry lateral indeed.'

That's when Erika suddenly pipes up. 'Fabrizio's had an amazing idea,' she goes, then she looks up at him – honestly, *adoringly*? 'Do you want to say it or will I?'

'No,' *he* goes, loving being the centre of attention. 'I sink effery-one is enjoy the party.'

Erika blurts it out anyway. 'Let's all go to Paris!'

This is the type of dude he is, see – always has to be the centre of attention, always has to be the hero of the hour. We all know people who are like that.

I'm like, 'I think people are pretty happy *here*, thanks, Fabrizio.'

But the old man has to go and let me down. 'Paris?' he goes. 'What, tonight?'

The focker's like, 'Yes, I haff plane een Dublin Airport. We can be een Paris een two hours.'

The old man turns around and catches Helen's eye. She's dishing out the mozzarella sticks and the miniature dim sums – she's a bit tanked, to be honest. 'Did someone say Paris?' she goes.

The old man's like, 'Yes! Tonight!'

'But you couldn't take us all, could you?'

Fabrizio goes, 'Of course. The plane, eet has rum for thirty.'

The word about Paris spreads through the gaff like I don't know what. Everyone is suddenly up for it. It's like their minds have suddenly been taken over.

'Let's just do it,' seems to be the general vibe. 'It's been nothing but doom and gloom. When was the last time we did something spontaneous?'

I go, 'You're forgetting one basic fact. It's going to be, like, midnight by the time you get there. Everywhere's going to be shut.'

Fabrizio laughs at that. 'Thees ees Parees we harr speaking of. Hat meednight, the night ees jost beginning.'

Helen goes, 'Oh, Charles! We could dance all night, then have breakfast by the Seine!'

I told you she was jorred. But they *all* are – on whatever vibes this focker is giving off. It's like they're actually hypnotized. They're all, like, heading for the door, like it's suddenly 2006 again – everyone forgetting that they have kids, jobs, responsibilities, mortgage arrears.

They're not the only ones conveniently forgetting about their real lives, of course. I'm suddenly thinking about what Louisa de Groot told me before she focked me out on my ear and made me sleep in my cor. Half of them are already out in the hall, throwing their coats and jackets on when I decide to hit Fabrizio with what I know. It's about time someone brought these people to their senses.

So I go, 'Maybe your wife would like to come with us?'

Oh, that puts a sudden halt to his gallop.

He's like, 'What?'

And there's, like, instant silence in the room, by the way.

I'm there, 'Er, your *wife*? Or have you forgotten that you're actually married to a woman called Lorena Something-something – because you *seem* to have, leching over my sister there, trying to be the big-time hero of the hour. I'm just saying, maybe this woman you're married to would like to come to Paris. I mean, where the fock even *is* she?'

'Lorena died three months ago, Ross.'

It's actually, like, Erika who says it? And there's, like, gasps in the room.

She's there, 'In a riding accident.'

The room is suddenly full of people going, 'Oh, you poor thing. You poor, poor man,' although not to me, but to him. And Fabrizio just stands there, soaking up the sympathy.

One or two are giving me serious daggers as well – including Erika.

'I don't like to theenk too much about eet,' *he* goes. He's even got tears in his eyes. Oh, he knows how to play a room.

One thing's for certain, though. Paris has been totally forgotten about. It's like everyone has suddenly snapped out of the trance they were in. The people who managed to get as far as the front door are hanging their coats back up and trying to remember where they left their drinks. A fair few of them are just, like, staring at me, hating me for ruining their fun.

'Hey,' I go, 'I didn't know the dude's wife was dead. You lot would want to cop onto yourselves. Carrying on like a bunch of focking teenagers. It's supposed to be a recession, can I just remind you?' and then I go out to the kitchen to grab another beer.

Sorcha goes, 'Oh my God, Ross, you are a total snob – and I'm *talking* total here?'

Which is horseshit, of course. If I *was* a total snob, I certainly wouldn't be standing around this shop shooting the shit with her, among the magnetic can openers (€2) and the Australia-to-US plug adaptors (€1) and the grey crimplene under-bed storage bags (€3) and the plastic Hallowe'en masks (50c) even though it's focking April.

I *could* say that to her, of course, but I decide not to. It's bad enough that Honor is hiding in a corner of the shop behind a pair of oversized aviators and the breathing mask that her old dear bought during the SARS scare of 2003.

'It's not being a snob to want the best for my son,' I go. 'I mean, these people are focking pond-life. They'd live off you. They look at *me* and they see focking yoyo signs.'

She goes, 'Ross, don't talk about people like that, especially in front of . . .' and then she sort of, like, nods silently in Honor's direction.

Honor's not even listening, though. She's, like, lost in focking Twitterworld.

'I'm telling you, Sorcha, these people could count the change in your pocket from the upper deck of a moving bus. Focking low-lifes. And to think, his last girlfriend's old man was a doctor! I blame Tina for this, you know.'

'But didn't she tell you she didn't like Shadden's family?'

'Yeah, no, I blame her for raising him on that focking council estate. Jesus Christ. When we were kids, we played hide and go seek. Ronan played hide and go fock yourself. Is it any wonder that he got mixed up with a family like that?'

Honor looks up from her iPhone. It turns out she *was* listening all along. She's like, 'BION, Dad – Mom is totally down with the povs these days.'

Sorcha tells her not to use that word. 'And take off that silly mask, Honor.'

'No. I don't want to catch something.'

I don't say it to Sorcha, of course, but I think the kid has an actual point. The whole shop smells of dust, wrongly spelt *eau de colone* and desperation.

Sorcha is suddenly talking over my left hammer to a group of

English girls who are giggling at the hen's night accessories. 'There's fifty percent off the iron-on faux diamanté transfers (€1),' she goes, giving them the pitch. 'And the Last Night Out sashes (€2) and the L-plate deely-boppers (€2) are Buy One, Get One. Oh, and with every €5 spent, there's a free Hottie Whistle!'

All the birds are there, 'What?'

One of them is alright looking – the rest are focking lagoon creatures.

'A Hottie Whistle,' Sorcha goes, producing one from a little bowl on the counter. 'When you're all out in, like, Busker's and one of you sees a goy who's, like, totally hot, you do this . . .'

She puts the whistle in her mouth and gives us three or four serious blasts on it.

All of the girls laugh. Whereas *I* could focking cry. A year ago, she was standing in the exact same spot telling the likes of Aoife Cogan and Laura Whitmore that – I don't know – a playful hot-pink bow adds a much needed pop of colour to an Oscar de la Renta gown. Or that *the* best summer layering advice anyone can give you is to steer clear of matchy-matchy and keep your colour palette soft. And now she's reduced to this – pushing pink Stetsons (€3), shot glasses on a neck chain (€2), lollipops shaped like penises (€1) and Hottie Whistles (50c, or free with every purchase of €5 or more) to packs of focking hounds.

The girls – and I'm using that term loosely – say they'll have a think about it and they might come back, then they drift out of the shop, still giggling like dopes.

'See?' Honor goes, without even looking up. 'Your STBX is *down* with the povs.'

I'm like, 'Honor, go easy on your mother, will you? She's actually doing her best.'

Sorcha thanks me with a smile.

But then Honor – again, without looking up – goes, 'Did she tell you that Rosanna called in? And that she – OMG – burst into tears when she saw what Mom had been reduced to. Er, *awks* much?'

I'm there, 'Are we talking Rosanna Davison?' because I'd wade five miles up a crocodile-infested river just to drink that girl's bathwater.

'She did *not* burst into tears,' Sorcha goes. 'She was in shock. Ross, you know how much Rosanna loved my shop . . .'

I'm there, 'She was never out of the focking place.'

'Well, she hadn't actually heard that it was closed down. She came in earlier to see could I order her this – oh my God – *amazing* violet Marchesa mini that Diane Kruger wore to the premiere of *Pieds nus sur les limaces* . . .'

'And saw you selling seven-piece screwdriver sets (€3) and magic brush and matching shoe horn gift packs (€2)! Jesus, the poor girl.'

Honor goes, 'It would have been lollers if it wasn't so traj.'

I'm there, 'And she actually *cried*?'

Sorcha's like, 'She didn't *exactly* cry? She was concerned about me, that's all. I was like, "Rosanna, it's okay. This is just what I'm doing now. I'm honestly happy. And I'm really well – especially *within* myself?" '

I'm like, 'Poor Rosanna, though. I must text her.'

It's as I'm saying this that a customer suddenly arrives at the counter. It's a woman. Nice as well. I don't think she's that *unlike* Adrianne Palicki? Sorcha switches back to sales assistant mode.

'How are you finding everything?' she goes.

See, she's still got the clothes shop patter.

'I have a complaint,' the woman goes.

Sorcha's like, 'Oh?'

'This shampoo,' she goes, then slaps this, like, two-litre bottle (€1) down on the counter.

Whatever's actually inside it is the colour of, like, French mustard.

Sorcha goes, 'Did it not do what it says on the bottle?'

The woman's there, 'I don't know. Because I have no idea what it says on the bottle. The only word I recognize is shampoo. Everything else is in, I don't know, Indian.'

'I think it's actually Farsi,' Sorcha goes. 'I recognize some of the script. A really good friend of mine represented Iran in the Model UN at school.'

'It made my scalp bleed.'

'What?'

'My scalp bleed – when I tried to wash my hair with it.'

Now *my* instant reaction would be, 'What the fock do you expect for a euro?' Honestly, it's the size of a lorge bottle of Coke! Except Sorcha is unbelievably professional.

'I am *so*, so sorry,' she goes. 'Okay, the first thing I'm going to do is give you your money back . . .'

'The money isn't the issue . . .'

'No, I insist. Okay, there's your euro. Now, I'm going to promise you that I'm going to investigate this thing fully.'

'Well, I already made an effort,' the woman goes. 'There's a telephone number on the back of the bottle there – presumably for the manufacturer. I dialled it, but the number isn't valid. The country code doesn't even exist.'

'Oh! My God!'

'You really shouldn't be selling it, though. It couldn't have passed any kind of safety checks. I was washing my hair and there was actual blood on my palms. I just thought I'd say it to you.'

'Well, thank you – for being so understanding as well.'

'I just wouldn't like to think of it happening to anyone else. Especially someone old.'

Off she goes with her euro – the focking busybody. Honestly, I'd have run her – I don't care what she looks like.

Honor sniggers behind her little mask. She's like, 'Er, *totes* embarrassing?'

Sorcha just ignores her and tells me she's going to ring Mr Whittle, the owner.

She goes, 'Ross, will you do me a favour? Get those bottles off those shelves – quickly!'

'Hello,' the voice on the other end of the phone goes. It's some dude. 'Is that Ross?'

I'm like, 'The one. The Only.'

'Oh, good,' he goes. 'I'm just wondering can you help me. I've got a bit of a seepage problem.'

'Excuse me?'

'Yeah, I've got big pool of standing water in the laundry room. The thing is I know a *little* bit about plumbing? I shut off the water, disconnected the washing machine and checked the pipes. They're definitely not leaking. But if I mop up this water, I'll come back in maybe an hour's time and there'll be another puddle.'

I just go, 'For fock's sake.'

He's there, 'Did I get you at a bad time?'

'Er, kind of.'

I was actually on the jacks, reading a four-page feature in one of Sorcha's magazines about the shocking rise of the sub-zero model – the photographs were making me hungry for borbecue spare ribs.

'You're in the middle of something?'

'Well,' I go, 'I do be very busy, so I do – with the plumbing and that.'

He's there, 'I did hear that. You're obviously good.'

'You're a mate of David's, are you?'

'He'd be more a friend of a friend. But he did recommend you. Said you were definitely the goy to solve our little mystery.'

'Sorry, er, Bud – like I said, I'm up to me bollicks, so I am.'

'I'd pay you top whack.'

'Er . . .'

'Five hundred euros.'

Five hundred snots? I'd nearly be focking tempted if I didn't have Regina's money possibly coming.

'No, I'm soddy, so I am.'

'Seven, then. It's just I'm worried about the water and the electrics, especially with the kids running around.'

'I'd, er, love to help you out, Bud, but you'll have to try someone else.'

'Fair enough. God, you must be good to be in that kind of demand – especially with the way the economy is now.'

They're all, like, glued to his bullshit story.

'Hin my head,' he's going, 'I know that to wheen Olympic gold medal, I must jomp clear round. Very last fence – Erika, you remember thees, because you watch eet on television – may horse, *Azara's Fox*, she cleeps the top rail weez her back hooves. I hear eet rattle and I ham sure I hear eet fall. I sink, "The gold medal – eet is surely go to Hans-Georg Marschall now." But then I hear the roar of the crowd. Hand I look over my shoulder like thees and I sink, "I ham Olympic champion! I ham Olympic champion!" '

Everywhere I focking go these days, he seems to be hanging around. Erika's sitting there in, like, total awe of him. I can't help myself, of course. I end up going, 'That's a great focking yorn. Real edge-of-your-seat stuff, Fabrizio. Or should we all just call you Fab?'

Not one person in the room backs me up, by the way.

In fact, Sophie goes, 'I thought it was an – oh my God – *amazing* story.'

She's obviously got a serious wide-on for the dude – like everyone else apparently.

I'm like, 'Yeah, no, but it was, like, seven focking *years* ago? Get over it already would be my basic attitude.'

Chloe laughs and goes, 'Coming from the man who wore his Leinster Schools Senior Cup medal around his neck for, like, *ten* years? *And* that was only, like, rugby.'

I can't believe what I'm actually hearing. 'Only, like, rugby? I didn't hear you complain back in the day, when you were panting around after me like a focking dog after a meat truck – the two of you, in fact.'

I turn to Erika for a reaction, but she doesn't even laugh – and she supposedly *hates* Chloe and Sophie?

And do you want to know what the worst thing is? I actually rang Fionn tonight to see did he fancy going for a pint – *being* the supportive friend. He told me to swing into his old dear's gaff, where it turned out there was, like, a *porty* in full swing?

They were all there as well. We're talking JP and Oisinn. We're talking Chloe, Sophie and Amie with an ie. We're talking a whole focking host of others, including Fabrizio – looking pretty focking ripped, I'm prepared to admit, under just a bottle-green, classic-fit, Ralph Lauren airtex.

I was like, 'What the fock is going on here?'

It turned out that, unbeknownst to me, there'd been – get this – a *polo* match? Focking polo! Some friends of Erika have a team that plays every Sunday afternoon somewhere up near Kilternan and they were supposedly short a player. So in steps Fabrizio to try to be the hero of the focking hour. He's supposed to have played unbelievably well – but, then again, who are any of this crowd to judge?

Then it was all back to Fionn's old pair's gaff for cake – oh, it's also his old dear's birthday, by the way. Nothing *but* birthdays this month?

Obviously, I was like, 'Why wasn't I included in any of this?'

I didn't even get a proper answer.

Erika pulls me to one side then. She does it with her eyes. Sort of, like, indicates the door out into the hallway, then expects me to follow her. Which I do. I try to get along with people.

'Why are you being so hostile?' she goes.

I'm like, 'Hostile?'

'To Fabrizio.'

I laugh. 'You don't see it – that's what makes it even horder for me to watch.'

'See what?'

'What he's doing.'

'What *is* he doing?'

'Coming over here with his polo and his cricket jumpers and his private jet. He's looking for a new wife, Erika.'

'Don't be ridiculous.'

'Hey, one player knows another player – don't forget that.'

'Ross, we're old friends. That's all there is to it.'

'I just don't want to see Fionn get hurt. The poor focker's had too much of that in his life already.'

'I'm not *going* to hurt Fionn. I love him, Ross.'

'I love him as well – as obviously a friend.'

'I love him more than I've ever loved anyone before.'

'So you say.'

She ends up just shaking her head in – I'm possibly making this word up – but *exasperation*?

She goes, 'Why do we always have to be like this, Ross?'

I'm there, 'Like what?'

'At war with each other.'

'Because you've always hated me – even going back to when we were teenagers.'

'But we're brother and sister now. Could we not try to . . .'

'What?'

'I don't know – *re-imagine* our relationship?'

'Re-imagine it? I don't know. I suppose.'

She reaches for my hand and just holds it. It's actually lovely. She sort of, like, stares into space then and ends up getting a little bit teary. 'I was so worried about you.'

'Worried?'

'When you were in the hospital. I was scared you wouldn't pull through. I was convinced you were going to die. I kept saying to Fionn, "I'm never going to get the chance to talk to him again, Fionn." You looked . . . so frail, Ross. I mean, I prayed. Can you imagine *me*, Ross, actually praying?'

'Not really, no.'

'Well, I did. And then this miracle. You woke up. And you got better. And I remember thinking, "We've been offered a second chance here. Things are going to be different. He's my brother and I'm going to make sure I cherish every single day that I have him in my life."'

'So what happened?'

She sort of, like, laughs. 'I don't know. Within two weeks, I was back wanting to smash your face in every time you opened your mouth.'

'Thanks.'

She gives me the big doe eyes then that any male would find hord to resist. 'Can we make the effort, Ross – as in both of us? Let's not do things to deliberately antagonize each other. Let's . . . let's end the war.'

I'm there, 'Okay.'

She smiles at me, lets go of my hand, then gives me the most amazing, amazing peck on the cheek, even though that's *all* it is?

She goes back and rejoins the porty. I follow her into the living room. She wanders over to Fionn and they end up kissing – this is, like, in front of everyone? – then having a bit of a cuddle. I'm still not buying it, though.

Fabrizio is tapping away on his laptop – a focking MacBook as well – with Chloe and Sophie sitting either side of him on the sofa, looking over his shoulder, again, pretty much *adoringly*?

'Hafter today,' he goes, 'my competitive yooces are once again flowing. I feel I most jump. I ham look for meet – een Belgium, een Germany . . .'

I think, sorry, Erika, I actually can't take any more of this.

That's when Fionn's old dear – who's always been a huge, huge fan of mine – pipes up. 'Okay, who's for birthday cake?'

And it's while everyone is banging on about how much they – oh my God – *love* chewy icing that I turn around to Oisinn and JP and go, 'I'm going to shit on his laptop.'

Oisinn reacts like he thinks he might have *misheard* me? He's there, 'Okay, say that again.'

I laugh. 'I'm going to shit on his laptop. Then close it. It's called a waffle press.'

'I know what it's called, Ross. I went to UCD as well, remember?'

'Did you? Because you'd never know it from the way you're refusing to back me up on this thing.'

JP throws his five cents' worth in then. 'Ross, I'm not a hundred percent sure . . .'

'Hey,' I go, 'he's got it coming to him – no one can deny that. He's been poking me with a stick since the day he arrived. This is just my way of saying, hey, welcome to big school.'

As everyone drifts out to the kitchen, I grab the MacBook off the table – it's, like, one of the white ones as well! – and I head for the Josh Ritter under the stairs. In the hall, I end up running into Eleanor. I didn't know she was even here. Maybe she's just arrived for the cutting of her old dear's cake. I say hello – it's nice to be nice – but she tells me I'm a wanker, then follows the rest of them into the kitchen.

I go into the jacks and I do the business. I've had one in the chamber for about an hour. I pull the toilet seat cover down, lay the laptop down on it, open it up, then – there's no *nice* way of saying this – but

I crimp one off. It's a focking beauty as well. A real work of ort. It seems a shame to close the laptop and ruin it. But I do anyway – my stomach turning cortwheels as I feel and hear the sudden squelch.

I tip back into the living room and put the thing back, then I join everyone in the kitchen.

Fionn's old dear hands me a piece of cake, then Fionn's old man – another huge, huge supporter of mine – asks me how Sorcha's getting on with the new shop.

I don't even get an opportunity to answer because Sophie is, like, straight in there. 'Oh my God, I heard she's running one of these, like, euro stores in the unit where her *shop* used to be? Er, *random?*'

I'm like, 'How is that random?'

She goes, 'Oh my God, Ross, don't be so defensive. I'm just saying – it must be, like, *such* a huge comedown for the girl.'

I'm there, 'Not as big a comedown as telling Rob Soames that you're on the Jack and Jill, to try to get up the spout and trap him into a relationship with you.'

She actually did that once – Sorcha told me – and it quietens Sophie immediately down. Erika smiles at me across the room, as if to say, fair focks, she had that coming.

Oisinn tries to change the subject then. 'So, Mrs de Barra,' he goes, 'did you get any nice presents,' and then he adds, 'for your forty-fifth?' which is a nice touch, even I have to admit.

Oh, he can turn it on, don't you worry about that.

She laughs, then goes, 'I wish it *was* forty-five! And it's Andrea – I've told you boys that before. Well, as it happens, Ewan bought me a wonderful holiday. We're calling it a second honeymoon, aren't we, Darling?'

I look at Fionn's old man and I go, 'You dirty dog – get in there!' because you can say literally anything to them. They're actually cool like that.

'The Maldives,' *she* goes.

I'm like, 'The Maldives!' and I laugh. 'You filthy focking animal, Ewan!'

She goes, 'I must show you the hotel,' and then all of a sudden – I swear to fock – it feels like the world has suddenly slowed down. Because she goes, 'Are you finished with my laptop, Fabrizio?'

JP – standing immediately behind me – goes, 'That's what I was trying to tell you, Ross, that I'm not a hundred percent sure it's *his* MacBook?'

My face turns instantly hot and I can feel my bowels sort of, like, grumble – even though I've just emptied them out.

'I'll get it,' Chloe goes, big focking smiley face on her.

Then it feels like the kitchen is suddenly spinning.

Ten seconds later, she's back. She hands the laptop – still closed – to Fionn's old dear, who goes, 'We're staying in these little over-water bungalows that are absolutely fabulous . . .'

She opens it up.

'. . . you can step off your balcony, you know, right into the . . .'

She screams and at the same time drops it. Which means everyone in the kitchen is suddenly staring down at the floor at it – a big turd, bet into her spanking new white keyboard. Sophie also screams – which *I* think is a bit OTT. Most other people make do with just repeating the words 'Oh! My! God!'

Fionn's old pair – this'll tell you what they're like – they can't believe that someone would actually do something like that *deliberately*? The old dear even goes, 'How would something like that have got in there?'

See, they think the world is basically a good place.

I, of course, suddenly see an *out* for myself. I think, just go with the bizarre accident line and crack on to share everyone's basic surprise and disgust.

Except that's when I catch Eleanor's eye. She's staring at me, smiling – her eyes wide with, I suppose, delight. I know she's going to enjoy this moment. She possibly deserves it. 'I saw Ross going into the bathroom with it a few minutes ago.'

Fionn puts his head in his hands. Erika just closes her eyes, like she's trying to wish me out of actual existence.

Fionn's old dear goes, 'Did . . . did *you* do this, Ross?'

I look at Fabrizio. He's got a big focking smirk on his face and I'm beginning to think the whole thing was possibly a set-up.

'Ross,' it's Fionn's old man who finally goes, 'I think I speak for everyone here when I say I would rather you left this house right now and didn't come back for a very long time.'

Sorcha's face lights up – enough to nearly, I don't know, illuminate the entire of her old pair's attic.

'Oh! My God!' she goes. 'Do you remember these?'

I'm crawling around the boards on my hands and knees looking for the light switch. I find it and flick it and suddenly it's bright and I notice that Sorcha's holding one of those old-style white Fisher-Price telephones with a big smiley face on it and wheels and a bell inside that, like, rings when you put your finger in one of the number holes and turn the dial.

I'm like, 'Yeah, I didn't have one, though.'

She's in, like, shock. 'You didn't have one of these? Oh my God, Ross, *everyone* had one of these!'

'*I* didn't. The old dear spent all her money on booze and uppers, remember. The old man used to just buy me, like, rugby gear, rugby balls, blah, blah, blah.'

'Oh my God, Ross, that makes me really sad.'

'Hey, I loved my rugby, Sorcha. Still do.'

She asked me to help her clear all of her old toys out of her old pair's gaff. They're obviously not going to have room for them when they finally sell this place and move into an aportment, which is why they've asked Sorcha to come and take whatever she wants to hang on to.

It's like the *Late Late* focking *Toy Show*, there's that much stuff. All it's missing is a couple of dozen tap-dancing kids and Tubs in a focking sweater.

There's, like, boxes of Care Bears and My Little Ponies and all Seven Dwarves and bikes of every size and colour. There's a duck on a lead with legs that spin around on a wheel and every board game you can possibly think of and an Airedale terrier that you push around – for some reason – on a trolley. And there's, like, doll houses of every shape and size. Actually, Sorcha obviously had a decent-sized property portfolio before every other focker on this side of the city had one.

'Oh my God! My Easy-Bake oven!' Sorcha suddenly goes. 'I used to spend hours playing with this. Oh my God, I'd really love it if Honor was interested in this stuff.'

I'm there, 'Kids aren't into, like, playing any more, though, are they? It's, like, iPhones rather than toy phones.'

She laughs. 'What do you think she'd say if I brought this downstairs to her now? Or my Petite 990 over there!'

'She'd go, "Er, *lame* much?" '

'Or she'd go, "OMG, Mum! I heart it muchly! Hashtag – get a life!" '

And we both fall around laughing, even though what we're actually laughing at is what a little bitch our daughter has turned out.

I'm there, 'Has she got her head around the idea of you managing the euro shop yet?'

'I don't think so. But also I don't *care*? We're all having to, like, share the pain, Ross.'

'You hear people saying that alright. What was the deal with the shampoo, by the way? Did you get to the bottom of it?'

'No, I haven't been able to get Mr Whittle on the phone. He's, like, away on *business*?'

'Will he not have a shit-fit when he finds out you took it off the shelves?'

'I had to make a decision, Ross, weighing up the commercial interest against the potential threat to public health. Sometimes in retail you have to make those calls.'

I just nod, then I stort checking out this mad-looking thing – it's, like, a doll's head and shoulders that you throw slap on.

'So is there any sign of this gaff being sold?' I go.

She's like, 'No. The bank want them to lower the asking price. They don't think anyone's going to pay three point five million for it in the current climate. *They* just want it sold. But so do Mum and Dad, of course.'

'Have they got somewhere else to live yet?'

'Oh, yeah, they've found this – oh my God – beautiful apartment in The Beacon.'

'The Beacon? Jesus!'

'There's nothing wrong with The Beacon, Ross.'

'Hey, no offence, Sorcha. I'm just saying, the Vico Road to The Beacon is the same distance as The Beacon to, I don't know, sleeping in the focking doorway of Foot Locker.'

'It's actually got two bedrooms,' she goes. 'I mean, it's a sensible-sized home for a couple of their age. As my dad said, they don't *need* this much space?'

I'm there, 'I suppose,' at the same time thinking, good enough for the focker.

Sorcha looks suddenly frustrated then. She's like, 'I don't know what to keep.'

I'm there, 'Keep it all. There's fock-all in the attic in Newtown-pork Avenue.'

She goes, 'I can't keep it all. It'd take – oh my God – ten trips in the cor to bring all of this.'

I'm there, 'I'd *do* ten trips.'

'Would you?'

'Sorcha, I'd do pretty much anything for you.'

'And I'd do pretty much anything for you.'

'Well, I've seen the proof of that, remember.'

She all of a sudden spots something under a pile of something else. A teddy bear. Obviously an old favourite judging from the squeal she suddenly lets out of her.

'Steve Biko!' she goes.

I laugh. I remember Steve Biko.

I'm like, 'You had him when we storted going out together. He was called something else. I remember you renaming him.'

'Oh my God, Ross, you used to knock him off the bed! Do you remember? When we'd be – you know . . .'

'I didn't like the way he sometimes looked at me.'

'You used to say, "You don't need Steve Biko any more, Sorcha – you've got me." '

I did actually say that. My seduction technique and my kicking technique were the only two things in my life that I wasn't totally and utterly shit at.

I suddenly notice that she's looking at me – and she's looking at me in *that* way? Slowly, our hands creep towards each other, along the dusty boards until our fingers are, like, touching. We sit there just staring at each other, a blizzard of dust blowing between us, and I realize in that moment – as if I ever doubted it – that I'm still in love with this girl, and she's still in love with me. Our heads move closer together until our lips are no more than an inch apart.

Then her old man sticks his big, fat barrister's head through the trapdoor and goes, 'How are you getting on up here?'

And Sorcha pulls away from me, like I'm suddenly toxic, which I suppose, in the eyes of my soon-to-be-ex-father-in-law, I am.

I'm going to be honest, I'm a bit hurt.

'I'm going to give it all away,' Sorcha goes. 'I'm sure there's children in hospitals who would be delighted with it. I'm just going to keep one thing.'

And she pulls Steve Biko close to her chest.

Honor says that Pippa Middleton is a bitch.

I laugh. I know a lot of these supposed parenting experts would probably say that it's not the right thing to do, but it's still funny.

'Why is she a bitch?' I go. 'I have to say, from this angle, I'd be a fan.'

'Because everyone knows you're not supposed to upstage the bride on her big day. It's, like, DEGT.'

'DEGT?'

'Don't Even *Go* There?'

I'm there, 'But she can't help it, I suppose, if she's just naturally hotter than Kate.'

'Oh my God,' Honor goes, 'she *so* could have toned it down, though.'

This is us watching the Royal Wedding, in case you haven't figured it out. Sorcha's spitting feathers at having to miss it. The famous Mr Whittle rang from Cyprus, where he seems to spend a lot of his time. He has her watering down bottles of screen washer fluid (€1 for three) and he refused to even let her bring a TV in.

Speaking of feathers . . .

'Who the fock is that?' I go.

Honor laughs. 'That's Princess Eugenie, Daddy. But wait till you see Princess Beatrice.'

'Oh my God, it looks like she's got a focking lobster on her head.'

Honor's there, 'I know! She's – oh my God – bet-down as well. If she ever becomes a mother, can I have one of her puppies?'

Now it's my turn to laugh.

Then she goes, 'Is Ronan staying here tonight?'

I'm there, 'I don't know. I can't keep track any more of whether he's staying here or in Finglas.'

There's all of a sudden a ring at the door. I go out and answer it. It's, like, Hennessy. There's no hello, no pleasantries, nothing. He just goes, 'She's upped her offer.'

I'm there, 'Go on.'

'Two hundred thousand.'

'Two hundred thousand yoyos?' I go. 'For nearly killing me?'

'It's just a fucking offer,' he roars at me. 'I'm not telling you to take it! I'm just keeping you informed!'

'Oh. Sorry. Cool. Could you not have, like, told me that on the phone?'

He looks at me like he can't believe my stupidity. 'You think this is something we should talk about over the phone? What have you got in your fucking head?' and then off he storms.

I wander back into the living room, sorry I even spoke.

'OMG!' Honor suddenly goes. 'Princess Mathilde – you should have saved that dress for the panto season!'

I end up laughing. Have to. It's funny.

That's when she suddenly turns and looks at me. 'Daddy, do you think you might stay?'

I'm like, 'What?'

'Stay – as in, here, with us?'

I take, like, a deep breath. Kids and their questions. I'm there, 'I don't think so, Honor. Come on, we told you it was, like, a temporary thing, didn't we?'

'But you and Mummy love each other, don't you?'

'Yeah. Big-time, in my case.'

'Why don't you just get back together, then?'

'It's complicated, Honor. There's no way her old man would ever let it happen.'

She turns back to the TV. I can see her little face all sad. She's hurt. It's easy to forget, because she's such a bitch, that she can be actually quite sensitive.

'Who the fock is that?' I suddenly go, pointing at the screen. 'It looks like someone's upholstered a pilates ball, then stuck orms, legs and a head on it.'

Of course that just melts Honor's hort.

She's like, 'And did you see Victoria Beckham? She looks like an air hostess. *Emergency exits are at the front, middle and rear of the aircraft!*'

I'm, like, nervous. About how she's going to react. She might be cool with it. She's plunging the coffee. Blue Mountain. The good shit. Because it's Sunday. I suppose we both knew that this day would eventually come.

I walk over to her. Even the little bit of a limp I had has gone – a sure sign that it's possibly *definitely* time?

She hands me my coffee and she smiles at me. She asks me if I enjoyed the match yesterday. Leinster beat Toulouse in the semi-final of the Heineken Cup, which is the reason I'm hanging this morning.

I tell her they were focking unbelievable. Then suddenly I hear myself say the words.

'I was thinking – it might be time for me to maybe move out.'

Sorcha's like, 'Move out?'

I'm there, 'Yeah.'

If I'm being honest, I'm waiting for her to ask me not to. She doesn't though.

'When?' she just goes.

'I was thinking maybe when I came back from, like, Fionn's stag?'

Two weeks, in other words.

She thinks for a few seconds, then she acts like it's suddenly *the* best idea she's ever heard. 'Yeah, no, you should. You're back on your feet again now. We said it was only temporary, didn't we?'

'Exactly.'

She just nods then. 'Honor's going to be disappointed.'

Maybe it's Honor I'm actually thinking about. As in, our conversation the other day? The longer I stay here, the more she's going to get her hopes up – like me – that something could actually happen. And long term, that's not fair on her. It's not fair on anyone.

Sorcha's there, 'Where will you go?'

I'm like, 'Back to the old Den of N. Equity.'

'Your aportment?'

'Hey, it's all fixed up. Haven't seen it myself, but the old man says it's – what was the word he used? – *habitable*?'

She goes, 'Amazing,' although she seems – I'm going to be honest – a bit disappointed. She suddenly decides that we should have biscuits and reaches into the cupboard for the Traidcraft stem ginger cookies – it's classic avoidance.

I'm there, 'Are you sure you're okay with it? As in me moving out?'

She's like, 'Yeah, no, I've just got one or two things on my mind, that's all.'

'Do you want to talk about them? A problem shared is a something, something, something.'

'No, I'm going to have to get used to dealing with my problems on my own again.'

I'm just there, 'You'll never have to do that, Sorcha,' and I genuinely mean it.

She sort of, like, shakes her head – like she *knows* she's being ridiculous?

'Look,' she goes, 'it's just I called out to my mum and dad's house yesterday and they were showing someone around – as in, a prospective *buyer*?'

I'm like, 'Hey, I thought you were cool with it now – as in, them selling the gaff?'

She stares sadly into the distance. 'I *thought* I was? I mean, they were *so* a nice couple. *She's* an intellectual property lawyer and *he's* a consultant in respiratory and critical care medicine.'

'Okay, I'm going to say fair focks.'

'But they have a daughter, Ross, and she's, like, four, maybe five? And when she saw the piano, she was like – oh! my God! So they asked if *it* was, like, *also* for sale? And without even thinking to ask me, Dad said they'd include it as part of the sale price.'

I end up just nodding. 'Obviously pretty focking desperate to sell.'

'Ross, that was the piano that I learned to play *The Heart Asks for Pleasure First* on.'

'But they're possibly not going to have room for it if they're moving into an aportment, Babes.'

'But the thought of another little girl sitting down at that piano with *her* daddy . . .'

I can see her eyes storting to fill up, so I get in there fast and give her a hug. Her bathrobe is soft and smells of Lenor – as in, the Sensual Infusions one?

'It's all about letting go of the past,' I go. 'It's about looking to the future.'

She's like, 'What if you're too scared to let go of the past?' I don't *think* I'm imagining this – she's holding onto me pretty tight. 'What if you're too frightened to face the future?'

I'm, like, waiting for her to say it – as in, let's do it, Ross. Let's give this thing another go. Except she doesn't. And then my phone all of a sudden rings and she lets go of me. It ends up being Tina.

'Howiya,' she goes.

Jesus, that accent of hers would drain the focking colour from your hair.

I'm just like, 'Hey, Tina.'

I decide not to admit that she was right about the Tuites – wouldn't give her the basic pleasure. So instead, I just go, 'Ro did well in his mocks, didn't he?'

We're talking nine As, by the way. That's as close as I'm going to come to admitting I was wrong about anything.

She's like, 'I toalt you he was well able for it, ditn't I?' And then she goes, 'Is there any chaddence of getting him back, be the way?'

I'm there, 'Tina, is there any way you could maybe talk slower?'

'Ine aston, when are you senting him home to he's mudder.

174

You've had um tree nights. Ine nearly arthur forgetting what he looks like!'

I suddenly cop it.

'Yeah, no,' I go. 'You know what he's like when he gets his nose stuck in those books.'

'Tell him to at least text me if he's coming home for he's thinner today. Ine doing Yorkshire pootens, so I am – he's favourite.'

'Yorkshire puddings!' I go. 'Cool. Talk to you soon . . . Okay, bye.'

Sorcha looks at me, her eyes narrowed to basic slits. 'Is everything okay?'

I'm like, 'Yeah, no – everything's fine. Anyway, I'm heading out for a bit.'

She goes, 'Where?'

'I said I'd meet Fionn for a bit of brunch in Dalkey. Just to run through the old rules of engagement for the stag.'

So I get in the cor and I get on the road. There's fock-all traffic about, what with it being ten o'clock on a Sunday morning, which means I'm there in, like, five minutes – ten at the very most. I get out of the cor and in I go. The old place hasn't changed much, I notice. It's actually like I've never been away.

There's two facts I should possibly tell you at this point, because they're both pretty relevant to the story. The first is that I'm not *in* Dalkey? I've been giving Fionn a wide berth since I had a Joe Schmidt in his old dear's laptop. The second is that, despite what Tina thinks, Ronan hasn't been staying with us. In fact, I haven't seen him for, like, a week? But I take a punt on where he *has* been staying – based on what *I'd* have probably done when I was a teenager.

I stand outside in the hall and I listen carefully. I hear talking. I hear laughter. Then I put my shoulder against it – the door of my bedroom in Rosa Porks.

Now, I've seen a few things in my life, as you well know. I kind of thought the world had lost its ability to shock me. But no. Even though I kind of know now what's been going on behind my back, the sight that greets me when I burst through that door shocks me to my literally core.

Ronan and Shadden are in my bed, going at it like two farmer's dogs on subsidy payment day.

I'm not proud of this, but I end up just screaming. I can't even say I scream in, like, a *manly* way? Then *she* screams as well – as in, Shadden – whereas Ronan just rolls off her, pulls the duvet around the two of them and goes, 'Moy! Fooken! Jaysus!'

I turn around – this is hordly my finest moment either – and I just run out of the place. And I keep running. I'm like Forrest focking Gump. I can even hear Ronan behind me, going, 'Rosser! Rosser, come back!'

5.

For the love of Blod

Some dude on the news says the Dáil has been debating the findings of the Nyberg Report, which found that lax oversight by regulators and the Government, flawed lending decisions by the banks and an unquestioning consensus regarding a soft landing for the property market were the main reasons behind the collapse of Ireland's financial sector.

I'm sitting at the bor in Kielys of Donnybrook Town, trying to get my head around *yesterday's* events, wondering could the same group of experts explain to me what actually happened.

Well, I *know* what actually happened. But could they help me understand it?

He's only, like, fourteen years old. I know I was an early storter myself. And kids now are supposedly a lot less innocent than *we* were. Shadden's obviously a couple of years older than him as well. And, having met her old pair, maybe I shouldn't be surprised.

But then I keep coming back to the same basic fact. He's still only fourteen.

I'm three pints in and on the point of actual despair when I suddenly hear a familiar voice behind me go, 'I should have known I'd find you here.'

I literally freeze.

I wouldn't be a big believer in, like, God and blahdy blah? I do believe in *something* – just not something that wants me pissing my time away down on my knees telling him how focking great and wondrous he is. If you're great, you don't *need* to be told – take it from someone who knows. But one thing I genuinely do believe is that Father Fehily is up there looking after me, pulling the actual strings. How else could you explain why my best friend in the world is suddenly standing in front of me?

I end up nearly hugging the poor focker to death. I'm going, 'What the fock are you doing back in Ireland?'

Christian just laughs. 'I can tell you, it's a long time since anyone has been this pleased to see me!'

'It's just – I don't know – unexpected, that's all.'

'Well, we were planning to come home in June for Fionn and Erika's wedding. I had a lot of holidays built up – been working twelve- and fourteen-hour days for, what, two or three years now? Lauren and I just figured, why don't we go home for a couple of months? Make it worth our while.'

'Hey, you focking deserve it, Dude. The pair of you. Even though Lauren wouldn't be my biggest fan in the world. Where is she, by the way?'

'She's gone to visit Sorcha.'

I go, 'Cool,' at the same time pulling a wad of notes out of my pocket. 'A pint of Responsibly, I'm presuming.'

He goes – and this is a genuine quote – 'No, I might just have a Coke or something.'

I'm not letting him away with that shit, though. It's obviously a habit he's picked up in the States, where you can't go on the lash for two weeks without every focker trying to tell you that you've got a drink problem. I remember that from my Jier.

'Two more of these,' I tell the borman.

Christian can roll his eyes and shake his head all he wants. He's having a pint and that's the end of it.

'Is everything okay, Ross?' he goes.

This is when he's only, like, two sips in and I'm already ordering another for myself. I'm like, 'Big-time.'

'You just seem, I don't know, on edge or something.'

Christian knows me too well. An outhalf can never lie to a goy who's played inside-centre to him. That's just a basic fact of life.

So I end up just blurting it out. 'I caught Ronan on the job.'

Christian's whole face just drops.

He's like, 'What?'

Considering the shit that we got up to back in the day, it's saying something that he's shocked.

'Hord at it, Christian.'

'But he's only . . .'

'Who are you telling? I mean, I knew they storted early on that side of the city. But it seems like only yesterday that I was buying him that replica pistol for making his Communion. *They grow up so quickly*. I used to think that was some shit that people just said.'

'Where did this happen, Ross?'

'In my aportment. He's been using the thing as a shag pad while I've been recuperating in Sorcha's. Oh, he was very clever about it as well. Asked if he could stay with us on the odd school night – to save him trekking across from Knackeragua every morning . . .'

'So there were nights when Tina thought he was staying with you goys – and you thought he was back home with Tina?'

'Exactly. Sow confusion. And he obviously whipped my key and made himself a copy as well. He's already thinking like a sixteen-year-old.'

Christian looks like shit – I don't know if I mentioned. He's honestly aged about five years since the last time I saw him. His hair is receding in a major way and there's a fair few flecks of grey in what's left.

'Are you sure,' he goes, 'he was definitely, you know, *doing* it?'

I'm like, 'Dude, I walked in on them.'

'Jesus! And what did you say to him?'

'Nothing. I ran out of there.'

'You ran?'

'Well, I sort of, like, screamed – *then* ran?'

'You screamed, then ran.'

'That was about the size of it, yeah. Didn't exactly do myself proud.'

'You've had a chat with him since, I presume?'

'Not really. To be honest, I've been kind of, like, *avoiding* him?'

'What?'

'He's been ringing me all day today *and* yesterday. Obviously wants to talk about it.'

'Ross, do you not think it should be the other way around?'

'Excuse me?'

'Do you not think *you* should be looking to sit down with *him*?'

See, this is why it's great to have Christian around. He's hord but he's fair – and a lot of what he says makes actual sense.

I'm like, 'Possibly. But I'm not sure I could face it, Dude.'

He gives it to me straight then, like he always has. 'That's the thing about *being* a parent, Ross – you don't have a choice in the matter.'

'Go on, keep talking to me like this. This is all good shit.'

'Do you not think it's time you manned up? Started acting with a bit more focking maturity?'

'Okay. Jesus. Point taken. I'll give the kid a bell and have the big father–son chat with him.'

Except Christian's on a focking roll now and it ends up turning into a bit of a lecture. 'You got shot, Ross. You could have died . . .'

'Hey, I take your point. You were worried about me. It's nice.'

'Well, I thought it might have been a life-changing experience for you.'

'It was in a lot of ways.'

'No, it wasn't. You've just picked up where you left off before. All these stories I'm hearing about you. The way you treated Fionn's sister . . .'

'Hey, I never made that girl any promises. And get that pint into you – you're drinking like a focking girl.'

He goes, 'Do you not think your dick has got you into enough trouble, Ross?'

There's a port of Christian that will possibly never forgive me for having sex with his old dear all those years ago.

I'm there, 'If you're talking about me being shot, they don't even know for sure that it *was* my dick? They still don't actually know who shot me, remember?'

But he continues on having a serious go at me.

He's like, 'Did you take a shit in Fionn's mother's laptop?'

'Okay,' I go, 'five years ago, that would have been considered hilarious – explain to me why it's suddenly not.'

'Because you're thirty-one years of age, Ross! The world isn't a focking playground any more. It's a big scary place where people get hurt!'

Jesus Christ. Twenty minutes ago, I was actually happy that this dude was home. But then, roysh, I suddenly realize that what the dude is really trying to say here is that he loves me and he can't handle the fact that I very nearly died.

I put my orm around him and I go, 'Hey, I think I'm hearing you, Christian. I'm definitely hearing you. And don't you worry – I'll apologize to Fionn. Get him back onside. I'm thinking of making the Heineken Cup final in Cordiff the actual stag.'

He goes, 'It's not just Fionn. It's about time you stepped into the adult world.'

I'm there, 'Okay, I've taken it on board. And don't you worry, me and Ro are going to have the big chat – that's also definite. We'll sit down over a couple of beers . . .'

He's like, 'Beers?' on it like a bonnet.

I'm there, 'Couple of glasses of orange juice, then. And we'll talk.'

He gives me one of those, like, withering looks you always hear talked about. Then he stands up – my best friend in the world, remember – and without even saying a word of goodbye to me, or offering to get a round in himself, just walks straight out the door.

'I've brown water coming out of my pipes.'

This is some random dude's idea of a conversation storter.

I'm there, 'Sorry, do I even know you?'

I *was* flicking through the paper, looking at a photograph of Nigella Lawson on her holidays, thinking how unbelievable she looks – even *in* a burkini.

Now I've got some focking joker on the phone interrupting my, let's just say, train of thought.

'I was told you were the man to solve the problem.'

'Were you?'

'Yeah. I thought I might have had rust in me pipes – except I rang the fella we bought the house from and he said the piping was all replaced two years ago. Galvinized iron.'

'Yeah, look, I can't help you, I'm afraid.'

'Sorry?'

'I'm, er, not *in* the plumbing game any more?'

'Really?'

'Yeah, no, I got out of it.'

'That's a pity. There's a friend of mine who works with the brother of a guy whose plumbing you fixed – he raves about you. Says you're an expert.'

'That's nice to hear. But my plumbing days are behind me, I'm afraid.'

'Ah, that's a shame. So what are you going to do now?'

I decide to just tell him the truth.

'I'm going to focking hang up on you,' I go, 'and then I'm going to rub one out looking at Nigella Lawson on Bondi Beach.'

I'm there, 'How did Lauren seem to you? When she called out to see you the other night?'

Sorcha seems surprised by the question.

She's like, 'Fine. Why do you ask?'

This is us in the Euro Hero shop, by the way.

'I don't know,' I go. 'It's just Christian seemed, I don't know, different.'

'As in?'

'Well, he used to be a bit of crack for storters. But he comes into Kielys – haven't seen the dude in over two years, remember – and he storts laying into me about the way I'm living my life. Told me I needed to possibly grow up. He doesn't even call me Young Sky-walker or Padwan Learner any more. He also came very close to calling me a bad father.'

'He and Lauren have been under a lot of stress, Ross – especially with Christian's job.'

'*Am* I a bad father, though?'

'No, Ross – you're an amazing, amazing father.'

'That's what I thought. There's his focking proof, then.'

I'm helping her to unpack a box of those freaky-looking gold cats (€3) that wave at you from the counters of Chinese takeaways.

'But Christian possibly *does* have a point,' she goes. 'You *could* do with growing up a bit. I heard about an incident that's supposed to have happened in, like, Fionn's mum and dad's house? Oh my God, I don't even want to *think* that it might be true.'

'It's probably exaggerated, Babes. You know what people are like.'

I stort stacking the cats on the shelf, at the same time wondering who the fock is going to even buy them.

'I'm just saying,' she goes, 'you could possibly do with maturing a bit. I mean, you still refer to your arms as guns.'

'Cannons. I call them cannons.'

'And you snigger every time I tell you I'm getting a facial.'

I try to hold in the laughter in, but it's no use.

She's like, 'See what I mean? Have you even talked to Ronan yet?'

'About?'

'About him being sexually active, Ross.'

'Oh. No, not yet. I'm going to, though.'

'Well, there's an opportunity to prove that you've grown up. And, by the way, you also need to get over this obsession you have with your sister getting married.'

I'm there, 'Why am I suddenly getting lectures from everyone? You're as bad as Christian. And anyway, Erika getting married isn't what I'm obsessed about. It's *him*. This so-called Fabrizio.'

'Well, you really need to get over *him* as well.'

'Oh, don't worry. I told Fionn. Well, I left one or two voice messages for him – just to say, look, I've done everything I possibly can, as a friend *and* as a best man. I'm not going to say another word. And then when the dude finally does make his move and runs off with Erika, I'm going to be there to say I told you so and help you pick up the actual pieces.'

'Well, hello!' this voice all of a sudden goes. We both turn around at the exact same time.

It ends up being my old dear.

'My . . . word!' she goes. 'Look . . . at . . . this . . . place!' like she's just stepped into Buckingham focking Palace. Or the factory where they make Grey Goose vodka.

'Hi, Fionnuala,' Sorcha goes and it's suddenly air-kisses and all the rest of it. 'Do you like it?'

The old dear's there, 'It's fabulous!' even though she knows as well as I do that if Sorcha wasn't managing this place, she'd have already stuck a focking picket on the door. 'Look at all these wonderful . . . *things* you're selling.'

She pretends to check out the rain ponchos (€1) and the soaps shaped like golf balls (50c for a pack of three) and the flip-up address books (€2) with the focked springs – and she cracks on to be impressed.

'What the fock do *you* want?' I make sure to go.

She's like, 'I *beg* your pardon!'

'Beg all you like. What are you doing here?'

Sorcha rushes straight to her defence, of course. 'Ross, don't speak to your mother like that.'

She's so easily taken in by people that it's sometimes frightening.

'She obviously wants something,' I go. 'I just haven't figured out what it is yet.'

The old dear's there, 'How dare you! I'm here to support my daughter-in-law – *and* friend! – in her new business endeavour, whether your cynical little mind believes it or not.'

I notice that she's trying not to breathe in too deeply. She storts picking up things she's supposedly going to buy.

'Don't listen to him,' Sorcha goes. 'I've actually just been telling him about how he needs to grow up.'

The old dear, of course, is delighted to have Sorcha as, like, an ally. She makes sure to give me a big focking smile. She has a face like a focking Jack Russell drowning in a bathful of tomatoes.

Again, I decide to stay out of it. I'll be proved right in the long run.

What I do instead is nip into the back of the shop, to the little office where Sorcha usually goes when it's quiet to do, like, paperwork and order stock. The thing is, roysh, that I held the fort for her at lunchtime and I couldn't help but notice that she came back with a bag from, like, Molton Brown.

I have a root around for it and I end up finding it, along with her handbag, in the second-from-bottom drawer of the filing cabinet.

I whip it out, pull the little ribbon and look inside. There's, like, three bottles. One of, like, Indian Cress Instant Conditioner. One of, like, Relaxing Yuan Zhi Bath and Shower Gel. And one – happy focking days – of, like, Radiant Lili Pili Hairwash.

I hang onto that one and put the rest back.

Then I tip into the little staff toilet just off the office – the one with 'Not For Customer Use' on the actual door. I open the bottle and tip the entire contents down the sink. Then I give it a good rinse out. I have a bit of a chuckle to myself as I'm doing it, thinking, Molton focking Brown – you'd hordly know Sorcha owes however many Ks it is to the Hilary Swank.

In the corner of the toilet are the twenty two-litre bottles of shampoo that the two of us removed from the shelves a couple of weeks ago after that woman came in complaining of a scabby focking head. I grab the actual one she returned, bring it over to the sink and use it to fill up the Lili focking Pili bottle.

I screw the top back on, dry it off and stick it in my sky rocket. Then I head back out to the shop.

The old dear's going, 'So it's taxis everywhere for the next twelve months – until I get my licence back.'

Sorcha goes, 'Oh my God, that is, like, *so* unfair,' as she storts ringing the old dear's items through the till. An eighteen-piece, nickel-plated Allen key set (€3), a *Great Train Journeys of the World* five-DVD boxset (€2), a set of thirty-seven assorted doilies (€2) and two tea towels (€1 each) with – focking hilarious, this – CORK: CITY OF CULTURE 2005 on them.

How can the woman say she's *not* up to something?

I watch her go to pull out her plastic, then I just go, 'Er, no credit cords, I'm afraid.'

She's like, 'What?'

I'm there, 'You heard. It's only if you spend a Brody Jenner or more.'

Sorcha smiles sweetly at her and goes, 'Sorry, Fionnuala, he's right. Oh my God, I'd love to make an exception in your case – but Mr Whittle's very strict about it.'

The old dear storts rooting in her bag, going, 'I must see if I have any *euros*,' and she says the word like it's some ancient focking currency that no one's used for, like, a hundred years. In the end, she can't find any. 'How much does it come to, Sorcha?'

'It's actually *nine*?'

'Oh,' she goes, 'why don't I take another of those marvellous City of Culture tea towels – that'll bring it up to ten,' and she hands over her platinum cord, all focking delighted with herself.

Sorcha bags up her shit and off she goes – the demented old hag. Sorcha ends up having a bit of a go at me then. She's like, 'Ross, you only get one mum. You really should make a better effort with her.'

I crack on to be suddenly all full of regrets. 'That's a good point,' I go. I'm sure you can picture the sincerity in my face. 'Especially when you think how close I came to never actually seeing her again. I'm actually going to go and apologize to her,' and I chase out of the shop after her.

I see her tipping down the steps and towards the doors onto South William Street and I call her. I'm like, 'Excuse me!' and she turns around with a big guilty face on her. I swear to fock, she was about to dump all the shit she bought into the bin just beside the door.

I reach into my jacket and I produce the Molton Brown bottle. 'You, er, forgot your free gift,' I go.

I hand it to her. The first thing she does is she checks the spelling on the bottle to make sure it's not a Chinese knock-off. She is such a focking snob.

But then who am I to talk?

'Yeah, no, it's the real deal,' I go.

She goes, 'Oh,' genuinely surprised. 'Lovely!'

Then she cocks her head to one side and sort of, like, smiles at me at an angle – which is what she does when she's trying to get all *in* with me?

She's like, 'Ross, why can't you and I be friends?'

I crack on to be just as sad about it as *she's* cracking on to be.

'I don't know,' I go. 'I'm always asking myself that basic question.'

She's there, 'Perhaps I *should* have come home when I heard that you were shot. Maybe throwing myself into my screenwriting work was my way of coping with what happened to you.'

She's turning it on in a major way.

I probably end up surprising her by just going, 'Maybe I could make more of an effort as well.'

She's delighted to hear that, of course – whatever it is she wants from us.

She's there, 'Let's both do that, then. Put the past behind us. And let's have dinner soon.'

And through the doors she goes, crossing the road and heading up that little laneway that leads to actual Grafton Street, walking in a way that she probably *imagines* is sexy?

I tip back around to the shop. I can hear, like, raised voices coming from it, even from the little newsagent at the top of the stairs, so I end up quickening the pace and pretty much *running* back?

There's a dude in the shop, a big, fat, sweaty focker – in his midtwenties, I'd say – and he's giving out yords to Sorcha. He's practically jabbing his finger in her face and going, 'Who facking told ya to do it?' because he's, like, *English* from the sounds of him? 'Who facking told ya, eh?'

Poor Sorcha's on the verge of actual tears. 'I decided I couldn't wait until you came home from Cyprus.'

'So you took va decision – va facking unilateral facking liberty – to just go ahead and facking do it.'

I step in between them. I know in the past I possibly haven't treated Sorcha the way she deserved to be treated, but I'd do focking time to protect the girl – and I'd do it happily.

I just go, 'Whoa, Pilgrim – what's the deal here?'

I don't know *where* I get Pilgrim from – I like it, though.

He's there, 'Who va fack are you?'

I square up to him – wouldn't take much to deck him. I'm the man who Frankie Sheahan once described as one of the five toughest-tackling backs he's ever played against – a second cousin of Oisinn's overhcard him say that in Flannery's in Limerick one night.

'Who am I?' I go. 'Who the fock are you?'

Sorcha's there, 'Ross, please, I can handle this!'

I don't listen to her, though. I just stare the dude down and go, 'Are you looking for a crack at the title? Are you, Player?'

Sorcha tries to pull me away, giving it, 'Ross, this is Mr Whittle, the owner of the shop.'

I'm there, 'I don't care who he is. No one speaks like that to my still technically wife.'

Sorcha's like, 'Ross, please! I *need* this job.'

The fat focker has the balls to actually sneer at me – he honestly couldn't be any older than twenty-five. 'Listen to va gell,' he tries to go. 'She's tawking sense.'

Sorcha shoulders me out of the way then and goes, 'Just to tell you, Mr Whittle, I tried to contact the manufacturer.'

'You what?'

He's one of those, I don't know, cockney wide boys – like you see in *EastEnders*.

'I rang the number on the bottle,' Sorcha goes. 'But it's no longer active.'

'*I'm* in contact wiv va manufacturer.'

'And what's he saying? I presume he shares our concerns?'

'Va stuff has been tested – not vat it's any of your facking business.'

'Well, can he provide us with certification to that effect?'

'Eh?'

'This woman's scalp was actually bleeding.'

'Look, vare's naffink to warry abaht – va shampoo's awight. It were a rogue one, is awl.'

I go, 'One rogue one recognizes another, I suppose,' which is unbelievably clever for me.

He knows he can't beat me physically, roysh, so instead he goes, 'Do you want *'er* to be still working 'ere tomorrah?'

I don't even answer him – wouldn't give him the pleasure.

He turns back to Sorcha then and goes, 'Be a smart gell – get vem facking bottles back on vem facking shelves. Uverwise, you're facking sacked.'

★

I can't even look the kid in the eye.

'Being a father,' I go, 'is a tough job, Ro. Don't get me wrong – it's actually the best job in the world. The positives would definitely outweigh the negatives – for me, anyway . . .'

He goes, 'You're babbling, Rosser.'

'Am I? It's possibly just nerves.'

He hops up from the table. 'Will I get you a beer so?'

I'm like, 'No, no – leave the beers, Ro . . .'

Sorcha's taken Honor to Dundrum for the afternoon so we can have the big father–son chat. I'm beginning to wish we could have, like, swapped roles, though.

'Alright, fock it,' I go, 'get me a beer.'

He actually grabs *both* of us a beer.

'Now, breathe, Rosser,' he goes, handing mine to me. 'Just breathe.'

Which I try to do. It definitely does help.

'Okay, look,' I go. 'I remember the first time my old dear caught me conkers-deep in some young one. I was probably a year or two older than you, in fairness. Anyway, the old dear ended up having a total focking knicker-fit. So I don't think my reaction was unusual.'

'You ren, Rosser.'

'I know I ran.'

'You screamed and then you ren.'

'Okay, thanks, Ro – I know what I focking did. The point I'm try-ing to make is that it was basic shock. I'm *still* in shock, if you want the truth. No one expects to walk into a room one day and catch one of their kids on the case. Especially a kid of your age . . .'

'I'm fourteen, Rosser.'

'And you've no idea how young that actually is, Ro. I mean, God, it seems like only yesterday that you were watching cartoons and shouting, "Doorty scum fooks!" at the Gorda Emergency Response Unit on the Ballygall Road.'

'I was a kid. Ine not any mower.'

'You are, Ro – you just don't realize it. And maybe your old dear and that dickhead McGahy are to blame for this.'

'How?'

'For pushing you. For telling you to sit your Junior Cert. a year early. I mean, what's the actual rush here? Look, Ro, I'm the last person in the world who should be dishing out advice. I've got shit for brains – that's an established fact. But one thing I definitely would say to you is this – don't be in such a hurry to grow up.'

He nods his little head, then goes, 'I love her, but.'

'Who?'

'Shadden.'

'You don't know that, Ro.'

'I do, but.'

'Look, you've a lot of years and – believe me! – a lot of women ahead of you. Wait'll they get a load of you in UCD, if that's where you end up going.' Then I sort of, like, chuckle to myself. 'You'll go through that Orts block like a bad focking catchphrase.'

He's like, 'Shadden's the only geerl I ever want to be with, but.'

'But, Ro, I wouldn't be any kind of father if I told you that it was cool for you two to be having, like, *sex*?'

'*She's* sixteen, but – she's not gonna wait arowunt until Ine old enough.'

Sixteen? Her focking body clock is hordly ticking! Jesus, what is it with this generation?

'If she genuinely loves you,' I go, 'she will. And do you know what, Ro? Sometimes? It's actually nice to wait.'

I realize how focking ridiculous that sounds coming from me, even while the words are still in my mouth.

Ronan cops it too. 'That's funny. You're heerdly a good exampiddle. Sure you're always hopping in and ourra bed with diffordent boords.'

That's, like, straight from his old dear's mouth.

I'm there, 'A lot of that gets blown out of proportion, Ro.'

He goes, 'But Ine only wit one geerl. I only ever want to *be* wit one geerl – and that's Shadden.'

He knows how to argue, this kid. I suppose I *am* on seriously shaky ground here.

I'm like, 'Ro, is there *anything* I can say to convince you that what you're doing is not a good idea?'

'No.'

'Well, just to let you know, you can't use my aportment any more.'

'Why not?'

'Because I'm moving back in there when I come back from the Heineken Cup final . . . So I'll have your key, please.'

He huffs and puffs, then fishes it out of his pocket and hands it to me.

'Ro,' I go, because I'm on a definite fatherhood roll now, 'I need to ask you another question?'

'Shadden washed yisser sheets.'

'No – Jesus focking Christ – no, that's not what I'm wondering. What I'm wondering is . . . are you being careful?'

'Yeah.'

'So you're actually using . . .'

'Course I fooken am.'

'Good. That's a huge relief. Because the last thing you want to do with a girl from a family like that is end up pupping her, Ro. And I don't mean that with any disrespect to your mother.'

He suddenly stops mid-sip. 'Here, you're not going to tell her, are you?'

'Who?'

'Me ma. About, you know, me and Shadden?'

'No,' I go, 'I'm not going to tell your mother.'

He smiles at me. 'That's because you're not a rat.'

'No, Ro, it's because I know she'd probably find a way of blaming me.'

Even to the most innocent question, Hennessy reacts like he wants to grab me by the back of the neck and smash my head through the actual wall.

All I went is, 'You must be delighted to have Lauren back home, are you?'

Lauren, as in Christian's wife. She's, like, Hennessy's only daughter – his only kid, in fact.

He keeps looking over his shoulder. 'Yeah,' he goes, 'whatever you fucking say.'

I'm there, 'Yeah, no, I heard they're actually back living with you. I'll tell you something as well, I'm going to make sure Christian has a good time in Cordiff. No prostitutes, though. That's a promise I'm happy to make to your daughter.'

That's when he basically turns on me. 'Your fucking head is all over the place,' he goes. 'Get in the fucking moment.'

'I'm *in* the moment. No better focking man.'

'Just fucking concentrate on what you're being asked. And give the answers like I coached you.'

The door behind us all of a sudden opens and in walks Shane Harron, who I'm sick of the focking sight of at this stage.

'Gentlemen,' he goes, which is his way of saying hello.

Hennessy is straight on his feet. 'I would like to object, formally, to the way my client is being hounded by you fucking people.'

The man is good. I presume that's why the old man has stayed friends with him for so long.

The cop goes, 'There's no need for objections. We're not in a courtroom, are we?'

'*You* will be. Believe me. Why have you dragged us all the way out here to Malahide again?'

'Because the investigation is being conducted from Malahide.'

'And you couldn't interview him someplace else? My client is a busy man.'

He's pushing it there.

The cop pulls out a chair and sits down on the opposite side of the table to us. 'Would either of you two gentlemen like a cup of tea or coffee?'

I turn and look at Hennessy. I don't know *why* I need his permission. I'm there, 'I could possibly use a coffee.'

'You're not having a coffee,' Hennessy goes – this is without even looking at me. God, he's a cranky focker. 'You're not having a coffee because you're not going to be here long enough for it to even cool.'

Then he looks at the cop dude. 'You said on the phone you had new information.'

'We *have* new information, yes.'

'Well, you better have some new questions.'

'Oh, we have some new questions as well.'

'Then shoot for the fucking stars, Detective.'

The cop dude looks at *me*, then. 'Hedda Rathfriland has changed her story.'

This seems to come as news to Hennessy, because he goes, 'Changed her story how?'

The cop dude keeps focusing on me, though.

'Often happens, you see, when someone's lying and they know their lies aren't being believed. They'll start adding details, even changing details – try to put a new, how would you say, *construction* on events, one they hope you *will* believe.'

'So what's she all of a sudden saying?' I go.

'Oh, she's suddenly remembered a whole lot of things. She didn't just walk in and find you bleeding to death in the kitchen like she initially claimed. She's saying she actually heard the gun go off now – as she was coming through the front door. Then she heard the back door open and the sound of feet running away from the house, along a covered passageway that leads to a side entrance into the property. Do you see the significance of the covered passageway?'

'No.'

'Huh?'

'I said no.'

'It explains away the absence of footprints.'

Hennessy's in there like a shot. 'What the fuck has any of this got to do with my client?'

'I thought it might refresh his memory.'

'He already told you, he can't remember anything.'

'Well, neither could Hedda until this morning. Now she can remember it all. And in blueprint detail. She's saying that when she heard the gun go off, she ran to the kitchen. She ran *to* the kitchen – not *away* from it. Brave girl, you'd have to say. And she found you lying there. A stuck pig. Bleeding out, all over her mother's nice clean floor.'

'Again,' I go, 'I don't remember anything.'

'But before she went to check on you – and to phone for an ambulance – she had the presence of mind to run to the window and get a good description of the two men who shot you. She's only just remembered that she did this – and sure, isn't it good that she did?'

'I wish I could help you – I really do.'

He reaches into his inside pocket and produces a piece of A4 paper, folded in three. He opens it out and goes, 'Will I read the description to you anyway? Sure it might dislodge something. I mean, look at everything *she's* after remembering.'

I'm there, 'Go on, then.'

'They were both about six foot four in height,' he goes, reading directly from the sheet, 'and they were both wearing black boiler-suits and balaclavas.'

I nod slowly. 'Yeah, no, it's definitely not ringing any bells with me.'

'Of course it's not ringing any bells. They don't exist. Two fellas, six foot four in height, wearing black boilersuits and balaclavas – it's straight off a *Crimecall* reconstruction.'

Hennessy goes, 'They might exist or they might not exist. You heard my client – he has no memory.'

The cop just nods, at the same time smiling to himself in a if-that's-the-way-you-want-to-play-it kind of a way. He goes, 'I don't know why you're covering for her, Ross. At a guess, I'd say you're trying to extort money from her mother with the aid of this gentle-man beside you.'

Hennessy goes, 'That's fucking slander, right there.'

The cop just carries on talking to me, doesn't address Hennessy at all. He's like, 'The girl is falling apart, Ross – just like her story. And your story is going to fall apart, too. It's just a matter of time. And then I'm going to make sure you're charged with withholding information vital to the investigation of a serious crime. And I'm going to try very hard to send you to jail.'

I'm there, 'I really wish I could be of more assistance,' even though inside I'm suddenly shitting it. 'I'll keep racking my brains, though – that much I can promise you.'

Hennessy all of a sudden stands up. He stares the dude down and goes, 'That all you got, Pilgrim?'

Pilgrim! *That* was where I got it.

The cop's there, 'That's it for now.'

Hennessy laughs, then sort of, like, gestures with his head for me to stand up – which I do.

On our way out the door, the cop goes, 'It's only a matter of time, Ross. This girl won't hold out another week.'

Neither of us says anything – this was agreed beforehand – until we're back in Hennessy's cor and a good mile away from the actual cop shop.

I'm sitting there in the front passenger seat, seriously crapping it, until Hennessy turns around to me and goes, 'Hey, that went good.'

Now, I might be as thick as a focking fire door, but I fail to see how anyone could think that went actually well. I'm there, 'Er, did you not just hear what the dude said? Hedda's falling aport.'

'She's not falling apart. The kid's strong.'

'How do you know she won't suddenly, I don't know, crack?'

'Because I'm fucking coaching her as well.'

'What?'

'Hey, you and I have got a lot of money invested in keeping her out of jail. She cracks – that's our money gone. So Regina agreed to let me coach her while our negotiations are continuing.'

I laugh. 'So that was *your* story? The dudes with the balaclavas. Because *he* doesn't seem to have bought it.'

'Doesn't matter whether he buys it or not. They've got four separate witnesses putting Terry and Larry outside the Rathfriland home earlier in the day.'

'That's true. Because they found out I was actually staying there.'

'That's why there's one or two Guards working the case still saying it was a hit.'

'So, what, *they* believe that Hedda's had amnesia up until now?'

'She never said she had amnesia. She told them she kept quiet because she was scared of reprisals. Hey, the poor kid just found her mother's lover bleeding to death on the kitchen floor. She was terrified.'

'Let's hope she sticks to that story.'

'Oh, she'll stick to it – she doesn't want to go to jail. And she's a hard-headed little bitch.'

'I know. She tried to kill me, remember.'

He laughs. Then he slaps my thigh – pretty hord, it has to be said – and goes, 'You did good today. Real fucking good.'

And I realize it's the first time that Hennessy has ever given me a genuine compliment. And it was for breaking the law.

The Big O says how times have changed.

And they've changed alright. The last time Leinster were involved in a European Cup final, we *flew* over. *And* we stayed in, like, a five-stor hotel. This time we're on the actual – and I still can hordly bring myself to say the word – *ferry*? We've still no Lemony Snickets and we're staying in a B&B that looked so depressing even on the website that I won't be surprised if they ask us for our shoelaces when we're checking in.

Yet another example of how the recession is affecting people right the way across the board.

I'm like, 'Times *have* changed alright. Ain't no bout-a-doubt it. How are you doing, Ois? As in, like, *generally*?'

He's there, 'Yeah, I'm good. Bit weird living with the old pair still. "What time will you be home?" Never expected to be answering that question at thirty-one years of age.'

He looks well, though – the best of the five of us, aport from obviously me. Bankruptcy actually suits him. It's like a definite weight has been lifted.

He goes, 'I've got to find a job, though.'

I'm there, 'Are you even *allowed* to earn money?'

'I'm just talking about something small. Cash in hand. It's not even *for* the money. It's more for my self-esteem. Hate feeling like a useless prick.'

This is us standing out on the deck of the HSS *Stena Explorer*, by the way. Getting the boat is as working class as owning your own snooker cue or living in a tower block named after a mortyr. I offered to pay for everyone's flights, but they all said no.

Pride and blah, blah, blah.

JP arrives back, wobbling across the deck of the ship, clutching another twelve cans of Sensibly. He's singing, 'True love. You're the team I'm dreaming of. You were sent from up above. And I'm gonna be . . . True Blue, Leinster, I love you.'

He's been seriously tanning it as well. He got through his stash from the O'Briens on Marine Road within half an hour of boarding. He looks at me, all glassy-eyed. 'I love my province,' he goes.

I laugh. I'm there, 'I love it too, J-Town.'

'No,' he goes, 'I really, *really* love it. *All* of it, Ross. The Hill of Tara. The Cooley Peninsula. Bray Head . . .'

'Come on, Dude, we've all had a few drinks.'

'Kilkenny Castle. Blanchardstown Shopping Centre . . .'

See, JP is the one I really worry about. The woman he drove to the motor showroom, hanging onto her own windscreen wipers for her life, obtained a judgement against Last Resort Asset Reclaim last week for €190,000 (plus costs)and the company was immediately liquidated. So now he's also on the scrapheap.

And he's obviously missing Danuta, his ex, who focked off back to Russia when my old dear scuppered her plans for a cash-for-gold outlet in Foxrock. He definitely loved her, even though she was as mad as a focking spoon.

I think back to how happy he used to be, when he was with Hook, Lyon and Sinker. He sold half the current Leinster squad their first gaffs. Some of them will be playing rugby well into their focking fifties to pay for them as well.

I'll have to make the effort to see the dude more.

'Oisinn,' he goes, hanging out of the Ois's Helly Hansen, 'there's two birds over here – I was talking to them at the bar – *gagging* for it!'

I look over. There's two birds leaning against a wooden post, in Leinster jerseys. They're gagging for it alright. I'd say rugby was still a focking amateur game the last time anyone touched either of them in a sexual way. One has a body like a sack of wet washing. The other looks like something I'd draw with my left hand.

Oisinn seems to like what he's seeing, though. 'Ross,' he goes, 'would you mind?'

I'm like, 'Yeah, no, you goys fire away,' somehow managing to keep a straight face. 'You saw them first.'

I end up just heading off in search of Fionn and Christian. I find them on the other side of the boat, leaning on the gord rail and staring out to sea, like the pair out of focking *Titanic*.

They're talking about, I don't know, some shit or other.

'Nyberg said it himself,' Fionn is going. 'The bank guarantee scheme was based on deficient information – the Government didn't know the banks were going to have solvency problems.'

Christian is shaking his head, like he thinks the whole thing is a focking disgrace – which it quite possibly is.

I go, 'Alright, goys?' because I've already picked up on the fact they're still both a bit *off* with me?

They're both like, 'Ross.'

I'm there, 'So are you back talking to me, Fionn, having ignored my calls for, like, weeks now?'

I actually had to go through either JP or Oisinn to make the stag arrangements with him.

'I'm coming around,' is all he goes.

I'm like, 'Dude, I cleaned your old dear's computer for her, didn't I?'

Three hours it took me as well. With a focking toothbrush. I spent the entire time just gagging.

He goes, 'That's not the point, Ross.'

I'm like, 'Well, would you mind telling me what *is* the point?'

'The point is that she didn't expect somebody to come into her home and shit on her focking computer. She was kind of upset. She still is.'

'Did you tell her it was called a waffle press?'

'Why do you think that would help, Ross?'

'Okay, did you explain to her that I thought it was Fabrizio's laptop? He deliberately let me think it, in fact.'

He holds up his two hands and goes, 'Ross, I just want to forget about it.'

I'm there, 'Hey, I do too.'

'If you're going to be my best man, you need to let go of this obsession you have with Fabrizio and Erika . . .'

'I wouldn't have said it was an obsession as such.'

'It's becoming really annoying – for both Erika *and* me.'

For both Erika *and* me. What a tosser. I'm *on* his focking side – that's what he fails to see.

I'm like, 'Hey, I've already let it go.'

'I really hope so,' he goes.

I'm there, 'Dude, *it's* gone.'

I look at Christian and I sort of, like, roll my eyes. He doesn't even smile, though. What's happening to everyone?

'And one other thing,' Fionn goes, 'I don't want any stag party pranks.'

I'm like, 'What?'

'You know what I'm talking about, Ross. I don't want to wake up handcuffed to something with my head shaved. I'm serious about this. And Erika told me to say it to you, too. It's too close to the wedding. If anything happens to me, she's holding you personally responsible.'

I stare out to sea.

I go, 'For once, I'm *actually* going to respect your wishes.'

Fionn is a good mate. I can't tell you how much it hurts to have to lie to him.

She's, like, the best-looking bird in the pub – by a mile as well. Christian thinks she might be a Leinster fan, except I know better.

'If she was a Leinster fan,' I go, 'she'd have a pair of sunnies on her head.'

He's there, 'I suppose so, yeah.'

I'm there, 'There's no suppose so about it. She's definitely, like, Welsh. And a focking ringer for Olivia Wilde – at least from this distance.'

Oisinn arrives over with the round – fair focks to him. Except, roysh, him and focking JP have ended up bringing the two birds from the ferry with them to the actual boozer, which I personally think is bang out of order.

This weekend was supposed to be about just us – as in the *goys*?

The birds are a disgrace as well. The last time someone walked off a boat with two things that looked like that, it was when Noah led the focking rat monkeys off the ark.

Fock's sake.

JP's, at least, has a decent set of whoppers on her, even though her belly and handles are hanging over the band of her jeans like an untrimmed pie. Oisinn's has a rack like two Disprin on an ironing board and a focking head like a half-dissolved Berocca tablet.

'Ross,' JP goes, 'you remember Una and Marie from the boat, don't you?'

'Yeah,' I go, taking a sip of my pint, refusing to even look at them. 'Big-time. They definitely made an impression alright.'

They're from focking Carlow as well. I mean, there's literally *no* good news. And they're total focking bandwagoners when it comes to rugby as well. Oh, they go to all the Ireland games, but they probably think Les Kiss is a focking porn movie.

'So did you always want to be primary school teachers?' I hear JP go and I think, oh my God, I'm losing the actual will to live here.

Our first night in Cordiff is turning out to be a seriously damp squib. It's actually officially the shittest stag of all time. If there wasn't a match on tomorrow, I'd be already on my way back to Holyhead. Fionn is drinking – I shit you not – Lucozade because – get this – he wants to enjoy the game with no hangover. Which means he's not going to be drinking during the day tomorrow either. Which means tomorrow night is going to be his only night on the actual lash. Christian, meanwhile, is drinking like Sorcha's granny, which is to say slowly and with lots of visits to the toilet to piss.

I just decide, fock it – I'm going to have a crack at the Olivia Wilde lookalike. This night is beginning to feel like a slow focking death. So I announce my intentions to the goys.

'She *is* beautiful,' Christian, at least, acknowledges.

I'm just like, 'I hear you borking, Big Dog. Later, losers!' and I just wander over to her.

I don't think it would be an exaggeration to say that there's suddenly a serious buzz in the bor. There's, like, two hundred Leinster fans in the place and their eyes have been out on basic stalks all night looking at her. Yet no one has plucked up the courage to go over and have a crack at her.

I smile and just shake my head. See, this is the cross I have to bear. The weight of an entire province's expectations. I know how Jonny Sexton and the rest of the goys feel.

'Hey,' I go, laying it down like my name's Chris Brown. 'I'm Ross.'

She looks even more like Olivia Wilde up close.

'Oh,' she goes, delighted I've come over. 'I'm Blodwyn.'

I obviously burst out laughing.

'Sorry,' I go, 'that's a new one on me. And I've known a lot of girls in my time. In fact, you should have seen the job that my soon-to-be-ex-wife and I had trying to come up with a name for our daughter. It couldn't be the name of a girl I'd been with in the past, see. Sorcha's a bit funny like that. Anyway, we ended up having to go through five books of baby names.'

She laughs then.

'You're funny,' she goes, except she pronounces it 'Funnay'.

The Welsh accent is not *that* unlike the Cork one?

She's there, 'Blodwyn was may grandmother's neem, see – means whait floawah.'

'Well,' I go, 'it's a pleasure to meet you – White Flower.'

You can picture Fionn, Christian, Oisinn and JP, I'm sure, just lapping up the show from the other side of the bor – in pretty much *awe* of me?

Blodwyn – I know, *I'm* still laughing as well – introduces me to her three friends. Their names go in one ear and out the other. All I remember is that they haven't got a vowel between them – it's like the three shittest Scrabble hands in history.

They're nothing much to look at either, so – while continuing to be my normal chorming self – I concentrate most of my eye contact and my chat-up lines on Blodwyn. I tell her a bit about myself and, well, she ends up being putty in the hand. No more than half an hour has passed before I've basically propositioned her – asked her if she fancies popping outside for a breath of air, which would be a famous manouevre of mine back home.

She's like, 'Where are you stee yen?' and I think, okay, this is a bird who doesn't need the whole I'm-having-trouble-breathing-in-here seduction routine.

'We're actually staying in some little focking grief-hole on Castle Street,' I go.

She's like, 'Way don't we go back to yooers, then?'

I have to say, I love a straight shooter. She says her goodbyes to, I don't know, Qqqqwwpt, Tfvvlllm and Nsxxxggg and I wander over to the goys to say the same to them.

There are Leinster fans in that bor actually high-fiving each other having watched what I've just pulled off. It's like, 'See? It's not only Munster who do impossible dreams!'

I turn to Fionn and I go, 'Remember the rule – if you hear the bed rockin', don't come knockin',' which I know is going to seriously piss him off. He was the one who said we should all get a room each – he knows from past experience that doubling with me means usually walking the roads till dawn.

Christian goes, 'Are you bringing her back to the B&B?'

I'm like, 'Does Brent Pope shit in the woods?'

And that's when I notice that he's grinning at me like a Billy focking Barry kid. So are Fionn, Oisinn and JP. *And* the two sea monsters.

It's immediately obvious that there's something wrong with Blodwyn.

I'm like, 'What's the deal? What are you all laughing at?'

'What's that on her ankle?' it's JP who goes.

I follow his line of vision. It's, like, an ankle bracelet. 'Yeah, no,' I go, 'Sorcha was saying the other day that chunky jewellery was, like, *in* this year? Or was it out? I don't know. I never really listen.'

That's when Fionn turns around and goes, 'It's an electronic tag, Ross.'

I suddenly feel all of the blood drain from my face.

I'm like, 'What?'

'She's been electronically tagged,' he goes, obviously delighted to have something over me after the whole laptop incident.

It's all of a sudden obvious to me why every Leinster fan in the place is high-fiving each other and laughing like the Heineken Cup is already won.

JP storts losing the run of himself then. 'I wonder what she did?' he goes. 'Hey, she could be on parole for, like, killing her ex-boyfriend.'

Oh, fock.

'Or cutting her cheating husband's balls off.'

I don't even have time to come up with an exit strategy. Because before I know it, Blodwyn is suddenly standing in front of me, going, 'Are we go wen, then?'

And all I can think is, I can't tell her no, because that'd mean losing face in front of all these people – most of whom idolize me.

So what I do is I end up just smiling through it. I just go, 'Yeah, no, let's hit the road, Blod,' and I make sure to get her the *fluich* out of there.

On the walk back to the B&B, though, I end up having to ask the question.

I go, 'That thing on your ankle . . .'

She laughs. 'It's just an electron neck tag,' she goes – no attempt to hide it or anything.

I'm there, 'Okay, do you mind me asking *why* you're wearing an electronic tag? And should you even be out tonight?'

She shakes her head like it's a ridiculous question that she's forever having to answer. 'You're worse than my bleddy probation officer, you are! No, I should tent be out tonait. But I were gasp pen for a drink – satisfied?'

I'm not, of course. What I really want to know is, like, what did she do? But then I don't want to ask the question for fear of what I'll find out. Maybe she *did* off her last bloke. Or, I don't know, beat his scrotum with a meat hammer. And maybe *I'm* next.

But against that – like I said – she *does* look like Olivia Wilde.

So I bring her back to the B&B and make a decision to try to, like, block *out* the ankle bracelet?

Of course, I've been so distracted by it that I end up totally forgetting about the unsightly focking mess that is my ab region. I take

my shirt off over my head and Blodwyn immediately covers her mouth.

She's like, 'Jesus!'

I suddenly realize what she's talking about.

'Oh,' I go. 'Er, I actually got shot?'

She's there, 'You could have bleddy warned me,' and I'm thinking, yeah, you're one to talk about focking full disclosure, aren't you?

I'm there, 'Does it bother you?'

She uncovers her mouth and goes, 'No . . . no, it doesn't bother me. Fact, I quate lake ett. It's sexay in a way. I've nefare been with a man with a scar before.'

I find that hord to believe.

She's there, 'It's very disting weshed really. I don't want to be with a man with a body like a bleddy Ken doll.'

So she takes off her top and I make an immediate grab for the goods. And Blodwyn storts going at me – honestly – like a dog with a bag of rubbish. But I can't get that bracelet out of my head. There's, like, a little red light on it that keeps flashing and – I don't know – *illuminating* the room at, like, five-second intervals. I try to close my eyes, except then I can actually *feel* the thing, vibrating against my orse.

I keep losing my steel, if you know what I'm saying. I'm shooting pool with a length of wet spaghetti.

She's like, 'What the fuck is the matt tare?'

I'm there, 'Okay, I'm sorry, but I'm going to have to come straight out and ask you – what actual crime did you commit?'

She goes, 'Way is *that* import tent?'

'Because I don't want the cops suddenly bursting in here.'

She laughs. 'The cops? How would they know I was hee are?'

I nod at her ankle. 'That focking thing, of course?'

She laughs – even *horder* this time? 'They can't use it to treck may. Jee suss! Is that way you kept looking up at the skay when we were walk ken here from the peb?'

'Possibly.'

'You were look ken for a helicopter – weren't you?'

I don't deny it. 'Yeah, no, I've possibly watched too many Matt Damon movies – who hasn't?'

'They can't use it to treck may! It's linked to a base station in may house – they just know when I've gone oat. Broken the terms of may parole . . . Stop look ken so worried, will you? I nick things – that's all. I'm a shoplift air.'

I'm like, 'Oh, thank God for that.'

'A professional shoplift air – a recidivist offendare.'

'You don't know how relieved I am to hear you say that.'

'What did you thenk I was?'

'You don't want to know, Blod. You honestly don't want to know.'

After that, I relax. Blodwyn ends up being a cracking little rattle, in all fairness to her – she rides like she owns the actual patent on it. And let's just say I don't exactly let my province down either.

Eight, maybe ten hours later, I wake up. It's pure instinct, roysh, but I make an immediate grab for my wallet. It's still there. Blodwyn's in the bathroom, putting her face back on.

'Morn anne,' she shouts out to me, when she hears me stirring. 'Do you want to go for breck fest?'

I *love* the accent, I'm going to have to admit it.

I'm like, 'I, er, might actually take a raincheck on that one, Blod. I'm supposedly meeting the goys.'

She's not a happy bunny when she hears that. She's there, 'I beg your part ten?'

I'm like, 'Hey, neither of us can have any complaints. Great night. No promises. Use and abuse. Blah, blah, blah . . .'

She goes, 'Oh no you don't!'

'*Excuse* me?'

'You're not treat ten may like some bleddy hook air. If you can spend the nait with may, then you can spend the bleddy morning with may as well. And that's the end of it.'

'You're saying you want to come to breakfast with *us*?'

Someone tell me this isn't focking happening.

'Yes,' she goes. 'I do.'

I'm like, 'But it's going to be all rugby talk. Ways in which we think we can hurt Northampton. Ways in which Northampton could possibly hurt us. Blahdy, blah. Wouldn't be a hundred percent sure it'd be your cup of tea.'

'You don't even know may. How would you know what may kep of tea is?'

This is a focking disaster.

I go, 'Fair enough – come if you want to come. Except don't blame me if you end up being bored shitless.'

I head into the bathroom. I stand on the toilet bowl and try the window. Except it's like she can read my mind.

'Tough leck,' she goes to me through the door. 'It's got bleddy bars on the outside.'

The goys are waiting for me, as arranged, in the Trade Street Café. When they see me walk through the door with *her* trotting behind me, their faces light up like it's Christmas come early. What they should say – if they were any kind of mates, of course – is, 'Sorry, Blodwyn, this is an actual stag – goys only and blah, blah, blah? You need to hit the bricks, Baby.'

Except they don't. They sense my instant discomfort and they, like, seize on it. They're giving it, 'Lovely to meet you, Blodwyn,' and all the rest of it.

She sits down in what would have been my place and I end up having to, like, tramp around the restaurant to find a chair that's not being used. I eventually manage to grab one and I end up having to sit at, like, the edge of the focking table.

By that time, they've already done the introductions and Blodwyn's asking them if they had a good night last night.

I don't know if it's necessary to tell you that she looks a hell of a lot less like Olivia Wilde than she did twelve hours ago. Isn't that always the case? That's the reason I never do breakfast.

I'm going to level with you here – she actually *disgusts* me now? She's still wearing last night's clothes and the ankle bracelet, I notice, is drawing a lot of attention from the other, I don't know, diners.

Why would she even *wear* a mini dress with that thing? As in, what the fock is wrong with just jeans until her parole ends?

The waitress who comes to take our order notices it and her eyes stay fixed on it for maybe a few seconds too long, because Blodwyn goes, 'Have you got a fuck ken prob lemm?'

The waitress, who obviously shits it, says no and storts taking our orders. It's, like, full fries all around, except for Fionn, who ends up ordering the croque-monsieur – on his own focking stag.

I'm nearly giving up at this point.

'The bleddy looks I keep get ten in this place,' Blodwyn goes. 'I was tell en your friend here that I was only ever done for nick ken steff. From shops – professional.'

Fionn especially nods, like she's just mentioned that she's a focking surgeon or something.

'She shouldn't have even been out last night,' I go. 'She's supposed to have, like, a six o'clock curfew?'

JP goes, 'So, like, what'll happen?'

She's there, 'Probably send me back to priss zen for a month or two. I don't *gev* a shet. I needed a good nate out. A bleddy good see-yen-to as well. Anyway, they'll have to ketch may first, won't they?'

'I have to say,' Oisinn goes, 'I'm really glad Ross brought you along.'

They're focking loving this – all of them. It's probably the first time Christian's been properly happy since he came home from the States.

'Well,' she goes, 'he didn't want to. Trayed to get red of may – cheeky bast ted.'

Christian goes, 'That doesn't *sound* like you, Ross.'

'Yeah, no,' I go, 'I was just trying to explain to her that we were probably all going to be giving our analysis.'

She goes, 'I'll tell you what I think he was fray tend of. That I'd give *may* analysis – of hez perform ants.'

Jesus Christ. They all laugh.

JP goes, 'You weren't a hundred percent satisfied, then, Blodwyn?'

I'm like, 'Goys, can I just remind you, there are people trying to eat in this restaurant?'

She laughs. 'Has a cock like a roll of bleddy pound coins,' she goes.

The goys are nearly on the floor pissing themselves. I probably don't need to tell you that.

'It was a bit lake give ven blood really. I felt a tany preck but it were all over very queckly.'

That even gets guffaws from a few other tables.

Our coffees arrive. It's Fionn who actually says it. And I could actually focking kill him, best man or not. 'Ross, why don't you bring Blodwyn to the match?'

I'm like, 'What?'

The others get in on the act then. 'Yeah,' JP goes. 'Have you ever been to a rugby match, Blodwyn?'

'No,' she goes. 'Nev fair.'

I'm like, 'Yeah, no, it'd be great to be able to bring you – but I doubt if you'd get a ticket at this late stage.'

Except the mate of my old man's who sold us ours when we met him in that pub in Holyhead insisted on us taking six – and the goys know it.

'But we've got a spare,' Fionn goes.

This is obviously his payback for what happened in his old pair's gaff that day. And a lifetime of other shit.

He goes, 'Blodwyn, you *should* come – it's going to be an amazing atmosphere.'

'I would lev to kem,' she goes. 'Thank you, boys!'

She turns to me then and she's like, 'It looks lake you've got may for the day, Ross.'

Of course, I know I'm going to end up being the laughing stock of the Leinster crowd if I turn up in the Millennium Stadium with a bird wearing a mini dress and a monitoring bracelet and smelling like cocktail hour last night.

I'm sitting there thinking, okay, I have to focking get out of this. And that's when they finally walk through the door. Not a moment too soon either. They look a bit confused at first – not sure where they're supposed to be looking. But I make sure to give them a holler.

I'm like, 'Over here, Officers!'

Blodwyn has her back to the door. Her face just drops.

One of the Feds just lays his hand on her shoulder. 'Hello, Blodwyn – are you going to kem quietly, then?'

She's not, by the way. 'You fuck ken bas ted!' she practically spits at me across the table. 'When did you call them?'

I'm there, 'When I went off to get a chair for myself. In fairness, Blod, I did try to tell you that I don't do next mornings.'

'So, what, you call the fuck ken police on may. I'll be sleep pen in a priss zen cell tonate because of you.'

I just shrug. 'What can I say? That's how seriously I take my rugby.'

She reaches across the table and slaps me hord across the face. It's a real focking stinger as well. The two cops grab her from either side and they end up just dragging her out of the Trade Street Café and into a waiting cop cor.

She kicks and screams the whole way – and offers me a few of the usual comments: 'You have a tany pea ness,' and blah, blah, blah.

The four goys are looking at me, pretty focking wide-eyed it has to be said. I know what they're all thinking: Who the fock would do something like that?

I take a sip of my coffee, then I shout over to the waitress, 'Cancel one of those fries, would you?'

It's over. I mean, it's only half-time but it's still over. That'd be, like, the *general* view?

It's not my view, though.

I'm reminding Fionn and Oisinn, just like I'm reminding Christian and JP, about some of *our* comebacks. We were, like, thirty-five points down against Pres Bray once – in albeit a friendly – and we still managed to win.

'We *let* them get thirty-five points ahead,' Oisinn goes, 'just to see could we reel them in. We were ripping the piss.'

'My point still stands,' I go. 'Do you think Leo Cullen is down there in the dressing room, telling the goys to just try to keep the score respectable? Of course he's focking not. He's telling them what I'm telling you. It's only 22–6. We're better than Northampton. If they can score twenty-two points in the first half, we sure as hell can score twenty-two points in the second half.'

The goys are getting a sudden reminder of why I was such an amazing captain back in the day. In fact, my words end up giving a lot of Leinster fans in the crowd a genuine lift.

I hear one dude turn to his old man and go, 'His name's Ross O'Carroll-Kelly. He could have been one of the best players Ireland ever produced.'

It's really stirring stuff.

The teams run out again. I'm there, 'Come on, Leinster!'

Fionn is chatting to some random dude beside him. I catch the tail end of the conversation. 'It'll be interesting to see,' he goes, 'how each of the banks reacts to Noonan's demand for a board renewal plan.'

I end up totally losing it.

'That's it,' I go. 'Oisinn, give him your hip flask . . .'

'I told you,' Fionn tries to go, 'I'm not drinking.'

'You *are* focking drinking. Board renewal plans? On your focking stag? Take that focking hip flask. And, JP, give him a can. Give him two cans.'

Fionn ends up having no choice in the matter, roysh, because the rest of the crowd gets in on the act, all going, 'Drink! Drink! Drink! Drink!' and of course he *has* to do it.

It's focking rugby.

Then Christian, on the other side of me, goes, 'Here, give me one as well,' meaning a can, and it's great, roysh, because at long last it feels like it's an actual stag.

And that's when Christian decides to finally open up to me. 'Ross,' he goes, 'I'm sorry I've been a bit . . .'

I'm like, 'You've been a miserable bastard is what you've been.'

He nods. 'I know. Look, I shouldn't have sounded off at you that day in Kielys. I'm sorry.'

I laugh. 'After everything we've been through together over the years – do you think an apology is even necessary? It's, like, no *focking* way.'

'It's just, well, I've got a lot on my plate right now.'

I'm there, 'Hey, at least you're doing better than the rest of us. Four focking unemployed layabouts.'

'Ross,' he suddenly goes, 'I got the sack. I got sacked from my job.'

I'm there, 'Dude, did you just say what I think you said?'

He nods. 'We're not home for a holiday, Ross. We're home for good.'

A roar goes up. Jonny focking Sextime. A try. Only four minutes of the second half gone. People are slapping me on the back, telling me I was right and that I obviously know my rugby. Then he nails the conversion – well, off the focking post, a possible sign that it's going to be our day.

I turn back to Christian. A good two or three minutes have passed. I'm like, 'So you're saying George Lucas sacked you.'

'It wasn't George Lucas as such . . .'

'Hey, don't stort defending him, Christian. If I ever run into him, he's getting decked.'

'Look, the casino's turnover for its first two years of operation was about seventy percent lower than we projected.'

'But that's the whole world economic thing. It's shit everywhere at the moment – that's what everyone seems to be saying. Did you explain that to him?'

'*I* was the project manager, Ross. *I* was the one who went seven hundred million dollars over budget building the thing in the first place. That's the way the corporate world works. You're paid the big money, you carry the can when it all goes wrong.'

I'm presuming he walked away with a nice wedge. It's still heavy focking shit, though. That's what I actually say to him.

'Dude, that's heavy focking shit.'

'And then . . .'

'What?'

He looks over both shoulders like he's suddenly just remembered that he's in an actual rugby stadium. 'Look,' he goes, 'I'll tell you another time.'

I'm like, 'Dude, you can't do that. What is it?'

He lowers his voice to practically a whisper. 'Lauren and I.'

'What about you?'

'We're in trouble, Ross. Our marriage, I mean.'

'You're shitting me. I thought you goys were solid as a rock.'

He shakes his head. Then he goes, 'I'll tell you about it again – when we get home.'

I end up just stunned into silence for a few seconds. Then I go, 'What are you going to do?'

He just shakes his head. 'Long term, I don't know. Short term . . . I'm actually going to take your advice and start enjoying this weekend.'

'That's the focking spirit,' I go.

He knocks back a mouthful of the old wonder stuff.

And then suddenly . . .

Yes! Sexton's going to get over again. Do it! Do it! Yes!

The crowd goes literally ballistic. Talk about a turnaround. Everyone's, like, hugging each other and – I'm not going to deny it – there's a fair bit of high-fiving going on as well.

Oisinn has Fionn in a headlock and the poor focker's glasses are on the floor somewhere. JP – I swear to fock – is in tears, although he's been drinking since before breakfast. I put my orm around Christian's shoulder – in a strictly rugby type of way.

If the boy puts the ball between the chopsticks, it's a two-point game, with more than twenty-five minutes to go and the momentum with us.

There's, like, silence.

I look at Jonny Sexton. I remember he rang me up once looking for advice. He would have been playing Leinster Schools Junior Cup with Mary's at the time and I would have been a serious guru to him. I remember telling him that there'll be days when rugby feels like work. But then, very occasionally, there'll be days when you feel you could slot those kicks over from anywhere on the pitch with a venti latte in one hand and not spill a focking drop. I can see from the cut of him that he knows what kind of day this is going to be.

He nails the kick.

And in that moment, we know. It's like when you're doing a hundred and forty on the Stillorgan dualler and there's some muppet in a Subaru Signet in the inside lane up ahead doing, I don't know, whatever the actual speed limit is – they're still in front of you but you know you're going to pass them.

I turn to Christian and I go, 'These fockers are an example to all of us. Never stop believing that things can get better.'

I cop another look at Fionn. His glasses are gone and he doesn't even give a shit. He's only been drinking for, like, twenty minutes and he's already half mashed. He never could hold his pop.

It suddenly feels like the old days again. Like we're all back together and we're all on the same page. 'Goys,' I go, 'this is going to be a night to remember.'

We arrive back from the hospital at eight o'clock in the morning. The woman who owns the B&B does a double-take when she sees me pushing Fionn through the reception area in a wheelchair.

'Do you have, like, a lift slash elevator?' I go.

She's too in shock to even answer, just stands there with her mouth open, like Sorcha's granny trying to pick up *Fair City* on our Frigidaire microwave.

I'm there, 'I'll take that as a no, then,' and I end up having to literally carry the focker up three flights of stairs in a fireman's lift.

Which is hord. I mean, that plaster cast on his leg has got to weigh, like, half a stone by itself.

I lay him down on the bed. Which is a lie. I actually drop him. And that's what causes him to finally wake up.

'Jesus, no!' he eventually storts going, when he finally gets his bearings. 'Jesus, no!'

So would you if you woke up, four weeks before your wedding, with your leg in plaster from ankle to hip, and literally no memory of what actually happened. Even with no glasses and bucket-loads of drink still swilling around in his bloodstream, he can make out the shape of the trouble he's in.

He's like, 'What . . . what happened?'

What happened was Leinster won the Heineken Cup and we ended up having one of those nights – know the one that's one too many and make it a focking double! It was truly one of the great nights, with all of us – especially me – in truly outstanding form. We're talking banter o'clock here.

Fionn's storting to actually cry. He's like, 'She's going to kill me.'

I laugh. I'm like, 'Do you honestly not remember what happened?'

He storts cradling his head in his hands. One of those hangovers that knows your name.

'Just tell me one thing,' he goes. 'How long do I have to wear this thing?'

I'm there, 'The doctor said eight weeks.'

'Eight weeks?'

'I'm only quoting to you what the dude said.'

'Oh, Jesus Christ. No, no, no.'

'Get your head around it, Dude – you're going to be standing at the altar on those Storskey and Hutches. I'll show you how to use them if you want.'

'Erika's going to go . . .'

'Well, she'll just have to get her head around it as well. You're going to be wearing a cast in all the photographs.'

'Oh, God, no.'

He closes his eyes and shakes his head, slowly, from side to side, like it's a dream he thinks he can somehow wish away. But it's not. It's actual reality.

'What . . . Jesus, what happened?' he goes.

I laugh. I'm there, 'You don't remember the titty bor?'

'Tell me we didn't go to a titty bar.'

'Dude, we *went* to a titty bor. In fact, you were the one who insisted.'

'But I'm *anti* them.'

'Not with a few drinks on you, you're not. It was like, "When are we going to Private Eyes? When are we going to Private Eyes?" The others focked off – they couldn't listen to you any more.'

'Just tell me I didn't have a lapdance. Erika would not be happy.'

I laugh. 'Dude, you were *performing* lapdances. There were men putting five-pound notes in the waistband of your – I don't know, whatever the fock those things were that they cut off you at the hospital. Focking slacks.'

He looks confused. 'So how did I . . . actually, what's even wrong with my leg?'

'We're talking about a straight break across the tibia. That's according to the doctor who X-rayed it. For some reason, you thought it would be a good idea to climb the pole.'

'How am I going to explain this to Erika?'

I look at the clock on my phone.

'Well, you've got about five hours to sleep on it,' I go. 'We're heading for the ferry at lunchtime. I'll come back for you around one.'

He's there, 'This is going to seem even worse when I'm fully sober.'

I decide to just leave him to his misery. I pull the door behind me and I set off to grab myself an early-morning pint somewhere.

There's fock-all wrong with his leg, by the way. This is his payback for trying to stitch me up by offering Blodwyn the spare ticket. And for telling me that there were to be no pranks.

So what *actually* happened?

It's pretty simple. Like I said, we ended up having a great night out. There were pints involved and you can take it there were shots involved too. Ended up in a club called Whispers. Two or three in the morning, the goys storted to peel away. Christian was off his tits – he obviously forgot how to drink while he was in the States – and was the first to head back to the B&B. JP and Oisinn met up with the gruesome twosome from the ferry and ended up going back to *their* hotel.

But a lot of fun was had. It was just like the old times, in fact. Like we were all seventeen again.

I'd actually forgotten all about Fionn. I was chatting to these three student nurses. None of them were great – I mean, they are *all* bringing muffins to the picnic – but I was in that kind of form where that didn't actually *matter* for once? I was happy just to talk away. I was actually trying to explain Jamie Heaslip to them – to sum the dude up in an actual phrase.

In the end, the best I could do was, 'If this dude ate alphabet spaghetti, he would shit the word class.'

That's when one of them turned around and nodded at some dude in the corner, fast asleep, with his forehead on the table in a puddle of Cointreau. 'Is *e* awright?'

They were all from Manchester, even though they were, like, *based* in Cordiff?

I laughed. 'It's cool,' I went. 'He's with me. It's *his* actual stag I'm on? I actually thought he'd focked off back to the B&B.'

And that's when the idea suddenly came to me.

I was like, 'How much would I have to pay you to put his leg in a plaster cast?'

I knew it was wrong, even as I was saying it. But there's a bad streak in me that was always there and I accept that I'm probably never going to change.

The three birds were in a little bit of shock. They were like, 'Purr is leg in plasti? Will we heck as like!'

They were all a bit *Coronation Street* knicker factory actually.

I was like, 'What if I offered you a grand?'

A grand, of course, is a game-changer – in any focking currency.

We managed to get him outside and into the back of an Andy McNab. I had to put, like, three different cords into the ATM, but I managed to get them their money. Then we were suddenly bound for Cordiff General, with Fionn babbling away in the back about how much he loved his fiancée – 'She's the kindest, most sensitive, most intelligent . . .' – before he eventually conked out again, like I figured he would.

He slept like a baby while the three birds set his leg. Evil bitches as well – they even gave me a bottle of, like, placebo pills for him. Tell him to take one three times a day, they said. He'll be convinced that they're what's keeping his pain away.

They also taught me the word tibia. I wrote it down on the palm of my hand just in case Fionn started asking questions – which he did, of course.

So now I find an early house called The Widow Hutton. I wander in, order a pint of the Master, then sit at the bor, trying to decide how to play this thing.

I finally decide that I'm going to keep it to myself for now. Let the focker stew. It'll teach him a lesson for trying to stitch up the Ross-meister General.

It's, like, just after midday when my phone suddenly rings. I check the screen and it's, like, Sorcha. So I end up answering it.

She's all, 'Hey, Ross, how was the stag?'

I laugh. 'Er, pretty eventful,' I go. 'Let's just say that Erika's in for a bit of a surprise when she sees her supposed fiancé.'

This, for some reason, seems to go totally over her head.

'Did you enjoy the match?' she goes. 'Leinster played – oh my God – *so* amazing, didn't they?'

The girl wouldn't know a rugby ball if it hit her in the focking head.

'They *were* incredible,' I go. 'Probably one of the best days of my life.'

She's there, 'Okay, I'm glad you're in such good form, because I've got a couple of things to tell you.'

I *already* don't like the sound of where this conversation is headed. I ask the borman for a JD and Coke.

I'm like, 'What are you talking about, Babes?'

'Okay, your mum called into the shop again yesterday. Oh my God, Ross, did you know she's losing her hair?'

I end up having to hold in the laughter. I'm like, 'Really?'

'I'm not being a bitch, Ross, but it's falling out in actual clumps.'

'I think alopecia might actually run in her family. I've seen photographs of her grandmother. Her head looks like a focking Easter egg. Is that what you're ringing to tell me?'

'No, what I was ringing to tell you is that you were right. She *did* want something.'

'What did I tell you? I can read that focking woman like a Mr Man book.'

'She wants Honor to be in her movie.'

'What?'

'Ross, she wants her to play the lead. Little Zara Mesbur. Hallmork are coming to Ireland to make it next month.'

'Well, what kind of shekels are we talking?'

'We didn't discuss money. I told her I'd have to think about it, but it would probably be a no.'

'You said that? Do you mind me asking why?'

'Because Honor is – oh my God – spoiled enough as it is. I don't want her turning into one of those little Hollywood brats.'

'To be honest, I think she's pretty much already there. Anyway, is that everything?'

'No, I've one more thing to tell you.'

'Okay.'

'Now, brace yourself, Ross . . .'

'Go on.'

'Your aportment building has been evacuated.'

I'm like, 'Evacuated? Rosa Porks?'

'Rosa Parks, Ross. It's been declared unsafe for human habitation.'

I could be wrong, but she sounds actually happy to say it.

'Something to do with foundations – they're saying they were, like, compromised when they carried out that controlled explosion on the unfinished blocks. It was all over the news last night. They're saying they might end up having to demolish the entire building.'

'You have *got* to be shitting me?'

'So it looks like you're going to be staying with us for a little while longer.'

6.

Don't cry for me, Orgentina

Eleanor and David are back together again. Not only that, she told the poor sap that she was no longer confused about her feelings for him and that she might like to spend the rest of her life with him after all. So they went back to Paris – I shit you not – and went through the whole focking routine again, same restaurant, same ring, except this time when she said yes, she didn't change her mind when they got back to the hotel.

Women. How are we supposed to know what they want when they don't even focking know themselves?

'Maybe she saw what else was out there,' Fionn goes, 'and she suddenly realized just how good she'd had it,' which is a definite dig at me. 'You should do it as a service, Ross. Girls who are having doubts, they spend a night with you, then they spend a week trying to get you on the phone, and then their doubts suddenly go away.'

I was actually going to tell him the truth about his leg this morning – it's been, like, two weeks now – but, after that crack, I'm going to let him stew for another few days.

This is us on the driving range in Leopardstown, by the way. We planned this little outing weeks ago. I haven't exactly brought my A game, it has to be said. My stomach hurts like fock when I turn my hips, which means I can't actually drive the ball. I'm kind of, like, scared I'll tear something down there. So I'm just, like, chipping balls, with Fionn just standing there on his crutches like a spare one, watching me.

'How's the, er, Jackie Degg?'

I'm a prick, I know.

He's like, 'It's not too bad. I mean, there's no pain. The pills are obviously doing what they're supposed to do. I'm just cursing my own stupidity, that's all.'

'Yeah, no, you were a focking idiot alright. It's shit for you.'

'I just can't handle my drink.'

'Dude, I've been pointing that out since we were, like, fifteen years old. I never asked you, by the way, how did Erika take it?'

My guess is she shat halibut. Her husband in an ankle-to-hip plaster cast on her big day – what bride wouldn't?

'Erika was fine with it,' he goes, using his crutch to roll another ball across the mat to me. I bend down and stick it on the tee, at the same time giving him one of my scoobious looks.

I'm like, 'Fine with you wearing that focking thing in all the photographs? You said she was going to kill you?'

'Well, obviously she's not happy. But it was an accident. She understands that.'

It doesn't sound like the old Erika who we know and guard our testicles around.

I'm there, 'Did you tell her you were in a focking lappy? Because *I* will if you don't.'

'She *knew* you'd bring me to a lapdancing club, Ross.'

I stort sizing up my next shot, a bit disappointed, if I'm being honest. I just think, fock it, I might as well tell him now. And I'm just about to when he goes, 'Obviously, it meant the suit had to be adjusted.'

I'm like, 'Adjusted? What do you mean adjusted?'

'I mean, I can't get a trouser over the cast obviously. We had to go back to the suit hire place yesterday and actually buy the suit that I was planning to rent. They're cutting one of the legs off it.'

Have you ever got that sudden feeling that a practical joke might have gone too far?

I'm like, 'Fock.'

Now is probably the time to tell him. He might even be able to ring the place and tell them to hold off. But he's going to go balls out when he finds out what I've done. And so is Erika, especially after all the talk of us acting towards each other like a proper brother and sister. So I end up just bottling it.

'So, er, how *is* Erika?' I go. 'I haven't seen *or* heard from her.'

He's like, 'She's fine. She's been away for two or three days.'

'Away?' I go. 'Where?'

And that's when he says *the* most unbelievable thing.

He goes, 'She went to Aachen with Fabrizio,' and he tries to make it sound less of a deal than it actually is.

I'm there, 'What?'

'Aachen, Ross. It's in Germany.'

'Yeah, I know where Aachen is, Fionn . . .'

I hadn't a focking clue where Aachen was, by the way.

I'm there, 'My point is that they went away together – are we talking just the two of them?'

'Ross, don't try to make something out of this. He had a show-jumping competition.'

'So?'

'And he asked Erika to go with him – as a friend.'

'In his jet?'

'What does it matter how they got there? Yes, in his jet.'

I actually laugh.

'And you're cool with that, are you? As in, you don't think anything happened between them?'

He closes his eyes then, like he's decided that he doesn't want to hear it, that he's sick of me even bringing it up. 'Look,' he goes, 'I know you've always had a problem with Erika and me being together. There's obviously a whole psycho-incestuous subtext to your feelings . . .'

'Hey, I'm not going to lie to you. I think she can do better than you – and I'm saying that as someone who really, really likes you.'

'And possibly a homoerotic subtext as well . . .'

'A what?'

'Look, I'm asking you, Ross – as my friend, as my best man, as my soon-to-be brother-in-law – can you please just lay off the subject?'

'Okay, I'm not going to say another word about it.'

'Just be happy for us?'

'Hey, I'm happy for you.'

He becomes suddenly serious then. He's like, 'I never thought I'd feel this way about a girl again. Not after Aoife.'

Aoife was his girlfriend who died – some would say the love of his life.

I'm there, 'Hey, I'm hearing you, Dude.'

'Since Erika and I got together, I've just realized how – I don't know – how much time and energy we waste on things that don't really matter.'

'As in?'

'Well, everything. Work. Wanting a better house, a bigger car. What I call the supernumerary of life. None of those things matters when you're in love. Her going to Aachen with Fabrizio might have bothered me once. But when you're in love – really in love – you're above those petty jealousies. Do you understand what I'm saying?'

'Not very often, no.'

He laughs. 'Her going away with a male friend. Me breaking my leg in a lapdancing club four weeks before our wedding. Even you . . .'

'Dropping a log on your old dear's computer?'

'Exactly. It's amazing when you're in love how easy it is to let things go.'

That's when I should tell him the truth about his leg. It's, like, the perfect opportunity. But, again, I don't. I just put the club head under the ball and send it maybe thirty or forty yords.

He's there, 'Speaking of letting things go, I heard about your apartment.'

I'm like, 'Yeah, no, they've been ordered to, like, demolish the entire focking building. I'm beginning to wonder am I possibly jinxed.'

He rolls me another ball.

'Well,' he goes, 'Erika and I are going to be away on honeymoon for three weeks . . .'

Mustique, by the way. A gift from Erika's old dear.

'If you want to crash in our apartment . . .'

He's, like, totally sound, Fionn. I'd never let him know that, of course. But he's possibly *the* most decent human being I know, which is the reason I don't want to see him focked over.

I'm there, 'Dude, it's much appreciated. I might just stay in Sorcha's, though, until I find a place to possibly rent. Thanks, though.'

'Well,' he goes, 'thanks for being my best man. And I have to say, I did enjoy myself in Cardiff. It was a great stag. Like old times, huh?'

'Majorly.'

'Despite, well, how it ended.'

I try to get him off the subject.

'Two European Cups in three years as well. Did you hear the rumour that Superman wears Jonny Sexton pyjamas?'

He laughs, even though he's probably already heard it.

'Oh, by the way,' he suddenly goes, 'can you do something for me? A best-man duty.'

Because the big day's only, like, two weeks away.

I'm just there, 'Name it.'

'Okay,' he goes, 'well, obviously part of your function is to make sure that everything runs smoothly on the day. The woman who's organizing the reception is called Annice Arnesson . . .'

I'm like, 'Annice Arnesson? Jesus, she sounds like a complete ride.'

'She's from Denmark'

'She *is* a complete ride, then. Fock!'

'Annice has broken the day down into ten-minute blocks and she's drawn up a schedule of what should happen within each of those ten-minute blocks. I want you to liaise with her to make sure it all runs with military-style precision on the day.'

'Oh,' I go, 'I'll liaise. I'll give her a bell. Better still, I might even swing down to Powerscourt to meet her in person.'

'Just . . . be professional,' he goes.

And I think – er, who's he telling?

I recognize the tune. It's definitely Karunesh – Sorcha has everything that focker ever put out – although I don't know if it's off *Zen Breakfast* or *Osho Chakra Sounds*. Either way, it's doing the job. I can't remember the last time I saw Sorcha and Erika looking so chilled.

They're in the actual Ritz-Corlton, in one of the private treatment rooms – the bride and her bridesmaid – enjoying a Luxury Retreat Signature Day Spa Package. I took a drive down here to run through one or two things with Annice, who turned out to be a focking disgrace, by the way – the kind of ugly you'd have to throw a stick at to get rid of the following morning. Tight hair and an underbite. A serious waste of petrol.

Anyway, I just thought, since I'm here, I should show my face in the ESPA and say hello to the girls. It's obviously frowned on, roysh, but I slip around the door when I see the therapist pop out of the room to go for a slash.

And that's how I end up in here, listening to – that's it! – *Layers of Tranquillity* and looking at my wife and sister, in the – I don't know – flickering candlelight, lying face-up on adjoining beds, under just a couple of towels, their eyes covered with moist heat-therapy warming masks and their faces covered with what looks and smells very much to me like hummus.

If I had a bag of kettle chips now, it'd be lunch sorted.

That's what I'm just *about* to say, when Erika – totally out of the blue – goes, 'So I hear Ross is going to be staying with you for a little while longer?'

And that's when *I* should go, 'Er, sorry, girls – I'm in the actual room here.'

Except I don't. I decide to just stand where I am and have a sly listen to what Sorcha has to say.

'The entire building was an actual deathtrap,' she goes. 'They're saying it could have come down like a deck of cords.'

I watch a smile suddenly tug at Erika's nacho dip facemask. She goes, 'You must be secretly delighted, though, are you?'

Sorcha doesn't answer either way, just goes, 'Oh my God, I can't see your face – what's that in your voice?'

Erika *properly* laughs this time?

'I'm just saying, it must be nice for you having him around all the time.'

Sorcha – suddenly all super-defensive – goes, 'Well, he's amazing with Honor.'

'And what about with you?'

'I'm not going to deny it, Erika, he's been – oh my God – *so* supportive during the whole row with my dad over the house. He was the one who told me to give them a chance to apologize. He can be actually *sensitive?*'

'Do you want him back?'

Sorcha acts all offended then. 'Oh! My God! I can't believe you're asking me that!'

They were obviously throwing the focking champagne down their necks earlier.

'Come on, Sorcha – what's the alternative? You can't spend the rest of your life sitting in on your own, sieving bits of cork from the last bottle of wine in the house and Google Image Searching pictures of Gordon D'Arcy.'

Focking D'Arcy! I end up nearly blurting it out as well.

Sorcha goes, 'Oh my God, I'm sorry I told you that now. And it was Rob Kearney, just for your information.'

That's even worse. These are two girls – can I just point out – who hated Clongowes almost as much as *I* did?

Sorcha goes suddenly quiet then and I take that as my cue to stort tiptoeing towards the door. I have my hand on the actual handle when I hear her go, 'I nearly kissed him.'

Erika's like, 'Who?' the delight obvious in her voice. 'Rob Kearney?'

'No, not Rob Kearney. I'm talking about Ross.'

Erika's like, 'Oh my God!' like it's suddenly goss.

'I'd just cleared all my old toys out of Mum and Dad's attic and I was a bit upset and – I don't know – he was just so sweet . . .'

'Well, you know how I feel. I never knew *what* you saw in him.'

My own focking sister!

Sorcha carries on putting my case, fair focks to her. 'And – oh my God – he has been *so* supportive of me in my new job.'

'Supportive in what way?'

'He comes and helps me stack the shelves. He chats to me when the shop is quiet. Then, well, a few weeks ago . . .'

'Go on.'

'Mr Whittle came in and storted giving out yords to me for taking that shampoo I was telling you about off the shelves. He was, like, screaming at me and I was – oh my God – actually *scared*? The next thing, Ross just stood between us and I just felt – er, *hello*? – *so* safe.'

'Did Ross hit him?'

'No . . . but I was almost secretly hoping he would . . .'

Erika laughs. 'And you with your peace credentials.'

'I was thinking, punch him in the face, Ross. Punch him in the face!'

'Oh my God, you marched in all those Anti Iraq War protests!'

'I know – does that make me a hypocrite?'

Oh, shit. The therapist bird is coming back. I can see her through the frosted glass in the door, walking this way.

Okay, she cannot find me in here. It's just not an option. I stort looking around the room. There's, like, a glass door about ten feet away. I don't even have time to think. I whip it open and I'm straight through it. I manage to pull it closed behind me just as she's stepping back into the room.

It's only then that I realize I've stepped – fully clothed, by the way – into the focking sauna.

'How are you getting on, ladies?' the therapist one goes.

Sorcha's there, 'Oh my God, that massage was *so* amazing. Would it be possible to change the CD, though?'

Fock, I'm thinking – how long are they planning to be in here? Jesus Christ, I'm already sweating like Josef Fritzl on *MTV Cribs*.

'Do you have *Heart Chakra Meditation Two*?' Sorcha goes.

The woman's there, 'I think I do.'

'That'd be amazing. Erika, will we move over to those two beds next to the sauna?'

You have *got* to be shitting me!

They plonk themselves down on the loungers right outside the door. Which means I'm literally trapped in here, the sweat focking blinding me.

I hear Sorcha go, 'So how was your trip?' and she doesn't actually mean anything by it. It's, like, an innocent question.

Except Erika ends up totally flipping. She goes, 'Why the fock does everyone keep asking me about my trip?'

This is in the supposed relaxation suite, remember.

Sorcha's there, 'I was only asking . . .'

Erika goes, 'You weren't asking, Sorcha. You were implying.'

I'm suddenly having to strip down to my boxers. Which is a feat in itself. My chinos are actually stuck to my focking legs.

'I wasn't implying anything,' Sorcha tries to go.

Erika's there, 'Well, everyone else is. My mum. My dad. It's like, "How was your trip?" and what they're really asking is, "Are you still marrying Fionn?" '

'*I* wasn't asking that.'

'For fock's sake. I'm allowed to have friends.'

'I know.'

'I don't know why people can't just mind their own focking business.'

Jesus Christ, I'm dehydrating fast in here. I'm going to literally focking die if I don't get a drink now. I end up just grabbing the bucket with the ladle in it. I hold it with my two hands and I knock back – whatever the fock it is – maybe a litre of warm, probably sweat-drenched water. But I don't *give* a fock. It's a matter of life and basic death.

Outside, there's, like, a pause in the conversation. A long one. Maybe thirty seconds. Then Erika goes, 'I'm sorry, I'm just a bit tense. It's probably nerves.'

Except Sorcha's known Erika too long to be fooled by her.

'Well, if I believed you before,' she goes, 'I certainly don't believe you now. Something did happen in Aachen.'

'Nothing happened in Aachen.'

It doesn't convince Sorcha and it doesn't convince me. Or what's left of me. I lie on the floor, staring at the wooden beams above me, seeing literally spots.

I have no idea, roysh, what kind of a look passes between them, but it's Sorcha who speaks next. 'Oh my God, you're still in love with him. Erika, you're getting married in, like, ten days' *time*?'

'I'm well aware of that, Sorcha.'

Sorcha's there, 'Oh my God, so Ross was right all along?'

There had to be a reason why Erika wasn't pissed off about Fionn's leg ending up in a cast. Or even the idea of him going to a lappy. And that reason is obviously guilt.

Jesus Christ, I feel like I'm about to die here.

'No, Ross was *not* right, Sorcha. Because I'm marrying Fionn.'

'He's a lovely guy, Erika. It would – oh my God – devastate him.'

'I told you, I'm *going* to marry him.'

'Well, I'm just saying it as your bridesmaid. He's the most dependable person in the world. And he's, like, so in love with you. You would be *so* secure, Erika. Look, this Fabrizio thing, it's probably just a wobble.'

Erika takes a deep breath – actually, it's more like a sigh – then she says she's going for a swim. Sorcha follows her out to the Swarovski crystal-lit pool.

I get back on my hands and knees again, push the door and manage to somehow crawl out of the sauna and towards the aromatherapy shower fifteen, maybe twenty feet away. I wave my hand in front of the motion sensor, then I lie there on the tiles, letting this – I think it's a word – but *torrent* of peppermint and relaxing lavender water just pour over me.

I even drink about a litre of the focking stuff, literally sucking it up off the shower floor.

After about ten minutes under the water – lying there, still in just my boxer shorts – I stort to feel something close to human again. And I lie there, with my back against the cold and, like, soothing wall, thinking more and more about what I just heard.

This is no wobble. As I've said all along, Fionn *is* the focking wobble. Something happened between Erika and Fabrizio in Aachen. And if I ever get the strength to pick myself up off this floor, I'm going to find out what it was.

I come downstairs for breakfast to find Hennessy in the kitchen – get this – having a casual root through the laundry basket, basically inspecting Sorcha's underwear. He doesn't even have the decency to stop when *I* walk in on him?

He goes, 'Someone's written on your car again,' holding a purple V-string to the light – it's *like* a thong but it's not *actually* a thong?

'No,' I go, 'that's been there for a while.'

He's like, 'This is fresh paint. Capital letters. Just says "Prick".'

I'm there, 'Okay, that actually *is* new.'

He laughs.

I snatch the V-er out of his hand and move the basket out of his reach.

That's when he turns around and goes, 'She's offering a million.'

I'm like, 'Okay, are we talking about Regina now?'

'No, we're talking about Jane fucking Fonda. Who the fuck else are you trying to extort seven figures from?'

'Look, chillax, will you? Okay. A million. I mean, yeah, no, it's obviously a lot less than I wanted.'

'Yeah, well, I think we're gonna have to come down some.'

'She took my old man for one point seven, can I just remind you?'

'Lot of it's spent. Look, I think I can push her to one point two.'

I'm like, 'One point two?' cracking on to be basically disgusted. 'I'll tell you what, Hennessy, why don't I give her a bell myself? Just to let her know that I'm not going to be dicked around on this thing. Hearing my voice again might even bring her to her sudden senses.'

He suddenly rips into me. 'If you even attempt to contact that woman, I will personally put you back in hospital.'

'It's just this thing seems to be going on forever.'

'I will put you back in that fucking hospital. Except this time, it'll be long-term care.'

'Fair enough. I just mentioned it as a possible option.'

'Well, it isn't a possible option. So get it out of your stupid fucking head.'

He storts making his way towards the door then.

'*I'll* tell you how we're gonna play this thing,' he goes. 'I'm gonna tell her we want one point four. But then a week or two later, I'm gonna let her know that we're prepared to take one point two. Then this thing dies.'

He doesn't ask me what I even think. He's not actually *looking* for my permission? He's out the door and up the path before I've said another word, a pair of Sorcha's blue plaid cotton ruched-back hiphuggers hanging from his pocket.

'It's *so* an amazing offer,' Sorcha goes. She's got the good Denby out, I notice. 'Especially, Fionnuala, coming from you. I mean, you are, like – oh my God – *so* an inspiration to me . . .'

The old dear's delighted with that comment. Her hair is still falling out – that's the other thing I notice. There's, like, one humungous bald spot around the crown of her head that she's doing her best to hide.

'So is the combover *in* for women this year?' I make sure to go. 'Or is that just an LA thing?'

Sorcha rushes to her defence, of course. 'Ross,' she goes, 'should you not be over there plunging the sink?'

It's blocked. She's been on at me for, like, two days to sort it out. She says she'd do it herself except it's – oh my God – *eeewww*!

I wander over to it and grab the plunger, which Sorcha brought home from work (€1). The old dear just sips her coffee, all delighted with herself.

'Like I told you,' Sorcha goes, 'I think Ross and I – *as* Honor's co-parents – are already concerned about her behaviour. She can be – oh my God – *so* bold and we're partly to blame for possibly spoiling her. What Honor needs – especially at a time when we're all suddenly having to scale back our expectations – is as normal a childhood as possible.'

Yeah. That's why our Vietnamese nanny is collecting her from her very expensive primary school and bringing her to her Italian *bel canto* singing class.

I don't say that, though. I just keep on plunging.

The old dear goes, 'Well, as a mother myself, Sorcha, I have to say that I completely understand. I'm disappointed, naturally. But only because I think Honor would have made a fabulous Zara Mesbur.'

Sorcha gives her the sad eyes and goes, 'You *do* understand – don't you, Fionnuala? – that I would love to say yes. Especially because it's you. I mean, you're, like, one of my top three female role models. You're – oh my God – *so* empowering.'

'Yeah,' I go, 'you're like a fat, bald Beyoncé.'

Sorcha's there, 'Ross, your mother has a dermatological condition!' She's such a suck-orse.

'Ignore him,' the old dear goes. 'It's what I always do. Anyway, forget about it, Sorcha. I just felt I had to ask. There's no doubt that little granddaughter of mine *has* something. I mean, I hope you don't mind, but I showed one or two of her photographs to the director that Hallmark have hired and he said, "I have to get this kid in front of a camera." That's a direct quote I'm giving you.'

Sorcha sad-smiles her again, then pushes the biscuits at her. 'What do you think they'll do now, Fionnuala?'

'Oh, I expect they'll cast some precocious US child-actor in the role. With one of these frightfully fake "stage-Oirish" accents.'

'Oh my God, I hate when they do that in movies.'

I look over my shoulder, just as the old dear is biting into a Fox's Golden Crunch. It's like watching TJ Miller get eaten by the focking monster in *Cloverfield*.

'Look,' she goes, 'I understand completely what you're saying, Sorcha. I've *lived* in Hollywood, remember. I know how difficult it is to be one of these – what's this the supermarket tabloids call them? *Supermums.*'

That gets Sorcha's instant attention.

The old dear goes, 'I mean, I said to Gwen Stefani recently . . .'

'Oh! My God! You *met* Gwen Stefani?'

'Yes, of course. And she just happened to be with *her* little two.'

'Kingston and Zuma?'

'That's them. They were all having babyccinos in that little Starbucks on Pico and Robertson. I said, "Gwen, I don't know how you do it – combining your singing career and your work as a high-end fashion designer with your role as a mother to two children who are constantly in the public eye and yet who've turned out to be so well behaved and well adjusted." And she said to me, "Fionnuala," because she's read three of my books, "it takes a very, very strong woman to do what I do." '

I stop plunging and go, 'Sorcha, she's trying to get inside your head,' because people don't realize, roysh, how focking manipulative the woman can be.

Sorcha goes, 'There was actually a whole article in one of my magazines recently about Supermums.'

I'm there, '*She's* obviously read the same orticle – that's what this is about!'

'There was a photograph – oh my God, *so* cute – of Max and Emme, as in Jennifer Lopez's kids? They were just, like, hanging out with their mom. And the caption was like – oh my God – look how *actually* normal her kids have turned out, *despite* being always in the limelight?'

The shit storts coming up the plughole then. Bits of food and all sorts of crap.

I've one eye on that and one eye on what's happening behind me. The old dear fake-smiles her. 'But you have far too much on your plate, Sorcha, with this . . . *amazing* new shop of yours.'

She's trying to make her feel shit about herself – and from the look on Sorcha's face, she's actually succeeding.

'It could turn into a career,' Sorcha tries to go. 'Mr Whittle's hoping to have, like, six stores just like it by the end of the year. A company expanding that quickly is going to need senior executives . . .'

'Well, that's where your future lies, then, Sorcha.'

'Mr Whittle said I'm doing a very competent job, Fionnuala. In fact, we've put the whole shampoo thing behind us.'

The old dear goes, 'What shampoo thing?'

Shit.

I have to think fast.

'Shut the fuck up!' I hear myself suddenly roar.

'Ross!' they both go at the exact same time.

Then Sorcha's there, 'Ross, what *has* gotten into you today?'

I wave the sink plunger at them in what could possibly be described as a threatening manner and – obviously just bluffing – I go, 'My daughter will not be appearing in any Hallmork movie – and that's the end of it!'

And that's when I look up and notice Honor and Linh standing in the doorway of the kitchen.

Honor goes, 'What Hallmark movie?'

'*A daughter may outgrow your lap,*' the old man goes, '*but she will never outgrow your heart.*' He looks at me over the top of his reading glasses and he's like, 'What do you think?'

He's going to have a hord job selling that one to me after the total and utter freak attack that Honor ended up having in the kitchen yesterday when she was told that she wasn't allowed to star in *Mom, They Said They'd Never Heard of Sundried Tomatoes.*

Screamed the focking house down. She called her mother – I swear to fock – a bitch and a pig in a pant-suit. And when I told her that she was being possibly unfair, she turned on me. She went – this is, like, word for word – "Oh my God, you're so lame. I'm actually embarrassed that you're my father." '

So a daughter may outgrow your lap, but she will never outgrow your hort – that's a difficult one for me to swallow right now.

'Who even said it?' I go.

The old man's got his big book of quotations open on the desk in front of him.

He's there, 'It just says Author Unknown. But there's another one here that I rather like, too. *The father of a daughter is nothing but a high-class hostage. A father turns a stony face to his sons, berates them, shakes his antlers, paws the ground, snorts, runs them off into the under-brush, but when his daughter puts her arm over his shoulder and says, "Daddy, I need to ask you something," he is a pat of butter in a hot frying pan . . .*

'Quote-unquote, Ross. And that's Garrison Keillor, if you don't mind! Man or woman, I couldn't tell you. Isn't it wonderful, though?'

He's supposedly getting his thoughts together for his father-of-the-bride speech. He closes the book, looking pretty focking pleased with himself, and goes, 'I am indeed blessed, Kicker.'

I'm like, 'What the fock are you talking about?'

He goes, 'With my daughter, naturally.' And then he throws in, 'And my son, of course,' as a definite after-thought.

I'm there, 'You'd want to lay off the focking brandy, do you know that?'

'Well, it's just the thought, Ross, that in five days' time, I'm going to be walking her up the aisle – as her father – to deliver her into the care of a fine young man who truly loves her and whom she truly loves. Do you know, I think I'm becoming rather emotional here. Can you imagine what I'm going to be like on Saturday, Ross?'

'I'm presuming you won't have half a bottle of XO in you, will you?'

'She's never held it against me, you know?'

He's *seriously* hammered. He's supposed to only drink in, like, moderation because of his hort condition.

I'm like, 'Who?'

'Your sister, Ross. For not *being* in her life for all those years. For never telling her the truth that I was her father. And that's . . . that's a miracle, Ross. That she's given me – her father – the opportunity to try to make up for all those squandered years . . .'

I'm like, 'Yeah, whatever,' except I'm kind of laughing.

'Look at how she's turned out, Kicker! Tell me that's not a miracle! She's kind. She's caring. She's sensitive . . .'

He checks his notes.

'Did I mention thoughtful?'

I'm there, 'She certainly puts on a good show,' at the same time thinking about what she probably got up to with Fabrizio in France or Germany or wherever the fock Fionn said that Aachen even was.

'And now I'm going to walk her up the aisle – as her father!'

I hear the front door suddenly slam. At first I presume it's just Helen – back from dinner in Peploe's with Fionn's old dear, who seems to have become her bezzy mate all of a sudden. But then the study door opens and in walks – speak of the devil – Erika herself.

She looks incredible, especially for a girl with all the shit that she's obviously got on her mind.

I think I remember Sorcha mentioning that *everyone* was going to be mixing tan with white this summer.

I'm like, 'Hey,' playing it cool at first, 'I thought I would have heard from you.'

She looks at me like I'm pork luncheon meat. She's like, 'What?'

I'm there, 'Yeah, no, when Fionn came home from Cordiff with his leg in a jocker, I thought you'd be straight on the phone to me. That big focking plaster cast is going to be in all the photos. I expected you to go ape-shit. You must have a lot on your mind.'

From the way she looks at me, I can tell she's trying to work out whether Sorcha spilled. In the end, she obviously decides that I know squat because she goes, 'Do you ever wonder what your life would have been like, Ross, if you'd been given enough oxygen at birth?' which is weak by Erika's normal standards.

The old man – he really is shit-faced – goes, 'Oh, yes, of course! Poor Fionn's leg! I said it to Helen. DEGT, Girl! There'll have been horseplay. One of these impromptu rolling mauls that I've seen Ross do – him and his chaps.'

Neither of us even looks at him.

'Speaking of horseplay,' I go, turning up the heat, 'how did you get on in Aachen?'

Erika goes, 'What?' except she says it in a really, like, *defensive* way? If that's not a guilty conscience, then I don't know what is.

I'm there, 'Horseplay – wasn't Fabrizio supposedly jumping?'

'Oh,' she goes, 'yeah, no, he got on fine.'

'Good ride, was it?'

'What?'

'As in, where did he finish?'

'Oh, he, em . . . he won.'

'Did he?'

'Yeah.'

'Well, then I'm going to *say* fair focks.'

It's the old man, though, who comes out with *the* most interesting line of the night. 'Unfortunately,' he goes, 'he's going to miss the big day.'

I'm like, 'What are you talking about?'

'Well,' he goes, 'he's had to go to – where was it, Darling?'

Erika's like, 'Stockholm.'

'Yes, that's it,' the old man goes. 'For some training camp or other. Terrible shame, of course. I think we'd all grown rather fond of Fabrizio.'

I'm there, 'Yeah, no, I'm certainly shocked to hear he's suddenly off the scene.'

Erika just stares me out of it, but decides not to take the bait. Instead, she turns to the old man and goes, 'Did I leave my phone here this afternoon?'

He pulls a face like he's racking his brains for the answers. 'I did see it,' he goes, 'and now I'm trying to think where.'

Then he says he's almost sure it was in the living room and he staggers out of the study into the hall, with Erika following him – one hand on his back to make sure he stays upright, the focking drunk.

I carry on sitting there for, like, a minute or two, then all of a sudden I hear a phone ringing on the old man's desk. It's coming from underneath his *Irish Times* special supplement on the Euro Zone debt crisis.

The call is coming from the house, which means that Erika is probably dialling it herself to see can she hear it ringing.

And that's when it suddenly pops into my head. Like all my best ideas, it comes to me in, like, an *instant?*

I know I have to be quick here, because I can hear Erika go, 'It's coming from your study.'

I go into her contacts and I delete my name and number. Then I go into Fabrizio's details and I change his number to, like, *my* number? Which means, of course, that when *she* texts *him*, it's going to come to me. And when *I* text *her*, she's going to think it's from Fabrizio.

It's wrong, I know. But then so is marrying someone you don't actually love.

No sooner have I finished screwing around with her contacts list – and, I suppose, her life – than she steps back into the study. She just snatches the thing out of my hand.

I tell her it was under the old man's newspaper. She tells me I'm a fucking orsehole and it's obvious I'm never going to change. Then she's gone.

Shadden wants to apologize. I tell Ronan it's already forgotten, except he still insists on putting me through it.

In she comes, into the kitchen, while I'm trying to make myself a bacon sandwich. The really focked-up thing is that *she's* actually a lot more comfortable talking to me about it than I am talking to her. I'm supposed to be, like, the adult here, yet I can't even look her in the eye.

I'm there going, 'Forget about it, Shadden. We were all young once. Blah, blah, blah.'

But she's like, 'Age is not an excuse. What we did – using your apartment like that – it was very disrespectful. And that's not how I was raised.'

I feel like going, 'Er, I've *met* your focking old pair, remember.'

Except I don't. Instead, I go, 'Yeah, no, that's cool, Shadden.'

Ronan's there, 'She has something *for* you, Rosser,' because I still can't even look at her.

It turns out to be, like, a bottle of wine – either an expensive one or a cheap one that she picked up in Aldi and just stuck into a bag from Mitchell & Son's. My guess is the first, roysh, because, unlike her old pair, she actually has a bit of class about her. And that's what I don't *actually* get? I mean, it's pretty obvious that her family *aren't* what my old dear used to call PLUDs – or People Like Us, Dahling. And yet, in fairness to her, Shadden very, very nearly is.

She goes, 'I'm so sorry and I hope you'll accept this bottle of wine along with my apologies.'

It's actually impossible not to like this girl. But, at the same time, I'm thinking, how could a father like Kennet turn out a kid who's, like, so different?

Ronan looks at me and goes, 'That you two squeer, then, is it, Rosser?'

I'm like, 'Yeah, we're square. Thanks, Shadden.'

Then off they trot. On the way out of the gorden, I hear Ronan go, 'See, I toalt you he was sowunt,' and I can't tell you how amazing that makes me suddenly feel.

I head back to bed with my bacon sandwich. Middle of a weekday afternoon – who could blame me? I put it on the old bedside locker and I whip out my phone.

I lie there just staring at it, thinking long and hord about what I'm going to write – what message I'm going to send to my sister from this great friend of hers who's supposedly only plutonic.

In the end, roysh, I go with a simple 'X'.

I get nothing back for ages. In fact, I finish my sandwich and watch the entire of 4 *Live* and *The Daily Show* before she comes back to me with 'Stop!'

I think, stop? Okay, that could mean literally anything. It could mean *actually* stop. Or it could be, like, playful.

I take a punt. It's probably rushing the conversation along but I just go, 'I really enjoyd wot happend in aachen.'

She's straight back this time with, 'Dont say that.'

I'm like, 'Why not?'

And she's like, 'Shouldnt hav happend.'

My hort, I have to admit, is beating in literally double time.

I'm there, 'I want you erika, i will come back to ireland for u.'

She goes, 'I dont want u to come back, u shud never hav come here in the first place.'

I'm there, 'I love u.'

There's no instant reply back to that one either. It takes a good half an hour and I'm just on the point of following it up with 'X' when she goes, 'Its too late Fabrizio.'

'Hello.'

'Is that Ross?'

'Yeah.'

'Do you do pipe insulation?'

'Fock off!'

Sophie says she was – oh my God – *so* the skinniest person in Krystle last weekend. At the same time, she's having a nosey around the shop, sort of, like, sniggering to herself at the plastic boules sets (€2) and the tea bag squeezers (€1) and the Happy Bar Mitzvah cards (50c) as long as your name is Mensch and the dog bowls (€1) as long as your dog's name is Mensch as well.

Chloe is holding up this, like, plaster saint (€2) and asking Sorcha who it's actually supposed to be? Sorcha says she thinks it's Saint Bridget and Chloe says – oh my God – she didn't realize that Bridget was *actually* good-looking?

They're only in here to rip the piss. All of them. Especially Amie with an ie, who keeps holding up various things – like the Mary McAleese 1997 Presidential Election Souvenir Book (€1) and the cocoa-dusted Christmas truffles (50c) with the best-before date of 31 August – and going, 'Get it or regret it!' while the other two cackle like focking witches, which I suppose is what they are.

Poor Sorcha is, like, pleading with them to put shit down. She's going, 'Girls, are you going to buy something or are you here to just mock?'

I'm about to run the three of them out the door when all of a sudden my phone beeps. It's, like, a text message from Erika.

It's just like, 'Im sory about last nite, just v emotional rite now.'

I think about what my reply is going to be for a good thirty seconds. Then I go, 'Its ok, i wud forgive u anything,' and then I throw in a little 'x' obviously just to keep up the illusion.

She hits me back with, 'This is gdbye Fabrizio, please, i realy dont want there to be any contact btwn us, its not fair on fionn and its not fair on u or i either, hav a gr8 life x.'

Sorcha goes, 'Who are you texting, Ross?' at the same time snatching a CD of the Swarovski Orchestra playing forty-one *National Anthems of the World* (€1) out of Amie with an ie's hand.

I'm there, 'Er, no one really.'

I decide then that I'd better go big with the next one because I'm obviously losing the girl here. So I just go, 'Erika I love you x o x.'

It's a good, like, three minutes before she replies. And while I'm waiting to hear back from her, a woman walks into the shop in, like, a belted trenchcoat, carrying a men's leather briefcase.

She storts scanning the shelves, taking a huge interest in the jelly moulds in the shape of rabbits (€1) and the boardgames with the sun-bleached boxes (€2) and the bags of – I shit you not – banana-flavoured coffee (€1 for two kilos).

My phone beeps. Erika again. 'I love you too Fabrizio but this is the way it has to be, pleas respect that.'

I decide to get right to the hort of the matter with my next one. 'U dont love fionn – i know that for a fact, if u dont love him u shudnt marry him x x.'

She comes back with, 'This is the same ground we went over in aachen. You and I are in the past, please let me go and let me get on with my life.'

The woman who walked into the shop a second ago suddenly steps up to me. She's like, 'Hello, could you tell me is Sorcha O'Carroll-Kelly around?'

Sorcha looks up from the toaster pockets (€1 for four) that she's arranging on a revolving rack and goes, 'I'm Sorcha O'Carroll-Kelly,' obviously not sensing trouble the same way I do.

The woman sticks out her hand. 'Helen Tuffy,' she goes. 'I'm a social worker.'

Sorcha gives her the old wet fish. She's like, 'A social worker? Is everything okay?'

I can see Chloe and Sophie and Amie with an ie are suddenly all ears.

'Can we talk somewhere a little more private?' the woman goes.

She's bet-down, by the way. She actually looks like if your face could have period pains.

Sorcha goes, 'Do you want to come through?' and she leads us into the little office at the back of the shop.

'Oh,' Sorcha goes, 'this is my husband, Ross, by the way. So what's this concerning?'

The woman gives us both a big patronizing smile, then goes, 'Well, part of my brief is to investigate situations in which children might be at risk.'

Sorcha just looks at me with her mouth wide open. It reminds me of the time I tried to explain the bonus try system to her. She's like, 'Ross, what's going on? Is she talking about Honor?'

I'm there, 'Yeah, what are you talking about? Honor's not at risk.'

'Well,' she has the actual cheek to go, 'that's what I would like to determine. I suppose the term "at risk" as we would classically understand it would involve either abuse or the threat of it. In recent years an increasing proportion of my workload has involved investigating cases where children are at risk of poverty.'

You can imagine how that goes down with Sorcha *and* me.

I'm like, 'Poverty?'

The three girls must be listening at the door, roysh, because I hear Chloe go, 'Oh! *My* God!'

Sorcha goes, 'Honor's not at risk of poverty. She . . . she plays the viola. Ross, tell her.'

'Poverty,' the woman goes, 'has nothing to do with class – that's becoming increasingly true in the current climate.'

The woman puts down her briefcase on Sorcha's desk, flicks the two catches and whips out this, like, blue folder, which I take to be our file. Sorcha looks at me, then goes to mouth something, except she can't think of anything to say, even silently, so she just shakes her head, her eyes just filling up, like this is her worst possible nightmare.

'So,' the woman goes, 'how long have you been operating this . . . *discount* store?' and she says discount store like she might as well be saying crack den or knocking shop.

Sorcha doesn't get a chance to answer because I don't let her. I'm just there, 'Okay, what focking business is that of yours?'

She's full of it, this one. She's there, 'I'm just doing my job.'

'And so is my wife. In very difficult focking circumstances. And she's doing it to put food in our daughter's stomach and keep a roof over her focking head. And you dare to come in here with your folder and your stupid focking questions about poverty.'

'I'm bound by law,' she tries to go, 'to investigate all complaints of possible neglect.'

I'm like, 'Whoa, whoa, whoa – complaints?'

Sorcha's there, 'Who complained?'

The woman goes, 'I have to treat that information with the utmost . . .'

'Tell me who was it?' I go, because I've already got a pretty good idea.

'That's confidential information and that's how it'll be treated.'

I look at Sorcha. I'm there, 'I know exactly who it was. It was my old dear.'

Sorcha's like, 'Why would Fionnuala do something like that?'

I'm there, 'Out of spite. Because you told her to shove her stupid movie up her orse.'

'Your mum wouldn't do something like that, Ross.'

I turn to the woman. 'It *was* her, wasn't it?'

Her face says it all. 'I have no desire to enter into a guessing game with you,' she tries to go.

I end up just losing it with her.

I'm there, 'Okay, you've had your meeting,' and I snatch the file out of her hands. I shove it back into her briefcase and slam the thing shut. Sorcha doesn't say a word to me. She's still in shock.

I morch back into the shop, with the woman following me, going, 'You're not helping your daughter's situation.'

I walk to the door of the shop and I fock the case out into the middle of the Powerscourt Townhouse Centre, nearly decapitating some poor focker sipping a coffee in Pygmalion.

'This isn't the end of the matter,' the woman goes. 'There'll be a home visit.'

'Make sure and give us plenty of notice,' I go. 'I'll bake a focking cake.'

I turn around. Sorcha has drifted back into the shop. She's in, like, total shock, but she tries to put on a brave face by continuing on working. She storts rearranging a rack of pocket umbrellas (€1) according to colour.

Sophie goes, 'Oh my God, Sorcha, is everything okay?' and she says it with, like, a big smirk on her face.

I turn to the three of them – we're talking Sophie, Chloe *and* Amie with an ie – and I go, 'Do you want to see yourselves out, or do you want to take the same route as that woman's focking briefcase?'

I'm watching *The Morning Show with Mortin King and Sybil Mulcahy* and at the same time I'm back sex-texting my sister. Actually, that's not a *hundred* per cent true? I don't put sex on the table straight away. I decide to, like, build up to it. Our last conversation ended with her telling me to let her go so she can marry Fionn. But I know that deep down that's not what she really wants.

I'm in Dublin. That's actually what I text her first. I go, 'Erika im here x.'

She texts me straight back just a question mork, which I take to mean, 'What?'

So I go, 'Im here – here to stop u makin the biggst mistake of ur life xxx.'

She goes, 'Ur in ireland?'

'Yes x.'

'Fab u shouldnt hav come back, I told u not to come back.'

I go, 'I cant stop thinkin about u x x.'

She's there, 'Do u think its any diffrent for me?'

I go, 'I think about u all the time. The way ur hair moves. Ur amazing legs. Ur beautiful eyes. I think about ur soft lips against mine. Ur tongue in my mouth. Then some of ur clothes especially the realy tight stuff u somtimes wear x.'

I wonder have I possibly pushed her too far then, because for maybe five minutes I don't get anything back. I just sit there and carry on listening to Sybil chatting to some poor fock with Blue Skin Disorder – a disease that only affects one in, I don't know, billions. It's actually quite funny.

Then my phone beeps and it ends up being Erika again. And let's just say the conversation becomes suddenly very inappropriate. 'I want to feel u inside me,' she goes.

She's got a mouth on her like a toilet seat in a bus station when you get her going. But there's no denying that I've *also* got the gift of the gab when it comes to this kind of shit. It's not long before the conversation has descended into the usual back-and-forth of your something-somethings make me all something-something and I wouldn't mind blahdy-blahing all over your blahdy blahdy blah-blahs.

Erika ends up giving every bit as good as she's getting, by the way. It's actually *she* who mentions meeting up – she didn't put up much of a fight in the end, as I suspect she didn't in Aachen – then it's me who suggests maybe getting a room, even for just an hour or two.

She goes, 'The westbury @ 6' – the girl who's supposedly marrying one of my best friends in the world in, like, two days' time.

I know exactly what I'm going to do. I go, 'I will see you there x.'

The day passes slowly. I spend the morning and afternoon watching TV and sort of, like, quietly congratulating myself on my ability to talk any woman in the world into bed, even if it is an actual blood relative and nothing is probably going to happen.

Sorcha rings from work to say that Linh was just on to her. She collected Honor from school and the kid ended up having another focking piss-fit.

'She's locked herself in Linh's cor,' Sorcha goes.

I'm like, 'The Kia?'

She ends up losing it with me. 'What does the make of the cor matter, Ross? She's refusing to open the doors until Linh promises to bring her to Dundrum Town Centre.'

'I didn't know those cors even *had* central locking, that's all. So where are they now?'

'In the cor pork of Mount Anville.'

'Okay. Well, why doesn't Linh just pretend she's going to take her to Dundrum, then as soon as Honor opens the door, tell her to go and fock herself?'

I can tell from Sorcha's silence what she thinks of this idea. I might as well have suggested hanging our daughter out of an upstairs window by her focking ankles. If you want my opinion, that might actually be worth considering. I wouldn't imagine Blanket Jackson has turned out to be half as big an orsehole as our daughter is.

'What,' Sorcha goes, 'and fracture her trust in adult authority figures?'

Jesus Christ.

I'm there, 'She's only playing up, Sorcha, because of this movie thing. We possibly shouldn't keep giving in to her.'

I hear Sorcha sigh. Then she goes, 'Okay, I'll tell Linh she can bring her. But just for a fro-yo and a quick look around BT2. And possibly Harvey Nichs,' and then she hangs up, leaving me just shaking my head.

I go back to thinking about Erika. I need to stay focused. As the time of our supposed date approaches, I stort to get the old butterflies-in-the-tummy feeling, which I put down to pretty much nerves.

At five o'clock, I grab a quick Jack Bauer, then I get dressed up – even have a splash of the new Tom Ford. I don't know why I go to all the effort. I suppose when you're acting, you sort of, like, go into character, don't you?

Then I tip out to the cor.

I point the Lambo in the direction of town. I try to come up with a gameplan. That's what big players do. I'll knock on the door, I think, then when she answers it, I'll have my iPhone out and I'll go, 'Expecting someone else, were you?' and I'll film her reaction.

Then, I don't know what I'll do. Probably show the footage to Fionn. Maybe even stick it up on YouTube.

Erika texts me just as I'm porking. She's like, 'Room 108. Waiting for you x.'

That's when I stort to feel a little bit bad. The old conscience is suddenly having its say. But then I remind myself why I'm actually doing this. Me and Fionn have had our differences over the years. But we played rugby together and I don't want to see him marrying a bird who's going to end up dumping his orse – if not now, then for the next Fabrizio Bettega who breezes into town with his Aviators and his cricket jumpers and his bullshit words.

Fionn deserves better, the ugly fock.

So I wander into the Westbury. I walk up the stairs, past reception and into the, I suppose, elevator. Then I hit the button for the first floor.

The doors open again and I wander down the corridor. I'm doing the right thing stopping this whole sham. I've been saying it from day one that they weren't even suited, except no one was listening to me.

I find the room. I pause for a second, just to whip out my iPhone, then I call up the camera app and I knock.

Through the door, I can hear Erika go, 'Just a second,' the excitement obvious in her voice.

Then she reefs it open.

I don't *get* the reaction that I'm expecting? Instead of being, like, shocked, she ends up being, I don't know, crushed.

It's hord to explain but, as it dawns on her what's actually happened here, it's like all of the energy that basically *is* Erika suddenly leaves her – happens right in front of my eyes – like the air being suddenly let out of a balloon.

It's straight away obvious that this time I've gone too far.

See, Erika and I have always been frenemies, from way back, even before we found out we were brother and sister. But the thing is, I've never managed to get the better of her until this precise moment. I can honestly say that this is the first time I've ever properly hurt Erika – and I don't like the way it makes me feel.

I'm suddenly remembering what she said to me that day in Fionn's old pair's gaff. How she prayed I'd pull through when I was in a coma and things were looking touch and go. How she wanted us to finally stop hurting each other. How she wanted us to have an actual brother–sister relationship.

I know now that all of that is suddenly gone. It's gone forever.

'Erika . . .' I try to go.

She just shakes her head, not saying a word, just standing there in – I can't help but notice – some very sexy night attire.

I watch her eyes fill up with tears.

Now, I've seen a thousand birds cry. I'm a hord dog to keep on the porch and women's tears just go with the territory. Most of them cry because they can't have what they want – they learn it in the pram – and once you understand that, you become kind of, like, *hordened* to it?

But this is different. I've genuinely hurt this girl – I've cut her to the core – and I know that there's nothing I can say that's ever going to fix it.

I try anyway. That'd be me all over. I go, 'I just wanted to stop you and Fionn making the worst mistake of your lives.'

She shoves me in the chest and I fall back against the wall of the corridor. Then she slams the door. But I can still hear her through, like, three inches of solid wood, sobbing her hort out, in her underwear.

Fionn laughs. He says I'm more nervous than he is and he's the one supposedly getting married. He asks me if I'm okay and I tell him of course – why wouldn't I be?

'Even last night,' he goes, 'when we were having those few pints in Finnegan's, you just seemed a bit on edge.'

JP tries to be the funnyman then. 'Even when he found out they had the same father,' he goes, 'I don't think Ross ever gave up hope that he'd be standing where you're standing today.'

This, for some reason, is considered hilarious. Even Christian and Oisinn end up going red in the focking face from laughing.

'It's not that,' I go, 'I'm just possibly nervous about the whole speech thing.'

Which is horseshit, of course. It's because I haven't seen or heard from Erika since the Westbury two nights ago. I've left, like, twenty messages, but she hasn't returned any of my calls.

This is all of us stood in Donnybrook Church, by the way. Fionn's still on crutches. Still in the full-leg cast. Fock it. I never did get around to telling him the truth. In my defence, it's been quite a week.

'Give us a flavour,' Oisinn goes.

I'm like, 'What?'

'Of what to expect. What stories are you going to tell?'

'Er . . .'

Christian goes, 'What about the time Charlie Bird turned up at the school on the day of the Leaving Cert. results to interview the

Castlerock student who got maximum points. And you pretended you were Fionn . . .'

I have to admit, that *actually* happened. I even ended up on the *Six One* news, going, 'I don't understand it myself, Chorlie. I'm usually a total dipshit.'

All the goys are laughing. Even Fionn. I'm thinking, is he going to be still laughing in, like, twenty minutes' time?

I turn around and look at the, I suppose, *congregation*? I spot Eleanor and David sitting in the second row and I think, fock – I toally forgot *he'd* be here today.

Have you ever felt that the world is, like, closing in on you?

The dude is just, like, staring at me, his eyes narrowed, a confused look on his face, like he knows that he knows me – it's just he doesn't know where *from*?

I can see him even nudging Eleanor, who's looking pretty fine, it has to be said, in the exact same Marchesa midi that Sorcha was looking at recently in BTs, a sideswept fringe that I have to admit is super-flattering and a diamond on her finger that's almost as big as the knuckleduster I confiscated from Ronan when he was, like, eight.

And speak of the devil. I spot *him* as well, two rows behind – him and Shadden – love's young dream. He's mouthing something to me, which I'm pretty sure is 'Bent', his favourite term of abuse for me.

'She's late,' I go.

Fionn's like, 'Who?'

'Who do you think? Who are we waiting for?'

'Ross, it's only five past one. The bride is traditionally late. You should have taken a valium or something.'

Fionn's old dear comes over then and storts fussing with his buttonhole and telling him how handsome he looks. I end up opening my big trap, of course. I'm there, 'Did you like the job I did on your computer, Andrea?'

Her mouth just drops open. The others – *including* Fionn – actually snigger.

I'm there, 'Sorry, it wasn't meant to come out like that.'

The look she just gives me. This is a woman who used to be one of my biggest fans, bear in mind.

What time is it now, I wonder? I stick my hand in my pocket and whip out my phone. I've had the thing on silent. So it's only then that I notice. Thirty-four missed calls. All from either the old man's home number or Sorcha's mobile.

Shit.

'I, er, need to go for a hit and miss,' I go.

Fionn just shakes his head. He's like 'The third since we got here. I don't remember you being this nervous on your *own* wedding day.'

I stort walking back down the aisle with an honestly sick feeling in my stomach.

I notice the old dear shuffle in – late, just to be the centre of attention. She's wearing – hilariously – a wig. A bad one as well. I've got an important call to make but I still take the time to go, 'You know you've got roadkill on your head?'

She goes, 'I know it was you, Ross.'

'The focking whiff of booze off you as well. Grey Goose would want to start putting childproof lids on their bottles.'

'My dermatologist said it wasn't Molton Brown in that bottle. What was it?'

'Probably Jeyes Fluid. I don't *give* a fock. It was funny.'

'How could you do that – to your own mother?'

'Yeah, this coming from the woman who rang social services and told them that my daughter was at risk of poverty? Anyway, I actually don't have time for this.'

I step outside into the church cor pork and ring the old man's number. It's *him* who answers. He sounds in a total panic as well.

He goes, 'Ross, have you heard from your sister?'

I'm like, 'What?' and I can feel my hort beating suddenly faster.

'She's missing, Ross.'

I'm like, 'What do you mean *missing*?'

In the background, I can hear Sorcha pleading with Honor to put on her dress.

Honor's going, 'Are you deaf or something? I *said* I'm not wearing it. Daddy said I didn't have to.'

The old man goes, 'The cars are here, Ross. Waiting outside. And no sign of her. The woman came to do her – what was it, Sorcha?'

I hear Sorcha go, 'Manicure.'

'We had to send the woman on her way,' the old man goes. 'Had to tell her the truth. No one's laid eyes on the bride since ten o'clock this morning. Told her mother she was popping out for five minutes. Never came back. I've phoned all the hospitals. Her mother's up the bloody walls, as you can imagine. Just a moment, Ross. Sorcha wants a word.'

He hands the phone over.

'Ross,' she goes, 'what's going on?'

I'm like, 'Why is everyone asking *me* that question?'

'Because you told Honor she wasn't going to have to wear her dress because there wasn't going to *be* a wedding.'

'I'm trying to remember did I actually say that.'

'Ross, you know something.'

'I honestly don't.'

'I came over here last night. We were supposed to have, like, a girls' night in? Just me, Erika and Helen. Erika was upset about something. She was being – oh my God – *so* weird. Anyway, I told her about the way you handled that social worker in the shop and she said she never wanted to hear your name mentioned again.'

'That *is* a bit random alright.'

'I'm not saying it's random. I'm saying I got the definite impression that it was something that you either said or did to upset her.'

I realize I have to get her off the phone. I've got to go and somehow break the news to Fionn that Erika's not actually coming. I wander back into the church, trying to come up with, I don't know, a formula of words – a way of telling him what I know without actually admitting my *role* in the whole thing?

I stand at the back of the church and I look at the dude, waiting there on his crutches, the old *banterus maximus* flying between him and Oisinn and Christian and JP. I realize that this moment is going to be the last time he's happy in a long, long time.

I stort making my way towards him and he can tell straight away from my face that something has actually happened. And then I realize that he's not looking at me at all. He's looking over my shoulder, beyond me. I turn around and it's suddenly obvious why.

Erika is standing in the doorway of the church.

She's wearing her Louboutin riding boots that apparently cost two Ks in Saks in New York, then just jeans, a black blazer and a white tee. Although it's what she's *not* wearing that has the entire congregation suddenly whispering among themselves.

She's not wearing her wedding dress.

I look at Fionn's face, just frozen in horror. It's like he knows what's coming – he's about to get squashed into the focking ground – but there's nothing he can do to get out of the way.

Erika storts making her way up the aisle, the sound of her boots echoing in the silence.

Clip, clop. Clip, clop. Clip, clop. Clip . . .

She, like, maintains eye contact with him the entire way.

I look around at the shocked faces in the congregation. People talking out of the corner of their mouths. Bad news spreading fast. Fionn pushes his glasses up on his nose. It's like he's already bracing himself for the hit he knows is coming.

I wish there was something I could say to stop this happening. Already, I can hear people going, 'Poor guy.'

She seems to take forever to reach the altar. When she finally gets there, she stops directly in front of him, looks him straight in the eye and goes, 'I'm sorry, Fionn.'

He can't even look at her. His head is down. He's there, 'Erika,' and he says it in a sort of, like, *pleading* voice? 'Jesus, Erika.'

But she just shakes her head. 'Fionn,' she goes, 'I can't marry you.'

The gasps ripple through the congregation as she confirms what we've probably already known for the past thirty seconds.

I watch him nervously chew his lip. Then he nods, sort of, like, knowingly.

'Fabrizio?' he goes.

She continues just staring him down, no expression on her face.

'I love him,' she goes.

Doesn't give a shit what anyone else in the room thinks. She's back to being the old Erika we all remember from way back.

The poor focker just nods. Knows it's game over. Nothing to be said.

Erika's there, 'I'm just so sorry I put you through all of this.'

Behind me, I hear Chloe turn to Sophie and go, 'Oh my God, I *knew* she was going to pull something like this?' and Sophie responds by going, 'I can't believe I hit my focking catwalk weight for this day and the bitch hasn't even looked at me once.'

Fionn's old dear is going, 'What . . . what's going on?'

Fionn's oblivious to all of that, of course. It's as if he and Erika are alone in the church. 'So something did happen in Aachen,' he goes.

Erika's like, 'It happened before Aachen, Fionn. At least in my heart.'

He's there, 'So, what, is he here? Parked in the bus bay outside, is he, with the engine running?'

'He's in Stockholm,' she goes. 'I rang him this morning.'

Fionn ends up having to steady himself on his crutches. 'This morning? *That's* when you decided?'

'I'm meeting him there tonight. Then we're going to live in Buenos Aires.'

I don't know if that's a real place or if she's just trying to throw us all off the scent.

He's just like, 'Erika, please. Don't do this to me.'

But she just goes, 'I'm sorry, Fionn. You didn't deserve this. After everything you've been through. You showed me nothing but love. But I wouldn't have been happy with you. And you wouldn't have been happy with me.'

That's what *I've* been saying since the day they got together. I'm suddenly realizing that by pulling the stunt I did, I actually persuaded her that her rightful place was with Fabrizio. Not that I get any thanks for it.

She tells Fionn she's sorry one final time, then turns to me and goes, 'I never want to see or speak to you again.'

Then, with her shoulders back and her nose in the air, Erika walks back down the aisle, out through the church doors and out of our lives, possibly forever.

There's, like, uproar the second she's gone. Everyone's turning to each other and just, like, shaking their heads or rolling their eyes and saying they knew it, they knew she was capable of doing something like this and they said it all along.

Except I was the only one who *actually* said it?

Fionn's old dear is crying in a sort of, like, high-pitched moan and Fionn's old man has his orms around her, basically having to hold her up.

I notice that Fionn and the rest of the goys are just staring at me.

It's actually Fionn who goes, 'What did she mean, Ross?'

I'm there, 'Sorry?' all innocence, of course.

'Why did she say she never wants to see or speak to you again?'

'Possibly because this is what I predicted would happen. And she hates seeing me proved right.'

But Fionn's a smort cookie.

'You knew this was coming,' he goes. 'That's why you've been so on edge.'

Christian turns to me and goes, 'Why didn't you say something?'

That's when Eleanor's David suddenly pipes up. 'I've just realized who the best man is! He's our plumber!'

Have you ever had a moment like that when all of the focus is suddenly coming on you, and I don't mean in a good way?

Someone turns around to him and goes, 'He's not a plumber. He used to be a rugby player. He actually could have been one of the best if it wasn't for injuries and all the rest.'

'Well,' he goes, 'he knows a lot about plumbing as well. I can tell you that for a fact.'

Fionn, Oisinn, JP and Christian form a kind of circle around me. They're all giving me serious daggers.

'You knew,' JP goes, 'and you let it go this far?'

I'm there, 'Look, I didn't know she was pulling out of the wedding.'

JP's like, 'What did you know?'

I turn around and I look at Fionn. 'I found out that something happened in Aachen.'

Fionn's like, 'How?' and I just think, fock it, tell him. Put it out there. Erika's left me to clean up her mess. Why should I bother protecting her?

'Look,' I go, 'I've been sort of, like, sex-texting her . . .'

There's, like, gasps from everyone in the church.

I'm there, '*Pretending* to be Fabrizio, let me just add – just in case any of you lot think it's weird.'

Fionn's there, 'What?'

'Yeah,' I go, 'and let me tell you something, Fionn, she was giving every bit as good as she was getting. Okay, I'm not going to go into the gory details. Definitely not in a church. But I managed to get out of her an admission that something had gone on over there.'

He shakes his head. 'I trusted her.'

'Then I upped the definite ante in the texts. *I want to do this to you. I want to do that to you.* Blah, blah, blah.'

'How could I have been so stupid not to see what that guy was here for?'

'A lot of people were taken in by him, Dude. Wasn't just you. Anyway, I arranged to meet her in the Westbury – again, pretending to be him – for an hour or two of sweet loving.'

That's when Fionn ends up really losing it with me. 'And you didn't tell me any of this? You're my best man and you let me come here today to be humiliated?'

And that's when I hear David turn around to Eleanor and go, 'Hang on. If *he's* Fionn's best man, how come you didn't recognize him when he came around to fix the heating?'

Fionn does something then that I decide to immediately forgive him for, on the basis that his hort has just been ripped out of his focking chest.

'Wise up!' he screams at David – this is without even looking at the dude. 'He wasn't there to fix the heating. He was having sex with Eleanor – you walked in on them.'

There's, like, a huge collective intake of breath. I'm telling you, Erika knew what she was doing getting the fock out of here.

David, it turns out, can't accept that this day isn't *about* him?

He's like, 'I've been recommending you to people,' with a sort of, like, disappointment in his voice.

I'm there, 'Yeah, can you stop focking doing that, by the way? I've been getting, like, four or five calls a week.'

'I also gave you two hundred and fifty euros!'

There's a fair few gasps at that as well – although I do hear one of Fionn's elderly relatives go, 'That's very reasonable, isn't it?'

He goes, 'I gave you two hundred and fifty euros – for sleeping with my girlfriend . . .'

I'm like, 'You'd actually broken up at the time, can I just remind you?'

'And you fucking took it from me.'

He jumps out of his pew and makes a run for me. Oisinn, JP and Christian manage to grab him before he can throw a punch and they basically wrestle him to the floor, then sit on top of him, while he struggles and calls me every name under the pretty much sun.

Oisinn looks up at me and he's there, 'You know what, Ross? I'm really tempted to let him go.'

He's, like, disgusted with me. They *all* are?

JP's there, 'You're a focking disgrace, Ross. Allowing Fionn to be humiliated.'

Even Christian goes, 'I think this might be the worst thing you've ever done,' and that's saying something considering I once rode his mother.

The next thing any of us hears is the old man's voice go, 'What the hell is going on?'

He's standing at the door of the church, along with Helen, Sorcha and Honor, who's not wearing her flower-girl dress, I can't help but notice.

It's, like, Fionn's old man who breaks the news to him. He has to shout it, the whole length of the church. 'Erika's gone,' he goes. 'She's run off to Buenos Aires. With this *friend* of hers.'

The old man looks shocked to the point where I'm *actually*

worried about his hort again? His lips are moving like the clappers but there's no, like, *words* coming out of his actual mouth. Helen puts her orm around his waist and still he can't speak.

Erika, I just think, what have you done? It's going to be a long, long time before we're all over this.

I turn around to Fionn.

'On the upside,' I go, out of the corner of my mouth, 'your leg's not actually broken.'

7.

Gran Slam

Fionn's old dear stares at me, standing at the door, like I'm a focking axe killer. She goes, 'What the hell do you want?'

'I'm there, 'Hey, Andrea. I just called to, I suppose, apologize.'

She's like, 'Apologize?' her voice all, I don't know, shrill. 'Oh, good! I'm looking forward to hearing what an apology sounds like for what you've done to my family. Wait till I get Ewan, though?'

She storts calling Fionn's old man over her shoulder, turning the entire thing into a bit of a performance. She's like, 'Ewan! Can you come downstairs a minute, Ewan?'

I thought she'd be actually cooler than this. Like I said, she *used* to be a fan of mine? Her *and* him.

He suddenly appears at her shoulder, cops me standing there and goes, 'What the hell do you want?'

I'm there, 'Look, I know I ruined everyone's day.'

He goes, 'Just a day, was it?'

'Sorry?'

'That's all it was to you, then? A day?'

'No, I'm just saying . . .'

'You didn't just ruin a day, Ross. You ruined two of my three children's lives.'

'Do you not think that's maybe a *bit* horsh?'

I honestly didn't expect him to be this orsey towards me.

He goes, 'A week ago, my son and daughter were both engaged to be married. Now, both of their relationships are over. Because of you.'

David must have given Eleanor the straight red as well.

'Look,' I go, knowing I'm possibly digging myself deeper into a hole here, 'neither of those relationships was going to last, let's be honest here.'

Ewan goes, 'What?'

'I'm just saying, they were both on pretty shaky ground.'

'And that's for you to decide, is it, Ross? You get to play God? You get to say whose relationship is worthwhile and whose isn't?'

'Look, the whole Eleanor thing. I'm not taking the full blame for that. Two to tango. Blah, blah, blah. Fionn and Erika – yeah, I stuck my oar in. But it was only because I knew she didn't actually love him. I didn't want to see a really good friend of mine get hurt.'

Andrea laughs, except not in a good way. 'Well, guess what, Ross? He *got* hurt. And I don't think he'll ever get over this.'

Ewan puts an, I don't know, consoling hand on her shoulder. Then he goes, 'We were always very fond of you, Ross.'

I'm there, 'I was just thinking that. You were major fans.'

'When you were shot, we prayed for you. And even when we read all those scurrilous things about you in the newspapers, we stood by you – didn't we, Andrea? We said, that doesn't sound anything like the Ross O'Carroll-Kelly *we've* known for the best part of fifteen years.'

They *were* always very easily taken in. I'd probably have to use the word gullible.

'And what do you think now?' I go.

He doesn't answer for a second or two. It's like he's trying to make up his mind whether he should say it or not. Eventually, he goes, 'You come into our home. You defecate on my wife's computer. You sleep with our daughter, who was in a very vulnerable place, let me tell you. You tell my son his leg is broken when there's nothing wrong with it. Then you send these disgusting messages to his fiancée, who's also your sister, and you persuade her to run off with another chap. Huh! I don't know who pulled the trigger on you, Ross. But I'm sure they had a bloody good reason.'

'Don't say that.'

'I'm saying it. The newspapers were right. However it happened, you brought it upon yourself. Andrea and I have no doubt about that.'

I end up just nodding. It's obvious that I'm not going to be able to get them to see things from my POV.

So I just go, 'Is Fionn even in?'

She laughs, as if it's the most ridiculous question she's ever heard. She looks over her shoulder at her husband and goes, 'Where does he get his confidence?'

'He's gone away for a few days,' Ewan goes. 'With Oisinn and JP.'

Oisinn and JP?

I'm there, 'Where've they gone? Do you know did they go on the honeymoon?'

'What?'

'Because I know Mustique was booked.'

'No,' Andrea goes, 'they didn't go on the honeymoon.'

Actually, it *would* have been a bit *Sex and the City* had they done that. They've probably just gone down to Crosshaven, where the de Barras have always had a holiday home.

It's weird thinking of the three of them down there and me left behind in Dublin, outside of the circle of trust for the first time.

I'm there, 'Can you give him a message?'

Ewan goes, 'A message?'

'Yeah, no, it's just he's not returning any of my calls.'

'Are you surprised?'

I'm there, 'I suppose not.'

He goes, 'I suppose not,' sort of, like, imitating my voice. Then he goes, 'I doubt Fionn will ever want to lay eyes on you again. And that's exactly how we feel.'

Then he slams the door in my face.

I'm helping Sorcha unpack a consignment of elasticated ergonomic knee supports (€1 for a pair) that's just arrived and neither of us is saying very much at all.

It's, like, a week since the wedding that never was and Sorcha has barely said a word about it. And I'm cool with that. She's one of the few people who isn't blaming *me* for what happened?

From the one or two things she *has* said, it's pretty obvious that she feels let down by Erika. She left her in the house in her bridesmaid's tan – her supposed best friend – and did a runner without even a word of goodbye.

I know she was crushed by that. She's been listening to a lot of Sufjan Stevens for the past few days and talking about – if you can believe this – the *impermanence* of things?

We finish putting out the knee supports and I ask her if she wants me to get storted on the *Toy Story 2* sticker books (50c) or the cinnamon and ylang-ylang lip salves (€1 for a pack of three).

She goes, 'No. Let's take a break, Ross. You've been – oh my God – so amazing this morning,' and we wander over to the cash till and sit down on a couple of high stools.

From out of nowhere, she suddenly goes, 'I heard you called to Fionn's house last night?'

Word travels fast in this town.

I'm like, 'Yeah.'

'He went away with JP and Oisinn. They're in Crosshaven – that's according to Lauren.'

'Christian's another one who's not returning my calls, by the way.'

'How were Mr and Mrs de Barra with you?'

'Let's just say I did not get a good reception.'

'What did they say?'

'*He* pretty much said I deserved what I got when I was shot.'

'That doesn't sound like Mr de Barra.'

I laugh. 'I think I bring out the worst in people, Sorcha.'

Of course, *she* comes rushing to my defence immediately. 'That's not fair, Ross. And it's not fair what he said. They still don't know who shot you. Did you tell him that?'

'Er, no. He actually did most of the talking. I didn't get to say a huge amount.'

'He's obviously upset.'

'*You* don't seem to be. Not with me.'

'You did a terrible, terrible thing, Ross . . .'

'Oh.'

'But you did it for the right reasons. To show Erika in her true light.'

'I suppose I *was* the one who was saying all along that something was going on between them. But no one was listening to me. That's why I had to get the actual proof.'

'The way you did it was horrible, Ross.'

'Okay.'

'But you stopped them both from making the biggest mistake of their lives. Everyone will see that in time – Fionn and Christian included.'

'Keep talking to me, Sorcha, because this is all good shit you're saying to me.'

'Well, what would have happened if you hadn't done what you did and they'd actually gotten married? Six months, a year down the line, she'd have run off with somebody else. That's just what she's like.'

'You seem pretty down on her.'

She laughs, then shakes her head – I'm going to use a word, even though it's probably not one – but *ruefully*?

'Nearly twenty years of friendship, Ross. I stood by her during – oh my God – everything. And in the end she left me looking like a fool.'

'She probably thought you'd try to talk her into going ahead with it – as in, the wedding?'

'Well, I knew she was having some pre-wedding jitters. But if I'd known they were actual doubts . . .'

She doesn't finish her sentence. She sort of, like, stares sadly into the distance, then – after ten seconds of silence – says she thinks she's changed her mind about Honor appearing in *Mom, They Said They'd Never Heard of Sundried Tomatoes*.

She says it just like that. Out of the blue. Last week it was a bad idea. This week it's a great idea. But that's women for you. They'd walk around in flippers and a focking Robin Hood hat if Marc Jacobs said the look was suddenly *in*.

'What's brought this on?' I go.

She's there, 'I don't know. If it's something she really wants to do and we stop her, she might grow up – I don't know – resenting us.'

'I thought we were worried about her becoming even more of a bitch than she already is.'

'It could actually have the opposite effect, Ross. Acting might be her thing. She's going to be on her holidays in a couple of weeks – the whole summer stretching out in front of her. This could give her an actual focus.'

'I suppose.'

'And I'm not going to deny it, the money *is* a factor.'

'What kind of shekels are we talking, by the way? Has the old dear even mentioned?'

Sorcha goes, '*Hello?* The money wouldn't be for us,' and she says it like this fact should be somehow obvious to me.

I'm like, 'What do you mean?'

'The money would be for Honor's future.'

'Her *future*? That sounds a bit heavy, Babes, if you don't mind me saying.'

'It *is* heavy, Ross. I was talking to my dad yesterday. Did you know that the fifty billion euros it cost to bail out Ireland's banks is more than the entire amount the country has received in social and cohesion funds since joining the EU?'

'I, er, suspected it was in that ballpork alright.'

'As my dad said, Ross, we've basically mortgaged away the next century. You have to wonder what kind of future the world is going to be facing by the time Honor leaves Mount Anville. The money would be put in trust for her, to see her through college and maybe help her to one day get a foot on the housing ladder.'

But I think I know what this is *really* about? I was rooting around in one of Sorcha's drawers yesterday and I found some pictures she'd cut out of *Closer* or *Look* or any of those magazines she buys. It was, like, all mothers and daughters. It was Meg Ryan with little Daisy True, eating cupcakes sitting outside Sprinkles in Beverly Hills. It was Jennifer Meyer, having fun with Otis and Ruby in a playground in Santa Monica. It was Rachel Zoe, shopping for clothes with little Skyler in Kitson Kids on Robertson Boulevard.

All images of glamorous mothers with their equally glamorous children being happily snapped by the paparazzi. Sorcha still fantasizes about having a life like that. It's certainly the relationship she'd love to have with our daughter.

And, well, it's in pretty stork contrast to the afternoon she has ahead of her, putting humungous 'Reduced to Clear' stickers over the 'Promotional Purposes Only – Not For Resale' warning on three hundred *Best of Hulk Hogan* VHS cassettes (€1).

You couldn't blame her for wanting a bit of joy in her life.

I'm there, 'Look, I've no real problem with it any more. To be honest, my only real issue is that I don't want to give my old dear the satisfaction.'

'Ross,' she goes, 'I know you still think it was her who rang social services.'

'I don't think, Sorcha. I know.'

'Fionnuala wouldn't do that.'

'You have no idea what kind of evil that woman is capable of – and I'm saying that as her son.'

I hop up off my stool. I need the shitter. I'm like, 'I'm just going to, er . . .'

She goes, 'Just do it, Ross. You don't need to make an announcement.'

I go into the office at the back of the shop, then into the staff toilet.

It's while I'm on the bowl, of course, that I end up doing a lot of my best thinking. And it suddenly occurs to me, while I'm dropping a lobster in the pot, that I must find out from Hennessy what the latest is with Regina and the payoff. Because to be honest, roysh, I'm getting a bit pissed off waiting. I mean, this happened last, what, November? It's already the start of June and still focking nothing.

His phone rings, like, eight or nine times, then goes straight to his voicemail. I leave a message.

I'm like, 'Hey, Hennessy – it's, er, Ross here. As in, Ross O'Carroll-Kelly? I'm sorry I didn't get a chance to, er, chat to you at the wedding last week. Obviously, I had one or two other things to deal with. I was just wondering was there any news on that other thing? I think you know what I'm talking about – obviously can't say too much on the phone. Blah, blah, blah. Maybe you'd give me a shout back and tell me if there's any update. Blah, blah, blah.'

It's just as I'm hanging up the phone that I hear this roar from outside on the shopfloor. It's, like, a man's voice, going, 'Why dint you fackin ring me?' and I straight away recognize it as Mr Whittle.

Up go the chinos. I don't even bother wiping up. I just morch straight out to the shop, where the dude has Sorcha – I swear to fock – backed into a corner, literally cowering.

He's going, 'Why are social fackin services sniffing around my fackin shop?'

Someone's obviously told him. Maybe someone from Pygmalion. I know he sometimes has his lunch in there.

Sorcha goes, 'It was nothing to do with the shop, Mr Whittle,' clearly focking terrified, by the way. 'They had a report that my daughter was at risk of, like, poverty?'

'You still should have fackin rang me. Better still, don't bring your fackin problems into my fackin shop. Got it?'

'Yes, Mr Whittle.'

'Now – anuver fing – why int vat shampoo fackin shifting?'

'I don't know. It's obviously just not a big seller.'

'It ain't vat – you've been fackin wawnin people off it.'

That's actually true – she has. Poor Sorcha doesn't know how to lie, though.

'I've just been telling people that it's not one of the *better*-quality hair care products that we stock?'

He goes, 'Who va fack are you to tell people vat? You little fackin kant.'

I suddenly make a big show of clearing my throat. And Mr Whittle turns around and sees me for the first time. I can tell from his face that he's getting ready to say something along the lines of, 'Oh, look who it is!' except he doesn't manage to get even one word out.

I hit him. Full in the face. And the noise of it.

Boomf!

It's like kicking the perfect penalty, see. It's all in the way you connect.

His eyes go suddenly vacant – it's obviously sleepybyes time – and his legs stort disappearing underneath him. He staggers backwards and crashes into a display of seventeen-nation euro coin-collector albums (50c) and plastic footballs with, like, Manga characters on them (€1), which always travel the same distance no matter how hord you kick them.

Sorcha screams. She's obviously never seen a man so well and truly decked.

Mr Whittle manages to squeeze six words out through his suddenly swollen lips.

'Get your fings,' he goes. 'You're fackin sacked.'

'*So* lollers,' Honor goes, staring at her mobile phone and, at the same time, cracking up laughing. 'Pixie Geldof looks like a J Cloth in that maxi. Er, hashtag – is it *dark* where you dress?'

I actually laugh myself – forget the movies, she actually belongs on the stage – then I go, 'Give me a look, Honor,' basically just showing an interest. But she pulls her phone away, then brings it – and her breakfast – over to the kitchen table to sit.

She's still in a serious snot with us for pulling the plug on her being in the movie – she doesn't know yet that Sorcha's changed her mind.

'Er, what was all the shouting about last night?' she suddenly goes.

That's the reason I got up early to make Sorcha breakfast, by the way.

I'm there, 'Your mother was upset. She, er, lost her job yesterday.'

'OMG!' she goes, obviously delighted. 'Er, GR to BR – that's what I say.'

'Well, she's mostly upset with *me*, as it happens – basically because I decked her boss.'

'Shut! The Front! Door!'

'It's nothing to be proud of, Honor. Violence. Blah, blah, blah. That's why I'm going to bring her breakfast in bed. How do you make pancakes, by the way?'

'*Excuse* me?'

'It's flour and milk and I'm pretty sure something else. Check is there anything on the internet about it, will you?'

She says something under her breath then, which sounds to me like, 'Do it yourself. I'm not your slave.'

The kitchen door all of a sudden opens and in walks Sorcha.

Honor, without even looking up from her phone, goes, 'Gratz, Mom! I hear we're a no-income family again!'

She really *is* a little bitch.

Sorcha totally blanks her and walks over to the island, where I'm hilariously trying to cook. This'd be one for my critics to see. I've got pots and pans and all sorts of shit out.

'It was going to be a surprise,' I go. 'I just couldn't remember what the other ingredient was supposed to be.'

Really calmly, she goes, 'Ross, you know I've always been opposed to violence in all its forms.'

I'm there, 'I suppose.'

'My special study topic for Leaving Cert. history was Jean Jaurès and the French anti-militarist movement in the years leading up to the First World War.'

'Oh, yeah.'

'One of our daughter's middle names is Suu Kyi.'

'I know.'

And that's when the most incredible thing happens. She leans in, plants *the* most unbelievable kiss on my cheek and goes, 'But thank you for hitting that horrible man.'

You should *see* Honor's face, by the way. She's in total shock. I look at her as if to say, that's where a little bit of chorm gets you, Kid. You should try it some time.

I watch Sorcha take the eggs out of the fridge. I'm thinking, eggs! *That* was it!

She storts cracking them into the bowl and goes, 'Honor, your father and I have some news.'

Honor's just, 'Yay, Mommy!' except not actually meaning it, just being a little wagon. Her nose is back in her phone, in fact.

Sorcha's there, 'We've decided to let you audition for your grand-mother's movie.'

Honor's reaction – the delight on her face – would make you nearly want to give in to her all the time.

She's like, 'Really?' suddenly a different girl. 'Oh! My God! Are you serious?'

Sorcha smiles at me. It makes such a change to see our daughter genuinely happy for once.

'I spoke to Fionnuala this morning,' Sorcha goes. 'The director – his name's Ford M Peret – he wants to see you on Monday morning for a screen test.'

Honor jumps up from the table, runs to her mother and throws her orms around her legs. She's like, 'Thank you, Mommy. Thank you, Mommy. Thank you, Mommy.'

I watch Sorcha smile and just stroke her hair, the first genuine affection I've seen between them in I don't know *how* long? Sorcha just looks at me and mouths the words 'Oh! My! God!' as in, 'Can you believe this is even the same girl?'

Honor goes, 'Richelle Hanney in my class is going to be *so* jealous. Oh my God, she is *such* a bitch. *And* a retard.'

I laugh. I can't help it.

I'm there, 'Don't go getting ahead of yourself, Kid. You haven't even *got* the port yet.'

And Honor, with one hand on her hip, just looks me up and down and goes, 'I'm *going* to get it, Dad.'

The old man says all the talk now is of splitting the Euro Zone in two to solve the continent's debt crisis.

The poor focker would sooner talk about anything than what actually happened in Donnybrook last weekend. It's like it's too painful to even *go* there? He mutes the *Six One* news.

'How do you like that?' he goes. This is us sitting in *his* living room in Donnybrook, by the way. 'Our so-called friends in Europe cutting us adrift. Us and one or two others. They've already got a name for us, you know? Pigs! Quote-unquote. Stands for Portugal, Ireland, Greece and Spain. Oh, I'm sure they're all FOFLing and ROFLing at that one in the bloody corridors of the mighty in Berlin.'

He's hurting bad. Anyone can see that.

'Has she even been in touch?' I go.

He doesn't even ask me who I'm talking about. Just nods. Which means she's obviously at the forefront of his mind. Of course she is.

His only daughter doing a legger on her supposed wedding day. A seven-course meal for two hundred and twenty people paid for, on top of all the other money he wasted.

'Matter of fact,' he goes, 'she rang her mother last night. Not before time either. What's it been, a week? And all of us worried bloody sick.'

'You sound pissed off in a major way.'

'She told her mother she loves this other chap. Says they're planning to start a new life for themselves in Argentina. An equestrian school. Quote un-bloody-quote . . . She wouldn't even speak to me, Ross. Her own father. I said to Helen, "Put her on to me and I'll talk some sense into her. Buenos Aires indeed! There's a chap here – namely Fionn – who thinks the bloody well world of her and would probably *still* marry her if she came to her senses and just got herself on the next flight home!" Well, she hung up! Hung up, if you can believe that!'

I just nod.

'Well, if it's any consolation,' I go, 'I was the one who said this was going to happen. I knew that focker was a player. Or at least fancied himself as one.'

'What, the famous Fabrizio? Bloody confidence trickster. Yes, he pulled the wool over all of our eyes.'

'Er, not *mine*, if you remember?'

'Oh, yes, of course. You did your utmost to try to warn us about him.'

'Well, I could just see it coming. Fionn was like a full-back trying to play in the front row. And *she* was hitting the panic button in a big-time way. Wrong side of thirty. Happens to a lot of birds. They feel they just have to grab whatever's there.'

That's when he suddenly goes, 'I blame myself, you know. For what Erika did.'

I realize it's the first time either of us has said her name.

I'm there, 'I wouldn't go beating yourself up. She was always a focking bitch – years before you even knew her. And I'm saying that in her defence.'

'What she did, though, Ross – running off like that – well, it takes a degree of coldness. And is it any wonder she's like that? Given that her father watched another man raise her for twenty-whatever-it-was years, just a few miles up the Stillorgan dual-carriageway, and never said a word. Then he bumbles his way into her life. Suddenly wants to be a father to *her* and a husband to her mother. The bloody nerve! No, no, I keep telling myself – this one's down to you, Charlie boy.'

He seems so down in the dumps that there's basically nothing I can say to him. There's a ring on the doorbell then. Helen must answer it, roysh, because the next thing I hear is Hennessy's voice in the hall, basically sympathizing with her.

'I'm so ashamed of her,' I hear *her* go. 'To put Fionn through that. Not to mention her poor father. He's in there watching television.'

The next thing I know, Hennessy's stuck his head around the living-room door. 'Come on,' he goes, 'we're going out.'

The old man's like, 'Where?'

'I don't *care* where. Somewhere we can get a drink. You've been stuck in this house for a week. You can't hide from the world forever. Get your fucking coat.'

The old man suddenly brightens up. He performs, like, a salute, then goes, 'Message received and understood,' although it's actually just a front he's putting on. 'I shall get my coat *and* hat. Leave you two alone for a moment to – no doubt – debate Ireland's future either inside or outside the euro.'

Then he focks off out of the room, leaving me there with Hennessy.

'What the fock?' I go. 'Did you get my message?'

He's there, 'Were you on the fucking toilet when you left that?'

'I, er, might have been. How did you know that?'

'Because I could hear your fucking plops. What the fuck is the matter with you?'

This coming from a man who I watched steal a pair of my wife's Diana Vickers.

I'm there, 'I, er, just wanted to find out what the Jackanory was – as in, has Regina agreed to a deal yet?'

He goes, 'Didn't I tell you not to ring me? Didn't I tell you just to leave it the fuck to me?'

'I'm sorry. I just got a bit, I don't know, *unpatient?*'

'Well,' he goes, 'you'll be happy to know then that we reached a deal.'

I have to admit, I feel a wave of sudden relief that it's finally over. 'Okay,' I go. 'How much are we talking?'

He's there, 'One point four.'

'One point four?'

I feel the two ends of my mouth turn upwards into a smile.

'So congratulations,' Hennessy goes. 'You've just become a fucking millionaire. And for the first time in your life, you did it without Charlie's help.'

I'm sitting on the edge of her bed, watching her throw on her BCBGMAXAZRIA black tailored jacket and skirt and her classic black Miu Miu courts that haven't been out of their dustbag since she bought them three Christmases ago.

I might even buy her another pair when my money comes through – my way of saying thank you for putting me up.

She checks herself out in the full-length mirror, first standing sideways, then front-on with one hand on her hip, then sideways again.

I always loved watching Sorcha get ready.

She can't make up her mind about her hair. She ties it back, then puts it down again, then decides that back is actually better, although I wouldn't rule out one or two more changes of mind before she leaves the house.

'Who was your letter from?' she goes, then she immediately regrets asking me. 'Sorry, I didn't mean to be . . .'

I'm there, 'Yeah, no, it's cool. It was just from the management company.'

'Of your apartment? Oh my God, have they said what's happening?'

'Yeah, they're going to knock it down.'

'That's, like, oh my God!'

'I know.'

She sad-smiles me.

She goes, 'Ross, you can stay here until you get yourself sorted.'

I'm there, 'It'll only be a few more weeks. I'll rent somewhere until I find out what moo I'm getting from the insurance.'

She puts her hand on my shoulder and goes, 'It's been so lovely having you here,' then gives me a peck on the forehead and I've suddenly got a sausage on me that wouldn't look out of place hanging in the window of the German Butcher's Shop in Aghadoe.

She asks me how she looks. I tell her seriously foxy and then I realize that that's probably not the look she was aiming for, so I go, 'Er, very businesslike,' and this seems to please her a bit more.

'By the way,' I go, 'Erika finally got in touch with Helen.'

She doesn't even look at me, just grabs her Yves Saint Laurent clutch and goes, 'I've decided I don't want to hear that girl's name ever again.'

'The old man's blaming himself,' I go.

She's there, 'Well, he shouldn't. Erika hurts people, Ross. That's what she's always done.'

'They're setting up, like, an equestrian school – her and that dick. That's the talk anyway.'

'Like I said, Ross I'm not actually *interested*?' and then she shouts, 'Honor, are you ready?'

Honor's already standing by the front door waiting. She's been up half the night, learning her lines for her screen test. She goes, 'Yes, I'm ready, Mom,' and she says it so politely that I end up having to tip out to the landing and have a look over the banister to check that it's even her.

Thirty seconds later, I'm standing at the door, waving them off and wishing them luck.

I go back inside. I have the sudden feeling that things are on the definite up again. I've got, like, one point four mills on the way, minus whatever Hennessy's cut is going to be. And no one can say I don't deserve it after what Regina and her mad bitch daughter put me through. The stomach and the tops of my legs are pretty much fully healed. Yeah, you could read me like a map of the London Underground, but five hundred sit-ups a day have given me back my washboard stomach and the scorring has made me look more – you'd have to say it – *interesting*? My nightmares have pretty much stopped and I haven't heard from the Feds in weeks. The old home life couldn't be better. Honor's like a new kid – or at least far less of a bitch than she was last week – and I can do literally no wrong in her mother's eyes.

All I need to do now is sort things with Fionn and the goys. I suddenly remember that it's, like, JP's birthday next weekend. So they'll all be in Slattery's on Saturday night for pints as usual. I'll go along and sort it with my usual gift of the gab. Cometh the hour and blah, blah, blah.

I go back to bed then and I end up sleeping for, like, five or six hours straight. I wake up, feeling pretty groggy it has to be said and also storving. I make myself a bacon sandwich and I watch a bit of TV. Then I decide to ring Ronan. The Junior Cert. exams stort on Wednesday and I'm wondering how he's sorted for them.

He answers on the fourth ring, except his voice sounds funny, like he's trying to keep it down.

I'm like, 'Ronan?'

And he's there, 'Who wants to know?'

He's a focking entertainer, there's no doubt about that.

I'm there, 'It's me. Ross, Rosser, whatever.'

He goes, 'Ah, soddy, Rosser. Howiya?'

'Are you in the library or something, Ro?'

'Er, yeah.'

'Two days to go, huh? So how are you fixed?'

'What?'

'Till your exams.'

'Oh, yeah. Ine, er, moostard, so I am.'

'Well, don't go breaking your neck,' I go, because I *am* still worried about Tina, and McGahy especially, putting too much pressure on him. 'It actually means fock-all in the bigger scheme of things. A bit like the Leaving Cert.'

'Feer denuff, Rosser.'

'I'll let you go back to the books, then, will I?'

'If you wootunt moyunt.'

'Well, best of luck anyway.'

'Thanks, Rosser. And tell Sorcha and Honor I said tanks for the keerd.'

'I'll pass that on. I genuinely hope you do well.'

Then I hang up. I grab one of Sorcha's magazines and I hit the jacks for old poop nap. I'm actually reading an orticle about mankles – shoes without socks is coming back as a look for men, someone seems to think – when it suddenly occurs to me that Sorcha and Honor have been gone for, like, eight hours?

I'm actually wondering should I be worried when all of a sudden I hear voices in the hallway downstairs – first, Sorcha mentioning that Tamara Mellon owns, like, eight thousand pairs of shoes, then Honor saying – not something sarcastic or hurtful for a change – but actually, 'Hashtag – er, *please* can I raid your closet?' and then the two of them stort giggling like a couple of teenage girls.

I'm thinking, okay, they've never had that kind of relationship before – obviously, what the fock?

Literally nothing could prepare me for the surprise that awaits me when I walk out of that jacks with Sorcha's magazine under my orm and head downstairs. They've *been* to Dundrum – that much is obvious from the bags. We're talking Hobbs. We're talking Coast. We're talking Fitzpatrick's. We're talking Karen Millen. And they've also hit Bucky's because they're both drinking frapps.

But that's not the surprise I'm talking about. The reason my jaw is on the pretty much floor is that they're both dressed in identical – what turn out to be – tangerine Baby Phat maxi dresses, blue-and-white-stripped ballet flats and humungous Jackie Os.

'She got the part,' Sorcha goes. 'They loved her, Ross. She's going to be playing a role that – oh my God – millions would kill for.'

And I look at Sorcha – playing Katie Holmes to Honor's Suri Cruise – and I think, she's not the only one.

Oisinn says that David McWilliams is on TV now advertising – get this – cider. He goes, 'What kind of message is that to be sending out about the Irish economy?'

Christian just shakes his head.

JP goes, 'It's back to the focking caves we're headed.'

They laugh. I missed that – as in, the banter.

I go, 'Hey, goys,' and the three of them suddenly look at me. They look like they don't know *how* to respond?

I'm just there, 'Happy birthday, Dude,' except JP doesn't immediately answer. He's being loyal to Fionn. They all are. I can understand that.

'Is he here?' I go.

Then I look over JP's shoulder and I spot him at the bor, getting the round in, in fairness to him. He looks well. And I don't mean it in *that* way – I just mean considering.

I sort of, like, sidle up to him, then I go, 'Hey, Fionn – how was Crosshaven?' and he turns and looks at me but he doesn't actually *say* anything? He just give me, like, a hord stare.

It's time to grovel. I realize that.

'Dude,' I go, 'I just want to apologize for, well, what happened. Telling you your leg was broken. Although obviously it was more than that. Sending those sex texts to Erika. That was bang out of order, I accept. Then, going further back, giving your sister the treatment. Even shitting on your mother's laptop. I'm apologizing for it all, Fionn. I focked up. I focked up in a major way. But I want you back . . .'

I actually find myself getting a bit emotional, which actually surprises me.

I'm there, 'I want you back as a friend. And I'm going to do whatever it focking takes to make that happen . . .'

He just goes on staring at me and not in a good way.

I'm like, 'Dude, I'll do what I did when Aoife died. I'll just keep ringing you. Day and night. I'll sit on the stairs outside your aportment until you eventually agree to talk to me.'

I watch his face suddenly soften. He shakes his head.

'Ross,' he goes, 'I know you did what you did with some vague thought of what was best for me buried among your other motivations. But that doesn't excuse what you did. I'm sorry, it just doesn't. That whole scene in the church – you set that in train, Ross. All of it.'

'I know.'

'That . . . humiliation.'

'Dude, I honestly can't apologize enough.'

'But you've been doing it all our lives, Ross. Screwing me over. Any opportunity you get.'

'Well, that's all going to stop now. I can promise you that much.'

'And yet I always forgave you. Why was that?'

I'm there, 'Probably because I care about you like a brother. Just as I do Christian, JP and Oisinn. It's the same shit, my friend.'

He nods. I think I even see a tiny hint of a smile.

He goes, 'It wasn't the worst thing that could have happened that day, Ross.'

I'm suddenly thinking, okay, this sounds more positive.

He goes, 'The worst thing would have been if we'd actually gotten married. I wanted to believe that she was in love with me. But she wasn't. And I wouldn't have known that if it wasn't for you.'

I'm there, 'That was actually going to be my next point.'

He cuts me short. 'It doesn't make you a hero, Ross. Far from it. But, like I said, I realize, in your own twisted way, you were looking out for me.'

I'm there, 'I was. The whole time.'

He goes, 'So . . .' and then he lets it hang there for a few seconds. Then – it's *the* most amazing thing – he suddenly sticks his hand out, offering to shake mine. I end up being pretty overcome.

I go, 'Fock that,' and I end up just grabbing him in an actual bear hug. It's a definite moment, there's no doubt about that.

Behind me, I hear JP, Oisinn and Christian burst into a round of applause. The vibe is very much, Hey, the Rossmeister General is back and normal service has resumed.

They were obviously listening to the entire conversation as well, because I hear Oisinn go, 'Probably because I care about you like a brother,' and 'I want you back! And I'm going to do whatever it takes to make that happen!'

JP and Christian crack their holes laughing. I pull away from Fionn and he's laughing as well. And even though the joke is technically on me, I end up just joining them.

Someone has written the words 'Rich Prick' across the side of my cor. Except this time, judging from the bottle they've left on the bonnet for me to see, they've written it in, like, brake fluid, which means it'll have eaten into the actual bodywork – I remember that from my Senior Cup days – and there's fock-all that Nudger or anyone can do about it, except get me two new doors.

Or burn it out for the insurance.

I wouldn't mind, roysh, but this is on, like, Newtownpork Avenue in the middle of the day. Where the fock are the Feds? That's what I want to know. And it's as I'm thinking this that I happen to notice one, sitting in the cor immediately behind me. My old friend Shane Harron. Fock. I was only thinking how long it'd been.

I get into my cor and I go to stort her up. Except *he's* too quick for me. He's suddenly standing next to me on the road, tapping my window. I wind it down, though just an inch, or two at the most. Cops always hate that, I can tell you from experience, especially when they've pulled you over for speeding.

He doesn't seem in the mood to have the piss ripped out of him, though.

He goes, 'Open the fucking window,' which I straight away do.

I'm there, 'You're not dragging me out to Malahide again,' just to let him know that I'm not in the mood to be dicked around either. 'And I'm not answering any questions without my old man's solicitor being present. You have his number, don't you?'

He leans down to my level, then he goes, 'Did he get you a good deal?'

I'm like, 'Excuse me?'

He's there, 'You know what I'm talking about. How much did he get for you?'

I just go, 'I don't know what you're talking about,' which is the answer I rehearsed with Hennessy.

He sort of, like, laughs to himself – like it's a *private* joke?

He's there, 'Well, you're in the clear. I've been moved to another case.'

I'm like, 'I don't know what you're talking about.'

He practically roars at me then. 'Ah, will you give over with your nonsense. I know what you did. I'm just telling you, you got away with it.'

'Whatever.'

He laughs, again to himself.

'*Whatever* is right. They think it was Terry and Larry Tuhill's fellas who shot you.'

'Who thinks?'

'My superiors.'

'Yeah, no, I wonder will we ever find out for sure.'

Hennessy would kill for me going off-script, but I can't actually resist the temptation.

'*I* know for sure,' he goes. 'I know Hedda Rathfriland shot you. But you won't give us the positive identification we need because you're blackmailing her.'

'That's an opinion.'

'Huh?'

'I said it's an opinion.'

'That's right. It's *my* opinion. But, like I said, the good news for you is that I've been moved to another case.'

I'm there, 'I'll miss you.'

'I doubt you will. But you're in the clear. For now.'

He actually says it with a bit of, like, *menace* in his voice?

I'm there, 'What does that mean?'

He goes, 'I'll get you, Ross. Eventually. I'm going to make it my life's work.'

I wind up the window and leave him just standing there – as pissed off as I've ever seen a man.

She's quiet. And that's unusual, because the one thing you'd have to say about my daughter is that she's always got something to say, even if it's just, '*What* is Nicola Roberts wearing? Hashtag – my eyes, my eyes!'

It could be just nerves.

I check her out in the rear-view mirror. She's sitting on the back seat, reading through her lines, which Sorcha highlighted for her. Those fluorescent yellow morkers always remind me of my glory days, when I was working my way through Dublin's grind schools like a focking shoplifter through Hector Greys.

'We'll definitely remember this day,' I go. We're pulled up at the lights outside the Radisson St Helen's. 'Your first day in movies.

We'll all remember this day in twenty years' time, won't we? When you're up there collecting your first Oscar!'

Jesus Christ. It scares me how like my old man I'm beginning to sound.

Sorcha turns to me and goes, 'Let her concentrate, Ross.'

And I'm there, 'Cool,' because I can see that the kid is in the zone.

Fifteen minutes later, roysh, we're pulling up on, like, Mount Street. The opening scene of the movie is being shot in Merrion Square, which they've, like, closed off for the day. Sorcha opens the back door for Honor, who's wearing a humungous pair of Dwyane Wades, I notice, and her Cappuccino faux fur jacket, even though it's June and focking roasting.

They wander on ahead while I feed coins into the meter. I've got my copy of the script under my orm and I end up having a quick mosey through it while I'm waiting for the dude at the security barrier to find out why my name isn't down on the accreditation list.

The opening scene looks pretty straightforward. It's September 1998 and Zara Mesbur is on her way to Montessori for the first day of term. They're, like, using Little Roedean's as well – as in, her old school – so it's like she was born to play the port. Zara is moody – again, *made* for her. Her mother asks her what's wrong and Zara says that it said on the news this morning that the American markets have expressed concern at the increasing level of debt default, especially in the area of sub-prime lending. Zara asks if it's going to affect them and her mother says of course it won't.

I know my old dear wrote it. But it's not actually bad compared to a lot of the shit you see on Hallmork.

I eventually get through the security barrier and I spot Honor and Sorcha, who are already deep in conversation with this bird who, even from, like, thirty yords away is a ringer for Elisabetta Canalis. She's American – the accent is a definite giveaway as I get closer – and whatever she's been saying seems to be muesli to Sorcha's ears, judging from the smile on her face.

'Because I know what you're thinking,' I hear the woman go. 'You're worried that your daughter's going to end up spoiled, right?'

'Well,' Sorcha goes, 'you hear such terrible stories about child stars – you only have to watch *E! News*.'

The woman laughs. 'Okay, you do *not* need to worry about that! It's my job here, on-set, to ensure that Honor gets everything she needs, but also to make sure that she enjoys her time on the movie and isn't adversely affected by the experience. We try to keep everyone in the real world as much as we possibly can.'

She turns to me then. 'Hi,' she goes, offering me her hand, 'I'm Fantasia . . .'

I *think* I actually laugh in her face. Fantasia. Jesus Christ.

'You must be Honor's father,' she goes.

I go, 'Yeah, I'm Ross,' and straight from the off, roysh, I'm thinking, I swear to fock, I am going to chorm this woman horizontal before this movie wraps.

Sorcha goes, 'Fantasia is a child-welfare liaison assistant.'

I'm like, 'Child welfare?' wondering is that not a *bit* OTT?

'She's worked with the likes of – who were they again?'

Fantasia goes, 'I've worked with Mila, Natalie, Reese . . .'

I'm there, 'I presume we're talking Kunis, Portman and Witherspoon . . .'

I masturbate way too much.

'That's right,' she goes. 'Just making sure their experiences in movies were positive.'

I turn to Sorcha. 'Well, those three have turned out alright, haven't they? I'm about to say fair focks here.'

'Well, okay,' Fantasia goes, 'why don't we go and meet Ford and the rest of the cast and crew, then I'll show you Honor's trailer.'

The kid has her own trailer – her face is suddenly lit up like a focking cruise liner.

To cut a long story short, that's what ends up happening. It's handshakes all round with a bunch of people whose names I'm never going to be able to remember again, then Honor is brought into her trailer to get into costume for the opening scene.

While she's doing that, I give Ro a quick bell. He has his final Junior Cert. exam this morning and I'm wondering how the others went.

He's like, 'Er, not bad, Rosser.'

I'm thinking, not bad? I don't know if that's him just being modest or if he found the whole thing genuinely more difficult than he expected.

'You're saying it wasn't exactly a piece of piss?' I go.

He's there, 'It's just heerd to know.'

I could focking kill McGahy for putting him through this.

I'm there, 'Still, nearly done, huh? Then you've the entire summer ahead of you. The Dubs. Blah, blah, blah.'

He suddenly remembers something. 'Here,' he goes, 'how's Honor getting on?'

I'm there, 'They're just about to stort shooting. It's very exciting, it has to be said. Honor in an actual movie – albeit a TV one that the old dear wrote.'

He goes, 'Tell her good luck from me, will ye? And tell her I'll Skype her later.'

I'm like, 'I'll do that. And best of luck today. Let's hook up this weekend. I haven't seen you in ages.'

He goes, 'Feer denuff,' and then he's gone.

All of a sudden, Honor arrives out of her trailer and she's, like, ready to go. It's immediately obvious that she's got her game face on, reminding me of a certain former schools rugby legend who shall remain unanimous.

Ford, the director dude, walks over to her and there's a bit of blah. Sorcha comes over to me and links my orm and tells me that she's *so* excited and isn't Fantasia *so* an amazing person. 'She's, like, totally allayed my fears about whether this is going to be a good or a bad thing for Honor's emotional development.'

After ten or fifteen minutes of everyone basically faffing about, it's time to roll. I can't honestly remember the last time I felt this nervous. Sorcha obviously senses it, roysh, because she grabs my hand, then gives it a squeeze, which is actually nice.

Ford – who's an oldish dude with, like, a grey goatee – shouts, 'Action!' and then we're suddenly off and running.

The first thing I notice – I have to mention – is that the woman playing Zara's mother, Susan – even *though* she looks a bit like Doutzen Kroes? – is an American actress putting on one of those begorrah and be-to-hokey Irish accents, like Nicole Kidman in *Far and Away* and Jonathan Rhys Meyers in, well, everything he's ever focking done.

Anyway, her and Honor – sorry, Zara – are walking along Merrion Square, basically just shooting the shit. It's like:

SUSAN: Are you okay, Little One?

ZARA: I'm fine.

SUSAN: It's just you hardly touched your breakfast, so you didn't. Och, you're not nervous about the gymkhana this weekend, are you?

Honor suddenly stops walking at the entrance to the school. She looks like she's about to burst into tears. I look at Sorcha. I'm like, 'What's wrong? Shit, something's up with her.'

Sorcha squeezes my hand to tell me to shut up, then, out of the corner of her mouth, she goes, 'She's acting, Ross.'

I'm like, 'What?' basically unable to believe that anyone could act that well. And that's not me, as her old man, being biased either. Everyone on the set is, like, looking at each other and just smiling.

ZARA: It's just . . .

SUSAN: Och, what is it?

ZARA: What it said on radio . . . on the news . . .

SUSAN: About the worryingly high level of debt default in the United States of America?

ZARA: Yes.

SUSAN: Why are you worrying your pretty little head about that?

ZARA: They said it could have a contagion effect, Mum – on, like, world financial morkets?

SUSAN: Och, it's nothing for you to worry about.

ZARA: Are you saying it, like, won't affect us?

SUSAN: Of course it won't. It's only an American thing, so it is.

ZARA: Do you promise?

SUSAN: Of course.

ZARA: Say it!

SUSAN: I promise . . . Here, put your little boater on.

'And cut!' Ford shouts.

There's suddenly a lot of American people high-fiving each other and going, 'Oh my God!' and, 'A star is born!'

I look at Honor, smiling and saying, 'Thank you,' to the various people telling her how wonderful she just was and I'm suddenly thinking, this is what she was born to do.

'Amazing,' a voice behind me suddenly goes. I turn around and it's, like, the old dear. I didn't even know she was going to be on the set. 'Congratulations to both of you.'

Sorcha gives her a big dramatic hug. 'Oh my God,' she goes, 'I can't believe I nearly denied her this amazing, amazing opportunity, Fionnuala.'

I notice Ford grinning over in our general direction. He catches Fionnuala's eye and says the kid is even better than Lindsay Lohan was at that age.

And Sorcha looks the happiest I've seen her in a long, long time.

We're being held behind a barrier, a hundred yords back from the scene of what promises to be one humungous explosion.

I don't know what I'm even doing here. Three times they've asked me to leave. They've asked us all to leave. Except, weirdly, we actually *want* to be here? Thirty or forty of us who invested our hopes and our dreams and our hord cash in Rosa Porks want to witness the exact moment when it's reduced to basically rubble. Christian goes, 'So what actually happened?'

It really is great to have the dude back in my life. He's come along to lend me a bit of moral support. And also because he saw a casino being taken down with dynamite when he lived in Vegas and it's the kind of thing he really wants to see again.

'They took down the three unfinished blocks last year,' I go. 'Same way. Controlled explosion. But it's supposed to have, like, compromised the foundations of our building. They said it was no longer *habitable*?'

Christian just shakes his head.

A dude in a flourescent orange bib and a hord hat tells us we shouldn't be here. Except no one moves. Then he tells us that if we choose to stay, it's going to be at our own risk, as if that's going to make a blind bit of difference to anyone.

I'm suddenly remembering the excitement when these aportments first went up. The big billboard on the M50 at the exit for Ticknock with the three photographs on it. A dude putting on cufflinks. A woman sipping a pomegranate bellini. A Newbridge Silver fork with a bit of asparagus on the end of it. Where is that bright future that we were promised now?

Someone has the idea of ringing for pizza. Which is what we end up doing. Half an hour later, two dudes arrive on little motor scooters carrying ten or fifteen of them.

I end up offering to pay for them all, which makes me a bit of a hero among the – you'd have to use the word – dispossessed.

Christian tears off a slice of Hawaiian for himself. We sit on the bonnet of my cor and he asks me what the deal is with the insurance. I tell him I don't know yet how much I'll be getting, but it won't be anything like the six hundred Ks the thing was worth when I first moved in.

I'm thinking that I really must make more of an effort with Christian. I haven't seen nearly enough of him since he came back from the States. I know he's got a lot on his plate. Can't have been easy being made redundant and he's already told me that all is not well between him and Lauren.

'We haven't talked in ages,' I go. 'As in, like, *really* talked?'

He straight away knows what I'm getting at and he just comes out with it. 'Lauren wants another baby.'

This would be in addition to Ross – or Ross Junior, as I call him.

I'm there, 'Is that not a good thing? You always said you didn't want your son growing up an only child.'

He looks at me like I've just said something ridiculous. He goes, 'How am *I* going to support another kid?'

I'm like, 'Dude, you'll get another job.'

'Ross, my last job was as the project manager of a themed casino that went almost three-quarters of a billion dollars over budget in the development phase and has been haemorrhaging money at a rate of about two million dollars a week since it opened. I'm not only unemployed, Ross. I'm unemployable.'

He has actual tears in his eyes. I honestly had no idea he was this low. I don't know what to say to him, so I end up saying the first thing that comes into my head.

I'm there, 'Could Lauren's old man not sort you out with a job?'

I'm thinking that a man as famously crooked as Hennessy has got to be able to pull a few strings.

Christian ends up basically losing it with me. 'I don't want to have to go cap in hand to my father-in-law. Jesus Christ, Ross, I wouldn't mind hanging on to the little bit of self-esteem I have left.'

It's bad enough that they're back living with him, I suppose.

The dude in the flourescent bib is back. He's telling us all that we need to block our ears when the explosion happens. He says he'll give us the signal.

I tell Christian I'm sorry. I wasn't thinking. No, he says, *he's* sorry. Then he goes, 'Have another baby? That's a laugh. Me and Lauren haven't . . .'

'What?'

'You know . . .'

'Jesus. How long are we talking?'

'Six months?'

Six months? Did he really just say six months? I don't think the internet had been invented the last time I went even six weeks without Ant and Decs.

He throws his pizza crust away then in a fit of – I'd imagine – frustration.

I put my orm around his shoulder. I'm there, 'Dude, things will . . .'

Except he just cuts me off.

'Don't say they'll get better,' he goes. 'Why do people always say that things will get better?'

'Because they have to.'

'They don't have to, Ross. They can get worse. They can get a lot worse.'

There's no point in talking to him. Not when he's like this. He'll be okay, though. He's got good people around him.

I look at the outline of my aportment building one last time and I try to remember how I felt the day I first moved in.

The dude in the bib goes, 'Okay, block your ears, everyone. You really should. For your own sakes.'

We all do as we're told.

The next thing, the earth suddenly shakes beneath our feet. A big cloud of dust seems to come up from the ground and then – with the loudest bang I've ever heard – the entire building disappears from the skyline forever.

'Can't think why you're surprised,' the old man goes.

I've spent the last twenty minutes boring the focking ears off him about Honor's performance on the set. And anyone else in Kielys who happens to be within hearing distance. I'm the typical proud dad.

'It's in the genes,' the old man goes. 'Lest we forget, you were an entertainer yourself, Ross.'

'Was I?'

'On the rugby field!'

'Oh, yeah. I was actually.'

'The consummate showman, said our friend Mr Thornley. Quote-unquote!'

That's when Ronan suddenly arrives.

He's all, 'Howiya, Grandda. Alreet, Rosser?'

I'm there, 'Coola boola, Ro. Coola focking boola.'

I promised to bring him for a drink when he finished his exams.

'So come on,' I go, 'don't leave me hanging? Do you reckon you passed?'

He just shrugs, playing it cool. He's there, 'Be heerd to say.'

'*Passed?*' the old man goes, handing him a glass of Coke. 'I should think – being your son, Ross – that *passing* the thing would repre-sent merely the base camp of the chap's ambitions. The base camp! Sorry it's not something stronger, Ronan. Should be champagne, of course, but they're a bit funny about underage what-not in here.'

I'm there, 'Be definitely champagne when you get your results, though. There's already a bottle in Sorcha's fridge.'

Ronan pulls a face like he's not counting his chickens, though. He's like, 'I don't know. We'll see,' ever the cool customer.

And it's then, totally out of the blue, that he turns around to me and goes, 'Here, you're not gonna be happy with me, Rosser.'

Obviously, roysh, I'm like, 'What are you talking about?'

He sips his Coke. 'Shadden's da's with me.'

I'm like, 'What?'

'He's looking for a space to peerk.'

'You're telling me he's coming here. To *actual* Kielys?'

'He's been ringing you, so he has. You've been ignorten him. He said youse arranched to go for a drink.'

'We did in our Billy Joels arrange to go for a drink. He suggested it and I pretended to have a problem with my coverage. Er, *not* the same thing?'

The old man goes, 'What the hell is wrong with him coming here, Ross? I must say, I'm rather looking forward to meeting the famous Shadden's father.'

I tell him not to expect too much – that way he won't be disappointed.

'And maybe stick your wallet in a safe pocket,' I go.

And Ronan, by the way, doesn't say a word in the man's defence.

The next thing, roysh, in he walks. You should see how he's focking dressed. The worst thing is that he's made an actual effort. He's wearing, like, a white dress shirt from obviously Dunnes Stores, with the top button done up – even though there's no tie with it – and it's tucked tightly into a pair of just basic jeans – no brand, no focking shape either – with the whole look touched off with a pair of – I swear to fock – just black slip-on shoes.

'Howiya!' he goes.

Howiya? Kielys has never heard the focking likes of it.

'J . . . J . . . Jaysus,' he goes. 'Moorder getting p . . . p . . . peerking arowunt here, idn't it?'

I just go, 'Yeah, you can be reasonably sure it'll still have all of its focking wheels when you get back to it, though.'

He doesn't even take offence at this. He just keeps grinning at me, like an inner-city community volunteer who's just found out that I'm the *Secret Millionaire*.

And do you want to know the *weirdest* thing? The old man is grinning at *him* in the same way that *he's* grinning at me. Then he goes, 'Kennet Tuite – as I live and breathe!'

And that's when I suddenly realize that they must know each other from prison.

'Cheerlie,' he goes. 'I doatunt believe it. I says it to Dordeen thudder day. I says to her, I was v . . . v . . . v . . . veddy good friends with a f . . . fedda insoyut whose second nayum was Accada-Keddy. Says I, I wonter are thee relayred?'

It took him that long to put two and two together? Jesus Christ, this focker's slower than *Avatar*.

The old man goes, 'So how the hell *are* you? Keeping your nose clean, I hope?'

'I have to, Cheerlie. Ah, you know yisser self – the kids were gettin to that age. All t . . . t . . . teenagers – wadn't feer on their mudder raising thum on her owen.'

The old man pulls a big understanding face.

Kennet turns to me then. 'Your f . . . f . . . fadder's a great man,' he goes, like he's telling me something somehow new. 'He was an un-fooken-beleafable support to the likes of m . . . m . . . me and a lot of utters in ta Joy. That's norra woort of a lie, Cheerlie.'

The old man goes all modest then. 'Well, we all muddled through – as best we could, I expect.'

'No, there was t . . . t . . . toyums in that jail, Cheerlie, when my spidit was veddy nearly b . . . b . . . b . . . broken, so it was. You were alwees the fedda on eer lanten you could go and have chat wit if you were feedin a bit down in y . . . y . . . yisser self. You safed me from a deerk place many's the toyum. A lot'd say ta sayum.'

This is how the night ends up passing. The three of them drinking Coke ('Ine off ta drink t . . . t . . . tis tree year, Cheerlie') and him and the old man – who's also off the drink because he's driving – reminiscing about their time inside.

It goes on for, like, three or four hours, until all of Kennet's stories begin with either 'I'll tell you now who's arthur gettin teddible strung out on ta gear . . .' or 'I'll tell you now who's arthur dyin, Lorta meercy on um . . .' and that's when I decide I've had enough.

If I wanted to hear that kind of shit, I'd go and sit on the focking Luas red line for an hour.

I tell them I'm gonna go and grab an Andy McNab. Kennet is immediately up off his stool. 'No neeyut,' he goes. 'Suren *I'll* drop you wheredever you're wanthen to go.'

I'm there, 'It's Blackrock actually. It's pretty far out of your way,' and of course the real reason I'm saying it is that I don't want him to know where I actually live.

'Would ye go onta fook ourra dat. Ballackrock, it's only ten bleaten minutes. Come on, Ro, suren I'll drop you back to Finglas as well, wha'?'

As he's saying his goodbyes to my old man, he goes, 'Moy thaughter and your graddenson, Cheerlie, wha'? Who'd of taught tat when we were doing isser stretch – not me, says you!'

The old man just laughs along like the sucker that he is. He genuinely doesn't see the bad in people. He's always quoting that line – which was one of Father Fehily's – that it's a far better thing to be disappointed by people than to be distrustful of them.

We step out of Kielys. The old man goes in one direction – he's porked in the little cor pork opposite – and the three of us go the other way. Kennet says he's way down, nearly opposite Donnybrook Fair. I end up stopping and orguing with him for a minute or two, *trying* to point out that I'd be nearly home in a taxi in the time it's going to take to walk to his cor. Except he won't take no for an answer. So we stort walking in that direction and I'm actually checking out the BeoSound 9000 in the window of Bang & Olufsen when it suddenly happens.

The first thing I hear, roysh, is the scream of brakes – it's, like, loud and piercing, almost like metal on metal. Then I hear *actual* screams, not to mention shouts. Then, all of a sudden, this 46A comes hurtling around the corner – obviously out of control – passes the fire station, mounts the path outside Empty Pockets and ploughs straight into the tree outside Marian Gale, basically flattening the focking thing.

'Fock!' I hear myself go.

Because my first thought is obviously whether or not the old man is okay. Then I notice that his Kompressor has gone and I breathe an instant sight of relief.

Ronan's obviously thinking the same thing because he goes, 'If we'd a left the pub toorty seconds later,' he goes, 'grandda woulda been a goner.'

I'm like, 'Thank fock.'

We watched the entire thing happen, bear in mind, from the opposite side of the street.

'It's a good job there was no one on that bus,' Ronan goes.

I'm there, 'Except for obviously the driver. He must have had, like, a *hort* attack or something?'

I go to say something to Kennet, roysh, and that's when I notice that he's lying face-down on the deck outside Borza's.

Obviously, roysh, I'm like, 'What the fock?'

Again, Ronan's on the same page as me. He's there, 'What! The fook!'

I get down to check on him. I turn him over and I'm giving it, 'Kennet! Kennet! Kennet!' at the top of my voice. 'Can you hear me? Kennet! What happened?'

His eyes are closed. He's totally out of the game. I'm actually slapping his face – like you see in *Holby City* or any of those – going, 'Kennet! Kennet! Can you hear my voice?'

Ronan's there, 'Might be shock, Rosser.'

I'm like, 'How could it be shock? He saw it happen the exact same way we did. Kennet! Come on! There's nothing wrong with you!'

That's when he all of a sudden opens one eye and goes, 'Shut the fook up, will you? It's a clayum!'

Then he goes back to playing dead.

I'm left in pretty much shock myself. Ronan is too, because we end up not saying a word to each other until the ambulance pulls

up – the full siren and everything – and Kennet is lifted onto a stretcher and loaded into the back.

One of the – I suppose – *attendants* goes, 'Do you know him?' and I straight away go, 'No, thank God,' and then I throw in, 'And neither does my son.'

Ro ends up letting me down, though – in a big time way. It must be the real thing between him and Shadden because he goes, 'He's me geerlfriend's da,' and then – as if that's enough of a reason – he climbs into the back of the ambulance and says he'll go with him to the hospital.

Then the ambulance roars off and I'm left standing there on my Tobler, just staring into space with my mouth slung open, like someone from Wicklow having the internet explained to them.

The speed at which the whole thing happened. We only left Kielys, like, ten minutes ago.

That's when my phone all of a sudden rings. I answer it without checking, hoping it's Ro, because I'm feeling suddenly bad about letting him go on his own.

It turns out to be Sorcha. Her opening line is, 'Are you sitting down, Ross?'

I'm like, 'Okay, why is that important?'

'Because,' she goes, 'I've got something to tell you and it might come as an actual shock.'

I'm there, 'Sorcha, after what I've just witnessed, I reckon I'm pretty much unshockable.'

'Okay,' she goes, with a definite have-it-your-way vibe, 'your grandmother's here.'

I laugh. Have to. I'm there, 'I don't have a grandmother.'

She's like, 'Er, your mum's mum?'

'Yeah,' I go, 'but she's been in a mental hospital for, like, fifty-something years. She's whacka-focking-doodle.'

'Well,' she goes, her voice dropping to a whisper, 'she's sitting in our living room.'

8.

Who's Suri now?

'She smells of wet tweed,' Honor goes.

Sorcha shushes her and reminds her that that's her great-grandmother she's talking about and she should at least keep her voice down.

Honor goes, 'Er, hashtag – sense of *humour* failure?'

The three of us are standing in the hallway. I'm struggling to get my head around the fact that beyond that living-room door is my oldest living relative in the world who I thought I was never going to actually meet.

'What the fock does she want?' I go.

Sorcha's there, 'Ross, *you* could keep *your* voice down too.'

I'm there, 'My question still stands. I mean, how did she even find us?'

She goes, 'I'm presuming the phone book. She knew that her daughter was Fionnuala O'Carroll-Kelly, the novelist . . .'

'So-called.'

'. . . and we're the only O'Carroll-Kellys listed in the 01 area.'

The old dear obviously knew what she was doing going ex-directory.

I'm there, 'So when did she get out of the funny form?'

She's like, 'Ross!'

'Sorry – when did she get out of whatever, I don't know, mental institution she was in?'

'That's, like, the big twist – she wasn't actually *in* a mental institution?'

That rocks me back on my definite heels. 'She's supposed to have been in there since the old dear was a little girl.'

'She was actually living with a closed order of nuns. In Wexford.'

'Wexford? Jesus!'

'The last of the nuns died a couple of weeks ago. Sister Edward. It was *her* brother who brought her here. The order has put the house and the lands up for sale. She has nowhere to go.'

'Whoa! Back up the hord drive here! Are you saying the woman's not even bananas?'

'Ross, I think a lot of people would take deep offence to the way you're characterizing mental illness.'

'Look, whatever the actual words are – you're saying she's, like, normal?'

Honor just sniggers. Sorcha tells her to go to bed. She has, like, an early stort tomorrow. They're filming in Carrickmines. Honor says oh my God, no way – she doesn't want to miss, like, a *minute* of this? Sorcha rolls her eyes, then turns back to me.

'No,' she says in, like, a whisper, 'I wouldn't describe her as normal. Eccentric might be more the word. She . . . she has no real concept of, like, *time* elapsing?'

'Okay, keep it simple, Sorcha – that's always been the way to get through to me.'

'She thinks it's still the 1950s, Ross. Or the early 1960s.'

'Jesus focking Christ.'

'Like I said, she's been living in a closed order. The world, as we know it, is a total mystery to her.'

'Well, she can't stay here.'

'I said it'd be okay as, like, a short-term thing? Just until she reconciles with your mum. The whole experience is going to be very traumatizing for everyone involved. And I did that mediation course when I was in UCD, remember – and it was actually *accredited*?'

Poor Sorcha. She's so nice – that's why people end up taking the piss.

'Look,' I go, 'she's not staying here and that's the end of it,' and at the same time I push the door and go into the living room.

The woman is sitting in *my* chair. It turns out that she's not one of the big grey afro types, like Sorcha's granny. Her hair *is* grey but it's, like, swept back into a bun, although the rest of her is pretty much what you'd expect – the cardy, the woollen skirt, the men's brogues and the unexplained bandage on her lower leg, which is visible through her half-inch-thick tights that Sorcha might well describe as adobe.

And she *does* smell of wet tweed. Honor got that much right.

I'm just about to tell her to sling her focking hook when she turns around and sees me for the first time. And this look of – I'm going to say it – *astonishment* comes over her face? I'm not making this shit up. 'Sweet Lord,' she goes, 'he's like a film star. He's like Cary Grant!'

And what can *I* do except turn to Sorcha and go, 'Alright, maybe she can stay for a few nights.'

Honor calls her mother a sap, then a wagon, then a sad sack. Then she goes, 'And whatever look you were aiming for with that dress, you missed it by a distance of from here to focking Jupiter.'

I really should chorge my old dear royalties for the number of lines in this script that she's ripped off from me. All those years, she must have been taking notes at the focking breakfast table.

I turn around and just glower at her – me and her are going to have words today. Her hair is taking hilariously long to grow back, by the way. She's following the scene really closely, silently mouthing all of the lines herself.

'Zara,' the mother goes, 'it doesn't matter how much you try to wound me' – another line that strikes me as pretty familiar – 'you're not competing in the gymkhana tomorrow and that's that. Now eat your dinner, like a good wee girl.'

I have to say, roysh, I'm really enjoying this scene. Honor – sorry, Zara – ends up shooting the mother the most unbelievable filthy I've ever seen.

ZARA: It's disgusting. I'd rather eat what's in the focking hoover bag.
SUSAN: 'Tis the first meat we've had in weeks. The International Monetary Fund are running this country now – who knows if we'll ever have it again.

Zara ends up pronging the meat with her fork. She saws off a piece, then takes it between her teeth. The face she pulls – you'd swear she was eating shit off a lollipop stick.

I turn to Sorcha. I'm there, 'She's good – there's no denying that.'

I can't tell you how actually *proud* of her Sorcha looks? She goes, 'I told her to channel her feelings from that time I gave her Tesco Value cola. Do you remember – when I had to take her to that stress counsellor?'

Some dude with an earpiece, a clipboard and a polo shirt shushes us, except he does it with, like, a *smile* on his face? So Sorcha, who does passive-aggressive like no other woman alive, smiles back and tells him under her breath that he has an attitude problem – a serious attitude problem.

This scene is being shot, by the way, in a bungalow in Carrickmines that has broken windows and smells of piss. In the storyline, Zara's parents were forced to trade down to this from their original home on, like, Serpentine Avenue.

I watch my daughter eat two or three mouthfuls of her dinner, then she pushes her plate away.

ZARA: That's all I'm eating.
SUSAN: That's fine enough for you. Sure 'tis your bedtime anyway.
ZARA: My bedtime? Oh my God, it's only, like, seven o'clock.
SUSAN: Do we have to go through this every night, Zara? We can't afford to heat the house, so we can't. 'Tis the only way to keep warm.

ZARA *suddenly stands up from the table.*

ZARA: Well, I'm going to say goodnight to Misty first.
SUSAN: Och, no – sure 'tis coming down by the bucketload out there . . .

They've got, like, a rain machine set up outside – obviously because an American audience couldn't believe it was Ireland unless it was focking pissing.

ZARA: I'm *going* to say goodnight to Misty.

She has, like, a stubborn look on her face that Sorcha and I straight away recognize. She opens the back door and steps out into the rain. The mother follows her outside, basically calling after her.

SUSAN: Come back! Zara, no! Come back in the house! Please!

We watch the next bit, what they call an 'exterior shot' in the movie game, on one of the little monitors. Honor – slash, Zara – pegs it through the rain to this pretty much coal shed at the back of the gaff.

SUSAN: Zara, come back! Let me explain!

Zara flings the door open. The shed ends up being empty. The camera sort of, like, lingers on the floor, which is strewn with hay, then it moves to an empty water trough, then to a saddle hanging on the wall.

Zara bends down to pick something up. It ends up being a horse shoe – I'm *presuming* one of, like, Misty's? She's standing there staring at it with, like, genuine tears in her eyes when her mother suddenly arrives at the door.

There's, like, a close-up of Honor's little face – she looks confused. Even lost. She's an incredible actress, no orguments.

ZARA: Where's my pony? Where's Misty?
SUSAN: I'm sorry, Zara – I was going to explain, so I was.
ZARA: We've . . . we've just been eating her, haven't we?
SUSAN: We had no choice, so we didn't. It was either that or starve to death.

Zara shakes her head in basically disbelief, just going 'No!' over and over again, until it finally builds up into a scream, which actually reminds of the first day Linh brought Honor into Euro Hero.

'And . . . cut!' Ford shouts, then everyone bursts into a round of applause. The clapping gets even louder as Honor steps back into the house, dripping wet, but smiling.

Ford gets up out of his little director's chair and just shouts, 'I love this kid! I *love* her!'

I'm not just saying this, but the look on Honor's face reminds me of myself back in the day. People are telling her how incredible she just was and, even though she's saying thank you, it's like they're not telling her anything she doesn't already *know*?

The old dear is clapping with her two orms fully outstretched in front of her, looking to be the centre of attention basically. She's going, 'Dahling, you brought tears to my eyes! Tears to my eyes!'

She gives Honor a hug. I end up just staring at the woman. Sorcha shoots me one of her warning looks. 'Now handle it sensitively, Ross.'

I'm there, 'Hey, you're talking to *Mister* Sensitive.'

'Like I said, it's going to be – oh my God – a huge shock to your mum's system. There's obviously a lot of pain there. And a lot of healing to be done.'

I'm just there, 'Trust me.'

Sorcha takes Honor off somewhere, I think Horvey Nichs, for lunch. I walk up to the old dear and I go, 'I want a word.'

She's there, 'Yes, of course – my lovely son!' because she likes to play happy families when we're out in public. 'Let's talk in my trailer.'

Sixty seconds later, she's sitting in front of a mirror in her dressing room, throwing on more slap and generally checking herself out.

'If your head was a rugby pitch,' I go, 'I wouldn't let the focking Clontorf J9s play on it.'

She doesn't even look at me – proving that what she said outside was just an act. She just goes, 'This is a happy day for me, Ross. I'm not going to let you cast your darkness over it.'

I plonk my orse down on this, like, ormchair in the corner. There's a book folded face-down on the little table in front of me. *The Brief Wondrous Life of Oscar Wao.* I pretend to flick through it. It's probably shit.

'Tell me about my grandmother,' I go.

She stops, her foundation sponge paused in mid-air about twelve inches from her face.

She's like, 'What?'

She actually reacts like it's the last thing in the world she expected me to bring up here today.

I'm there, 'My grandmother – I want to know about her.'

She goes, 'Well, what is it you want to know?'

I just shrug. 'It's just you never talk about her.'

'Well, there's nothing to say. The woman's doolally. Is that all you want, Ross, because Ford has asked me to make some revisions to a scene . . .'

'I wouldn't mind going to visit her.'

'What?'

'I mean, she must be, what, ninety-one, ninety-two now? I'd just hate if she died and I never got to actually meet her.'

'Ross, she's in a mental institution.'

'I know that. I presume they have visiting hours, though, don't they?'

'But . . . but she wouldn't know who you were. The last time I laid eyes on her was more than fifty years ago and she didn't even recognize *me*.'

'Still, though, I'd like to at least say I met her.'

'Please yourself.'

'So what mental institution is she in, then?'

'Excuse me?'

'What *actual* mental institution?'

'Ross, does this have to be now?'

'No, but I'm *asking* you now – where actually is she?'

She puts the foundation sponge down, then she puts on this really sad face, like she's got some terrible news she needs to break to me.

'I didn't want to tell you,' she goes, 'because you were going through a difficult time with your divorce and everything. But your grandmother passed away, Ross. Three years ago. Peacefully, in her sleep. A merciful end for everyone concerned.'

I just nod.

'That's funny,' I go, 'because she's in Sorcha's focking kitchen.'

The old dear's face just hits the floor. It's as if a ghost has just appeared. Which, in a way, I suppose it has.

I'm there, 'Oh, yeah. I left her half an hour ago, horsing into a big bowl of porridge. Focking Flahavan's. And I can tell you this much – she's very *much* alive. *And* she's actually sound. She's already a huge fan of mine.'

'It must be a mistake.'

'It's not a mistake. I mean, yeah, she's nutty as a focking noodle. But she's definitely not dead. There's ways of knowing, see. Like when you're sitting down and having an actual *conversation* with someone?'

'What did she say?'

'Oh, she'd tonnes of news to tell me. We had a serious catch-up.

Probably the biggest news of all was that she wasn't even *in* a mental institution. Well, she *was* – for a couple of years. But then she was released in – what year was it? – 1958? Except your old man didn't want her back.'

'How dare you! You don't know anything about the situation.'

'You abandoned her. A woman with serious focking head problems. And a bunch of nuns had to eventually take her in.'

She turns dog on me then. 'So,' she goes, 'what the hell does she want now?'

I'm there, 'Somewhere to live.'

She suddenly stands up. 'I don't have time for this . . .'

I'm there, 'Time for what? Time for a mother?'

She goes, 'Time for *that* mother,' and then she storms out – *the* most upset I've seen her since the time *VIP* used her photograph in a 'Still Sexy at Seventy' photo spread.

I don't even know her name.

'Aida,' she goes.

I'm there, 'So do I, like, *call* you that? Or do I call you Granny?'

'You can call me whatever you want.'

'It's just that Granny feels kind of weird.'

'Call me Aida, then.'

'Maybe I will so. Maybe I will.'

I'm putting clean sheets on her bed. I'm actually giving her my room. I don't mind sleeping in the boxroom – it's only going to *be* for a while.

'So I, er, spoke to the old dear today,' I go. 'Fionnuala? As in, your daughter?'

'Sure she wouldn't remember me.'

'Well, she knows she *has* a mother. I mean, everyone has a mother.'

'Never so much as a card at Christmas.'

'Look, I'm not a fan of hers myself. So feel free to talk here.'

'Christmases, birthdays – they all went by. Ten years. Nothing.'

'It's, er, a bit longer than ten years, Aida.'

'Ten years,' she just goes. 'So has your father a fine jawline, too?'

I'm stuffing her duvet into its cover when she says this and to be honest it takes me a bit by surprise.

I'm like, 'Sorry?'

She goes, 'Is he a handsome man? I'm just wondering where did you get your good looks? You certainly didn't get them from your mother.'

I crack my hole laughing. I'm there, 'I thought you hadn't seen her since she was a kid.'

'Sorcha gave me some of her books . . .'

Of course. Her photograph – focking horrendous – is on the inside cover.

'She's turned out like her father,' she goes. 'No chin. Eyes you couldn't trust. Like a Chinaman.'

I laugh even horder. I'm definitely going to remember that quote.

'But you,' she goes, 'you're like something from a picture house. Hollywood. I told you that. Cary Grant. Jimmy Stewart. Any of them.'

I just nod and accept it. It's a huge boost. She'd be good for your confidence. I button up the duvet cover, then shake it out. Then I move on to the pillows.

'Do they live close to you?' she goes.

I'm there, 'Who?'

She's like, 'Fionnuala and your father.'

I'm there, '*She* does. Just up the road in Foxrock. He lives in Donnybrook. They're, like, *divorced*?'

She sort of, like, tuts to herself. 'Divorced, is it?' Actually, it's more like a *chuckle*? 'Did they go to England for that?'

'No, they got it here.'

'But sure there's no divorce in Ireland.'

Now it's my turn to laugh. The news obviously didn't get much of a mench in the nuns' gaff. 'There is now,' I go. 'Me and Sorcha are actually getting one.'

Except *she* just shakes her head. 'You'll be a long time waiting for a divorce in Ireland.'

I end up just letting it go. I finish dressing the bed. Then *she* goes, 'Well, I think I'll say goodnight to you.'

I'm there, 'Fair enough, Aida. Porridge for brekky, is it?'

'What's that?'

'Do you want me to do you a bowl of Flahavan's again?'

'That'd be nice. Oh, you're such a lovely young man.'

'Er, thanks.'

'Such a lovely gentleman.'

You could end up getting a seriously big head from being around her. I say goodnight to her, then I step out onto the landing. I feel my phone vibrate in my pocket, so I check it and it ends up being Christian.

He actually sounds embarrassed. He's all, 'Look, er, thanks for the chat last week, Ross. I'm sorry if I was a bit . . .'

I'm like, 'Dude, don't even mention it. Er, *how* long have we been friends?'

'I missed that, you know. When I was in the States. Having you to talk to.'

'Well, I'm always here, Dude. I'm going nowhere – as McGahy used to tell me at school.'

He sort of, like, laughs.

'So,' I go, 'how are things? Any improvement, you know, since?'

He takes, like, a deep breath. He sounds upset. They've obviously just had a borney.

'Pint,' I just go. 'Kielys. Now.'

He's like, 'Ross, I'm tired of talking about it.'

I'm there, 'Then we'll talk about something else. Rugby. Women we wouldn't mind scoring. Old times.'

He's there, 'Okay.'

'You need cheering up, Dude – and I'm the man for the job.'

I tip downstairs. Honor and Sorcha are sitting at the kitchen table. Sorcha's going, 'I know you're hungry, Darling. Just keep sucking on the ice cubes until I come up with a way of getting us some food.'

They're doing a read-through of Honor's lines for tomorrow. At least I focking hope they are.

'I've, er, got to go out,' I go.

Sorcha's head shoots up with a definite look of disappointment on her face. I'm trying to work out is it, like, jealousy?

I'm there, 'It's actually, er, Christian I'm meeting.'

She goes, 'Oh,' and then, 'Is he okay?'

It's pretty obvious from the way she says it that Lauren's told her they're having problems. I love women, but they can't hold their piss.

'He's, er, cool,' I go. 'I don't know whether to do Aida's porridge tonight or in the morning. It's nicer – isn't it? – if you leave it soaking overnight.'

Sorcha's suddenly looking at me like I'm Aung San Suu Kyi – or *any* of her heroes.

I'm like, 'What? What are you smiling at?'

And Sorcha just goes, 'Ross, you are *so* an amazing person.'

The old dear sends out a text to obviously everyone in her contacts list going, 'Another earthquake in New Zealand. Watching it on the news. Christchurch devastated. Lol.'

This is the kind of shit that's important to her – what, a week after finding out that her old dear is back after fifty-whatever-it-is years and has nowhere to focking go?

There's things I *could* text back, but I don't.

Me and the old man are standing on the third tee box in Elm Pork. Ronan, who sliced his drive, is over to our right, searching for his ball in the rough.

I line one up and hit it sweetly, except I don't get any really power behind it. It happened on the first two as well. They were a good fifty yords short of where I'd usually put them. The old man cops it.

He's like, 'You okay, Kicker?'

I'm there, 'Yeah, no, I'm just a bit, I don't know, tight or something.'

What I mean is I haven't got my full movement back since the shooting. I can't really open up on my swing. The old man knows where I'm coming from. He was the same after his hort bypass.

'Do you want to call it a day, Ross? Get ourselves a couple of short ones in the clubhouse?'

I'm like, 'No, let's play. Just don't expect too much competition, that's all – from me *or* Ro?'

The old man laughs. 'I don't think the famous Ronan has his mind on his game, you know,' and then he shouts, 'I think it went further over, Ronan.'

As the old man is lining up his drive, I go, 'By the way, what do you know about my grandmother?'

He stops. He's like, 'Your grandmother? Do you mean my mother or your mother's mother?'

'The second one.'

'Sadly demented, Ross.'

'Really?'

'Regrettably so. Yes, she's been mouldering away – the poor old girl – in one of these institutions – oh, ever since your mother was a child. Very painful for all concerned.'

'Is that what you think?'

'Well, of course. Matter of fact, Fionnuala's last memory of her was sitting in the dayroom of whichever hospital it was – looking at her across a table. The woman was loop the loop, by all accounts. In the end, they had to give up going to see her – Fionnuala *and* her father.'

'Why?'

'Too upsetting, I expect. You've got to remember, Kicker, this was the 1950s. These institutions were terribly grim places. Abandon hope, etcetera, etcetera. And there *wasn't* any hope for poor old Aida, from what I hear. There was no hope of her ever snapping out of it. And I think Fionnuala and her father had to eventually bow to the inevitable.'

He assumes the stance again, then takes one or two practice swings.

I'm there, 'So what if I said that was all horseshit?'

He's like, 'Come again, Ross.'

'Every word you've just said to me – except the bit about her actually *being* in a mental hospital. What if I told you that she got out after a year and that *he* just didn't want her back?'

'Fionnuala's father?'

'Exactly. What if I told you that he basically abandoned her? Then she ended up living with a pack of nuns for, I don't know, fifty or something years.'

The old man is no stranger to secrets himself, but I can see that this has come as a genuine shock to him. He goes, 'Where's all this coming from, Ross?'

I'm there, 'She turned up on our doorstep.'

'What?'

'Yeah, no, she's actually staying with us until we can find somewhere else for her.'

'And what's Fionnuala saying?'

'She doesn't want to know.'

'Well, I find that very difficult to believe . . .'

I laugh.

'Well, you found it very difficult to believe that she'd tell social services that her granddaughter was at risk of poverty.'

'She wouldn't do something like that.'

'What, just like she wouldn't do something like this? Open your eyes. She's known her old dear was out there somewhere for however many years it's been. I'm pretty focking certain she knew exactly where she was as well. You know, she actually tried to tell me the other day that she was dead.'

'Well,' he goes, 'she was in shock, I expect.'

She lied to him about her mother for their entire married life and he's, like, still trying to see the good in her.

I let him finally take his shot. It's a good one as well. He'll end up birdying this hole – nothing surer.

'I'll, er, go help Ronan find his ball,' I go.

I wander over to him. He's, like, pulling back the long grass with the head of his club. The old man was right. His head's not in the game. I can take a pretty good guess where it actually is.

'So,' I go, 'what's the story with K . . . K . . . K . . . Kennet,' which is what I've storted calling him.

Ro nods his head and goes, 'He's gonna be alreet, so he is.'

I'm there, 'Of course he's going to be alright – there's fock-all wrong with him. What's the story with this supposed claim of his?'

'He's looking for a hundrit gerrand offa Dubbalin Bus.'

I laugh. 'A hundred Ks? He was, like, fifty focking yords away from the crash when it happened.'

307

'He's saying he was trun across the road.'

All I can do is just shake my head. 'Well,' I go, 'good luck to him finding a witness to back up that story.'

Ronan doesn't say anything.

'Don't do it,' I calmly go.

'He's Shadden's da, Rosser.'

'That doesn't mean you've got to stand up in court and lie for him.'

'He says it woatunt go to court – the insurance company will settle.'

'Only if *you* back up his bullshit story.'

'Not just me, Rosser. You *and* me.'

'No focking way.'

'He ast me to ast you . . .'

'There's no focking way I'm doing it, Ro. You can tell him that from me. I'm staying well out of it. And my advice to you would be to do the same thing.'

'It's heerder for me, but. He's me geerlfriend's fadder.'

'Well, he shouldn't have put you *in* this position,' I go, suddenly spotting his ball. 'And, much as I like Shadden, Ro, you should be asking yourself is this the kind of family you want to get mixed up with?'

He stares sadly at his ball. 'Can I trun it on the feerway?' he goes.

And I think to myself, no, there's a lesson in this for him.

I'm like, 'Sorry, Ro. You're going to have to play this one without my help.'

Aida wants me to bring her to Dalkey. Which is no biggie. She says she always loved it as a little girl and I just think, yeah, no, it might be nice for her to see it again.

She says her earliest memory as a child is staring across at Dalkey Island from Coliemore Horbour – this is in the Lambo, by the way, while we're on the way there.

I tell her *my* earliest memory is watching the old dear make a Bloody Mary using Ragù when she found out there was no tomato juice in the gaff.

She laughs, in fairness to her.

'Bloody Marys,' she goes. 'Is that what she drinks?'

I'm there, 'She'd drink anything once she could squeeze her big focking sink-plunger lips around the neck of the bottle. She's a serious lush. If they ever cremate her, it'll take them six days to put the blaze out.'

She goes into literally hysterics when she hears that.

'Oh, you're so funny!' she goes – again, *boosting* me. 'You're a funny, funny man!'

Then she points to the radio. She's like, 'Is that a wireless?'

I'm there, 'Slash radio, yeah.'

I turn it on for her. It's, like, Kesha – *We R Who We R*.

She listens to it with her face screwed up, like me trying to understand poetry. In other words, it's just focking noise to her.

'Do you like Ritchie Valens?' she goes.

I've never heard of the focker, of course. But then I don't want to hurt her feelings, so I end up going, 'One or two of his tunes I like, yeah.'

'And what about The Platters? I love The Platters. See can you find The Platters there on the wireless.'

This is as we're approaching the Glenageary roundabout. I go through the presets, although just to humour her more than anything. There's no Platters, although she doesn't seem too disappointed, because the next line out of her mouth is, 'Do you have anything to drink?'

That catches me a bit on the hop. I'm like, 'Drink? Er . . .' and then I remember my Leinster supporters hip flask in the glove comportment that I just topped up with XO from the old man's study.

'There's a drop of brandy in there,' I go, indicating it with a nod of my head. She whips it out, then opens it and knocks back a good lungful – it'd be a definite treble, measure-wise. Then she sort of, like, nods her appreciation – obviously no stranger to the hord stuff. The old dear obviously didn't lick it up off the floor – although she probably would if she ever spilled a drop.

'Are *you* a brandy drinker?' she goes.

This is as we're driving up Dalkey actual Main Street.

I'm like, 'The odd time. Usually if I'm at a rugby match – keeps out the cold and blah, blah, blah. My old man would have been a massive fan of the stuff – that was before the hort attack.'

'What's *he* like – your father?'

'My old man? He's actually alright – when he's not trying to be all palsy-walsy. He's actually a lot nicer than *her*.'

'Fionnuala?'

'Yeah, no offence.'

She knocks back whatever's left in the hip flask – it *was* actually full?

Then she goes, 'You don't like her, do you not?'

I'm there, 'Why would I? She's never had time for me. Kids in Chernobyl, Romania, anywhere that anything shit ever happened – she was always on it like a bonnet. But her own son? No, didn't have a minute for me.'

She looks at me sideways. Her eyes seem actually glassy – could be tears, or she could be just pissed.

'Well,' she goes, 'that's one thing that you and I have in common, isn't it?'

She's genuinely one of the soundest people I've ever met.

I pork on the side of the road, then I help her out of the cor and we walk slowly down to the actual horbour, her linking me all the way. There's a dude sitting on a bench on the pier reading the *Irish Independent*. A headline leaps off the page at me – 'Receiver Appointed to Superquinn'. He gets up and offers us the bench.

Aida goes, 'Did he look like a dirty foreigner to you?'

I laugh. She's obviously a racist, except in, like, a *funny* way?

'Er, I don't know,' I go.

'He'd the look of a Frenchman.'

'I think he might have been Irish, except just with dork hair?'

'I don't care much for the French. They put too much what's-this-it's-called in everything they cook. And they can't be trusted.'

We sit and stare at Dalkey Island for maybe five minutes before another word is spoken.

'I painted it,' *she* eventually goes.

I'm like, 'What?'

'The island. I liked to paint it – when I lived with the nuns.'

'What, you did it from just memory?'

'Oh, yes. All around here, in fact. Dun Laoghaire. Bray . . .'

'Bray? Jesus.'

'Killiney Bay. I lived here for a lot of years, remember.'

'You must have some memory, though – that's all I can say.'

'I do. For happy things.'

We carry on just sitting there. It's actually nice. It kind of feels like we're close to nature, if that doesn't sound too wanky.

'Yeah, no,' I go, 'I'm just thinking about a headline I saw in the paper there about Superquinn being supposedly focked. I hope they manage to save it – even just for Sorcha's sake. She's never out of the place. Loves the deli counter. It just shows you how bad things must be if even *it's* banjoed.'

'I blame Dev,' she goes.

It'll tell you the way my mind works that I just presume she's talking about the dude from *Coronation Street*. I'm like, 'Dev?' and I'm on the point of reminding her that he's not actually a real shop-keeper when she goes, 'Eamon de Valera.'

I'm like, 'Oh, *that* Dev! Yeah, you've got a definite point there – I'd have to agree.'

'The worst leader we ever had. Always fighting with England. We hate England more than we hate being poor. That's the Irish for you.'

'I suppose.'

'And now we're looking to join the Common Market.'

'Er, yeah.'

She tuts. 'That'll end in tears. Mark my words. Should have never got rid of the barges.'

We sit like that and chat for maybe another half an hour, then I suggest grabbing a bit of lunch in possibly The Queens. On me. I keep forgetting. I'm a focking millionaire – or I will be when Hennessy diverts Regina's money to me through the series of off-shore accounts he uses for 'cleaning currency'.

The place ends up being jammers, but we still manage to get a table out the front. We both order the chowder and Aida orders more brandy – just a double, this time – and that's when I suddenly cop Sorcha's old pair. *They're* actually leaving. They've stopped by a table a few feet away to chat to a couple who've just arrived. Sorcha's old dear is telling the woman how surprised she was by the risotto – which she never usually eats – while the old man is telling the dude that Spain and Italy are now in the same position as *we* were when we were bailed out by the EU and the IMF.

Then they go to move off and I give them a shout – nice to be nice, blah, blah, blah.

He looks at me like I'm a wet dog at a wedding.

I'm there, 'How the hell are you?' again just making the effort.

'We're well,' he goes, like he's pissed off about having to tell me.

Sorcha's old dear introduces herself to Aida, then *he* does the same. Except *he* actually goes, 'Yes, Sorcha told me that Ross's grandmother was staying now. I expect she's beginning to feel a bit outnumbered in that house.'

He's an orsehole. Sorcha wouldn't even be talking to him if it wasn't for me. I try to just change the subject, though.

'So,' I go, 'any news on the gaff?' because Sorcha was saying they'd dropped the asking price to one point five mills. I turn to Aida and go, 'They're having to sell their house on the Vico Road – I think Sorcha might have even mentioned it. It's a seriously nice gaff as well,' which most people would consider a compliment.

Not him, though.

He goes, 'What the hell business is it of yours?'

This is just as the waitress arrives over with our chowders.

I'm like, 'Hey, no offence, Dude. I'm just making general convo.'

Even Sorcha's old dear goes, 'Come on, Edmund!' but there's, like, no calming him down where I'm concerned.

'No offence?' he goes. '*You* are a permanent offence. You're like a little cockroach we can't seem to get bloody rid of. When are you planning to clear off out of Sorcha's life?'

I'm there, 'Er, my aportment's just been demolished, in case you didn't know.'

'And what the hell does that have to do with my daughter? I mean, can't you find somewhere else to go? A quarter of a million vacant properties in this country and you're still living in the home of the woman who's trying her darndest to divorce you. Infesting the place like vermin . . .'

It happens without any warning. Aida doesn't even bat an eyelid. She just picks up her chowder bowl and – I swear to God – turns it upside-down, tipping the entire contents all over Sorcha's old man's trousers and shoes. And this, by the way, is with the entire outside of The Queen's looking on.

He's like, 'What the hell do you think you're . . .'

Aida doesn't just sit there and listen to his shit, though – see, *she's* not scared of him? Instead – this is amazing – she looks the focker dead in the eye and goes, 'This here is my grandson. And you will never, ever speak to him like that again!'

He literally can't believe what's just happened. He's, like, staring down at his rhythms, going, 'What the hell . . .' because – whatever about the trousers – they're *actual* John Lobbs that he's wearing and now they're covered in bits of focking fish.

Aida goes, 'I'm ninety-two years of age. I don't know how much time I have left, but I don't intend to spend any of it listening to horrible little men like you.'

He goes to say something, but then he thinks better of it and just focks off, quoting the price he paid for his shoes as he squelches his way up Castle Street, Sorcha's old dear running alongside him, trying to calm him down.

I'm sitting there – I'm going to be honest here – literally on the edge of tears. I've never had anyone stand up to him for me, except Sorcha the very odd time.

'Thanks,' is all I can think to go.

She's there, 'Why does he speak to you that way?'

'He has his reasons. He thinks I'm a waste of space.'

'No one in this world is a waste of space. Don't let anyone put you down like that.'

Then she catches the waitress's eye over my shoulder and goes, 'We're going to need another bowl of chowder here. And another brandy.'

*

313

Sorcha's looking at me with her eyes wide open, waiting for an answer. She's there, 'Well?'

I'm like, 'Well, what?'

'I asked you a question, Ross. Did Aida throw a bowl of soup over my dad?'

She can't help but smile as she says it. It *is* funny.

I go, 'Yeah, no, it was actually chowder. You don't seem too pissed off.'

She shakes her head – *while* laughing. She's there, 'Well, Mum said he kind of deserved it.'

I'm like, 'He definitely did.'

This is just us having a coffee on the set, waiting for the afternoon's filming to begin. It's actually nice. Sorcha looks incredible, I should say. She and Honor arrived on the set this morning dressed in matching red Jeanne Yang summer dresses and I'm beginning to wonder is *she* getting more carried away by the whole movie thing than our daughter.

'I don't mind admitting it,' Sorcha goes. 'I was wrong.'

I'm like, 'That's always good to hear, Babes. About what, though?'

'About Honor. About her doing this. We're getting on, like, *so* well these days.'

'That's great news.'

'And oh my God, have you noticed her behaviour recently?'

I'm there, 'What do you mean?'

'She's become – oh! my God! – a different person, Ross. She's, like, *so* good. Even the way she speaks to me – she's, like, *so* mannerly.'

'That's good, isn't it?'

'She's found something she's – oh my God – so, so amazing at. It's like when I discovered debating in transition year.'

'She definitely seems to have settled down alright.'

'You heard what Mr Perret said, Ross. She's the best child actor he's ever seen. And he's worked with, like, Anna Paquin.'

'Yeah, no, Michelle Trachtenberg was also mentioned.'

'*And* Michelle Trachtenberg – exactly. Do you know what, Ross, I think we're also beginning to see our daughter grow.'

'Grow? What do you mean?'

'I'm talking about her personal growth. There's a real moral to the story your mum has written.'

'I know. Even during a recession, there's still money to be made from selling shit to people.'

'The lesson I'm talking about is that the current economic situation is affecting everyone – even people like us. Playing the part of little Zara Mesbur, *I* think, has helped Honor to see that. I really believe she's stopped taking things for granted.'

I'm there, 'Well, I'll be the first to say fair focks if that turns out to be the case.'

I all of a sudden spot Fantasia walking past, over Sorcha's right hammer, and I excuse myself – I actually go, 'Later, Gator!' – and I run after her. I end up *having* to run because she seems in a hurry. She's on her way to Honor's trailer with a big fock-off smoothie.

I'm thinking, okay, when did she stop being her welfare liaison and stort being her personal assistant?

I go, 'Fantasia!' because I can't see a pretty girl without hitting on her – it's, like, a mental disorder with me. I'm convinced of that. She stops and turns around. I'm there, 'I just want to apologize for my rudeness the last time we met.'

Elisabetta Canalis – that wasn't an exaggeration. Jesus, I'd put an exit wound in her.

She's like, 'Rudeness?'

She seems hassled – like talking to me is stopping her from being somewhere more *important*?

I'm there, 'Yeah, no – you're over here, foreign country, blah, blah, blah. I should have offered to maybe take you out for a drink, possibly even dinner. Helped you get settled in.'

She goes, 'Om . . .' and she keeps looking over her shoulder – she's actually a nervous wreck.

I'm there, 'Hey, if you're worried about cutting Sorcha's lunch, you don't have to – we're actually getting divorced.'

Oh, I've still got a few moves in the old repertoire. I don't think anyone needs to worry about that.

'Look,' she goes, 'we're only shooting for, like, two more weeks. I'm not sure it makes any sense to embark on something new.'

Embark on something new? Americans really need to get over themselves. All *I'm* looking for is to get her horizontal for an hour. I try to tell her that – not using those words, obviously. I go, 'You're pushing an open door, Fantasia. I'm a no-ties kind of goy . . .' and I give her one of my famous all-those-curves-and-me-with-no-brakes kind of looks.

Except she cuts me off and just shakes her head – like I'm threatening to carry out a bikini wax on her against her will.

She goes, 'I have to bring Honor her lunch,' and then she turns her back on me and disappears into my daughter's trailer.

I'm suddenly thinking, hang on, did she just drive all the way to Dundrum Town Centre for that smoothie?

Then, as I go to turn away, I hear a scream from inside the trailer. I go to look in the window, but as I'm walking towards it, the smoothie suddenly explodes against the inside of the glass. There's, like, mango, banana, yoghurt and – I'm presuming – low-fat milk suddenly dribbling down it.

And that's when I hear my daughter roar, 'I said I wanted an All Berry Bang – you useless focking bitch!'

'What are you doing?' Oisinn wants to know.

I'm, like, riveted to my phone. Which is something I'd usually give the others serious focking stick for, especially when it's supposedly a boys night out.

'I'm actually Googling Ritchie Valens,' I go.

That gets a few interested looks. This is in, like, the Merrion Inn, by the way.

It's JP who says what the rest of them are thinking. 'Why?'

'Because,' I go, 'my grandmother happened to mention that she liked him – and I'm just trying to find out if he's still alive and, if so, if he's playing in Dublin in the near future.'

The famous One F happens to be standing, like, ten feet away from where this conversation is taking place. And of course he knows his music like he knows his rugby – in other words, inside out.

'He's dead fifty years,' he goes. You know the way he talks. 'Same plane crash that killed Buddy Holly. Why don't you just bring her to Eddie Rockets?'

I'm like, 'What?'

'That's where you hear all that old stuff. Bring her to Eddie Rockets.'

That's actually not a bad idea.

I turn around to Fionn then. It's nice to see him out and about and just getting on with life. I make sure to include him in the conversation.

'Okay,' I go, 'here's another name she threw at me – and *you* might be the one to answer this one, Fionn, with your world-famous brain. Who's de Valera?'

Fionn's face just drops. He's like, '*Eamon* de Valera?'

I'm there, 'Eamon. Yeah, no, she definitely *did* say Eamon, now that you mention it.'

He looks at the others, then back at me. 'You don't know who Eamon de Valera is?'

He seems a lot more put out by this fact than I am.

JP goes, 'I wonder would they have any of *his* stuff in Eddie Rockets.'

Which everyone finds obviously hilarious.

'Actually,' I go, 'the joke's on you, J-Town, because I already know that he's some kind of politician.'

Fionn goes, 'Eamon de Valera is a former Taoiseach and President of Ireland, Ross. He led the fight for independence, supervised the writing of the Constitution and was one of the founding fathers of the state.'

I'm there, 'Hey, that's all you had to say, Fionn. And I'll remember that.'

Which I won't, of course. It's already gone from my focking head.

I catch Oisinn just grinning at me then.

I'm like, 'What the fock are you smiling at?'

He goes, 'You and your grandmother, Ross – it's nice.'

'She's actually a really cool person, Ois. I'm not being defensive. I'm just saying it as a statement of fact.'

'And I'm saying it's a really great thing to see, Ross – you two being friends.'

'Well, *I'm* just saying that she's a great bit of stuff. She's actually a good laugh. She doesn't take shit from anyone, including Sorcha's old man. And she's always boosting me, which is something I think I definitely need. Okay, she doesn't know what year it is half the focking time, but look at all the shit I'm learning just from, like, hanging out with her. I mean, de Valera! Jesus!'

It's at that exact point that my phone rings. I answer it, roysh, without checking the screen because I'm expecting it to be Christian, telling me whether he's going to get out tonight or not. Except it turns out not to be him. In fact, at first I don't know who the fock it is, although the five seconds of silence after I go, 'Hello?' *should* be an actual giveaway.

'R . . . R . . . Ross,' the voice eventually blurts out. 'It's K . . . K . . . Kennet Tuite.'

For fock's sake.

I actually *say* that. I'm like, 'Ah, for fock's sake.'

I step outside onto the road.

He's like, 'You alreet theer?'

'Er, yeah – just go ahead there, Kennet. And bear in mind that I'm not in an area with good coverage and you might end up getting cut off mid-focking-sentence.'

'Feer denuff. C . . . c . . . c'mere, what I wanna ast you – Ronan says you d . . . d . . . d . . . doatunt wanna g . . . g . . . go witness for me.'

I decide to just give it to him straight. It's easier that way. 'I'm more than happy to go witness, Kennet . . .'

'Ah, thanks be to J . . . J . . . Jaysus!'

'. . . but I'm going to tell them what I saw.'

'Soddy?'

'Which was you just focking threw yourself down on the ground – with fock-all wrong with you.'

'Ine saying I was trun, but.'

'But you weren't *trun*. And I'm not lying for you. And I don't want my son lying for you either.'

He's more than a *bit* taken aback by that?

'This is a t . . . t . . . turden up for the bukes. Suren we're practically famidy.'

'Er, no we're not practically family. Ronan just happens to be going out with your daughter – who I really like, in fairness to her. But that doesn't entitle you to involve us in your focking scams.'

'That's snobiddy – that's what thar is.'

'It's hordly snobbery to want my son to grow up *not* a criminal?'

'D . . . d . . . did you just call me a crimiddle?'

I'm like, 'Yeah, I focking did,' and then I just hang up on him.

I tip back into the pub. JP says that Christian rang him while I was outside. He said he won't be in. Him and Lauren are out looking at gaffs to rent, which sounds hopeful. Christian told me the other night they're also seeing, like, a marriage counsellor?

Fionn is suddenly keen to get everyone's attention. 'Okay,' he goes, 'since Christian's not coming . . .'

He sounds like a man who's about to make an announcement.

'I just wanted to tell you all something. I know this is short notice, but I'm going away for a while.'

It's JP who goes, 'Where?'

I think we're all expecting him to say Orgentina, to search for Erika.

But he's just there, 'Uganda. It's a teaching job that's come up.'

None of us says anything.

He goes, 'It's in Africa, Ross.'

I'm there, 'I don't know why you're focking directing that at me, Fionn. *They* didn't know where it was either.'

Oisinn probably speaks for us all when he goes, 'Why are you going to Africa? Is it because of what happened?'

He doesn't deny it. 'Of course. It's hard enough living in this town with reminders of Aoife everywhere. Now I've got the ghosts of Erika as well. I can't stay here. I know that.'

I'm there, 'When are you leaving?'

'Tomorrow morning,' he goes.

I'm like, 'Tomorrow morning?'

No wonder he was so keen to get us all out on a Thursday night.

'I know it's short notice,' he goes. 'I was only offered it a week ago.'

Oisinn's not a happy bunny. 'You were offered it a week ago and you're only telling us now?'

'I would have told you sooner, Oisinn, but . . .'

It's JP who goes, 'You thought we might try to persuade you not to go.'

Fionn just nods.

JP's there, 'So how long are you going to be away for?'

Fionn's like, 'The contract is for two years.'

'Two years?' Oisinn goes.

'I'll come home for holidays.'

'Do you not think this is a bit of an over-reaction, though? What Erika did – shit the bed – the girl's a bitch. Let's not mince our words. I can't imagine what you must be going through. But surely the place for you to be at a time like this is around your mates?'

See, Oisinn knows. It's pretty much the same speech I gave him when I persuaded him to come back from Monte Carlo.

Fionn's like, 'Thanks. Seriously – all of you. I know that what I'm doing seems a bit drastic. And it probably is. But I know that I need to do it.'

I suddenly realize how much I'm going to miss him. For the last year, or however long it was, all I kept banging on about was how Erika was basically too good for him. But suddenly I'm nearly tempted to say that it was Fionn who was too good for her.

I wish I'd been a better friend to him. Not just in the last year. But always. I want to say that to him, except I end up just bottling it.

Instead, I just go, 'Let's get shots.'

*

The old dear and Ford-whatever-the-fock are walking across the cor pork of the Silver Tassie, which is where all the trucks and the trailers are porked today, and they're, like, deep in conversation.

'What I'd like for this scene,' *she's* telling *him*, 'is to evoke the same sense of Dickensian tragedy that we all got seeing the streets of Mumbai, or wherever the hell it was, in *Slumdog Millionaire*. Same atmosphere. Same sense of pathos. Proud people pushed into doing desperate, desperate things to survive – and at traffic lights as well. I want people to look at Zara and her mother washing the car windscreens of strangers on the N11 and join up the dots. This is the catastrophe that has come from people trying to live above their station – mortgages for the bloody unemployed! – and how it's people like *us* who've ended up paying the price for it. And what a price. Squeegees!'

The dude's just nodding – I can't tell whether he agrees with her or whether he's just humouring her.

They see me and Sorcha standing there and it's suddenly all smiles and bear hugs and air-kisses galore.

Ford tells us that he's predicting huge things for Honor. 'She's going to be bigger than Saoirse Ronan,' he goes. 'And as for the writer, what can I say, but that I am privileged.'

She's obviously thrilled to hear that, of course.

You do have to keep reminding yourself that it's only a focking TV movie. You'd nearly feel like telling them all to cop onto themselves.

I notice her hair has almost completely grown back as well. So to stop her getting too full of herself, I stare at her and go, 'Against all that, you've still got a face like a ploughed field, though.'

Sorcha and *him* stort shooting the shit then about politics and blah, blah, blah. That's one of the amazing things about Sorcha – she can talk to anyone about anything and still *sound* intelligent?

The old dear decides to just ignore my crack about her face. So I go, 'Oh, your mother's fine, by the way – just in case you're wondering. I'm about to go home and make her lunch for her – which is something *you* should obviously be doing.'

'Ross,' she goes, making sure to keep her voice down, so her director mate doesn't hear, 'it would be like meeting a stranger.'

'What, meeting the woman who gave birth to you?'

'Ross, I'm not going to meet her and that's all there is to it!'

Ford M blahdy-blah is telling Sorcha that he doesn't think that dude Obama is going to get the support he needs to increase the US's debt ceiling and Sorcha just rolls her eyes and says that there are – oh my God – *so* many racists in the world, which is why everyone is suddenly *turning* against him?

I go, 'I'll, er, just go and see where Honor is,' because no one's seen her since she disappeared into her trailer, like, half an hour ago?

I *could* – possibly *should* – have told Sorcha about the incident with the smoothie. In the end I didn't. I don't *know* why? Maybe I was just so happy to see Sorcha and Honor getting on for once. Sorcha's been so happy with how it's all been going, I thought it was the last thing she'd have wanted to hear from me. I probably should add that I was still hoping against hope that the whole Mango Magic slash All Berry Bang incident was a one-off – that Honor had had maybe a stressy day or that it was, like, the emotion of the *scene*?

Anyway, I wander over to her trailer and I'm going to have to admit something here – before I knock, I end up having a listen at the door. And I can't believe what I'm actually hearing. Honor is tearing someone a new proverbial.

She's going, 'Is there something wrong with you? Are you special needs or something?'

'Honor,' I hear, obviously, Fantasia go, 'I tried everywhere for the sunglasses. They're not in the shops for another month.'

'Did you ring Ray-Ban?'

'No, I haven't had a minute. There's so much to do . . .'

'Okay, eyes glazing *over*?'

'Honor, I'm working sixteen hours a day . . .'

'Would you like some cheese to go with that whine?'

'Excuse me?'

'Oh, soz – I keep forgetting what a dizzy bitch you are . . .'

I've literally never heard a kid talk to an adult like it before – although me talking to my old dear is an obvious exception.

'Honor,' she goes, obviously trying to reason with her, 'I don't think I deserve to be treated . . .'

That's when I hear Honor go, 'Okay, you're still talking to me and I don't know why. Ring Ray-Ban this morning, then get me a skinny peach and raspberry muffin from Starbucks and have it waiting here for me when I finish this scene.'

The door of the trailer suddenly flies open, nearly taking the focking nose off my face in the actual process. Honor doesn't even notice me standing there. She just stomps past, muttering, 'Oh my God – person of *no* consequence?'

I'm left just standing there, rooted to the spot, thinking, what kind of monster have we raised?

I go into the trailer. Fantasia is on the sofa, curled up in what I'm pretty sure is called the fecal position, sobbing her literally hort out, her hands covering her face.

I touch her orm and she jumps like she's been, I don't know, *electrocuted*?

I'm there, 'It's okay, Fantasia – she's gone. She can't hurt you now.'

She throws her orms around me and hugs me and I end up just going with it. Hey, I like people.

'She's horrible,' she goes. 'I know she's your daughter, but she's the most horrible little girl I've ever met.'

I end up having to go, 'I know – she *is* an orsehole.'

'How did she get like that?'

'That's the thing – no one knows. We just have to accept it.'

She's still bawling, by the way. I'm a bit turned on here. She's wearing *Reb'l Fleur* – Rihanna's shit – which I have a definite thing for.

'In the States? The way she just spoke to me? That would constitute bullying.'

I'm there, 'It'd possibly constitute that here as well, Fantasia. Why don't you complain about her?'

And I'm not just saying that because I've a horn on me. Deep down I think I'm actually terrified of what Honor is turning into.

She goes, 'Who would I complain to? Ford?'

I'm there, 'I don't know. I suppose.'

'He's not going to listen to me. I'm just a spare wheel in the operation. I'm just here for compliance. He thinks your daughter is the greatest child star since Shirley fucking Temple.'

I go to pull away, roysh, but she tightens her grip on me. 'Just hold me,' she goes.

I'm there, 'Er, okay.'

'Just keep holding me.'

So I do. I hold her tight and I rub her back. I tell her everything's going to be okay. I might end up even having a word with Honor, I tell her, to ask her to even tone *down* the abuse a notch?

And as I'm saying it – you *know* me, I can't help myself – I'm staring down the length of Fantasia's very shapely back, checking out the white lacy sliver of knicker riding above the waistband of her skinny Made in Heavens.

Otis Redding. Martha & The Vandellas. Sam Cooke. Donovan. I mean, who's even *heard* of half of these fockers? Or even half of these songs? *Waterloo Sunset. I Just Don't Know What to Do with Myself. The House of the Rising Sun. I'd Rather Go Blind.*

It's like, whatever!

It's good to get out of the house, though.

'Beats sitting in,' I go, still turning the pages of the jukebox.

'Oh, there's nothing on that *Telefís*,' she goes, agreeing with me. 'Nothing but bad news.'

I'm like, 'Things *are* turning to shit out there alright – that's what you hear all these experts suddenly saying.'

'Oh, it's terrible, Ross. Emigration. Unemployment . . .'

'It's actually affecting a lot of my friends.'

'And sure John A. Costello is as useless as the other fella.'

'Er, yeah, I suppose.'

'Sure maybe the Russians will press the button,' she goes, 'and put us all out of our misery!'

She laughs.

I'm there, 'Maybe, yeah,' just going along with it, because she's obviously Tonto.

'I don't care for the Russians,' she goes. 'Another race I don't care for is the Chinese.'

Hope she doesn't object to them cooking her food because otherwise we're going to focking storve in here.

There he is. Ritchie Valens. *Come On Let's Go Little Darlin'*. I put the twenty in the slot and hit the buttons. H4. It comes on pretty much straight away and her face just lights up.

'Oh,' she goes, 'I like this song. Who sings this?'

'It's actually Ritchie Valens.'

'Oh, I like Ritchie Valens. Is that on the wireless?'

'No, no – I just stuck it on there on the old jukebox.'

She stares at the thing, like she's admiring it, but at the same time doesn't fully trust it – like the people of Wicklow when they stuck the second lane on the N11.

The waitress arrives over, the one who looks like a mix between Christian Serratos and Kylie Bisutti – I think she might be, like, Polish or something? I've always suspected she has a thing for me, on the basis that she always ends up being my waitress, no matter where I sit, and she gave me an extra portion of burger sauce once, to dip my fries in, then didn't even chorge me for it.

'I'm going to get my usual,' I go, 'which is a Classic with, like, bacon and cheese fries?'

Aida – this is focking hilarious – covers her mouth with her menu, then goes to me, within full earshot of the bird, 'I think someone's taken a bit of a shine to you!'

The poor girl is, like, totally morto. Or, as Honor would say, 'Er, awks much?'

At the same time, it's nice to have an independent witness to the fact – see, people think I'm exaggerating a lot of the time.

I'm there, 'Aida, what do you want to eat?'

She's like, 'What are *you* having, Ross?'

'A Classic – it's, like, a hamburger?'

'Oh, I'll have that,' she goes. 'I've never had a hamburger.'

Imagine that. Never had a focking hamburger. Jesus.

'With *also* fries?' the waitress goes.

I'm like, 'Yeah, she'll have the bacon and cheese fries as well. And two Cokes.'

She puts the order into her little machine thing, then focks off, shaking her little two-scoop orse as she goes.

'Did you see the way that girl was looking at you?' Aida goes.

I laugh. 'I did, yeah.'

'Like she wanted to eat you.'

'I'm glad someone else saw it.'

'Must happen to you all the time. You have such a handsome face.'

'There does seem to be something about me alright.'

'The way she was looking at you. It was lustful. And you a married man?'

'Technically, yeah.'

I stort flicking through the jukebox pages again.

'Did you meet at a dance?' she goes.

'Sorry?'

'You and Sorcha. Was it at a dance you met?'

'No, it was actually in Eddie Rockets?'

'Here?'

'No, it was the, er, Donnybrook one.'

We're actually in Stillorgan – I don't know if I mentioned.

She just nods. 'Was she very pretty?'

I laugh. 'There's things I *could* say, but I'd prefer to keep the conversation clean.'

She has a good old chuckle at that – she seems to find me one of the genuinely funniest people she's ever met.

'Yeah, she was incredible,' I go. 'I mean, she *still* is. You should see her when she's just had her roots done and she's got a bit of colour in her face. I mean, she'd knock serious spots off any girl – *including*, believe it or not, that waitress. Especially when she's been on the Weight Watchers as well. It's like, whoa!'

Aida nods – did you ever meet someone who just *gets* you?

'She's a lovely girl,' she goes. 'A lovely, lovely girl. Your daughter I don't like so much.'

I laugh. I end up having to. It's just because she's so straight.

'Yeah,' I go, 'she's a bit much at times.'

'Oh, she's a little *wan*, isn't she? Oh, I'd give her the birch! I would! Right across the back of her legs!'

She just cracks me up, this woman.

Six weeks ago, I'd never have believed I'd be sitting here on a Friday afternoon, listening to olden days music and basically chilling with my actual grandmother. It's amazing.

Our food suddenly arrives. Aida's eyes go wide at the sight of it. Never eaten a hamburger. My old dear and her old man have a lot to focking answer for. She's not afraid of it, though. She doesn't even wait to see what I do with mine. She just takes it in her two hands and horses into it – secret sauce dripping everywhere.

'Beautiful,' she goes, chewing away. 'Absolutely beautiful.'

I'm like, 'Yeah, no, I've been coming here since I was kid. In fact, we often did a runner.'

'A what?'

'Oh, it's where you just peg it without paying. It would have been me, Christian, Fionn – the dude I told you has just gone to Africa – JP and Oisinn. You scoff it down and then you're out the door.'

She loves that. She's laughing her head off.

It's when we're actually finished eating that she goes, 'So what's all this talk about you and Sorcha not being happy?'

I'm there, 'Like I said, we're actually broken up.'

'You don't look like you've broken up.'

'Yeah, no, that's because I got shot – I possibly mentioned – and then my aportment block got basically condemned. She's just putting me up until I get sorted.'

'No,' she goes, 'the way you look at each other – it's not like a couple who don't love each other.'

'Are you saying you've noticed that?'

'I've noticed the way you look at her and I've noticed the way she looks at you – yes.'

'Look, if there was a snifter of it, I'd be in there like you wouldn't believe. But, well, there's more to it than that. I'm a bit of a dirty dog, to be honest with you.'

She goes, 'Did you have other affairs?'

I laugh – it's just that phrase.

'You *could* say that, yeah. I was always at it.'

'But could she not forgive you?'

'She did. And I'm saying that in Sorcha's defence. Loads of times, in fact. Until she basically got a pain in her hole with it.'

She nods, roysh, sort of, like, *sadly*?

That's when the waitress with the serious wide-on for me arrives with the bill. Me *and* Aida both make a grab for it. *She* actually gets it – and not because I deliberately let her, as used to happen on dates.

I go, 'Okay, Aida, this is, like, *my* treat?'

And this look suddenly comes over her face. She scrunches the bill up into a ball and goes, 'Are we going to make a runner?'

I actually laugh. 'The phrase,' I go, 'is *do* a runner – and no, we're not.'

She looks crushed. She's like, 'Why not?'

I'm there, 'Because, er, I don't know – I'm far too old for that kind of thing.'

'Well, I'm not,' she goes. There's a real streak of trouble in her, which I'm only just beginning to see. I definitely approve of it. Then she stands up and she looks at me in a real, I suppose, *challenging* way? 'Are you with me?'

And I look at her and think, how focking mad would I have to be? I mean, here I am, a genuine millionaire – *and* at a time when a million snots is suddenly considered a lot of money – and she wants me to peg it for the sake of twenty-odd snots' worth of food.

And I just think, okay – why the fock not?

I nod at her and she turns and storts scuttling towards the door. I'm thinking, okay, she's obviously not going to be as fast on her feet as I am – better give her a good headstort. Let her get at least half-way across the cor pork, then make a bolt for the door.

But as Aida *reaches* the door, she turns around and shouts at me,

'Make a runner, Ross! Come on! Make a runner!' which, of course, gets everyone's immediate attention, including the staff.

I've suddenly got no choice. I'm straight away out of my seat and moving for the door.

Which doesn't go unnoticed, by the way.

I hear the workers shouting in various languages. Then, out of the corner of my eye, I spot this big – either Polish or Russian – security gord, with a mullet, a Barry McGuigan moustache and a leather Members Only jacket, come chorging out from behind the counter, his eyes focused firmly on me.

I probably don't need to say anything here about my famous burst of speed from a standing stort and my acceleration over the first twenty to twenty-five yords. It's been written about enough over the years – it's all there in the record books. But this security dude gets to see it up close for himself.

I'm suddenly out that focking door like someone's just shouted, 'Fire!'

Aida's a lot faster on her Reet Petites than I would have given her credit for. She's already flown past the window of Rocks and she's passing the door of McDonald's by the time I catch up with her.

'We need to seriously peg it,' I go. 'There's a possibly Russian security gord behind us.'

She can seriously move, though. She goes, 'Where did you park the car?' a not unreasonable question, in the circs.

'Shit!' I go. 'It's back there – outside the actual restaurant.'

I look over my shoulder. The security dude is a good twenty yords behind us and I'm thinking, okay, we should have enough time here to get around this next corner, then hide in the new Donnybrook Fair and maybe go back for the cor later when the heat is off. I've just remembered Sorcha said we needed Gouda anyway.

Except it's at that exact moment that this pain suddenly rips through the tops of my legs – obviously something to do with my gunshot wounds. I stop. Aida stops too. Maybe it's one of those little, I don't know, bullet fragments that's worked its way loose. The only thing I *do* know is that suddenly I can barely focking run – and now it's actually me who's holding Aida back.

'Quick, Ross,' she shouts. 'It's a dirty Russian!'

'Go on without me,' I tell her. 'Seriously – save your own skin. I'll just pay the dude. I'll tell him you saw the sign that said "Eat and Get Out" and you got confused.'

She's like, 'You will not!' and she grabs a huge handful of my blue Apple Crumble and goes, 'Keep going!'

The security dude is, like, ten yords behind us at this point, but I struggle on, even though I'm in literally agony and he's about five seconds away from grabbing me.

It's as we're passing the vacant unit on the corner that we get a sudden stroke of luck.

Well, *two* things *actually* happen.

The first thing is that me and Aida split up. She goes left, waddling off in the general direction of Nimble Fingers and the Stillorgan Leisureplex. I hang a right and stort running – or limping is possibly *more* the case? – across the cor pork in the general direction of Tesco.

The dude decides to keep after *me* – I don't know whether that's because he can see I'm a wounded animal or because he knows it'll be easier to prosecute a thirty-one-year-old man for doing a runner from a burger bor than a ninety-two-year-old woman.

He's, like, literally two steps behind me when the second break happens. He gets hit by a cor. Not creamed. It's only, like, a three-door Ford Focus and it's only doing, like, ten Ks at the time? But he still goes over the front of it and lands on the deck with a serious focking thud.

I keep focking running – don't you worry about that. But I'm struggling. I turn around just as I'm reaching the cor pork exit on the Kilmacud Road and I watch the dude slowly climb to his feet, then keep coming after me.

He's like that focker out of *Terminator* – except he's working for Eddie Rockets rather than Skynet.

I hobble out onto the road and I manage to get across to the other side. I'm standing outside Xtra Vision – totally focked – looking at him on the other side of the road, just waiting for a break in the traffic.

The game is up. I know it. He knows it.

I'm reaching into my pocket, in fact, for a fifty-yoyo note – which I'm going to tell him to keep, for the food and the hassle – when a taxi all of a sudden comes screaming to a halt right in front of me. The back door is thrown open.

Aida is sitting on the back seat, going, 'Get in!'

She obviously saw the rank. The driver, I notice, is cracking his hole laughing. It's pretty clear he knows the score.

Aida says it again – roars it this time. 'Get in!'

I don't need to be told again. I throw myself in and I pull the door behind me. The security gord slaps the roof of the cor as we pull off, the two of us rolling around the back seat, wetting ourselves with laughter – maybe even literally in Aida's case.

'We made a runner!' she keeps going. 'We made a runner!'

And I'm going to be honest with you – I can't remember the last time anything felt this good.

It's not long, of course, before I'm brought crashing back to earth. Because that's the way the universe works. It high-fives you with one hand, then with the other it grabs you by the bat and balls.

I'm actually just paying the driver, then helping Aida out of the cab, when my phone all of a sudden rings.

It's focking Tina on the other end. And straight away she storts giving me a serious mouthful. Her opening line, in fact, is, 'I want a woord wit you.'

I'm there, 'What about?' genuinely meaning it.

'Bout Ronan and Shadden.'

'Okay,' I go, 'hands up – you were right about her family. They *are* pretty much scum. But don't worry, I've already told the famous Kennet that I don't want Ronan being a witness to his so-called accident.'

There's, like, silence on the other end. Whatever she's ringing about, it's obviously not that. She goes, 'Did you know dat Ronan was having sex wit dat geerdle?'

I'm like, 'Er, what makes you think they're having sex?' trying to just bluff it.

'Because I fowunt a packera conthoms in he's pocket when I was lookin to boddow a cigarette.'

There's an awful lot of questions for Tina to answer in that sentence.

I'm there, 'Hey, I'm as surprised as you are, Tina.'

She's like, 'You loyer.'

'Excuse me?'

'He toalt me *you* knew. He said you toalt him it was alreet as long as he was keerful.'

'That's not exactly what I said, Tina.'

'So you *did* know.'

'Yeah, I knew. I caught them in the actual act, if you must know.'

'Jesus, Meerdy and Josuff.'

'And what I said to Ro was, look, I'd rather you *didn't* do it? But if you're going to, like, insist on it, then I'd prefer if you were careful. Which it sounds like they *were* being.'

'And you tink dat's de reet message to be givin to a fourteen-year-oalt boy . . .'

'Look,' I go, '*she's* sixteen. This is what kids of their age get up to. It's an unfortunate fact of life. You listen to *Liveline*, don't you?'

It's a stupid question. *Everyone* on that side of the city does.

'Dis is down to you,' she goes, 'and de kind of role mottle you are as a fadder.'

I'm not going to take that, though. You can question my record as a son – yeah, I wasn't great in that deportment. You can question my record as a husband – I came up short there, no orguments. You can even question my record as a rugby player – although mainly on the grounds of temperament rather than actual ability. But the one area of my record that is not open to question is my record as a father.

I'm like, 'You're bang out of order, Tina, and I think deep down you know it.'

'He fooken woorshups you – and he sees you sleepin arowunt . . .'

I can't listen to her being a basic hypocrite 'Tina,' I go, 'you were present at his conception, much as you like to forget that fact.'

'I was eighteen, going on nineteen.'

334

'Well, I'd only just turned sixteen. Shadden's age. And can I remind you that you played a full and active port in events. Jesus, the noises out of you!'

It's obvious she's not ready to listen to any of the points I have to make, though.

'Ine so fooken mad wit you,' she goes, 'I caddent even talk to you any mower,' and then she just slams the phone down on me.

'You did *what*?'

She's a bit taken aback, in fairness to her.

I just shrug. 'We did a runner,' I go. 'Sorcha, it's not a biggie.'

She was the head of the Justice and Peace group in Mount Anville, though – she'd regard that kind of thing as very much working class.

'I just don't understand why you would eat a meal in a restaurant,' she goes, 'and then leave without paying.'

This is in the kitchen the following morning, by the way.

I'm there, 'Because Aida wanted to know what it felt like.'

She just shakes her head. 'I'm going to go up there later and pay – what did you both have?'

I'm like, 'I don't want you to pay.'

'Why not?'

'Because then it won't have been a runner.'

'Ross, that means we can't go there to eat any more.'

'We'll just have to go to the one in Blackrock – or even Dundrum – until the heat's off.'

She sort of, like, smiles then, suddenly beginning to see the funny side of it. 'I can't tell whether you're a bad influence on her or she's a bad influence on you.'

Aida shouts from the hall. 'The car's outside.'

Sister Edward's brother, the dude who brought her here, is bringing her back down to Wexford this morning. She says she has a few things – loose ends, she calls them – to look after.

I walk her to the door and wave her off.

And it's at that exact point that the photographer pulls up outside.

Hallmork want to get some publicity shots of Honor and Sorcha leading a pretty much normal life, doing ordinary mother–daughter things, which is why the pair of them were up before the focking Air Coach this morning, sitting in Brown Sugar, getting their hair and make-up done.

I invite the dude in.

Honor sort of, like, floats down the stairs. The best way to describe the way she looks is that it's as if someone stuck Sorcha in a spin-drier with the heat setting too high and she ended up, like, shrunk. She's wearing the exact same – it turns out – Juicy Couture haphazard pink ruffle dress that Sorcha has on in the kitchen, with, again, chestnut ankle-high Uggs.

She's like, 'Hi, Daddy!' her voice full of sweetness – the way it usually is when she's being false. Then she goes, 'And you must be Mark,' and she, like, shakes the photographer's hand. 'You're very welcome to our home.' Then she leads the way into the kitchen.

'What a lovely kid,' the dude turns to me and goes.

He doesn't know the half of it, of course.

I'm there, 'She can certainly turn it on when she wants to alright.'

I stand around just watching while he snaps the two of them in a series of, like, scenarios. Sharing a joke while baking brownies. Having fun on the swing in the back gorden. Concentrating hord while doing Honor's Mandarin Chinese homework together – both of them with a full face of make-up.

And of course there's more focking costume changes than you'd see at a Lady Gaga concert.

Sorcha goes, 'Oh my God, Honor – for the swing shots in the gorden, you *so* should wear your Little White Dress – as in, the Monnalisa one? – with your pink Hunters.'

'Oh! My God!' Honor goes. 'Festival cool!'

It continues like this for the next pretty much three *hours*?

It's, like, snap, snap . . . Snap, snap, snap.

They're sitting quietly reading, they're tickling each other, they're splashing in puddles in the gorden, they're staring sadly at a leaflet that came in through the door from Trocaire. And it's 'Why don't you wear your white Armani tutu with your pink Cath Kidston tank – the one with the elephant on?' and 'What about your *Hello Kitty* tee with – oh my God – your pink *beret*?'

Sorcha is literally in her element. I think this is pretty much how she envisaged motherhood was going to be. I know I should tell her about Honor bullying Fantasia, but I just don't want to be the one to burst her bubble.

All of a sudden, there's, like, a ring at the door. It's certainly all go around here today. I go out and answer it and there's, like, a woman standing there, who I can't place at first, but who, after a few seconds, I realize is the social worker who called into the euro shop that day.

How focking long ago all of that seems now!

She goes, 'Hello, Ross,' and *I* end up just laughing – pretty much in her face. Because I suddenly realize that this is obviously the follow-up home visit she said she'd be making. And what a focking day to pick.

'Come in,' I go, sounding all welcoming. 'Sorcha, it's that social worker from a few weeks ago – just double-checking that our daughter's not at risk of poverty!'

This, the woman decides to ignore. I'm sure she must take shit from parents all the time – there's probably fock-all original that I can hit her with.

Although, judging from her expression, the sight that greets her when she opens the door of the kitchen *is* new.

Sorcha and Honor are sitting at the island, rolling cookie dough, but dressed up for a night out, while a photographer clicks away, moving around a floor that's, like, strewn with midis and maxis, ballet flats and kitten heels, and coats and ponchos and hats of every focking shape and colour.

'Does that look like a kid who's at risk of storving to death?' I go.

The social worker ends up having to agree. No option. She must feel like a total tit.

'Do you want to stay for coffee?' Sorcha goes. 'We're almost finished here, aren't we, Mark?'

'Er, no,' the woman goes. The kind of ugly – I think I mentioned –

that'd have you knotting your sheets together to escape out the focking window if you ever had the misfortune to wake up next to it. 'Whoever made the report, it's pretty clear to me now that they were being malicious.'

I'd say her dog fantasizes about other legs when he's humping hers.

I'm like, 'Malicious? Yeah, that *sounds* like my old dear alright. Also try *conniving* – if that's the right word.'

'I'm sorry to have wasted your time.'

Off she trots, out the door and into the cor with her little focking briefcase, leaving me just standing there in the hall, thinking about my old dear, how deeply focking evil she is and how she got her own way in the end.

Then something hits me. I don't know if you'd call it a moment of realization. All I know is that I'm suddenly stood there in the hall-way thinking something that makes me feel sick to my actual stomach.

It takes me a good ten seconds to pluck up the courage to even walk up the stairs. I don't want to know and at the same time I *do*?

I tip into Sorcha's room and I find the little pink file box where she keeps all the Bear Grylls. Household shit. Gas, electricity, blah, blah, blah.

Downstairs, I can hear her going, 'Honor, let's just do one more outside in your Missoni coat and your D&G moon boots.'

Then I hear the back door open, then slam shut.

I stort thumbing my way through the bills until I find the ones from O2. Then I find the bill for May 2011. We always get them, like, *itemized*? I run my finger down through the numbers she called. It's nearly all mobiles, so it should be easy to find one that actually stands out.

There it is. It's a 1800 number. I feel my hort suddenly quicken.

Outside, I can hear her go, 'Come on, Honor – let's pretend we're tending to the organic herb garden!'

I grab the phone on Sorcha's bedside locker and I dial the number. It rings five, maybe six times before someone answers.

'Hello,' a voice goes, 'the Irish Society for the Prevention of Cruelty to Children.'

I don't say anything for a few seconds – I'm, like, stunned into silence – then I just go, 'Sorry, wrong number,' and I hang up.

And I sit there for, like, a full five minutes, unable to even move. It wasn't my old dear who told social services that my daughter was in danger of poverty.

It *was* my daughter.

9.

To have and to have yacht

Aida's face lights up when she sees it.

She's like, 'What's this?'

I'm there, 'The dude in the Ort and Hobby Shop said it was called an easel. And that's a canvas. And those – you'll obviously recognize them – are brushes. And I don't think I need to tell you what's in those little pots. I got pretty much all the basic colours, then one called magenta and another called – believe it or not – *jade*?'

I'm standing over the cooker while she's pulling all of this shit out of the bag. I'm doing her a full fry, by the way. Fock the porridge. We're talking sausages. We're talking bacon. We're talking eggs, pudding, the lot. The old traditional death-row breakfast.

'But what are they for?' she goes.

I'm like, 'I thought you might like to paint.'

The way she smiles at me, I'm beginning to wonder am I the first genuinely nice person she's ever met.

I'm there, 'You were saying you painted all the time when you were living with the nuns. All from memory. I thought we might set you up in Dalkey, Dun Laoghaire, wherever – and you can paint what you actually see.'

'I'd love to see the bay from Killiney Hill,' she goes.

I'm there, 'Then Killiney Hill it'll definitely be.'

She smiles at me, roysh, and tells me I'm wonderful and I tell her to sit down, because I'm about to, like, dish this up.

She mills into her breakfast, can I just mention, while I bring all the, I suppose, ort supplies out to the cor. Then an hour later – and three visits to the toilet for Aida, because she's obviously excited – we're on the road and heading for the hill, me praying that the rain holds off.

'They were *actual* Superquinn sausages,' I go. 'That's the place I was telling you was in trouble. They're one thing about the Celtic Tiger that I think everyone would miss if Superquinn goes. That and the word *soupçon*, which you never hear any more. And calling gravy *reduction*.'

I'm babbling a bit.

She's like, 'German, were they?'

I'm there, 'Who?'

'The sausages.'

'Er, no, Irish, I'm pretty sure.'

'I don't like the Germans, the Spanish or the blacks.'

'Possibly keep your voice down if you're going say shit like that, Aida. I mean, obviously it's fine in the cor. But there wouldn't be many takers for those kinds of opinions any more.'

I've got the radio on – she's decided she likes the channels with talking on rather than actual music. There's someone banging on about the forthcoming Presidential election. Aida says she hopes that Sean MacEoin gets in and it'll tell you how much I know about world affairs that I couldn't tell you if he's an actual person or just someone from, like, the *olden* days?

We're flying along the Vico Road, the two of us just enjoying the scenery and – it has to be said – the company, when the sun all of a sudden comes out. It storts splitting the skies, in fact, and I can't help but think that this is like that movie that Sorcha loves, *Once* – except we're *in* my Lamborghini rather than *on* Glen Hansard's motorbike, and Aida's not as easy on the eye as Markéta Irglová and I'm saying that as a fan of both.

'Which is Sorcha's house?' she wants to know.

I'm there, 'What, Honalee? It's the one coming up on the right here.'

'What's this you call it?'

'Honalee. It's from that song, *Puff the Magic Dragon*.'

'I don't know it.'

'Yeah, no, Sorcha loved it as a kid. And her old pair let her name the gaff. That'd be a big thing out this direction. Here it is now – the big massive one with the turrets.'

'Merciful hour!'

I laugh. It *is* a focking eyesore. 'Stands out, doesn't it? Has incredible views, though, in fairness to it.'

I pork the cor on the road near the Druid's Chair, then we take the long path up, me linking her with one orm, then with the other struggling to carry the easel, the canvas, the bag with the brushes and paints in it and the collapsible stool that Sorcha bought when she queued overnight the time H&M storted stocking Sonia Rykiel.

It takes us a good twenty minutes to get to the top. I think that runner we did from Empty Pockets took a lot more out of us than either of us realized.

We, like, eventually get there, though, and I set everything up, and before I know it Aida is slapping paint on the canvas and smiling away to herself, happier than a bogger in Costcutter.

'So is it the same,' I go, 'as it was in your memory?'

She's doing that thing that ortist's do, where they close one eye and hold out their thumb – I'm pretty sure it's something to do with, like, *prospective?*

'It hasn't changed a bit,' she goes. Then, totally out of the blue, she's like, 'Will you do something for me, Ross?'

I'm just there, 'Hey – name it,' because that's just the kind of form I'm in.

'I'd like to meet Fionnuala.'

I laugh. 'Meet her? Why?'

'Because I'm ninety-two and I haven't long left.'

I'm like, 'Don't talk like that.'

'It's a fact. Will you talk to her?'

'You know I already did?'

'Yes.'

'And she said she wasn't interested. Said she didn't have the time, it'd be like meeting a stranger, blah, blah, blah.'

'I know what she said. Will you keep trying, Ross? For me?'

I'm like, 'Er, yeah, Aida – no worries. I don't know why you're bothering your orse, though.'

She says something that actually surprises me then. 'You're too hard on her, Ross.'

'Too hord on her? Yeah, try telling me that when you've spent an hour in her company.'

'I know you're saying she wasn't a good mother . . .'

'That's the understatement of the century. She's on the record as saying that she didn't even want me.'

'Well, maybe she didn't know *how* to be a mother – because she didn't have a mother herself.'

'Oh, she *had* a mother, can I just remind you. And she knew where you were for, what, fifty-odd years?'

I have a quick look over her shoulder at what she's done. It's actually not bad. You can make out what it is – that'd be my definition of whether a picture is good or shit.

'Don't blame Fionnuala for that,' she goes.

I'm there, 'You've changed your tune. I thought we both agreed she was a bitch. That was one of the first things that me and you had in common.'

'It was all her father's doing, Ross.'

'That's easy to say now. But he died focking years ago.'

'We didn't have a good marriage, you see. What with my episodes. And his obsession with money. Oh, he regretted ever marrying me – I knew that. And he used my committal to get out of it.'

'What, so you're letting the old dear *totally* off the hook?'

'She was just a little girl. Your grandfather wanted it to be just the two of them. And he got his way. He was a devious so-and-so.'

'A bank manager. I rest my case.'

She smiles. 'She used to write me lovely letters, though.'

'Letters? When?'

'Oh, when she was still a child. I came out of that institution that I was in – for all the good it did me – and I moved to Wexford, where I had a sister. That'd be your aunt Aileen, Lord have mercy on her. It was when she passed on that the Sisters took me in . . .'

'Yeah, no, you were saying about letters, though.'

'Oh, they were just letters – like any child would write. Telling me her news. How she was doing in school. That kind of thing. Every week, they'd arrive, without fail.'

I'm there, 'Stop. You're going to have me feeling sorry for her. And that's not a feeling I'm comfortable with.'

She puts out her thumb again and squints her eyes in the direction of Bray head. Then she goes back to dabbing the canvas with her brush.

'Will you talk to her again?' she goes. 'Will you do it for me?'

And the answer, of course, is obvious. I'd do pretty much anything for this woman.

So I tell her I will.

Then she mentions – totally randomly – that the Russians are a terribly cold-hearted class of people. 'Imagine sending a poor dog into space like that,' she goes. 'Oh, they'd press that button and they'd not think twice about it.'

Honor slash Zara is sitting in front of an unlit fire, wrapped in a blanket for warmth, with a worried look on her little face. Her mother is counting out shrapnel – mostly ten- and twenty-cent pieces – onto the focked sofa with the springs and the stuffing showing.

You'd have to wonder how the old dear dreams this shit up.

SUSAN: One euro twenty . . . one euro twenty, begod.

ZARA: I'm sorry. It's all I could get.

SUSAN: Och, don't keep blaming yourself, wee one. It's not your fault, so it's not. I explained it to you before – we're paying the price for the sins of a nation that was drunk on illusory wealth. But we both know what it means.

ZARA: No . . . Mom, please . . .

SUSAN: Zara, there's no other way.

ZARA: There must be . . .

SUSAN: Och, we're going to freeze to death, so we are. We need to buy coal.

ZARA: There's still things we can burn, Mommy. The front door.

SUSAN: We burned it last night.

ZARA: The back door, then.

SUSAN: And what happens tomorrow?

ZARA: I'll just work – oh my God – *twice* as hord?

SUSAN: You're working as hard as you can, so you are. Don't think I haven't noticed. Six o'clock in the morning until midnight is a long day, so it is. Unfortunately, the squeegee business is at saturation point. Especially since AIB and Bank of Ireland closed down. We need a Unique Selling Point, so we do. We need to offer people something a bit different.

SUSAN *produces a rusty screwdriver.*

ZARA: Mom, in the name of all that is good, please don't take away my eyesight.

SUSAN: Och, pretty soon, sweetheart, there's going to be precious little left in this country that's worth seeing anyway. You'll be better off blind.

ZARA: Mom . . . I'm begging you . . .

Her screams could literally turn milk bad. You can see everyone on the set – especially Sorcha – take an actual step backwards. Then she stops screaming and Ford M Peret shouts, 'Cut!' and there's, like, a round of applause that lasts for definitely a full minute and possibly even two.

Sorcha, who's literally bawling, runs towards Honor and just, like, throws her orms around her, going, 'Oh! My God! You were so amazing. *I* was even frightened for you?'

Honor fake-smiles her.

The old dear's all over her as well, going, 'I want to say not only congratulations, Honor, but also a sincere thank you – for doing such wonderful, wonderful justice to my writing.'

'Oh my God,' Honor goes, 'I just *so* heart the part.'

It'd make you nearly want to puke.

Behind me, someone – under their breath – goes, 'I wouldn't say no to five minutes alone with that screwdriver and that fucking kid.'

I turn around, roysh, and it ends up being Fantasia. She's pretty shocked, it has to be said, that I managed to hear her. She's like, 'Oh my God, I am *so* sorry. I didn't mean to . . .'

I'm just there, 'Hey, it's cool. I know she's been giving you a hord time.'

'Yeah, but I shouldn't have . . .'

'Look, she can *be* a bitch – I know that better than anyone. You wouldn't believe what I found out about her recently.'

Fantasia looks *and* smells incredible. She's going to be handing me my eyeballs back in a minute, because they're all over her bangers.

She's like, 'Oh my God, what happened?'

I end up nearly telling her about Honor ringing the ISPCC, except in the end I don't, because it feels – I suppose – *unloyal*?

'Oh,' I go, 'just another example of her being a complete and utter wagon.'

She closes her eyes and smiles and nods, all at the same time, like she totally understands what I'm saying.

'Well,' she goes, 'I've decided I'm not going to take it any more.'

I'm like, 'What do you mean?'

'What I mean is I'm going to do something about it.'

I'm there, 'If it's complaining you're talking about, I'm not sure that Ford's going to listen. He thinks she's incredible.'

She goes, 'So what? Okay, I'm not an amazing child actress who could potentially make hundreds of millions of dollars. But I'm still entitled to be treated with the same respect as any human being.'

'Er, if that's what your contract says,' I go, 'then I'd have to say fair focks, Fantasia.'

She's there, 'You see, it's not only me who Honor's been bullying.'

I'm like, 'What?'

'Shauna?' she goes. 'In, like, wardrobe? I mean, she's quite a heavy girl? Never lost the baby weight after having Harper and Moretz. Two weeks ago, they had a row over something – maybe some piece she gave Honor to wear. Do you know what Honor said to her?'

'No,' I go, 'go on.'

'She said, "You're so fat, your car has got stretchmarks."'

'Jesus,' I go.

I can't help it. It's actually one of my lines.

'And she told Trey – you know Trey from make-up? – she told him he was so far in the closet that he was practically an accessory bag.'

Mine.

'And Alanah? One of the interns? Honor asked her to get her

something – I think it was, like, a caramel steamer? – and she got, like, the wrong thing. Honor said to her, "Body by Fisher-Price, brains by Mattel."'

I'm like, 'These are all word for word, Fantasia, are they?'

'Excuse me?'

'I'm just saying, she definitely said all those *specific* things?'

'Look, I know it must be very hard for you to have to hear – as her father? But she said them. I've got them all in writing.'

She waves this, like, red folder in front of my face.

I'm there, 'In writing? That sounds heavy, Fantasia.'

'Bullying is a heavy subject. I've done, like, courses in the whole area of, like, human resources? The only way to tackle this kind of treatment is if we all sit down, write up our victim impact statements, then confront the bully *with* them?'

It's pretty obvious to me that Fantasia has suddenly lost the focking plot.

She goes, 'I've got testimonies here from fourteen members of the cast and crew, alleging abusive or inappropriate behaviour from your daughter . . .'

Oh, she's lost it in a major focking way. I'm not saying it wasn't without provocation. But the girl has gone loop the focking loop.

'And I am going to read these statements out,' she goes, 'at the wrap party on Friday.'

I'm there, 'You can't do that, Fantasia.'

She's like, 'What?'

'You can't do that to a not-even-six-year-old girl – albeit one who *can* be a bit of a bitch.'

'It's going to be like an intervention. It might be that Honor doesn't realize the impact of her behaviour on others. Maybe she will when she's confronted with all these things she's said.'

I straight away know that I can't let it happen. I can't let my daughter be publicly humiliated like that, even though I'm still majorly pissed off with her.

I immediately make it my mission – whatever else happens – to get that file from Fantasia.

I won't deny that I have a slightly selfish interest in it as well.

I doubt there's a single one-liner in it that didn't originate from my focking mouth. Sorcha knows my act inside out. If Fantasia storts reading that shit out in the middle of Residence, I'm going to get the definite blame.

'Another way to look at it,' I go, subtly trying to lift the file out of her hands, 'is that filming ends the day after tomorrow. You might never have to see the girl ever again.'

She quickly pulls it away from me – she can see what I'm trying to do. She might be mental, but she's not stupid. 'After what that little bitch has put me through?' she goes. 'Oh, I'm going to do everything I can to make sure that her first movie for Hallmark is also her last.'

Off she storms – fantastic orse, by the way, on top of her other obvious qualities.

The old dear comes over to me then. 'Ford just described my script as a Dystopian nightmare,' she goes.

I try to think of a clever comeback, except I can't – too much pressure – so I end up just giving her two middle fingers and going, 'I think *you're* the reason God *gave* me these babies.'

'You're not going to bring me down,' she tries to go. 'I'm in too happy a place.'

She goes to walk away.

I go, 'I need to talk to you about something.'

'Be quick,' she goes. 'I have some more rewrites to do for Honor's final scene.'

I'm there, 'It's about Aida.'

She screws her face up – I swear to fock – like she smells gas. 'Aida?' she has the actual balls to go. 'Who's Aida?'

I'm there, 'She's your focking mother, you scabrous focking whelk.'

That gets a few looks on the set, I don't mind telling you.

'Well, what about her?'

'She wants to meet you.'

'Meet me? That's preposterous. I told you. I don't even know the woman.'

'Even so. She's ninety-two and she's not going to live forever.'

'But what of it? We have no relationship whatsoever.'

'You and I have no relationship whatsoever. Doesn't change the fact that you're still my, unfortunately, mother.'

'But what could she possibly have to say to me? Or I to her? I haven't laid eyes on the woman since I was five years of age.'

I just go, 'But you wrote to her.'

She's genuinely shocked that I know that. I can tell from the look on her face – even *with* the two pounds of orse fat that she's had injected into her forehead and cheeks. She's there, 'What?'

'You wrote her letters,' I go. 'Until you were, like, ten years old.'

She looks away – obviously not comfortable with the subject.

I'm like, 'Yeah, I'm talking to you.'

When she finally looks back at me, I notice the most amazing thing – she's got, like, tears in her eyes. Bear in mind, roysh, that I've tried everything over the years to make this woman cry. I came to the conclusion that one of the many surgeons who've had a crack at her face must have stuck a needle in crooked and focked up her tear ducts. But they're suddenly working – in fact the water is, like, *streaming* from her eyes?

She goes, 'She remembered my letters.'

Then she brushes past me and heads off in the direction of her trailer, telling me that she wants to be alone.

I've always had a soft spot for Nudger. He's one of my favourite of Ronan's friends. One of my favourite working-class people full stop.

'Me ask ye a question,' he goes.

I'm there, 'Ask away, Nudger.'

We're in the little lock-up garage he rents, just off the old Marilyn Mun Road. They could shoot the Aladdin's Cave slot on *Crimecall* from in here, there's that much stolen shit in it. He's just given the Lambo another coat.

'Burn the bondholders' is the latest message – who *they* are, I have no focking idea.

He goes, 'Why are you still thriving around in tis ting?'

I laugh. I'm there, 'That's not a bad question, Nudger.'

'I mean, how many times is it Ine after sprayin it?'

'I think it's five.'

'Ine not tedding ye how to spend yisser money, Rosser, but ye'd have been berror off aston me to budden it.'

'I'm beginning to see that now.'

The first thing I'm going to do when my moo comes through from Regina is get myself a new set of wheels.

I'm like, 'Just as a matter of interest, what would you chorge for torching this thing?'

'It's the sayum as a spray job.'

'The same?'

That's actually good value.

I'm there, 'I'll tell you what, if it happens again, you can do it. Just burn the focking thing out.'

He's like, 'Can't say feerer. Be the way, I've haven't seen Ro for a few weeks.'

A lot of people would find it weird that a kid of fourteen has friends who are, like, more than twice his age. But I kind of like the fact that he's got the likes of Nudger, Gull and even Buckets of Blood looking out for him.

I'm there, 'Well, he's in love these days, isn't he? The famous Shadden.'

Nudger pulls a face.

I'm like, 'What?'

'Look, don't get me wrong,' he goes, 'she's a nice geerl, but I hate seein him gettin mixed up wid a famidy like tat.'

'Are you talking about her old man?'

'Ine talkin about him. Ine talkin about her brutters. Ronan's too smeert a kid to get mixed up wit the likes of that crowt. They're fooken doort boords, Rosser. Eveddy last one of tum.'

That says a lot. When someone who sets fire to things for a living thinks you're a scumbag, well, it's a bit like finding yourself one morning having breakfast with a stripper – you've got to ask yourself what you're doing with your life.

I'm there, 'Kennet's asked him to be a witness to some accident that I know for a fact he wasn't involved in.'

Nudger just shakes his head – this dude, by the way, has been in prison more times than I've had hot models.

'He toalt me,' he goes. 'And he feels wonther pressure to back up he's stordy.'

'I told him not to have anything to do with it.'

'But he's torden, so he is. Least he seemed to be the last time I sawd um. Seemed veddy thrubbled. And he wadn't at Croker last weekent.'

'What was on at Croker?'

'Te Tubs was playin. Semi-final of the Awdle Irelunt. Thee beat Duddeny Gall.'

'Jesus. I can't believe he'd have missed that.'

'Me eeder. As ye know, I do usually go to te Tubs matches wirrum. He's ticket went to waste.'

I tell him thanks for the info. I'll give the kid a bell – check he's okay. Try to properly talk him out of backing up K . . . K . . . Kennet's story.

I pay the dude, he hands me my keys and I hit the road.

I'm driving along and I'm about to ring Ro's number – I've even got the phone in my hand – when it suddenly storts ringing. I answer it, pulled up at the lights on – believe it or not – Dorset Street. It ends up being a dude called Barry Summoner, who went to CBC Monkstown back in the day and who now works in the Leinster Branch, doing fock knows what.

'Barry,' I go. 'What's the Jackanory? Joe Schmidt finally realize that I can do a job for him, even if it is as just back-up for Jonny Sextime?'

He laughs – obviously thinks I'm joking.

'Someone rang here looking for you,' he goes. 'I didn't want to give out your phone number, so I said I'd contact you and you could maybe contact her.'

I'm like, '*Her*?'

'Yeah, it was a girl.'

'Okay – intriguing. Wait a minute, why did she ring you?'

'Because you told her you played for Leinster.'

Shit. That's almost certainly true.

He goes, 'Can you not do that any more, by the way? It's not the first time it's happened.'

He's focking delighted to tell me that, of course. That'd be the whole Castlerock versus CBC Monkstown, us-versus-them thing.

'Fock you,' I go, 'just give me her focking name, will you?'

He's there, 'Okay. I had to write it down, because it was a new one on me. Her name is Blodwyn.'

My hort ends up nearly stopping.

I'm like, 'What?'

He goes, 'I think I'm saying that right. Blodwyn. She said she was from Cardiff.'

Fock. She's obviously out of the slammer.

'Anyway,' he goes, 'you should maybe ring her. She's very keen to get in touch with you.'

Sorcha sticks her wrist practically in my face.

'Smell that,' she goes.

I have a sniff. It *is* nice. Actually it's *very* nice?

I'm there, 'What even is it?'

'It's *Clive Christian No1*, Ross. It's the same perfume as Emma Watson wears. It's, like, *the* dearest perfume in the world – that's, like, *official?*'

I'm there, 'How much are we talking?'

'It's nearly three thousand pounds sterling for, like, thirty milli-litres . . .'

'Jesus.'

It's hord to believe this is the same girl who told Honor a few months ago that you could get away with wearing torn or worn clothes by being inventive with layering and adding a block colour underneath. I heard her actually say the words, 'We can all ride out this recession, Honor, if we make our wardrobes work for us – like Olivia Palermo and Kate Bosworth do?'

It's just nice to see her happy again.

'It was a gift,' she goes, 'from Ford. A bottle for me and a bottle for Honor. He has one for your mum as well, but there's no sign of her today.'

They're shooting the final scene on Stephen's Green. I'm there,

'Have you checked the No. 27? It's three o'clock in the afternoon. She's due her second bottle – of focking gin.'

She goes, 'Ross, don't be horrible.'

Apparently, Ford's been trying to get her on her mobile, but it's switched off and they end up having to go ahead with the scene – which she was supposed to be rewriting – because they only have permission to film until, like, half-four, when rush hour storts.

So it's like, 'Action!' and it's off we focking go.

A dude in a big red Honda Pilot pulls up at the lights outside the Sony shop and Honor slash Zara, like, emerges from the shadows, her bucket and squeegee in one hand and a white stick in the other, tapping her way towards the cor.

Sorcha leans in to me and goes, 'They're going to use some really sad Irish music for this scene. I suggested Caitlín Maude singing *Róisín Dubh*.'

I just nod. It's, like, whatever pokes your hontas, baby.

Honor puts the bucket down, then storts feeling the front of the cor, supposedly looking for the windscreen. She eventually finds it, then she storts washing it. The dude in the cor is just, like, staring at the lights, waiting for them to turn green – he *so* wants to be out of there.

Honor finishes washing the windscreen, then taps on the driver's window, looking for her moo. The dude flicks his hand at her – I suppose you could say *dismissively*? She taps on the window again. He winds it down with the intention of telling her to take her begging orse somewhere else, except he ends up getting a fright – we all do – when he sees her eyes for the first time. They're, like, pure white – they've obviously used some kind of contact lenses.

The light turns green and he goes to put the beast in drive. But then he suddenly stops and ends up having to do a double-take. Because he recognizes little Zara Mesbur – the twist is that he used to be her viola teacher.

And that's the focking end.

There's, like, a round of applause from the forty or fifty people film people and maybe a hundred members of the public standing around. Sorcha turns around to me and says she has an – oh my God – *amazing* Azzedine Alaïa dart shift dress for the wrap porty in Residence and that's what suddenly reminds me of my mission here today.

I make a subtle excuse – I tell her I need to take a shit – then I go off in search of Fantasia. All of the trailers – the entire movie circus, in fact – is porked along the Loreto side of the Green. I have a mooch around for fifteen, maybe twenty minutes, looking for her, except there's no sign.

Actually, I *do* need a Joe Schmidt all of a sudden. I think about tipping across to the Shelbourne – that and the top floor of BTs are the best spots in Dublin for a Shit and Run, that's a little tip for you – but I don't think I'd make it and I end up having to use one of the portaloos that they've got for mainly the crew.

In I go. So there I am, roysh, sitting there, crimping one off, when all of a sudden I hear Honor pass by the door going, 'Okay – surpassing all *previous* fock-ups?'

Then I hear Fantasia go, 'Honor, you need to understand the hurt you cause when you speak to people that way.'

She sounds like she's been crying. Definitely unhinged.

Honor goes, 'Yeah, whatevs. I'm just happy I'm never going to have to work with you again. That fact I love muchly. Insert happy emoticon here!'

Then she focks off, presumably back to her trailer.

I wipe up and I flush – come on, it's not focking Oxegen. Then I go outside. Fantasia is leaning against the railings of the Green, in literally floods of tears.

She looks incredible, by the way. She's wearing the exact same neutral silk sheath that Sorcha bought five of when she read that Max Azria was ditching his body-con aesthetic.

'Fantasia,' I go, acting the innocent. I'm still buttoning up my chinos, by the way. 'Is everything okay?'

She looks at me, her mascara all over the shop. Her face looks like a satnav impression of Blanchardstown – focking roads everywhere.

I immediately spot the red file under her orm.

'Your fucking bitch of a daughter just called me fat,' she goes.

I walk up to her and I put on my soft voice. 'You're anything but fat,' I go, except it doesn't sound as sleazy as you're possibly imagining it. 'Elisabetta Canalis was what I said when I first saw you and I'm standing by that analysis.'

There's no telling what a well-chosen compliment will do for a girl whose self-esteem is momentarily focked. Fantasia suddenly throws her two orms around my shoulders, hugs me hord and, in my ear, storts telling me that I am *so* a nice person.

I'm there, 'Hey, it doesn't cost anything to be,' and at the same time I'm giving the folder a bit of a tug, testing her grip on it.

It's wedged in there pretty focking tight.

'Like, have you ever read that book,' she goes, '*We Need to Talk About Kevin?*'

I thought it was a film, but I keep my mouth shut because I don't want to come across as stupid.

'Go on,' I go, 'keep talking.'

'Well, it's all about the conflict between, like, nature and nurture? And whether children can turn out to be little fucking monsters despite the best efforts of their parents.'

I give another tug, a firmer one this time, but she's not letting go of it. So I'm forced to try another tack.

I have a little sniff of Fantasia's hair, then I nibble her actual ear lobe.

She suddenly pushes me backwards – her hand on my chest – asking me what the hell I think I'm doing. Well, what she actually says is, 'I'm not sure that's appropriate.'

It did come out of nowhere, of course.

I look her straight in the eye and I go, 'I don't actually care what's appropriate any more. I've been keeping my feelings for you bottled up for, like, weeks now and I'm not doing it any more . . .'

Now, a girl in her normal state of mind would instantly recognize that as a line. But a girl who's been taking shit from a kid for practically the entire summer is going to take any little compliment that's coming to her.

'Elisabetta Canalis,' I go. 'I'm going to repeat what I said.'

And that's when I throw the lips on her – there and then, standing next to the railings on Stephen's Green, half-four on a Friday after-noon, on a packed focking street, with offices and all the rest of it emptying out.

She kisses me back. And it's pretty obvious from the amount of meat she puts into it that she wants me every bit as much as I want what's under her orm.

We kiss four, maybe five times, while she tells me that she's attracted to me too and I have another go at the file – it moves a little bit but she's still clinging on to it tightly.

I'm aware, of course, that someone – namely Sorcha – could walk by at any minute and interrupt this little romantic scene. So what I end up doing is I slowly turn Fantasia around – I basically slow-dance her from twelve o'clock to six o'clock – then I stort backing her across the pavement towards the chemical toilet.

She knows where we're headed as well, roysh, because it's actu-ally *she* who reaches behind her and pulls the door open, then we disappear inside and that's when it really kicks off.

Now I've had sex in a lot of toilets in my time – I went to UCD, for fock's sake – but never in an actual portaloo and I have to say, roysh, whatever about the focking hum, they're actually pretty roomy.

Fantasia pushes me down on the throne, hoicks up her dress and sits on me, her legs spread like bad news in a small town. As you know, I've never been one to kiss and tell – respect for a girl's dignity, blah, blah, blah – but she's suddenly coming at me like a focking spider monkey, hands everywhere, really putting on a show.

I'm not exactly disgracing myself either, can I just say – giving her the magic like Penn & Teller. I've got her dress unzipped at the back and I'm making sure to give her plenty of compliments, which birds *always* love when you're sorting them out.

It'll tell you what a great father I am that I'm only, like, fifty per-cent focused on the sex aspect of what's happening – the rest of me is thinking about freeing that file that's still stuck in the crook of her orm and sparing my daughter a humiliation that could, like, scor her for life.

It's as I'm undoing the clasp of Fantasia's bra that she finally lets go of it. I hear the thing fall and the sound of papers scattering across the floor. But she's enjoying herself so much at this stage – *and* of course the words of encouragement that I'm giving her – that she doesn't give a shit about it.

All she wants to do is sit on me like I'm *Secretariat* and ride me to focking glory.

I'm using my foot to try to, like, gather all the pages together and shove them into a corner, where I can subtly pick them up again when I'm on my way out the door.

But there's also a job of work to be done.

It's *as* she's undoing my belt, then yanking down my chinos – and I'm telling her that I don't know *how* Honor could think she was fat, just to boost her confidence – that I suddenly hear it.

It's, like, a *beeping* sound?

I'm there, 'What the fock's that?'

She's like, 'Who the fuck cares?' her breathing all funny.

My first thought is that it sounds like the reverse warning on an orticulated *lorry*?

'Just keep doing what you're doing,' she goes.

I'm like, 'Okay – do you want me to move onto the other one?'

That's when the beeping noise suddenly becomes more, I don't know, *urgent*? As in, it gets faster and definitely louder, then I hear all these roars – warning roars – and it's suddenly obvious that it *is* an orticulated lorry.

In the second it takes me to realize that, it suddenly hits the portaloo. The sound is like an explosion going off. It's like, 'Boom!' except really deep and really focking loud.

Actually, it's more like, 'Beddooom!'

The next thing that either me or Fantasia knows, we're being thrown through the air – her still, I don't know, *astride* me, like Ruby focking Walsh. We crash into the door, except the door is now the floor, because the toilet has been knocked focking over.

And you know what that means.

I'm lying on top of Fantasia with my chinos around my knees, the two of us listening to this, like, *gurgling* sound? Except it's not the gurgling sound that either of us is worried about – it's more what the gurgling sound is leading *up* to?

There's suddenly a second explosion – this one even louder – as the actual tank holding the you-know-what literally focking explodes, sending a flood of basically shit and piss and fock knows whatever else all over us.

My first instinct is to look for a way out, except the thing has fallen onto its front, so the door is obviously jammed.

Fantasia storts with the hysterics then. Actually, I wouldn't blame her – I'm pretty much on the verge myself, as this tiny space we're trapped in storts to quickly fill up with the bodily waste of every electrician, caterer and extra working on this movie today.

I probably don't even need to describe the smell. It's the worst smell you can possibly imagine, then with blue disinfectant added.

I'm basically gagging and it's possibly only the shock that's stopping me from actually puking. *She's* focking screaming, by the way – she's totally lost it. And that's when I notice the pages from her file – you'd possibly call it a *dossier*? – floating past my focking face.

It's, like, totally destroyed. Unreadable, basically. Well, I think, at least it's a case of mission accomplished.

I've no idea how long we end up being trapped in there. It feels like twenty minutes, although it's possibly more like three, before a bunch of crew members manage to roll the toilet onto its side and I kick the door open, sending a focking tsunami of vile-smelling piss and shit out onto the pavement.

Then we both crawl out – the two of us still in a state of pretty much undress, remember – to be greeted by a sea of, like, goggling faces. I manage to pick Sorcha's out straight away. Then – oh, fock – Honor's. They both look actually traumatized by what they're seeing. Everyone does, in fact.

Ford – what the fock is the M even for? – Perret steps forward from the crowd and goes, 'I can't even make out which one of you two is Fantasia.'

It's a total exaggeration, of course – even though we *are* covered from head to toe in crap.

Fantasia goes, 'It's me, Ford.'

He just nods, then goes. 'I thought so. You're fired!'

That's when Honor begins to see the *funny* side of it? She's going, 'Oh! My God! ROFL?!'

Now I've let Sorcha down enough times to be used to the look that's on her face at that exact moment in time. But what gets to me, *I* think, is the venom in her voice when she goes, 'Don't you even *think* about coming to Residence tonight, Ross.'

'I did this for you,' I try to go. 'For you and for Honor.'

Except by this stage, the entire crowd is just looking at me and, like, shaking their heads in disgust.

I finally get Ronan on the phone. I've been trying him all focking morning.

He's like, 'Howiya,' except he says it in a really, like, *hushed* tone?

I'm there, 'Hey, Ro – what's up?'

He's like, 'Ine history, Rosser.'

I'm there, 'What do you mean, you're history – has that focker threatened you?'

I feel my right fist instantly tighten – like it does when I see photographs of Jodi Albert with Kian focking Egan.

I'm there, 'He's going to be decked. Dude, I'm going to be like a focking Lithuanian corpenter in the good old days – I'm decking him quick and I'm decking him well. Threatening *my* son? I don't focking think so!'

'No,' he goes, 'I said Ine *in* history.'

'What do you mean you're *in* history?'

'Ine back at school, Rosser.'

'Are you? Already?'

'It's the foorst of September.'

'Is it? Well, you continue with your learning and blah, blah, blah then – I'll ring you later on.'

He's like, 'No, you're grant, so yar – the teacher hatn't arrived yet. I can talk for a second.'

'Okay, I'm just wondering what the deal is,' I go. 'I was talking to

Nudger the other day. He said you weren't at the Dublin football match.'

He's like, 'What Dublin football match?'

As a South Dublin father, I should be focking delighted, of course, to hear my son say those words. But I'm not, roysh, because I'm worried about him.

'Don't give me *what Dublin match*?' I go. 'It was the, I don't know, Celtic Championships Semi-final or some shit. Nudger ended up having to go on his own.'

Except he doesn't say anything.

I'm there, 'Is everything okay, Ro?'

'Yeah.'

'This isn't about the the packet of Dollymount whitefish your old dear pulled out of your pocket, is it?'

'The what?'

'The johnnies. Because if it is, I wouldn't sweat it, Ro. The woman's a focking hypocrite.'

He goes, 'I have to go, Rosser. Teacher's arthur walkin in.'

Imagine living practically your entire life and never even *seeing* video games. And yet Aida's taken to the Wii like her daughter took to the idea of Drambuie for breakfast. She's brilliant at the tennis. Well, not brilliant – I'm actually just about to beat her in straight sets – but there *have* been a fair few rallies. Long ones as well.

'Oh, you're very good at this,' she goes.

I'm like, 'Do you think?' because it's been, like, days since anyone has said *anything* nice to me. I'm still in the doghouse over the whole having sex with Fantasia in a chemical toilet incident. That's the amazing thing about Aida, though – she's a huge admirer of mine, no matter what I do.

When my one point something million snots comes through, I'm going to buy her – I swear to God – the present of an actual life-time.

'Just an observation,' I go. 'You don't actually *need* to swing your orms so wildly? If you just move the paddle with your wrist, it's the exact same effect.'

Of course, I'm a total wanker for only telling her that just as I'm about to serve for the match. I suppose that's just a mork of how seriously I take my sport and how competitive I *still* am? Then to prove it, I go and win the match with a fourth straight ace.

I'm like, 'Yeees!'

Honor – sitting in the corner of the living room with her nose, as usual, in her iPhone – goes, 'Er, *lame* much?'

'Is the game over?' Aida wants to know.

She's actually wrecked. She definitely hit a wall some time around the stort of the third set.

I'm there, 'Oh, *it's* over! You've been packed and dispatched!'

'Oh, thank God for that!'

Honor – again, without even looking up – goes, 'One of you two needs to take a shower.'

She's a little bitch and getting worse. Even though she does have a point. I told Aida she should possibly take the heavy cordigan off. The wool in it is like focking loft insulation – the thing doesn't breathe. But I still go, 'Honor, don't be rude,' just letting her know that she might be potentially a movie stor, but she can't go around saying whatever the fock she wants to people.

She goes, 'Whatevs.'

Aida says she's going out to the kitchen to get a drink.

I'm there, 'Hey, I'll get that for you,' but she's like, 'No, it's fine. I'll go.'

Sorcha's out there anyway – still giving *me* the silent treatment. She's focking great with Aida, though.

Aida's like, 'Errol Flynn's dead,' and this is, like, totally random.

Sorcha – she's just so amazing – goes, 'Oh, did he die? That's very sad.'

I'm pretty sure he's from, like, way, way back.

Aida's there, '*Captain Blood* was the one I liked him in.'

Sorcha's like, 'I don't think I've seen that one,' knowing that the way to handle Aida is to just keep talking to her like actually nothing's wrong and she'll eventually snap back to the real world.

'He was a dirty old man,' Aida goes. I actually laugh out loud. Can't stop myself.

I hear Sorcha go, 'Would you maybe have tea? It's very good if you've a thirst.'

Aida's there, 'Tea would be lovely.'

'Oh my God, I might even make some lunch. It's nearly two o'clock. Aida, would you mind asking Ross if he's hungry?'

And Aida – this is also amazing – goes, 'Would you not ask him yourself?' because she's obviously picked up on the atmos in the gaff over the last few days.

'Ross and I aren't speaking at the moment,' Sorcha goes.

I wander over to the living-room door for a better listen.

Aida's there, 'Well, isn't that just stupid?'

'Not if you heard what he did,' Sorcha goes. 'I couldn't even tell you what it was, Aida.'

This is another lovely thing about Sorcha. She *could* say that I was knocking the orse off some random woman on the side of the street in a metre of other's people's shit and piss. But she'd never, ever let you down like that.

'Was it another affair?' Aida goes.

Sorcha's like, 'What?'

'Did he have another affair?'

'Well, yes, actually.'

'But what do you care? You don't want him any more – or so he tells me.'

'It's more complicated than that, Aida.'

'I don't see what's complicated. I look at you and I see two people who love each other.'

I'd love to see Sorcha's face when she says that to her.

'Sure that much is obvious,' Aida goes.

Sorcha suddenly lowers her voice. 'I really respect what you're saying, Aida – and also your *right* to say it? – but there are, oh my God, major trust issues there.'

'The nanny, wasn't it?'

'Excuse me?'

'He said you walked in when he was having an affair with the nanny – a dirty Russian.'

You can nearly *hear* Sorcha trying to work out whether that's actually racist or not. She goes, 'She was from *one* of the former Soviet republics, yes. But Eskaterina wasn't the first, Aida. He was always at it.'

'At it?'

'I'm saying there were always other *girls*?'

'Before you were married?'

'Oh my God, yeah. He did the dirt on me, like, twenty times when we were just going out together.'

She doesn't know the focking half of it, of course. Add a zero to the end of that number and you're still not even in the ballpork.

'So why did you marry him?'

'I don't know. Maybe I thought he'd change.'

'And why don't you think he can change now?'

'Oh my God, Aida, all these questions.'

'You must have asked yourself that one. You forgave him all those other times, so why can't you forgive him again?'

'Er, *marriage*?'

'Ah, marriage!'

'I'm sorry, Aida, but loyalty and trust are two things that are – oh my God – *so* important to me? And when Ross did what he did, he fractured that trust.'

'Well, I'm only an old woman, so what do I know? Except that you're a beautiful, beautiful girl. And you're married to a man who's an auld fool – anyone can see that – but he's got so much love in his heart.'

I'm actually on the point of tears here. Imagine if Aida had been my old dear – as in, what would I have achieved in life if I'd had this woman in my ear pointing out my amazing, amazing qualities?

I'd probably be on the plane to New Zealand right now for the Rugby World Cup, with Rog and Jonny Sexton sitting across the aisle from me, sweating like James Gandolfini.

Although that's for others to say.

I end up having to run and sit down then, because I hear Sorcha suddenly coming. The next thing I know she's stood in the doorway. She goes, 'Honor, do you want some lunch?'

Honor's like, 'What is it?'

'I was thinking of doing my double tomato bruschetta,' Sorcha goes.

Honor's there, 'Puke!'

The little focking wagon.

'Okay, fair enough,' Sorcha goes, then she turns to me – this is having not spoken to me for, like, three days – and she goes, 'Ross, would you like some double tomato bruschetta?' and she says it in, like, such a nice way that I end up just nodding at her like the focking Churchill Insurance dog.

I'm like, 'Yeah, Sorcha – er, anything that's going.'

Oisinn is seriously ripping the piss out of me over the whole Fantasia thing – effluence is the new affluence and blahdy, blahdy, blah-blah.

Apparently, it's all over town, what happened.

He shakes his head – but at the same time *laughing*? 'You're never going to change, are you?'

I'm there, 'I wasn't aware there was any call for me to,' and it actually sounds genuinely amazing the way I say it.

I'm just looking at Oisinn then, wondering what the fock Father Fehily would think if he could see him now. We're talking bankrupt, we're talking back living with his old pair, we're talking driving his old dear's Ford Ka and now – most embarrassingly of all – doing odd jobs for literally cash in hand. And mainly – get this – dismantling decking.

It's, like, the new thing apparently. Back in the day – and I'm hordly the first person to point this out – every focker and their neighbour was having decking put in their gorden. Now, apparently, everyone's having it removed, either because it reminds them of their, like, shamefully decadent past, or because they've finally realized – at the end of yet another shit summer – that we live in a country where it pisses rain three hundred and fifty days a year and that, far from being a place to enjoy a bowl of stuffed olives and a bottle of *Châteauneuf du Plonk* on a balmy August evening, their deck has basically become a permanent shelter for mice and rats.

Oisinn was always way ahead of the curve.

He says he's honestly never been busier. Six jobs this week and another four next week. The one he's doing right now is in Cornelscourt. The thing is like a focking bandstand, which is why he asked me along to give him a dig-out.

So there I am, roysh, two o'clock in the afternoon, with a hammer in my hand, doing literally manual labour. The idea of it. I suppose this is what they meant when they said we were all going to have to adjust.

'Is this what they call a metaphor?' I go.

He's there, 'You mean for the end of the Celtic Tiger?'

'Yeah.'

'I don't know.'

'It kind of feels like one, though, doesn't it? The Fall of Deckland.'

I pull out a nail with the claw end of the hammer – you pick these things up quickly enough.

It's good to catch up with the dude. I didn't see half enough of him during the summer. He's like, 'How are things with you?'

I'm there, 'Yeah, no, same old, same old. Still living under Sorcha's roof.'

'Is your granny still on the scene?'

'Yeah. You're going to have to meet her, Ois. She's an amazing bit of stuff. I can do no wrong in her eyes. She even smoothed things over between me and Sorcha after the whole Fantasia and the Exploding Shithouse episode. I think she's genuinely trying to play Cupid between us.'

'And how are the kids?'

'Don't ask. The whole movie thing was a major mistake, although Sorcha can't see it. Honor's turned into an even bigger bitch than she already was.'

'Jesus, Ross, that's your daughter you're talking about.'

'Hey, I've never been afraid to call it, Dude. You wouldn't believe some of the shit she's been up to. Ronan's fine. Although I do worry about him. I still think they're pushing him too hord.'

'Who? McGahy?'

'Mainly. The kid just seems a bit, I don't know, elsewhere these days. Even his mate Nudger said it. Possibly worried about the Junior Cert. results next week. What about you, Dude? How are you – I don't know – *within* yourself and blahdy blah?'

'I'm the happiest I've been in a long, long time, Ross.'

'I hope you don't mind me saying, but I find that very hord to believe. I mean, you're wearing a tool belt. Jesus, I could weep for you.'

'Ross, this might be the first honest work I've ever done – even though it's obviously off the books. I love it. Being out in all weathers. It's kind of sobering. I generally start early . . .'

'How early are we talking here?'

'Half-eight some mornings.'

'Jesus Christ!'

'I even bring a packed lunch.'

'A packed lunch?'

'Yeah.'

'Like you see bus drivers eating?'

He laughs. 'I suppose so, yeah. Seriously, though, Ross. I wish it was still 2007. Who doesn't? And, yeah, I never expected these hands to ever have to do a hord day's work. I mean, that's how we were all raised. But I'm telling you, it's good for the old self-esteem to get up in the morning and actually have something to do.'

'I'll take your word for it.'

'I'm trying to get JP and Christian to join me the odd day.'

I'm just there, 'Good luck with that,' and then I decide to change the subject to something a bit happier.

I'm there, 'Do you remember that bird I rode in Cordiff with the electronic tag on her ankle?'

It's a stupid question, of course. Who's going to forget that?

'Blot When,' Oisinn goes – it's not a bad impression either.

I'm like, 'Yeah, no, she's trying to get in contact with me.'

His jaw hits the literally deck.

'What do you mean she's trying to get in contact with you?'

'Well, I'm presuming she's out of prison. She rang the Leinster Branch looking for a number for me.'

'The Leinster Branch? You told her you were in the Leinster squad, didn't you?'

I just nod. 'I even told her Rob Kearney calls me Guru – a new low, huh?'

He's not laughing, though.

'Ross, what if she arrives over here?'

'She's not going to arrive over here.'

'You don't know how pissed off she is – you got her sent back to prison.'

'Okay, even if she does arrive over here, how's she going to find me?'

'Ross, it's a small town. If she stopped ten people on the south-side, seven would probably know you.'

I think the figure is possibly closer to nine, but I let it go.

'What if you end up shot again?' he goes.

I'm like, 'Come on, Ois – how focking likely is that to happen? I mean, she told me herself, she's a sociopath, not a psychopath.'

Whatever the actual difference is.

I'm sitting in the Lambo, outside the gaff on Newtownpork Avenue, when out of the blue, the front passenger door opens and the old dear suddenly plonks herself in the seat beside me.

The first line out of her mouth is, 'Stop trying to think of something hurtful to say to me.'

I *was* about to say she looks like Hulk Hogan in drag.

'Well, what the fock do you want?' I go.

No introduction or anything – she's just there, 'My father stopped me.'

I'm like, 'What?'

'From seeing my mother,' she goes. 'He wouldn't let me. Didn't want it. Didn't approve.'

I actually laugh. I'm there, *'That's* your excuse?'

'It's not an excuse . . . Ross, couldn't you just listen to me? Why do you always feel the need to judge me?'

'Okay, then, let's hear it – the stage is yours.'

'The woman was doolally, Ross, that's what you have to remember. And my father, well, he was at the end of his tether – of course he was! She'd been that way since she was pregnant with me. Anyway, when they finally put her away – a blessed relief for him – I don't think he ever expected to see her again. I remember visiting her and the woman was just . . . I'm trying to think of the word here . . . *catatonic*. Yes, that's it. Not there. Eyes vacant. Mouth open. All that. It was terribly distressing, Ross. I mean, I was just a little girl. Five years old. To see your mother like that! Anyway, my father decided it would be better all round if we didn't go to see her any more.'

I'm there, *'Both* of you?'

She nods sort of, like, sadly. 'Like I said, he didn't ever foresee a day when she was going to get out of that place. Then – a couple of years later, it must have been – he got a call to say she was being released, discharged, whatever the politically correct phrase is. I think in his mind – certainly in his heart – he'd already said goodbye to her. He felt he couldn't go through all that again. Couldn't cope. Didn't see why he should. She had a sister in Wexford . . .'

I'm like, 'Okay, I'm going to have to interrupt you again. According to Aida, their marriage was in shit anyway. He was rubbing his hands when they stuck her away.'

She doesn't even deny it. She actually goes, 'There's probably some truth in that,' and this is a woman I've never heard say a bad word about her old man. 'I used to write her letters – when she was in the hospital, then when she was living with her sister. I was never sure she got them – and, if she did, whether she even understood them. That's why I got upset that day when you mentioned them.'

'I presume that's why you didn't show up to see your so-called movie wrap.'

She doesn't respond to that, just goes, 'Then one day, my father told me not to write any more letters. Just like that. From what I remember, she was going to be homeless again. This was around the time that the nuns took her in. Her sister couldn't cope with her, as it turned out – well, I don't think they ever got on. And my father, he thought there was going to be pressure brought to bear on him to take her back. I think I'd started asking a lot of questions as well. Oh, I was very precocious, even then. Why doesn't Mummy live with us? That type of thing. I expect he realized that sooner or later I was going to want to have a relationship with this woman. So he told me – no more letters. Told me to forget I ever had a mother.'

I'm there, 'From what I've heard about him in the past, he sounds like he was a complete and utter wanker.'

She doesn't deny it. 'What's she like?' is all she goes. 'I'm talking about Aida.'

I end up just shaking my head. 'She's focking fantastic,' I go. 'Unbelievable. I mean, my confidence has gone through the roof since she arrived on the doorstep.'

I have to be honest, roysh, I'm not expecting the next line that comes out of her mouth. 'I want to meet her.'

I realize it's the closest I'll possibly ever come to actually hugging this woman.

'She's not in at the moment,' I go. 'Sorcha's taken her to Dundrum Town Centre.'

She's there, 'I didn't mean now. I have a taxi waiting.'

I look in the rear-view. There's an Andy McNab porked behind me, with the meter running. Still hasn't got her licence back obviously.

She goes, 'Will you arrange it, Ross? For me?'

And for the first time in my life, I turn around to my old dear and go, 'It'd be an actual pleasure.'

Sorcha's old pair's gaff is finally sold. One point five mills! Back in the day, it was supposedly worth eight! They're, like, moving out today and Sorcha asked me to come with her to say, like, her final *goodbye* to the place?

I hold her hand the whole way to Killiney – that's one of the nice things about driving an automatic, I suppose. She's, like, silent for most of the drive, except when we pull up at a red light at Baker's Corner and she tells me that what I did in bringing Aida and my old dear together – the old dear's taking her out for lunch tomorrow – was, like, '*so* an amazing thing'.

Then, roysh, when we're halfway up Ballinclea Road she goes, 'And thank you for coming with me today. One thing I will never forget, Ross, is what an incredible, incredible person you can be,' the whole Fantasia business totally forgotten.

It makes me feel good like Gielgud, to quote the great Dricmeister General himself.

The gates of the gaff are open, which means I can turn off the Vico Road and drive straight up the gravel driveway for once. There's only, like, one removal truck porked in front of the gaff, which strikes me straight away as sad – that everything Sorcha's old pair have left in the world would fit in the back of that.

I know she's thinking exactly the same thing.

Most of their shit, they ended up either giving away or auctioning off to pay their debts. I know her old man's George III antique terrestrial globe and his Edward Delaney life-size famine figures would have looked focking ridiculous in a two-bedroom aportment in the middle of Sandyford Industrial Estate – but even so.

We step inside. The place has been, like, stripped *bare*? It's weird the way our voices echo around the big entrance hallway, which Sorcha's old man chased me through many times over the years, once after threatening to cut my throat with a nineteenth-century antique ivory letter opener, which is supposed to have fetched a fair few grand when James Adam stuck it under the hammer last week.

Sorcha has her little determined face on – like she's *decided* to be brave? But I can tell, roysh, that inside it's killing her. She pushes various doors and looks into various rooms – the kitchen, the dining room, the study, where she put in some serious hours, for not only her Leaving Cert. but also her degree – for all the focking good they were to her.

But she doesn't go *into* any room? She just, like, stands in the doorway of each and stares into it, like she's taking – I don't know –

a mental photograph. Or maybe she's just trying to remember them the way they were, because one thing's for certain – it doesn't *seem* like the old Lalor home any more?

She even says it. She's like, 'I thought it was going to feel different. Saying goodbye. It feels like I'm too late. Like it's already *gone*?'

We go up the big – I'm going to say – *sweeping* wooden staircase. Her old bedroom is the only room she *does* actually go into? She just walks silently around it, staring at the walls. It reminds me of the day that her boutique closed. Walking sadly around empty rooms. There's been way too much of that lately.

She looks out the window. 'Oh my God,' she goes, 'there's Mum and Dad!'

I was actually wondering where they were myself. It turns out they're having lunch on the patio. There's a real Last Supper vibe to it. I can see the Cavistons bags from up here.

I'm there, 'Do you want to go down and join them?'

She nods and at the same time smiles. 'Give me a hug first,' she goes.

In she comes – nearly ends up breaking my back she squeezes me so tight. Her hair smells of the Jackberry shampoo she always uses and I've instantly got one on me.

'Come on,' she goes, 'let's go down to them.'

It's *as* we're tipping down the stairs, roysh, that her sister's voice comes from her own room, going, 'Ross, could you help me with this box?'

I look at Sorcha, who just rolls her eyes. 'Go on,' she goes. 'Oh my God, she's always *so* last minute.'

Sorcha heads downstairs and I go into the room. It probably goes without saying that there *is* no box. The sister – I'm going to remember her name one day, even if it kills me – is sitting on the vornished wooden floor with her back against the wall – mini skirt, Uggs with tights and her sweater muppets practically bursting the seams of her baby-pink Abercrombie polo shirt.

She's there, 'Did you hear where we're moving?'

She doesn't seem a happy rabbit.

I'm like, 'The Beacon, yeah.'

'It's like, Oh! *My* God?'

'Handy for the Luas, though.'

She goes, 'That's what *he* said,' and *by* he I presume she's talking about her old man. 'You'll never guess what he made me do last week. He drove me around and made me hand CVs into actual shops.'

'That's, er, not a good buzz.'

'We're talking, like, Dunnes and Tesco, Ross. And – oh my God – O'Briens *off*-licence? He said that if I'm going to be living with them, I was going to have to make a contribution.'

'There's suddenly a lot of that around at the moment.'

She just shakes her head and at the same time laughs, like she can't find the words to describe how unfair this is to her.

Then she goes all serious again and she goes, 'Do you want to have another go of them?'

I presume she's talking about Statler and Waldorf.

'I, er, might actually pass on that.'

This seems to surprise her. She's there, 'Do you mind me asking why?'

I'm there, 'I'm just not a hundred percent sure it'd be fair to your sister.'

I know. It sounded weird coming out of my mouth, as well.

She actually doesn't seem to care that much. She's just like, 'Whatever.'

I tip downstairs, then outside to the gorden. It's a cracking day, it has to be said – especially for September.

Sorcha's old dear goes, 'Ross, will you have some Cava?'

I'm like, 'Too right I'll have some Cava,' except Sorcha's old man stares at me like he's weighing up in his mind what kind of, like, provocation it would take to allow him to legally kill me with his bare hands.

He goes, 'You won't have some Cava. Not if you're planning to collect my granddaughter from Mount Anville this afternoon, you won't.'

Sorcha's there, 'Dad! It's fine. Ross, I'll drive if you want to have a glass or two.'

I'm like, 'Actually, no, I don't think I will – although thanks for offering.'

'Well,' it's the mother who goes, picking up a plate, 'you'll have some prosciutto and you'll have some goat's cheese,' and she storts making me up a plate of, like, bits and pieces from the table.

Sorcha's there, 'Give him some of the Serrano ham as well, Mum – he really likes it.'

Serrano focking ham – they're certainly not *eating* like a family on the breadline.

Her old man, of course, hates seeing his two favourite women in the world making a fuss of an absolute waste of time like me. He just goes, 'They're a very good removal firm we're using,' aiming the words, for some reason, in *my* direction? 'I must give you their number, Ross, for when you decide to move on. Which is when, by the way?'

I just laugh in his face and go, 'Can I tell you something, Eddie my boy? Your other daughter just offered me a shot of her jobbers upstairs.'

No, I don't really say that.

I actually go, 'I'm going to buy probably another aportment as soon as the insurance money comes through for my old gaff,' and then I think about what Aida said, about not letting him talk to me like I'm a piece of shit any more. So then I'm like, 'Be careful what you wish for, by the way – you could end up with me as a neighbour.'

Sorcha and her old dear both crack their holes laughing. The old dear, in fact, goes, 'Oh, you asked for that, Edmund! You really did!'

He tries to change the subject then – focking raging, you can see it. He turns to Sorcha. 'How's Honor settling back in at school?' he goes.

Sorcha's there, 'Fine. I mean, it's going to be difficult obviously – after the *summer* she's had? I think she'd love to be home-schooled. But Ross and I explained to her, as her co-parents, that despite everything she's obviously got going on for her, we want her to have as normal a childhood as possible.'

He seems happy enough with that answer.

That's when I notice the old tyre swing that Sorcha was talking about before, hanging from the branch of a tree on the other side of the gorden. I pop a piece of prosciutto into my mouth and ask Sorcha if she wants me to cut it down. I'm there, 'I could hang it in the gorden in Newtownpork Avenue.'

He's pissed off, of course, that he didn't think of it first.

'Yes, I could go and get my shears,' he tries to go.

Sorcha's there, 'No. I honestly can't see Honor ever being interested in it. The people who bought the house – do they have kids?'

He's like, 'I've no idea.'

'Well, I hope they do,' she goes. 'And I hope they have as much fun on it as I did.'

She stands up then. She's obviously decided that we're hitting the road.

We say our goodbyes and I hop into the Lambo. Sorcha opens the passenger door, but then stops and has one last look at the place. Same thing – like she's taking a mental picture. Then she gets in beside me.

I hand her my iPod and I tell her to put in the earphones, which she does. I press play. It's, like, *Puff the Magic Dragon*, which I downloaded this morning, specially for her.

She doesn't say anything, just listens, as I ease the beast into drive and pull back out onto the Vico Road. That's when I feel her hand on my leg and I hear the sound of her quietly sobbing.

The old dear is standing at the front door with a face on her like something that Ronan would eat deep-fried in batter and served with a side of chips and onion rings. I don't comment on it, though, because she's obviously shitting herself. It's, like, a massive day for her.

'I thought I might take her to The Unicorn,' she goes.

I'm there, 'The Unicorn's a good spot.'

'Or what about The Gables? I want her to know something about me and who I am. I think The Gables says that more volubly than anything, don't you?'

'Look,' I go, 'it doesn't really matter *where* you bring her? All that matters is that you're, like, spending the day with her.'

'I'm just very nervous,' she goes. 'What am I going to say to her?'

I'm like, 'It won't be hord. Just talk to her. I told you – she's great.'

I open the door wider. She takes a breath, then steps into the gaff. I tell her she's in the living room.

The old dear goes, 'Come *with* me, Ross. You must introduce us.'

Which is what I end up just doing.

Aida has been sitting in her coat since about ten o'clock this morning and it's now after one. She's watching the news.

I sort of, like, clear my throat to get her attention. She looks at me, then beyond me, over my right hammer, and I end up not having to say a word.

'Hello, Fionnuala,' she goes.

And the old dear's like, 'Hello . . . Mum.'

I'm there, 'I'll, er, leave you to it, then,' and I sort of, like, moonwalk out of the room.

I feel genuinely amazing. I was the one who threw them together. But even genuinely amazing moments – I know from painful experience – last only so long.

I'm actually filling the kettle, just in case either of them wants a cup of tea or coffee, when the old man suddenly rings. It's mostly just blah to begin with. He's all, 'What an exciting day for your mother, eh?' and I'm like, 'Yeah, they're in the living room now,' and then he goes, 'Big day for Ronan, too. The latest scholar in the family! The Junior Cert. results are out this morning.'

I actually forgot it was today.

He gets all, I suppose, philosophical then. He goes, 'These are the moments, eh, Ross? The little oases of happiness in a sea of uncertainty.'

'Er, if you say so, yeah.'

'It was the worst day on the stock market last week since the dark days of 2008. Europe's in a right old state – as I'm sure you know – and America looks like it's going to lose its, inverted commas, triple A rating. But then you hear the news about Fionnuala and her mother being reconciled and, well, you just remember the things in life that matter.'

That's when he says it. Comes totally out of left field. 'By the way, did you hear about Hennessy?'

I'm like, 'Who?'

'Your godfather, Ross!'

'What? No. What about him?'

'Well, it seems *he's* taking the economic view that we need to spend our way out of this recession!'

I'm there, 'What are you talking about?'

'The chap's about to buy himself a yacht!'

I'm like, 'A yacht?' and then I actually say it again, 'A yacht?' as a horrible feeling suddenly comes over me.

'Oh yes! A hundred feet long, if you don't mind! Tastefully proportioned foredeck. Black-masked deckhouse and cockpit. Something, something, something. Oh, he showed me the photographs, Ross. As fine a piece of engineering as ever I've seen. Chops through the water like I don't know what. That's according to the bumf. Do you know how much it set him back?'

'How much?'

'One point four million!'

'You're . . . you're focking shitting me?'

'That's what I said, Ross. I said, "Hennessy, what are you thinking? This at a time when we're all supposed to be – what's the famous phrase? – sharing the pain? Tightening our belts and so forth?" I said, "What kind of message is this to be sending to ordinary people?" Well, he just laughed. "Fuck ordinary people," says our friend – oh, he can be terribly blue with the language . . .'

I feel sick. I really think I'm going to actually vom.

'One point four million!' he goes. 'I didn't even know he had that kind of money. A year ago he was nearly broke.'

Hennessy's not answering his phone. I don't know why I thought he would. I rang Christian and asked him about the focker's whereabouts and he said he'd gone to France to buy a boat.

It'll tell you what a nice goy I am that I'm still trying to give the focker the benefit of the doubt. I'm thinking, yeah, no, maybe it's not *my* money he's planning to spend.

Maybe the old man was wrong. Maybe he *wasn't* nearly skint? Maybe he had actual money stashed.

It'll tell you what a sucker I am, roysh, that when my phone rings when I'm driving into town in the middle of the afternoon, I answer it by going, 'Hennessy?'

Except it's not Hennessy. It's focking Tina. And from her tone, it doesn't sound like she's ringing to tell me what an amazing person she thinks I am.

There's no hello or anything. She's straight in my ear, going, 'What the fook is goin on?'

I'm there, 'Tina, I've got a lot on my plate slash mind at the moment. What do you want?'

I end up nearly crashing the cor when she turns around and goes, 'Ronan's arthur failing his Judinior Ceert.'

For, like, ten seconds, I think I've basically misheard her.

'Say that again,' I end up *having* to go.

'He failed, Ross. Every bleaten one.'

'What are you talking about?'

'NG. NG. NG. NG. NG. NG . . .'

It suddenly brings me back to my own school days. But I have to say it gives me no pleasure at all to find out that he's following in my footsteps.

'Okay, Tina, I take the point. But I'm definitely getting a vibe here that you think *I'm* somehow to blame for this?'

'Ine aston you what's goin on.'

'*You're* asking *me* what's going on? As opposed to yourself, who actually lives with him? Or your boyfriend, who sees him every day of the focking week in school?'

'There's somethin not reet wirrum.'

'Whoa, whoa, whoa. I was the one who argued *against* him sitting it a year early, if you remember? But you wouldn't listen. You had him down as Finglas's answer to Stephen focking Hawking. You pushed too hord and he cracked.'

'Tom said he failed them on poorpose.'

'And how would he know that?'

'Because he left effery exam arthur half an hour. Just wrote he's exam number on the front of he's answers buke and stayed the midimum amount a thime.'

'Well, what's Ro saying?'

'Nuttin. I can beerly get a woord ourrof um.'

'That's because he probably hates you for forcing him to do it. Anyway, look, I don't see what the biggie is. He can sit it again next year with the rest of the kids in his class.'

She storts roaring abuse at me then, which I decide I don't actually *have* to listen to? So I end up just hanging up on her, then switching my phone to silent.

I pork the cor in Merrion Square, throw some coins in the meter, then I walk around to the Shelbourne.

Five minutes later, I'm banging on her door again. I think you know whose door.

I knock three or four times – loud knocks as well – except at first, roysh, no one answers and I'm just about to walk away when I hear a woman's voice go, 'Will yee hold year harses – ay sad ay'm cawmin.'

The door is suddenly reefed open and there we are, standing face to face again.

Regina's opening line is, 'What the fuck do yee want?'

I'm there, 'Some answers would be actually nice,' and as I'm saying it, I'm looking over her shoulder and noticing there's, like, four suitcases next to the door, then another one open on the bed.

I'm like, 'Are you going somewhere?'

Regina goes, 'What bazness is thot of yours? Yee gat your prace. Noy leave us alone.'

A look must cross my face, roysh, because Regina's mouth suddenly drops open.

'He dadn't gav it to yee, dud he? That slappery wee bawsterd. Ay knee it.'

She suddenly storts calling over her shoulder to her daughter.

Hedda appears behind her.

She storts going, 'What the fock does he . . .'

Except Regina cuts her off. 'He didn't pee um. What did ay see to yee. Slappery bawsterd.'

She seems to think it's somehow hilarious.

I'm there, 'So you're saying you actually paid him?'

'Of course ay focken peed um,' Regina goes. 'Yee were thrattening tee go tee the Gords. Ay peed um sax months ego.'

'Six months ago?'

'Aye – back in Morch. One point savan mallion.'

'The full one point seven? The focker told me you were negotiating.'

The two of them crack their holes laughing, especially Hedda. She's a seriously bad egg.

'So hoy does it feel?' it's, like, Regina who goes. 'Yee trayed tee extort mornay from us and yee anded op gatting screed over yeersalf.'

I'm just there, 'No way. No *focking* way. Because you're going to pay again. I want another one point seven mills – this time delivered to me personally.'

'Awee tee fock wit yee,' Regina goes. 'Yee're naver gonnay *see* us agan.'

I'm there, 'Where are you going?'

It's, like, Hedda who answers. 'We're going to the States.'

I'm there, 'To live?'

'Tell him nathin,' Regina goes.

'Yes, to live.'

I'm there, 'How can you? You're still a suspect in an attempted murder investigation.'

Regina laughs. 'No, she's nat. There's no avidence against her. Yee sad yee con't remamber onythang. The Gords have told us she's nee longer even a sospact.'

I'm there, 'She will be if I tell them I've suddenly remembered everything.'

Regina just laughs at me and goes, 'And ay'll tell them abite yee and that solacitor of yours blackmeeling may. You'd get abite tan years in jeel, the pair of yee.'

She's right. And Shane Harron would make sure of it.

She goes, 'Yee jost have tee accapt that yee've been ite man-oovered. So goodbay . . . foraver,' and with Hedda – the girl who tried to kill me – sniggering away behind her back, she slams the door in my face.

10

Fahrenheit N11

'Why do you keep asking me about Hennessy?' Christian goes.

I'm there, 'Do I?'

He's like, 'Three times on the phone this week. And now again. I didn't think you even *liked* Lauren's old man.'

'Yeah, no,' I go, 'it was more the yacht I was interested in. Do you know did he buy it in the end?'

'I don't know.'

'Or did he end up having a last-minute change of hort?'

He's like, 'Do you want me to text Lauren?'

I'm there, 'Er, no, it's cool. How are things there, by the way?'

'Good,' he goes.

I'm there, 'Good?'

'Better.'

'Was it the counselling?'

'Talking to each other certainly helps. Fehily always said that, didn't he?'

'Talk, talk and keep talking.'

We both smile at the memory.

I look over at Aida. She wanted to see the famous Kielys and she seems to like it. She's chatting away to JP and Oisinn, telling them – if you can believe this – all about her wonderful daughter, Fionnuala.

They seemed to really hit it off, by the way. The old dear sent me a text message about two hours after they left the gaff, going, 'She can really drink!'

I remember thinking, yeah, you can afford to focking talk.

They ended up in, like, the Merrion Hotel for the whole day and a lot of the evening – the two of them arriving back to Newtown-pork Avenue in a taxi, already shit-faced, then they made a serious

Horvey Dent in the Sandeman's that Sorcha keeps in the medicine cupboard for whenever her own granny calls in.

'Hey,' Christian suddenly goes, 'did I tell you about my new job?'

I'm like, 'Job?' the concern clear in my voice.

'Well, it's more of a venture. I'm going into business for myself.'

'Here, it's not dismantling decking, is it?'

He laughs. 'No, it's not dismantling decking.'

'Because Oisinn has that morket sewn up. He even had focking J-Town over there working with him today.'

'No,' he goes. 'Have you ever heard of Footlong?'

I'm there, 'Is that the American submarine-sandwich place that's *like* Subway but *isn't* Subway?'

'Exactly. Well, Lauren and I bought a franchise.'

'What?'

'With some of my redundancy money. We're renting a shop unit on Chatham Street. We're hoping to be open this side of Christmas.'

I'm pretty focking stunned, it has to be said. I try to just jolly along with it, roysh, but I end up *having* to say something?

I'm there, 'You're going to be, like, making rolls for people? Processed meat and blah, blah, blah?'

'It's an amazing business opportunity, Ross. You should have seen the number of people at the open day in the RDS. They were all architects and car salesmen and solicitors and estate agents. They had nine hundred applications for just twenty franchises.'

I tell him fair focks, even though I know it's not the 'Fock, yeah!' that he's looking for.

There's, like, a TV on. Enda Kenny is babbling away about how things are basically shit for Ireland right now and people are experiencing tough times due to the incompetence and greed of a tiny elite. But then he talks about the Irish character and how Irish people, down through history, have always overcome hordship and had an extraordinary capacity to put up with shit without complaining too much.

'Oh, I hate Sean Lemass!' Aida suddenly shouts.

That gets a good focking laugh from the Kielys regulars, especially JP and Oisinn, who obviously think she's a riot.

She's not finished yet either.

'He wants to lead us into the Common Market,' she goes, 'and he'll not rest until he's done it. Sell us off to the Germans and the French and let those dirty foreigners decide what happens in this country.'

Then she turns to me and goes, 'That's it now – I've said my piece.'

The entire boozer is, like, breaking its balls laughing.

I'm just there, 'You called it, Aida! You called it!'

I decide to go for a hit and miss then. So I'm standing there and one of the bormen comes in and storts having a slash at the trough beside me.

'Oh by the way,' he goes, 'a girl rang here looking for you.'

I automatically go, 'Don't give her my focking number!'

It's amazing how those words just trip off my tongue without even having to think about it.

He laughs. 'We never do,' he goes – which they don't, in fairness to them. That's one of the reasons why it's the best battle cruiser in the world. 'Even though this one sounds like a looker. She had a funny name. What was it?'

I'm there, 'It wasn't Blodwyn, was it?' even though I already know the answer.

'Blodwyn – yeah. Welsh, she said she was.'

'How the fock did she end up ringing here?'

'She said she met you in Cardiff, but you got separated before you managed to exchange phone numbers. I thought, That doesn't sound like our Ross!'

'Okay, whatever – just get on with the story.'

'Well, she knew you were into rugby. So she just Googled "rugby pub Dublin" and up we came.'

Oh, she's focking clever, there's no doubt about that.

'So she rang and asked did any of us here know you,' I said, 'Know him?' He's never out of here.'

'Shit.'

'When he gave up the drink for Lent one year, we had to lay off staff.'

'Fock!'

'So do you want her number?'

'No. Bin it. And if she rings back, tell her I've emigrated.'

I tip back outside to Aida and the goys. There's, like, a brand-new pint waiting for me. I've got incredible mates.

Christian turns around to me and goes, 'So what's the story with you and Sorcha? There's no sign of you moving out of the gaff.'

'No, I'm still there.'

'You still have feelings for her, don't you?'

'Always did. I've never denied that. I mean, she was incredible when I was in the hospital, Christian. She was in there three times a day. She's one of the few people who genuinely gives a shit about me.'

'Do you think she'd take you back?'

'She probably would at the moment. She's very emotional.'

He just shakes his head, disappointed with me.

I'm there, 'No, what I mean by that is, you know, that we've actually grown closer since I've been back living with her. I've been an unbelievable support to her while she's been going through the whole shit with her old pair's gaff. Then the whole, as she calls it, co-parenting our daughter thing. Then her seeing the way I am with this little lady here. Dude, it's been intense.'

'What about you, though? Are you ready to be loyal to her?'

'Put it this way, her sister presented her rack to me the other day and I'd no even interest. How like me does that sound?'

'Not very,' he has to admit. 'How's Honor, by the way?'

I end up just shaking my head. 'I think me and Sorcha are heading for big problems with that girl.'

He's there, 'What do you mean?'

I've said it before and I'll say it again. It's great to have the dude back in my life.

I'm there, 'She's just a little bitch, Christian. The way she speaks to people. She was, like, bullying the shit out of people on that movie set.'

'Bullying them? She's a kid.'

'Dude, I saw it myself. And then on top of that . . .' and I sud-

386

denly drop my voice to a pretty much whisper. 'I don't even know how to say this.'

He's like, 'Dude, what?'

I'm there, 'Do you remember a few months back, when Sorcha was managing the euro store, and someone phoned the ISPCC and told them that Honor was a basic poverty risk?'

'Yeah, you said it was your old dear.'

'Well, it wasn't her for once.'

He looks at me totally blank-faced, then his mouth just drops open, like someone from, I don't know, Navan seeing escalators for the first time. He's like, 'You are focking joking me!'

I'm there, 'I'm not.'

'A five-year-old girl?'

'Dude, I found the number on her bill.'

'Jesus Christ! What did Sorcha say?'

'Well, obviously I never told her.'

'What do you mean *obviously*? Why would you keep that from her?'

'Because the two of them were suddenly getting on – for the first time ever. They had that whole Katie Holmes and Suri Cruise thing going on and Sorcha was, like, genuinely happy. I didn't want to take that away from her.'

He just shakes his head as if to say, you're my best friend in the world – you've got some genuinely amazing qualities – but there are times when I just don't understand your tactics.

What he actually says is, 'That's the reason why you and Sorcha will never work. Because you're not ready to be honest with her.'

It certainly gives me something to suddenly think about.

Christian's phone rings and he answers it. He puts one hand over his ear so he can actually hear.

He goes, 'Hey, Lauren,' and even just judging from the way he says it, I know those two are going to be fine.

Oisinn is telling Aida that Ireland are playing Australia in the Rugby World Cup this weekend and that's when I get a sudden idea.

I'm like, 'Let's all watch it in my gaff. I'll do a big fock-off breakfast. Be like old times. I'll even explain the rules to you, Aida.'

She says that would be lovely.

And that's when Christian – still on the phone – turns around to me and goes, 'He *did* buy the yacht, Ross,' and then he goes back to talking to Lauren. 'One point four million! I didn't think your old man had that kind of money.'

I jump off Dun Laoghaire pier onto the actual deck of the boat. There's, like, a real James Bond vibe to it, in fairness to me. Hennessy comes pegging it out of the cabin to see what the commotion is, except he seems almost *relieved* that it's me?

He even *goes*, 'Oh, it's you,' like he's not even embarrrassed by what he's done.

I'm there, 'What the fock is this?'

He's got a cigor between his teeth that'd have a field of broodmares playing dead. He takes it out of his mouth and goes, 'I knew you were stupid – but Jesus . . .'

'Yeah, no, I know what it *is* – as in, a boat? What I mean is, what the fock is your actual game?'

He's there, 'Little retirement present to myself.'

'Using *my* money?'

'Hey,' he goes, cracking on to be actually pissed off with *me*? 'It was never *your* money. You get that out of your fucking head right now. It was your father's money – money *I* helped make him.'

'Money *I* deserved for being basically shot. You're supposed to be my godfather!'

He just laughs, like it's nothing more than a meaningless title.

He goes, 'You think I was going to let you walk away with one point seven big ones? What the fuck use would that kind of money be to you? You'd have pissed it up against the wall.'

'No, I wouldn't. I might have bought, I don't know, shares with it.'

He laughs even horder this time, although I'm not a hundred percent sure why that's considered funny.

He goes, 'Oh, you'd have pissed it away alright. Like your rugby career. Like your marriage. Like the shredding business. Like everything that Charlie ever gave you. Jesus, it'd be fucking ethically wrong for me to let you have anything like that kind of money.'

I just shake my head. 'You've some balls,' I go, 'talking to me about ethics.'

He's obviously been to, like, Wind and Wave or one of those, because he's got all the new clobber as well.

'Let me show you something,' he goes and I end up following him into the actual cabin area, which ends up being big enough to pretty much live in. It's got, like, a master stateroom with a super-king bed in it, then two guest bedrooms, a saloon with, like, a home theatre, bor and dining area and a kitchen that you'd have to see to actually believe.

I don't understand the reason for the guided tour, though.

'Ain't she something?' he goes. 'Sailing performance meets luxury living. All my life I wanted a boat like this. I'm going to take this on the fucking ocean.'

I'm still in pretty much shock at the focking nerve of the dude.

I'm like, 'I'm going to tell the Feds,' and I say it like I'm expecting it to be a real game-changer. Except *he* doesn't even bat an eyelid, just fixes himself a massive drink from a decanter of brandy, without even offering me one.

'So what's your story?' he goes. 'I withheld information vital to a criminal investigation in order to extort money from the mother of the girl who shot me – and my solicitor ran off with my money? You'd do jail time. And a lot of it.'

'You focking . . .'

'No, you have no options here, my friend. Want to know why? Because I'm smarter than you. I'm smarter than you when I'm fucking sleeping. Now, if you don't mind, I would very much appreciate it if you would get off my fucking boat.'

Which is what I end up having to do. He puts this – I think it's the word – but *gangplank* down and I end up having to walk it, which feels somehow fitting.

As I'm walking back up the pier, Hennessy storts whistling *I'm Popeye the Sailor Man*, just to really rub it in.

I head back in the direction of the Pavilion and I decide to, like, grab a coffee from Insomnia. I end up getting, like, a cappuccino – a lorge one – then sitting with it at one of the little tables outside.

I have a couple of sips – a cracking blend, it has to be said – then I whip out my phone and dial the number.

Hennessy's right. He *is* smorter than me. But only ninety-nine point nine percent of the time.

Nudger answers on the fifth ring. He recognizes my voice straight away. He's like, 'Howyia, Ross, man?'

I'm there, 'Do you burn boats?'

He laughs. He's like, 'What?'

I'm there, 'I'm serious, Dude. Is it possible?'

He goes, 'I can burden athin you want.'

'Okay,' I go, 'I'd like you to burn an actual boat for me. It's, like, a big fock-off yacht.'

This gets one or two funny looks from passers-by. It's not the kind of thing you expect to hear walking into Meadows & Byrne.

He's there, 'Are ye wanthin me to make it look like an accident?'

I'm like, 'No, I want you make it look like someone was trying to make it look like an accident.'

He goes, 'Ine not foddying ye, Ross.'

And I'm there, 'I want you to make it look like it was an insurance job.'

I'm the first one to say that I think this Ireland team has at least one massive performance in them and definitely one massive result. Then everyone gets in on the act – Christian, JP and Oisinn – all saying that they think it's definitely possible, Australia aren't the same team without David Pocock and blahdy, blahdy, blah-blah.

The point is, though, I've been saying it since way before the World Cup even storted, during the summer, when they were playing pants. I was like, 'Goys, they're saving it – believe me,' which was a huge, huge call by me at the time.

This is all of us in the living room in Newtownpork Avenue, by the way.

'Is Nicky Rackard playing?' Aida goes.

I'm like, 'Er, who?'

I'm not the only one either.

'Nicky Rackard,' she goes. 'Oh, my father loved Nicky Rackard. Used to say he was the best hurler that Wexford ever produced.'

I'm like, 'No, this isn't hurling, Aida. This is, like, rugby, remember? This is the game that I could have made it at – if it hadn't been for injuries and one or two other things.'

The goys are all grinning away at me. It's obviously only half the story, of course – but, hey, she's an old woman.

The anthems come on. That's when Sorcha suddenly pops her head around the door and she's like, 'Breakfast is ready, everyone,' because it's one of those stupid o'clock kick-offs. 'Come and help yourselves . . . Aida, you stay where you are, I'll make you up a plate.'

We all wander out to the kitchen. I've honestly never seen a breakfast buffet like it – even in, like, hotels. We're talking pumpkin pie French toast, we're talking huevos rancheros, we're talking polenta and sausage hash, we're talking blueberry-ricotta pancakes, we're talking individual pineapple and raspberry parfaits. She's been up since half-five this morning cooking and I'm going to say fair focks. She's even done about a gallon of her lemon zinger cider and enough coffee to wake the dead in Shanganagh.

It's air-kisses all round. The goys all love Sorcha. She looks unbelievable, I should also mention.

She tells JP that she believes congratulations are in order. This is as he's helping himself to a matcha muffin.

I'm there, 'What's this about, Dude?'

He says he's decided to go back to college to study, like, auctioneering. 'Distressed properties,' he goes. 'That's where the future of this country is.'

I tell him that's focking great news.

The next thing, Aida lets a roar out of her from the living room. She's like, 'It's a goal!' and the goys all make a bolt for the door.

I stop, though, and say thanks to Sorcha for putting on such an unbelievable spread this morning. I'm there, 'And I really mean that, Sorcha,' and I give her a little peck on the cheek.

She goes, 'Oh my God – you are being *so* weird!'

I'm there, 'Hey, I'm just mentioning that I really appreciate it, that's all. The effort you went to. Blah, blah, blah.'

She laughs. 'Go in and watch your match.'

The goal turns out to have been a penalty, of course, and – fock's sake – it's Australia who've scored it. We're all like, 'Shit!' and then it gets even worse when Jonny Sexton misses a kick that I'd have put over with focking skis on my feet.

JP gives me serious daggers. He's a Rog man – I'm a Rog man, myself – but I'm also Sexton's number-one fan, remembering what he did to us when I coached Andorra against Ireland A back in the day. Made shit of us, basically.

Aida's full of questions, by the way. She's like, 'Why do they keep throwing it backwards?'

I'm there, 'That's just the rules of the game, Aida. Otherwise, it'd be basically just Gaelic football. And nobody would want that.'

Within a few minutes, roysh, I'm giving JP the finger, because Sexton not only kicks his next penalty from practically the next island over but then he puts over a drop-goal, just as casually as you or I would button our chinos, to put Ireland into the lead.

'Who's that fella with the ball?' Aida, at some point, goes.

I'm there, 'That's Brian O'Driscoll. He's the dude I showed you on the Credit Union ad.'

She's like, 'Brian O'Driscoll. And were you a better player than him, Ross?'

I just go, 'That debate will rage on and on, Aida.'

That draws one or two sniggers from the goys. But I turn to Christian – the main culprit – and go, 'The greatest player *ever* to play for Ireland and the greatest player *never* to play for Ireland. There'll always be comparisons. And there'll always be people who come down on both sides.'

'You're a lot more handsome than he is,' Aida goes.

I end up nearly choking on a mouthful of chorizo scrambled egg, I laugh that hord. 'It'd focking kill him to know that, Aida,' I go. 'I can tell you that for a fact. Goys, you're my witnesses that she said it.'

Fock! Sean O'Brien – who's having the game of his life, by the way – gets caught offside and Australia are suddenly level. Ireland are giving away a lot of silly penalties – I'm not afraid to say it – and we *could* actually be behind, even though our pack is totally kicking the shit out of theirs.

'We could actually win this game,' Oisinn goes, 'if we minimize the basic errors.'

I think that belief is pretty much there in all of us as the game reaches half-time and there ends up being, like, a stampede for the kitchen to fill our plates again.

Aida, I notice, is out to the world, but I decide to just let her sleep, because the old dear is going to be swinging by later to bring her to the Village at Lyons for lunch and a nosey around the gorden – she'll need her strength.

Honor's up, by the way. Sorcha's bringing her to Dundrum to spend some of her movie money – or at least stick a load of shit on her credit cord until the the moo comes through.

I'm there, 'It's shaping up to be a cracking match, Honor. Do you want to come and watch the second half with your daddy and his friends slash former team-mates? History in the making and blah, blah, blah.'

She's like, 'Er, DILLIGAC, Dad?'

And I'm just there, 'No, now that you mention it, you don't.'

Our back row end up putting in a shift like I've never focking seen before in the second half and they, like, seriously slow the Australian ball.

Ten minutes into the second half, Jonny Sexton gets a chance to put Ireland ahead and – pressure is for focking tyres! – he nails it and I just punch the air and tell the goys I'm storting to think all sorts of crazy thoughts here.

We're the better team – there's no doubt about that. I can't even remember the last time the Australians were even in our half. Then they concede another penalty. They're bottling it – you can see it – and they're bottling it in a way that would have to be described as majorly.

Rog takes the kick this time. Focking masterful. Through the posts it goes. Now it's, like, 12–6. JP cheers in a way that suggests that some basic point has been proven.

I end up losing it with him. I'm like, 'Why does it have to be O'Gara *or* Sexton?' and I pretty much shout it at him. 'Why isn't it possible to think that they're both great players?' and Oisinn and Christian end up having to call a time-out – tempers getting frayed, which I put down to the absence of alcohol and the, I suppose, enormity of what could possibly happen here.

Me and JP end up just shaking hands. 'Dude,' I go, 'I lost it. I'm sorry.'

And he's there, 'Hey, I don't want to hear sorry. All it shows is how seriously we both take our rugby.'

We're frustrating the fock out of Australia still. They just can't get any decent ball. Then they end up conceding another penalty right in front of the posts.

'If you are what you eat,' Oisinn at one point goes, 'then Paul O'Connell must have eaten a focking legend this morning!'

It's a cracking line that deserves every high-five it ends up getting.

O'Gara – look, every focker knows, I'm as big a fan of him as he is of me – kicks us 15–6 ahead with less than ten minutes to go and suddenly we're all thinking this is going to happen – this is going to be our actual day.

Except the Australians are now porked on our line.

I end up sitting there, just glued to the clock in the top-left-hand corner of the screen. I'm like, 'Is time moving slowly or is it just me?'

My phone rings. I answer it. There's, like, five seconds of silence on the other end. I'm expecting it to be some dude in India, coming bouncing at me off a satellite, asking to speak to the billpayer. I'm about to hang up when I hear a familiar voice go, 'Ross?'

I laugh. I actually laugh. I'm like, 'Fionn, how the fock are you? How are things in Umbonga?'

He's there, 'Uganda, Ross.'

'Uganda, then?'

'It's great. I'm teaching in this little village not far from Kampala. The kids are incredible. And, actually, I've been pleasantly surprised by the level of literacy . . .'

He suddenly stops, roysh, mid-sentence, and gets down to the real reason he's ringing.

'Who's winning the match?' he goes.

It's amazing. There he is, roysh, hundreds of thousands of miles from home, and he's thinking about us and probably secretly wishing he was here.

I'm there, 'Ireland are winning 15–6.'

He goes, 'What? How long's left?'

I'm like, 'Not long. Dude, stay on the line.'

Except he's ringing from, like, a payphone. They must still exist in Africa. 'It's swallowing the coins, Ross. I'm not sure how long it's going to give me. What's happening now?'

'We're under serious pressure, Dude.'

JP, Oisinn and Christian all suddenly roar. Tommy Bowe has intercepted the ball and he's got it tucked under his orm with, like, seventy or eighty metres of open road in front of him.

I explain all of this to Fionn, doing my best Ryle Nugent impersonation.

'He's eating up the ground like you wouldn't believe. There's, like, two Australians – can't even see who they are – closing on him.'

We're all there literally roaring at the TV, going, 'Run, Tommy! Run!'

Even Fionn is screaming it in my ear.

I turn to JP – the fastest rugby player I've ever seen in an actual footrace – and I go, 'Does he have the legs?'

JP scrunches up his face and goes, 'I don't think so . . . Shit!'

He gets caught. Just a couple of metres of grass too many. Except it doesn't matter. Because a few seconds later, the referee is blowing the whistle and me and the goys are suddenly going literally ballistic.

Fionn's there, 'Is that it?'

I'm like, 'Yeah. We did it, Fionn! We beat Australia!'

He just goes, 'Yes!' and then I hear, like, a beeping noise and he tells me that he's about to be cut off.

And I just go, 'Mind yourself, Fionn.'

There's, like, basic pandemonium in the living room. There's, like, fist pumps. There's, like, high-fives. There's, like, group hugs to beat the band. We're, like, dancing around like focking lunatics, with everything – me getting shot, JP and Christian losing their jobs,

Oisinn losing everything, even Fionn being jilted – totally forgotten in a moment of pure joy.

'We're going to make the focking final!' Christian goes – everyone now an instant believer.

He has me in a clinch at the time. And I'm hugging him hord and at the same time looking over his shoulder at Aida, just sitting there in my old ormchair, with her eyes gently closed and the most peaceful look on her face. And my hort, in that moment, goes from full to empty, because I suddenly know – as sure as I know my own name – that Aida is dead.

The old dear says she's sad that she never got to show her mother Monart – like she *owns* the focking place?

'We did discuss taking a spa weekend together,' she goes. 'Oh, she'd have loved the hydrotherapy suite down there – I know she would. Alas, it was not to be.'

And she's all dressed in black, by the way. The full grieving daughter act – the veil and everything. She only spent, like, one day with her. I'm about to point out that basic fact, except it's like she reads my mind.

'Silly to be all dressed up like this,' she goes. 'I mean, I only met her that one day.'

'She was still your mother,' I hear myself go, actually giving her the benefit. 'That's a fact that no one can change.'

She stares at me for ages then, just nodding, as if what I've said is somehow – I don't know – *deep*? Then she smiles. There's shit I could say here about crow's feet, but I don't bother.

That's for another day.

It's pissing it down – always seems to be in graveyards, doesn't it? The funeral was a small affair. It's how we all wanted it. Just me and the old dear, Sorcha and Honor, the old man and Helen, then Ronan as well, who's quiet – obviously still embarrassed about bottling his exams. And he needn't be – not in front of me anyway. My focking IQ seldom exceeds the room temperature.

The old dear puts up her umbrella and she invites me under it.

'She told me that you took her to Eddie Rockets,' she goes, 'and that you left without paying for your food.'

I laugh. I think that'll always be one of my favourite memories of her. That and throwing the chowder over Sorcha's old man's shoes.

I'm there, 'She was actually faster on her focking feet than I was, if you can believe that. I would have been caught if it wasn't for her turning up in a taxi at just the right time. *And* the security dude getting knocked down by the cor. The whole thing was pretty hilarious.'

'That's what *she* said. You know, I think she wet herself telling me that story?'

'Are you serious?'

'You brought her so much happiness in the last few months of her life, Ross.'

'Hey, I told you she was a great old bird, didn't I?'

She smiles. 'You know what she said to me? She said that nothing in her entire life brought her as much joy as that time she spent getting to know you.'

'She was certainly a fan – she made that very clear. But the feeling was definitely mutual.'

The rain continues just thundering off the umbrella. I can hear Sorcha, just within earshot, tell the old man and Helen that I haven't cried yet, which seems to concern her for some reason.

But I watch the old dear's eyes fill up.

'I want you to know,' she goes, 'that I'm grateful. If you hadn't talked sense into me that day, then I might never have had that time I did with her – short as it was.'

'Hey, it's cool.'

'I know we've never been close, Ross. I know you feel I've been distant at times and perhaps withholding . . .'

'Hey, I don't think this is the time or place for us to have a focking moment.'

'No. I expect you're right.'

'I get that you're grateful. But we're not about to stort being bezzy mates.'

'Point taken, Ross. Are you coming back to the house?'

She's got a big focking crew coming around – Delma and Angela and all her friends from her various campaigns *against* shit? They'll have been buttering bread since the focking dawn – it's the Irish way when someone dies, isn't it?

I'm there, 'Yeah, I'll come back for an hour or two.'

She nods at the two gravediggers – no fun for them standing out in the pissings – and they stort shovelling the earth over Aida's coffin.

The old dear links me and we walk back to the funeral cor. She's there, 'Are you travelling with us?'

I'm like, 'No, no, I brought *my* cor, remember?'

She ends up having to squint across the cor pork – too focking vain to wear glasses, of course.

'Oh, yes, of course. By the way, what *is* that written on it?'

Fresh this morning.

'It's like, "Prosperity for you means austerity for us!" and then, underneath, it's like, "Rich prick!"'

'My word!'

'Well, to be honest, I think I'm ready to say goodbye to it.'

I open the door for her and in she climbs. I slam it shut and she opens the electric window. She's there, 'I need to talk to you and Sorcha about something.'

'As in?'

'Today's not the day. It's important, though. We'll talk again.'

Helen and the old man wander over to us then. Helen tells me she's so sorry for my loss – she's an amazing person – and the old man says something, well, pretty similar.

'Speaking of loss,' he goes, leaning in and whispering, like he knows he possibly shouldn't be bringing the subject up here, 'I expect you heard all about your godfather's pride and joy?'

I'm like, 'No,' acting the total innocent, obviously.

'Up in flames, Ross.'

'You're shitting me.'

'I wish I was. Destroyed by fire before its maiden voyage. Oh, the chap's devastated, don't you know! The thing's a – what is it these insurance companies call it? – a write-off.'

'That's shit for him.'

'Except . . .'

'Except what?'

'Well, there's some question now as to whether he'll ever see a cent from them. Chaps they send out to investigate these things seem to think he did it himself for the insurance money. Preposterous, I know. But they seem to think there's evidence.'

'What a focking choker, huh?'

'Oh, you know what these insurers are like. Don't Even Go There, Girlfriend! Anything not to have to pay out.'

Deep down, I know that this won't be the end of it. Hennessy's not just going to take his medicine. He'll come back at me somehow. For now, though, I'm going to just enjoy it.

The old man's there, 'Are you coming back to your mother's?' He opens the door of the funeral cor.

'Er, yeah,' I go. 'I'll see you back there.'

Honor's like, 'I want to go with Granddad and Grandma,' and the old man's there, 'Well, GAMO, then – that's Get A Move On to the rest of you!'

They all climb in and off they go. And then it's only me, Sorcha and Ronan left.

'Hey,' I go to *him*, 'I appreciate you coming this morning. Again, I was sorry to hear about the exams.'

Sorcha's like, 'We both were.'

'Er, thanks, Rosser. Thanks, Sorcha.'

'There's no shame in bottling it, Ro. I tried to make the point that you were too young. But, if you remember, I got shouted down.'

He just nods – the weight of the world on his little shoulders.

I'm there, 'Seriously. Don't worry about it. Like I said to you before, just enjoy your childhood. Don't be in a rush to get old.'

He heads off – presumably back to school.

I go to get into the cor.

'Wait,' Sorcha goes.

I'm like, 'What?'

'Will we have a hug?'

'Er, yeah – whatever bloats your goat, Baby.'

Of course I realize mid focking embrace that what she's actually trying to do is see if she can make me finally cry. Because she storts going, 'She loved you, Ross. She really, really loved you.'

I pull back, hold her at orm's length and I'm like, 'I'm fine, Sorcha. I really am,' and then suddenly it's like we're back in the attic of her old pair's gaff all those months ago. Our eyes are just locked together. Except this time I don't hang around. I move in for the prize.

I kiss her on the lips. It's not all one-way traffic either. She kisses me back and she makes that funny sound with her mouth that I remember so well from the past – like a dog that can't get his dinner into him quick enough.

It's a good five minutes before she remembers herself. She pulls away and says we really should go – it's lashing rain and it's really not the most appropriate place in the world to be doing this.

I tell her I don't care about the rain. I'm there, 'What would you think of the idea of us getting back together again?'

We *are* both getting a serious soaking, by the way.

She goes, 'Back together?' like she's never even thought about it. 'Ross, we're getting a divorce.'

'Yeah, but what would you think of the idea of us *not* getting a divorce? Maybe having a second crack at the whole marriage thing instead?'

She reaches behind me for the handle of the door and pulls it open. 'Now is maybe the worst possible time to discuss this,' she goes. 'We have to recognize that our feelings are – oh my God – *so* raw right now?'

And she gets into my cor, leaving me standing there on my Tobler in the rain.

So it's, like, two weeks later – we're talking the middle of a Saturday afternoon in October – and I'm sitting in Kielys with the goys, none of us even drinking. I don't think any of us could be even orsed.

Ireland were knocked out of the World Cup by Wales this morning. The dream had looked definitely on. Beat Wales, then beat either France or England and we were in the final against possibly New Zealand.

Wasn't meant to be.

Still, at least there's a chance of my sleep patterns returning to normal now. All this getting up early in the morning and going to bed at a reasonable hour takes its toll on the body eventually.

But little do I realize – as I'm giving the goys my post-match analysis – that the final whistle is about to signal the kick-off of *the* craziest, most focked-up twenty-four hours of my basic life.

JP says that Renards is gone again. I suppose that's a good sign of how actually focked Ireland is. Nightclubs going out of business not once but twice. That and the fact that the Germans are supposedly running the country these days.

The goys are all in pretty good form, even allowing for this morning's result. They're all getting their shit together in one way or another. JP's back at college, studying auctioneering, and he's also doing the odd day helping Oisinn with the decking removal business, which seems to be going from strength to strength. Christian and Lauren will be opening the doors of the Chatham Street branch of Footlong in four weeks' time. You'd have to say fair focks.

I hit the jacks for a quick Douglas Percy and I end up getting a bit, I don't know, philosophical in there. I'm thinking, yeah, no, it hasn't been a bad old year as they go. I didn't die – that's a definite gimme right there. Okay, I didn't get my one point seven mills, but another way of looking at that is that it was never really mine to begin with. And I met Aida, the most amazing woman in the world, who – in the short time I knew her – softened up this tough old hort of mine to the point where I'm thinking that I might actually want to get back with Sorcha.

But then you know me. In eight hours' time, I'll probably be wankered drunk, helping some bird out of her Ireland jersey while telling her that Leo Cullen high-fived me coming out of Terroirs two Christmas Eves ago and called me 'Legend'.

I'll possibly never change.

I'm buttoning up my chinos and trying to make up my mind

whether I need to wash my hands or not, when all of a sudden I hear what would have to be described as a kerfuffle coming from outside in the bor.

It seems to be, like, one voice – a woman's voice – shouting something that I can't make out, then a load of other voices telling her to, like, calm down?

And suddenly – I swear to fock – I feel like my orse is about to give out. Because I realize that it's, like, Blodwyn. And from the pitch of her voice – speaking as someone who has pissed off, let's all agree, one or two women down through the years – it sounds to me like she's on the pretty much warpath.

I wander over to the door, open it a crack and look through.

It's Blodwyn alright. She's seriously focking mullered. She's got a bottle of wine in one hand and a glass in the other – she's obviously come from somewhere else – and she's, like, cross-examining Christian, JP and Oisinn, all of whom she obviously straight away *recognized*?

'Where's that bleddy friend of yours?' she's going. 'Where is he?'

She's totally shit-faced, staggering around the place like a dancing bear on a hot tiled floor.

Having said that, she actually looks well. I said Olivia Wilde back in May and I'm not taking it back. She's also lost a few pounds, which is always good. I remember her mentioning that she was always happiest at what she called her prison weight.

'I've just spent four months in fuck ken priss zen. Now where is that little bas ted friend of yours?'

She's still wearing the ankle tag, by the way. I get the impression that girls like Blodwyn are slow to focking learn.

The goys, in fairness to them, refuse point-blank to give me up. The problem – when you've made as many enemies over the years as I have – is that there's always someone who's more than happy to.

'He's in the gents,' I hear someone go. I'm pretty sure I know who it was as well. He went to, like, Clongowes and I don't think I need to say any more than that.

Her eyes immediately go to the door, which I'm still holding

402

about an inch open. I let it go, at the same time thinking, 'Fock!' and all I can hear then is the terrifying sound of high heels stomping across the hordwood floor towards the jacks.

I'm standing with my back against the wall, shitting myself – very nearly literally.

The door opens and there we suddenly are, face to face.

I say the first thing that pops into my head. 'Did you see your crowd did a serious job on Ireland this morning?'

The first thing that pops into my head is very rarely relevant to anything. The upside is that it buys me some time.

She's like, 'What?' genuinely thrown.

I'm there, 'Wales are in the semi-final of the World Cup. I'm saying well done.'

'I don't care about rogbay,' she goes. 'I've just spent four months in priss zen because of you, you fuck ken bas ted. And now I'm go wen to smash this glass into your fuck ken feece.'

I'm like, 'Not the face, Blodwyn,' and I swear to God, roysh, she smashes her wine glass against the wall – this is without even blinking – like you've seen in a hundred episodes of *Bad Girls* or *Prisoner: Cell Block H*.

'Oh,' she goes, 'I'm go wen to carve up them pretty fee chairs of yours.'

I'm like, 'Blodwyn, I'm actually begging you here. I'll give you money, anything you want. Just leave the face.'

She takes a step towards me then and suddenly the most incredible thing happens.

Some focking friend of humanity has managed to miss the trough completely and piss all over the floor. Okay, hands up, it was me. Blodwyn steps into it in her killer heels and she slips. She not *only* slips – she goes orse over tit in the air and lands on her back, cracking her head against the porcelain trough.

She's out of the game. I can see that immediately. I'm not sure whether it's the blow to the head or just the effects of the drink but she's, like, totally unconscious.

I stand there staring at her, lying on her back in, I have to say, a

403

very nice cocktail dress – she must have been in Leeson Street last night – and I think, okay, what's your move here, Maestro? And it ends up being a case of cometh the hour, cometh the plan.

She weighs nothing – what the fock do they feed them in prison? – and it doesn't take much for me to get her up onto my shoulder and carry her in, like, a fireman's lift through the door, then through the actual pub. You can imagine the roars of laughter, I'm sure, when the regulars see the Rossmeister General escape from what should have been a focking bloodbath in the jacks and emerge through that door carrying his would-be attacker – yet another woman scorned – over his shoulder like a sack of focking potatoes.

Oh, there's a swagger about me – don't you worry about that.

'She slipped,' I go, and then, with my free hand, I point at one of the borman and go, 'There's piss all over the floor in there – you'd better get it mopped up.'

Everyone laughs – even the focker from Clongowes who turned me in – and I walk out the front door, with everyone turning to each other and just going, 'Oh my God – another quote to remember him by!'

I carry her to my cor, which is porked at the front of Bang & Olufsen. Christian, Oisinn and JP are obviously pretty curious as to how I'm going to play this one because they follow me outside, going, 'Ross, what the fock are you doing?'

I'm there, 'Let's just say I've got a plan,' and I give them one of my cheeky little winks.

I pop the boot.

'Ross,' Christian goes, 'you're not putting her in there.'

He's wrong there. Because I am. I actually *drop* her in there? She's fine, though. She's going to sleep for hours. Then I slam the boot shut.

JP goes, 'Ross, she could have a concussion.'

This coming from the man who drove a woman to a cor show-room clinging onto her own windscreen wipers.

I open the passenger door and hop in.

'Okay,' it's Christian who goes, 'at least just tell us what's in your head.'

I'm there, 'I know you've probably heard me say this before, but this is one of my best plans ever. I'm going to drive to Dun Laoghaire . . .'

Oisinn's there, 'I think I already know where this one is going.'

'I'm going to buy a ticket to Holyhead, then I'm going to drive onto the ferry with Blodwyn sleeping like a baby in the boot. Then I'm going to get off and watch the boat set sail. I'm going to give it, say, an hour, then I'm going to ring the Welsh cops – directory inquiries, before any of you ask – and tell them that there's, like, a wanted woman in the boot of a Lamborghini on the way from Dun Laoghaire. With a bit of luck, the cor will never come back. I can save myself the three hundred snots that I told Nudger last night I'd pay him to burn the focking thing!'

'Ross,' Christian goes, 'is there any way we can persuade you that this is not a good idea?'

I'm like, 'Dude, you saw what she was like in there. This is a girl on the edge. Desire is obviously a major port of that. But she's already found out where I drink. There's fockers in there who wouldn't hesitate to tell her where I live. And I can't run the risk of her turning up on my doorstep. No, the best place for her is back behind bors. Now, are any of you coming with me?'

They all take a step backwards. Bear in mind, of course, that back in the day, they'd have been on it like a bonnet. Now, they've all got too much to lose.

I just go, 'Suit yourselves,' and I pull the door shut.

Five minutes later, I'm on the Ferris Bueller out of town, thinking, how focking mad is this? I'm sitting in a Lamborghini with a Welsh fugitive from justice in a very nice cocktail dress unconscious in the boot.

I'm just saying – the twists and turns that life takes.

That's when Sorcha all of a sudden rings. I answer by going, 'Hey, Babes, how's your day?'

She's like, 'Ross, can you come home?'

I'm there, 'I'm just on the way to Dun Laoghaire, Sorcha. Weird question to ask, but do you know what time the HSS sails?'

I don't notice the edge of whatever-the-fock-it-is in her voice. 'Ross,' she goes. 'I need you to come home now. Your mum is here.'

I'm there, 'Give her that bottle of Booth's London Dry under the stairs. It'll keep her occupied for a couple of hours until I get there.'

That's when she ends up totally losing it with me. 'Ross,' she goes, in a take-no-shit tone she hordly ever uses, 'get home *now!*'

Of course, the whole way down Newtownpork Avenue, I'm wondering what kind of trouble I could be in now? I run through the possibilities in my mind. It could be literally anything, from the old dear telling Sorcha about the real reason her hair fell out to this famous movie being cancelled by the studio because of a multi-million-dollar lawsuit for bullying against our five-year-old daughter.

Sorcha and the old dear are both sitting in the living room when I get there. The old dear has managed to find the Booth's, I notice.

The impression I immediately get is that Sorcha doesn't know what this is about yet either.

The old dear has her hands clasped together in front of her. She's loving her moment, of course. There's, like, a white A4 envelope on the coffee table.

I straight away fear the worst.

'Is this about Honor?' I go.

The old dear's like, 'Honor? No, of course not. It's about your grandmother.'

I'm like, 'Aida? What about her?'

'There were a couple of things you didn't know about her, Ross.'

I look at Sorcha, then back at the old dear. I'm there, 'Like what?'

'She was an artist.'

'I know she was an ortist. Jesus, I bought her paints and all sorts.'

'Oh! My God!' Sorcha goes, 'she painted Killiney Bay from the top of the hill. It's *so* an amazing painting, Fionnuala.'

The old dear flashes Sorcha her patronizing smile, which Sorcha doesn't realize is a patronizing smile, but it is. It definitely focking is.

She goes, 'Have you ever heard of an artist called Francis Weyermann?'

Needless to say, I haven't. Sorcha has, though. 'Oh my God, yeah,' she goes, 'you see his stuff in the window of, like, the Oisin Gallery, the Oriel, all those.'

The old dear just nods and goes, 'Aida *was* Francis Weyermann.'

I think we're both in equal shock, even though I wouldn't know one of the focker's paintings if you smashed it – Laurel and Hordy-style – over my focking head.

'I was as much shocked as you,' the old dear goes. 'Although the more I thought about it, the more sense it made. Certainly explains where my own creative streak comes from.'

I let that one go, but only because I want to hear the rest of the story.

'Anyway,' she goes, 'none of us knew, that there she was – my mother – in a nunnery in Wexford, painting these extraordinary canvases of places she only knew from memory, but which sold for thousands and thousands of euros. They say Bill Clinton has one, you know. And one of The Corrs who's not Andrea.'

I'm there, 'Okay, where the fock is all of this going?'

'She left quite a substantial estate,' she goes. 'When she left the nunnery, she had close to two million euros in a deposit account.'

I'm there, 'What? And where the fock is it now?'

She just smiles. She loves dragging out a story. You only have to read her books to know that.

'She spent it,' she goes.

I'm like, 'Spent it? What the fock could Aida have spent nearly two mills on?'

The old dear looks at Sorcha then. 'She bought your mum and dad's house.'

Sorcha's two hands shoot up and cover her mouth. She bursts into tears. The old dear reaches out and holds her hand. 'She wanted to thank you,' she goes, 'for your kindness. So she bought it for you.'

I'm like, 'Jesus focking Christ. That's some thank-you.'

Sorcha is just, like, sobbing uncontrollably.

I'm there, 'Can I just clarify something here – is it, like, between us?'

'No,' she goes. 'She bought it for Sorcha.'

Fair focks to Aida. See, she knew I'd have somehow managed to piss my share away. She loved me, but she also *knew* me?

I'm thinking, when did she do all of this? Then I'm thinking, shit, it must have been that day that Sister Edward's brother came and drove her supposedly down to Wexford. She said she had some affairs to sort out.

The old dear knocks back the rest of her gin.

I'm there, 'So why did she tell you all of this?'

She licks her lips, then puts the glass back on the table. She doesn't even lie, just goes, 'She was afraid I'd contest the will on the grounds that she was . . .'

'Bananas?'

'Well, yes. She had an inkling that she was going to die. Anyway, she asked me to please respect her final wishes and I told her I wouldn't dream of doing otherwise.'

She stands up. Her taxi is obviously outside. She strokes the top of Sorcha's head and asks her if she's okay. Sorcha can't even stand up to hug her goodbye. Can't talk, either. She's just too in shock.

The old dear leaves the envelope on the table – I'm presuming that in it are, like, the deeds? – and then she lets herself out.

We end up just sitting there on the sofa for ages, neither of us saying anything. Suddenly it's, like, seven o'clock at night and Sorcha goes, 'Ross, I really need to lie down,' which I think is a bit overly dramatic – all that's happened here is that someone's just given her a massive focking house – but I take her upstairs anyway.

She kicks off her slippers and lies on the bed, except *outside* the sheets?

I go to switch on her bedside lamp, except she goes, 'No, leave it. I want it to be dark. I want you to lie down as well, Ross.'

I'm such a focking idiot, I think she means in *my* room? I'm on the way out the door when she goes, 'Er, I mean *beside* me?'

I'm there, 'Er, okay.'

So we end up just lying there in the dork, staring at the ceiling – again, neither of us saying a word. Honor's having a sleepover in one of her friends' gaffs tonight and, after a short while, I stort thinking the obvious – could I actually get in here?

'What would have changed?' she suddenly goes.

I'm like, 'Excuse me?'

'If we did get back together, Ross – what would change?'

'Well, me for storters. *I'd* totally change.'

She's there, 'But I don't want you to change, Ross. That was one of the things that Aida helped me to see – that it was you I actually *fell* for? And not the ideal that I wanted to wish into basically *reality*?'

I'm like, 'So what would we be talking about here – an open relationship?'

I can nearly, like, hear her exasperation before she even opens her mouth. 'No, I am not talking about an open relationship,' she goes.

'Okay, don't fly off the handle, Babes. I'm just trying to establish what the rules would be.'

'The rules would be our wedding vows. Like they were the first time.'

'Oh, yeah.'

I'm pretty sure there's a copy of our Mass booklet downstairs in one of the kitchen drawers. I'll throw my eye over it later.

'All I'm asking from you,' she goes, 'is loyalty and honesty.'

I'm there, 'I can do that,' even though I do realize that it's a massive, massive, massive ask.

'No more lies,' she goes. 'No more secrets. No more hiding things from me.'

There's, like, silence then and there's suddenly a real is-there-anything-you-want-to-tell-me? vibe in the room. Or maybe I'm just imagining it because I actually hate silence.

But I end up just blurting it out – Christian was right – something I should have already told her.

'Our daughter,' I go, 'has turned into a horrible little girl,' and you can imagine, I'm sure, how difficult it is for me, as her father, to say that.

Sorcha's there, 'Oh! My God! For once, I actually *disagree* with you? I think she's calmed down a lot. I thought working on your mum's movie was actually good for her.'

I could just leave it at that. Except I don't.

I'm like, 'Sorcha, she's actually worse. There's some shit you don't know.'

She goes, 'What? Ross, you're frightening me.'

'I should have possibly told you this, but she was bullying the fock out of everyone on that movie set. Including Fantasia, who had a list of statements from other members of the crew that she was going to read out at the wrap porty – that's why I ended up having to bull the girl boss-eyed in that focking portaloo.'

There's, like, silence for maybe thirty seconds – then she goes, 'I think this total honesty thing is something I'm going to have to get used to slowly.'

I'm thinking, monogamy's not exactly going to be a focking cake-walk for me.

I go, 'There's something else.'

'What?'

I end up having to take a breath before I tell her. 'It was Honor who rang social services and told them you were working in that povo shop.'

I swear to God, there's, like, another thirty seconds of literally silence. Then she shakes her head and goes, 'No. No way,' just not *wanting* to believe it?

I'm there, 'Sorcha, I checked her itemized bill. I saw the number on it with my own eyes.'

She doesn't know what to say. Although when she thinks about it, she realizes that it's definitely true.

She goes, 'What are we going to do?'

I'm there, 'I think we need to bring her to see someone.'

'Ross, what did we do wrong?'

'Who said we did anything wrong? I think we've been amazing, amazing parents. We did possibly spoil her, though.'

'That's the end of it, then. No more movies for her.'

'I know.'

'What if she ends up resenting us, Ross?'

'I'm pretty sure she resents us anyway.'

'I can't take it in, Ross. It's too much for one night. The house. What you've told me about Honor. You and I.'

I'm there, 'I want us to face it together, Sorcha. Honor. The future. Everything. I know your old man will probably have a shit-fit, but I want us to try again. I think I'm actually ready for it this time.'

She doesn't answer. Not in words. I just feel her breath on my neck and her hand suddenly fiddling with the buttons of my chinos.

I'm still half asleep, thinking, who the fock would be ringing the doorbell at, what, nine o'clock on a Sunday morning?

'Ross, you get it,' Sorcha goes and I get this sudden flash of, like, realization of what it's like to be all of a sudden married again.

Whoever it is, roysh, they're pretty, like, *insistent* as well? They must have hit the bell, like, five or six times before I've got my dressing-gown on and tipped downstairs.

I open the front door, roysh, and it's only Nudger.

I'm like, 'Hey,' still only waking up if I'm being honest. 'What the hell are you doing here?'

He's there, 'Ine lookin for me money.'

'I paid you for the boat, didn't I?'

'Yeah, Ine lookin for me money for the keer.'

With everything that's been going on, I actually forgot that I asked him to do it. I'm there, 'Oh, yeah,' and I turn to head for the kitchen, where my wallet is – in the inside pocket of my Henri Lloyd, hanging on the back of one of the breakfast stools.

Except then I suddenly stop and I go, 'Oh, no! Oh, Jesus Christ, no!'

Nudger sees the look on my face and he straight away knows that something is seriously wrong.

'What's the strodee?' he goes.

I'm suddenly, like, fighting to even *breathe*? I'm there, 'Nudger, please tell me you didn't burn the cor out.'

'You fooken ast me to – you said to do it last neet.'

'I meant to, like, ring you to tell you it was off. Oh, Jesus Christ.'

'What's wrong?'

'Jesus focking Christ.'

I've got my head in my actual hands.

'Rosser,' he goes, 'what the fook?'

I'm there, 'There was a bird in the boot.'

He goes, 'A boord?'

I'm like, 'A good-looking one as well. Although I don't know why that's even relevant?'

He goes, 'Why the fook did you have a boord in the boot?'

He's obviously in just shock.

'It's not as dodgy as it sounds,' I go. 'She slipped in a puddle of my piss and I was going to put her on the ferry back to Wales. She's wanted by the cops over there.'

He puts his hand to his chest. I swear to fock, for a second, I think he's about to have an actual hort attack.

'Jesus,' he goes, 'I wootunt like that on me conscience.'

I'm like, 'What?'

'You're arthur killin someone, Rosser.'

I'm like, 'Well, you technically killed her, Dude.'

'I didn't know she was in there, but – you did.'

I step out into the gorden, going, 'No! Please, no! This can't be focking happening!' knowing full well, of course, that someone with my looks wouldn't last a week in prison.

I'm actually wondering how much money Nudger would want to take a bullet for me when, all of a sudden, I see something out on the road that has my hort instantly jumping for joy. I end up having to walk out to the front gate to make sure my eyes aren't, like, *deceiving* me? It's my Lambo – and there's fock-all wrong with it.

And that's when I hear the laughter. Two people's laughter. I turn around and there's Blodwyn and Nudger standing there and – I can't help but notice – holding hands.

I'm suddenly like Sorcha was last night. There's, like, too much going on. I can't take it instantly *in*? I'm like, 'What the fock?' or words to that effect.

'I toordened up last neet,' Nudger goes, 'to do the job and I hears all this fooken kickin and screamin comin from the boot . . .'

I look at Blodwyn. The dress is a mess, but she still looks well, in fairness to her. 'I'm sorry,' I go. 'I only meant to put you on the boat to Wales. Then – it's a long story – I ended up getting back with my wife and she ended up inheriting a house and between one thing and another . . .'

'I'd have been dead,' she goes, 'if Say Men hadn't heard may screams.'

Simon. I never knew his first name before.

He goes, 'She wanted to boorst ye, Rosser. I'd to talk her out of going in there and thragging you ourra the fooken bed. I toalt her you were sowunt as a powunt.'

'Thanks for the back-up,' I go.

I'm still, like, totally fixated on their two hands holding.

'Well,' *she* goes, 'we went for a drenk. Within aboat ten mannets, I was thin ken, "Where's he been hay den all may lafe?" '

My jaw is literally on the floor. I can instantly tell from the way they're looking at each other that they're in, like, love.

I laugh and just shake my head. I'm there, 'Can I just say fair focks, Nudger? You will not be disappointed.'

I don't know why I feel the need to let him know I've sampled the goods.

'I'm happy for you,' I go. 'Jesus, it's actually pretty emotional.'

'You're bleedy leckay,' she goes, 'that I've found a reason to stay out of priss zen. Otherwase, you'd be fook ken dead rate know.'

'Amen to that,' I go.

Then off the two of them trot, up Newtownpork Avenue – as *in* love as I've ever known two people to be.

I'm thinking I might go inside now and stick the kettle on. Make Sorcha breakfast. Then collect Honor from her sleepover – tell her that her movie career is over and stort imposing some discipline on her at last.

Probably won't tell Sorcha about Blodwyn. I know it's very early to be going back on my word. But what's that expression I heard before? Marriage doesn't thrive on full disclosure.

It's at that exact point that Tina pulls up outside in her shitty old 94 D Daihatsu Charade. From the look on her face – we're talking the proverbial kicked-in wheelie bin – she's ready for a row about something.

I go, 'Tina, you wouldn't believe the twenty-four hours I've just had. All I'm saying is, I'm not in the mood for any more surprises.'

She looks at me – mad enough to kill me – and goes, 'You'd bethor get in the mood. Because I found out what's arthur been eating Ronan the last few months. Congratulayshiddens, Ross. You're gonna be a grandfadder.'

Acknowledgements

Thanks to my editor Rachel Pierce, agent Faith O'Grady and the unique genius of the artist Alan Clarke. Thanks to Michael McLoughlin, Patricia Deevy, Cliona Lewis, Patricia McVeigh, Brian Walker and everyone at Penguin Ireland for your continued support. Thanks, as always, to my father, David, to my brothers, Vincent and Richard, and to my wife, Mary, for whom there aren't enough words.

He just wanted a decent book to read ...

Not too much to ask, is it? It was in 1935 when Allen Lane, Managing Director of Bodley Head Publishers, stood on a platform at Exeter railway station looking for something good to read on his journey back to London. His choice was limited to popular magazines and poor-quality paperbacks – the same choice faced every day by the vast majority of readers, few of whom could afford hardbacks. Lane's disappointment and subsequent anger at the range of books generally available led him to found a company – and change the world.

'We believed in the existence in this country of a vast reading public for intelligent books at a low price, and staked everything on it'
Sir Allen Lane, 1902–1970, founder of Penguin Books

The quality paperback had arrived – and not just in bookshops. Lane was adamant that his Penguins should appear in chain stores and tobacconists, and should cost no more than a packet of cigarettes.

Reading habits (and cigarette prices) have changed since 1935, but Penguin still believes in publishing the best books for everybody to enjoy. We still believe that good design costs no more than bad design, and we still believe that quality books published passionately and responsibly make the world a better place.

So wherever you see the little bird – whether it's on a piece of prize-winning literary fiction or a celebrity autobiography, political tour de force or historical masterpiece, a serial-killer thriller, reference book, world classic or a piece of pure escapism – you can bet that it represents the very best that the genre has to offer.

Whatever you like to read – trust Penguin.

read more
www.penguin.co.uk